Gate of Stars

P.G. BADZEY

DEDICATION

For all those who try to do what's right and true and just, no matter what
forces of this world are arrayed against them.
Do not be afraid. Help is coming.

Praise for the Grey Riders Series!

<u>Book 1, Whitehorse Peak</u>

"...Whitehorse Peak excels, standing out from the crowd of fantasy adventures...a riveting, emotionally powerful story line...vibrant with realistic action" – D. Donovan, *Midwest Book Review*

"…an excellent balance of worldbuilding and introduction,…fully lavish and exciting, with atmospheric moments of high, epic fantasy that smack of tradition and the old favorites, but then also more modern inclusions and plenty of witty humor… Highly recommended: fantasy fiction at its best." – K.C. Finn for *Readers Favorite* (5-star review)

<u>Book 2, Eye of Truth</u>

"…a real treasure … Think Dungeons and Dragons or Tolkien, throw in a dash of Patrick Rothfus … recommended for any reader who enjoys high fantasy spiced with a bit of mystery" — D. Donovan, *Midwest Book Review*

"… a charming and rich tale of magic, loyalty, friendship, and secrets, …. I enjoyed the complexities of the plot and characters, and their development and alterations as secrets are uncovered…good world-building…Danger, action, threats, and camaraderie will keep the reader engaged…" – K.J. Simmill for *Readers Favorite* (5-star review)

<u>Book 3, Helm of Shadows</u>

"…wraps its cloak of fantasy around an atmosphere of mystery and intrigue… Impressively vivid…" — D. Donovan, *Midwest Book Reviews*

"…an even bigger and better addition to the Grey Riders series… Helm of Shadows is an excellent addition that once again lifts the series to new heights: a highly recommended read for fantasy fans everywhere." – K.C. Finn for *Readers Favorite* (5-star review)

<u>Book 4, Assassin Prince</u>

"P.G. Badzey has created a complex, absorbing atmosphere …fast-paced and thoroughly engrossing… a compelling saga… satisfying action… whets the reader's appetite for more to come in later sequels." — D. Donovan, *Midwest Book Reviews*

"I am always delighted to return to the works of author P. G. Badzey and the fantastic Grey Riders series, and this new addition is no exception... As always, the worldbuilding and atmosphere are solid, and the closer we get to what is sure to be an epic conclusion, the less I want the series to end." – K.C. Finn for *Readers Favorite* (5-star review)

<u>Book 5, The Skull Gates</u>

"…rivals J.R.R. Tolkien's Middle Earth in cultural and genealogical complexity… will have fans clamoring for the saga's next chapter." – Kate Robinson, US Review of Books (Recommended)

"Badzey keeps this novel in perfect balance, shifting action to keep readers following the different threads of the story and giving each of the Riders time to shine with their unique skills, whilst also building to a fantastic magical conclusion. Overall, I would highly recommend The Skull Gates…" – K.C. Finn for *Readers Favorite* (5-star review)

CONTENTS

ACKNOWLEDGMENTS

The author would like to thank the Orange County (CA) Science Fiction Fantasy Critique Group (Melissa Sokol, David Wake, Jamie Kamlet, Chris Lillja, Joy Pixley, James Takos) for their invaluable and helpful criticism, humor and encouragement. Your expertise and insights have helped me become a better writer and have made this book possible.

The author is also indebted to Matt Bostic for the excellent chapter thumbnails, Eugene and Dora Badzey for their superior editing and Veronica Badzey for her superb typesetting and formatting. You helped me make this the quality novel it is.

"Be strong and courageous; do not be afraid or discouraged, for the Lord your God will be with you wherever you go."
– Joshua 1:9

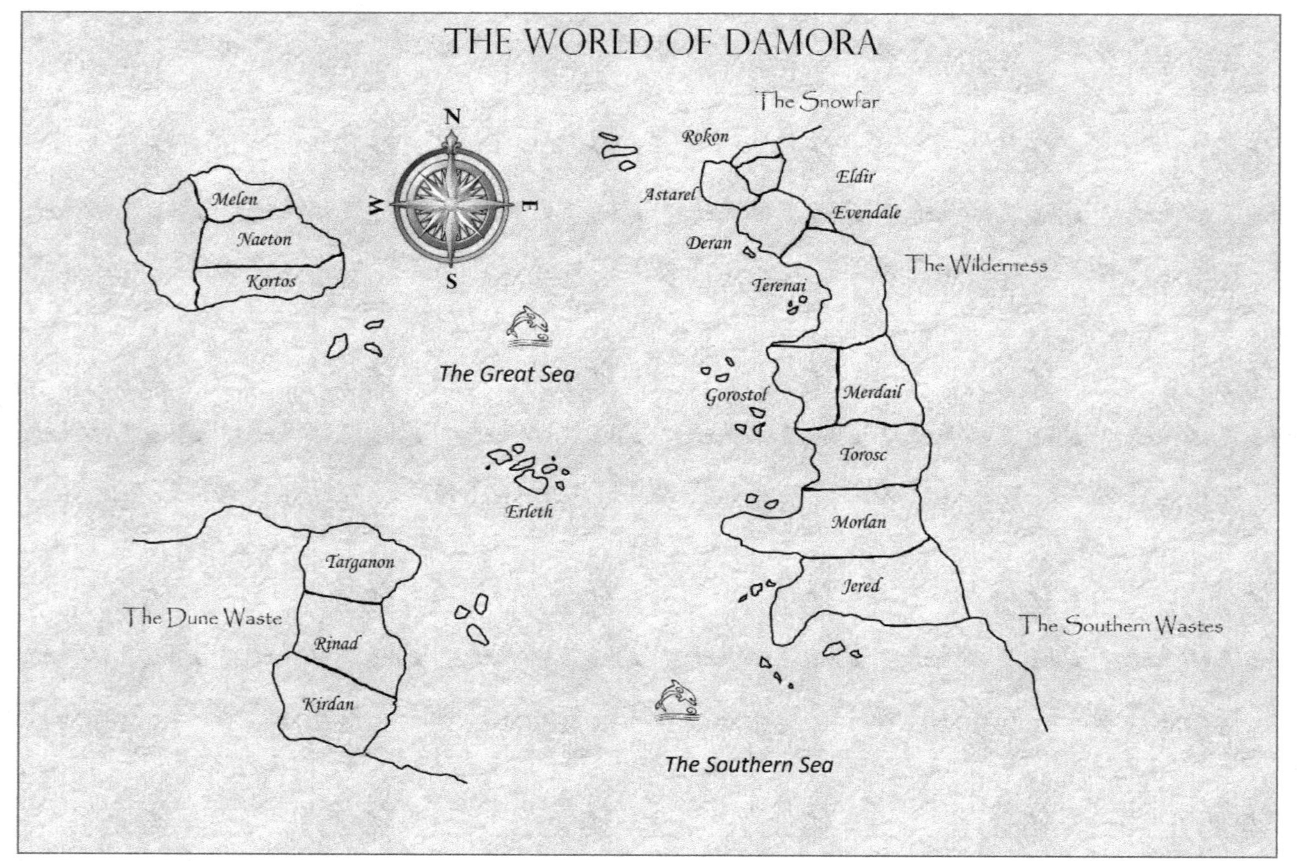

THE WORLD OF DAMORA
N
W
E
S
Melen
Naeton
Kortos
The Great Sea
The Snowfar
Rokon
Astarel
Eldir
Evendale
Deran
The Wilderness
Terenai
Gorostol
Merdail
Torosc
Morlan
Jered
The Southern Wastes
Erleth
Targanon
Rinad
Kirdan
The Dune Waste
The Southern Sea

DERAN AND EVENDALE

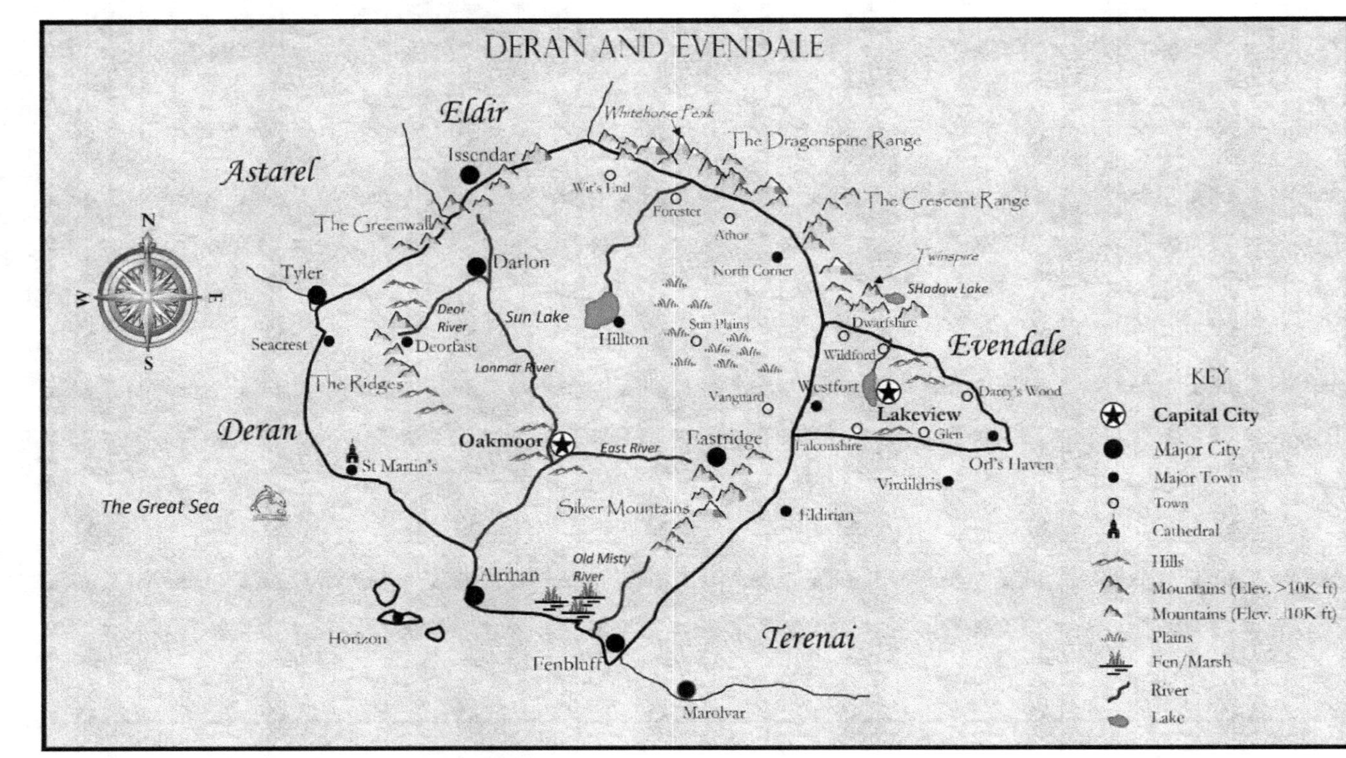

THE ELVEN EMPIRE OF TERENAI

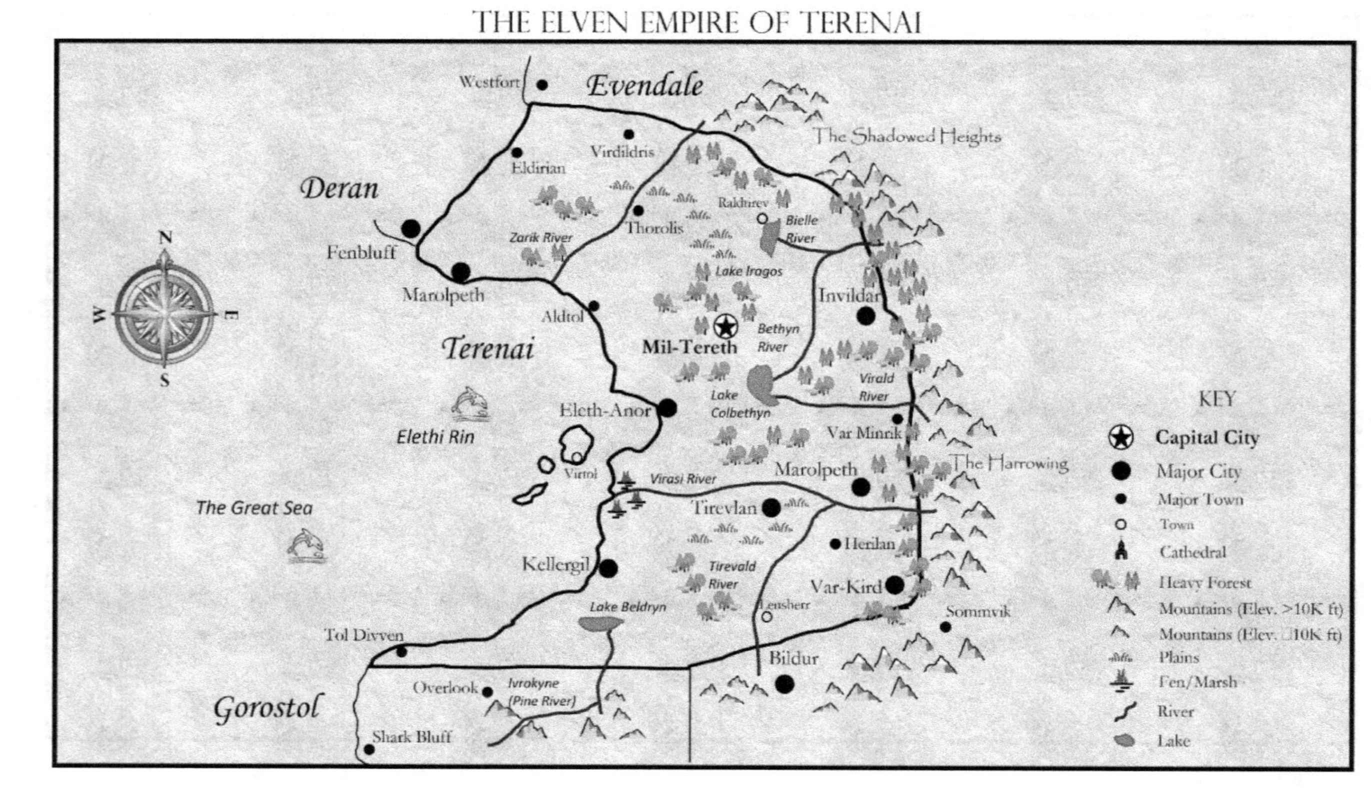

THE REPUBLIC OF GOROSTOL

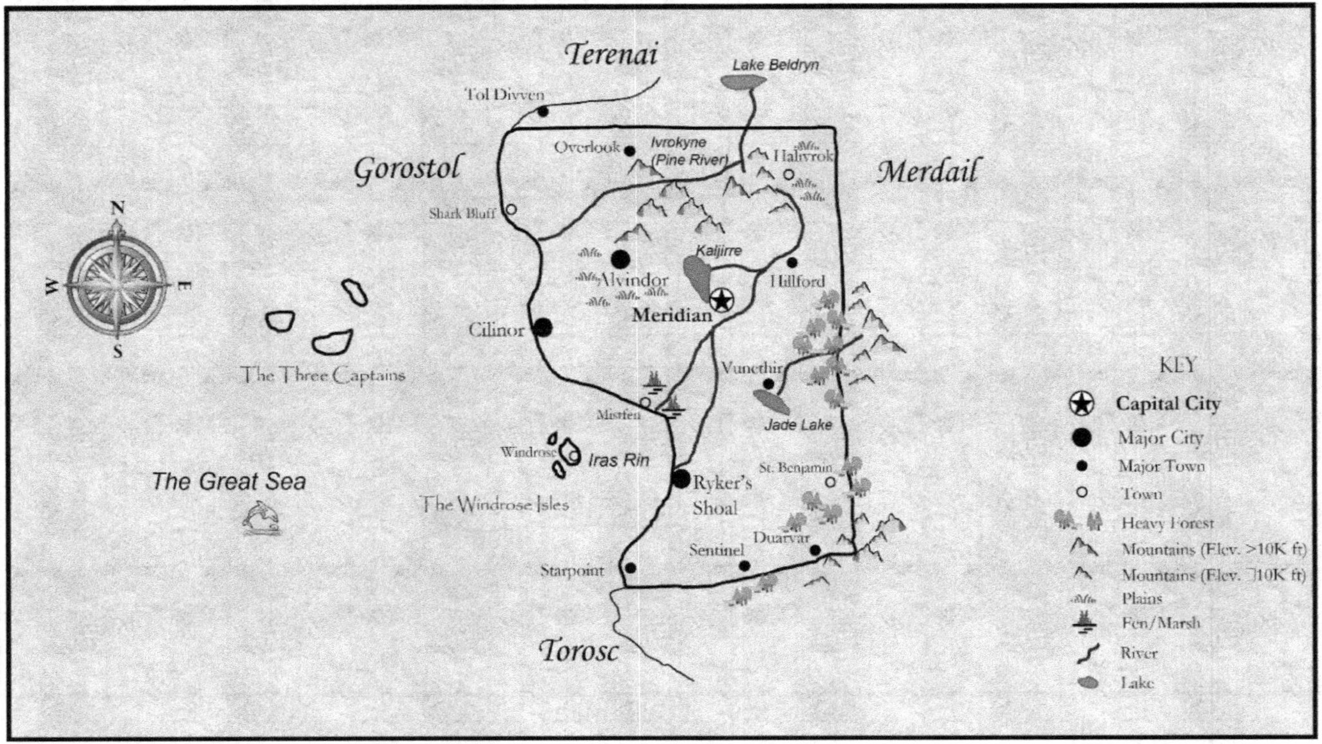

THE REPUBLIC OF TOROSC

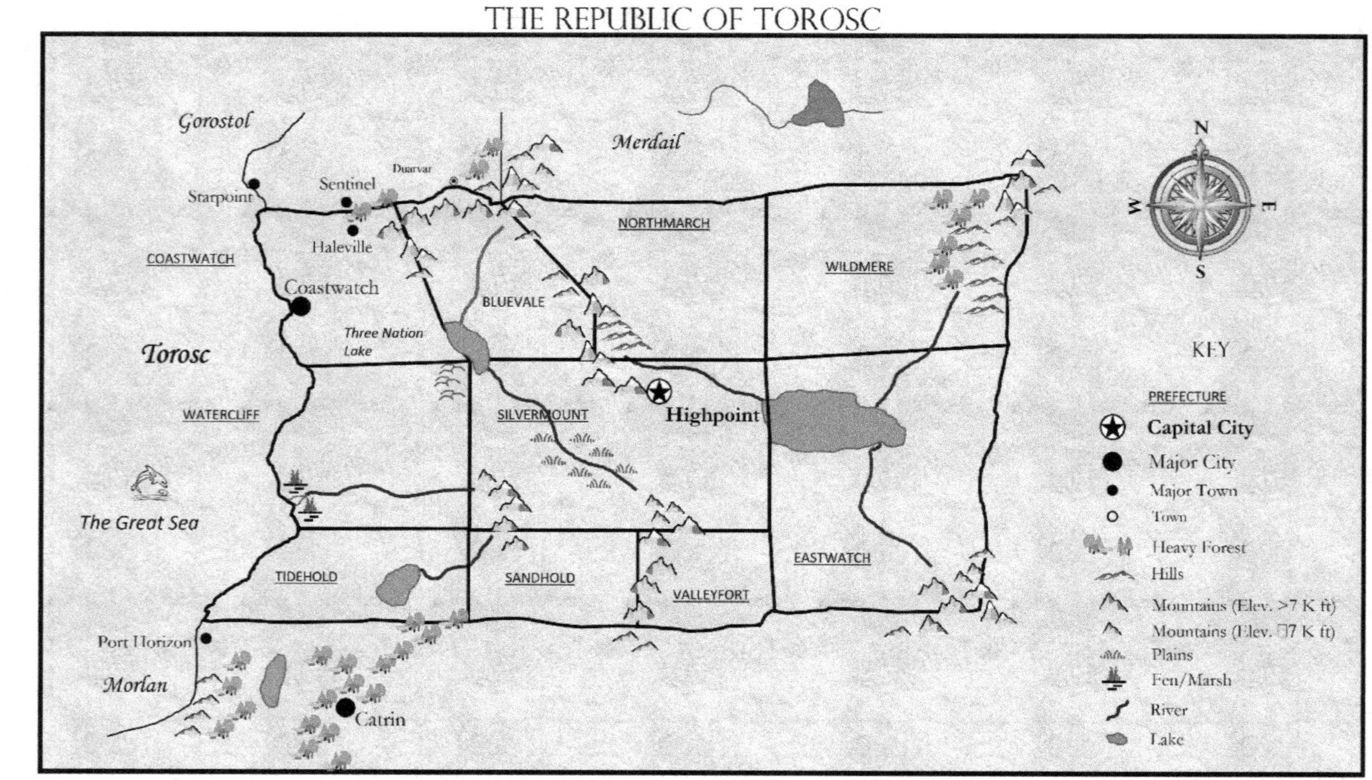

COASTWATCH PREFECTURE, TOROSC

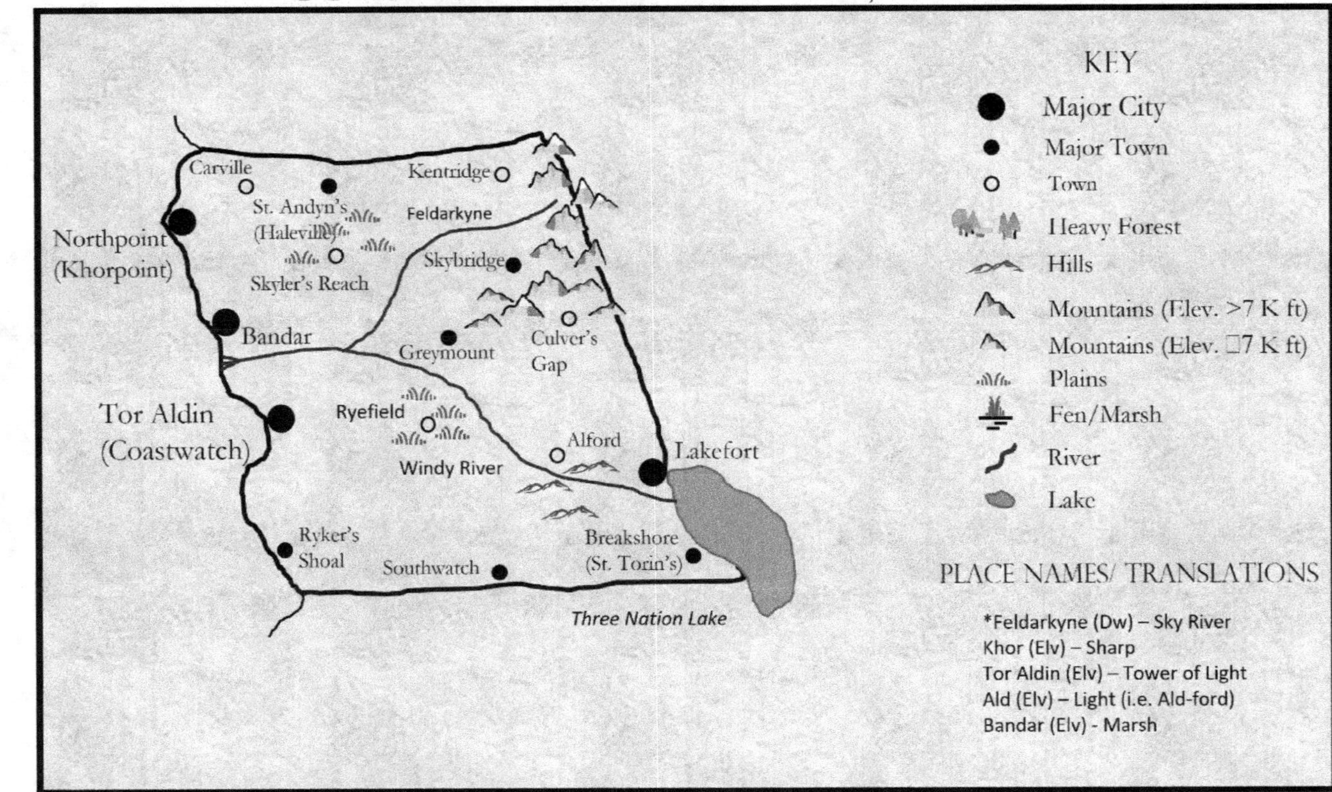

Chapter One – Important Visitors

"Lord Golvadu?"

Golvadu Fellhammer, Second Archon of Torosc, frowned. He slapped his scalpel and forceps down on the laboratory table. "I said I wasn't to be disturbed!"

"Y-Yes, Your Power, but- but- "

Golvadu waited. Morning sunlight streamed in the tall windows of his personal library and birds chirped outside on the terrace, but no further words came from beyond the door.

He shrugged, turning his attention back to the tiny, human-like figure lying spread-eagled on the specimen plate under his examining glass. Only a foot long, the hill-sprite's eyes fluttered closed and her chest ceased its labored breathing. The iridescent shine on her dragonfly wings faded even as he watched.

Damn it! How can I study the shitty things if they keep dying on me? And with all these infernal interruptions…

Golvadu spat a string of creatively worded obscenities. Tossing down his tools, he stood and stumped to the door. He waved his hand to cancel the warding spells, then yanked the portal open.

His human servant trembled in the foyer, eyes wide and face pale.

I should get a dwarven servant. Golvadu mused. *At least we'd have something in common. Useless, short-lived humans...*

Golvadu waved a hand and his servant jerked up into the air like a marionette, hovering just under the door lintel, eyes bulging.

"This had better be good," the Archon growled.

The servant managed to nod despite the vise of magical energy holding him.

Golvadu considered tormenting him further, then decided he didn't have the time. Something had frightened the man more than the prospect of punishment. He released the servant, who dropped back to the floor and leaned against the doorjamb.

"Well, what is it?" Golvadu snapped.

"A-a-visitor."

"That's why you interrupted my experiment? Are you daft? We have visitors all the time. Have him wait in the audience chamber. I'm busy."

"She came in through the Skull Gate, Great One," the servant managed, perspiration beading on his forehead. "And she demands your presence."

Golvadu frowned. "Another daemon entered through the Gate. So what? We've been seeing fifteen of them a day. And what daemon would dare demand anything from me?"

The servant merely shook his head.

Golvadu pressed his lips together in a firm line. "You're trying my patience. I'll have your skull in my display case if you don't —"

"One of the Royal Ones..." the servant managed.

An unearthly chill settled on Golvadu and his heart skipped a beat.

No. That's not possible.

"Robe of Office," he announced. From a coat rack next to his worktable, a mantle of shimmering indigo floated towards him like a giant bat. He held out his arms to the side and the robe snapped down around his stout frame. More than two dozen bone-white sigils flared briefly on the fabric.

Opening a silver-chased wooden coffer on a side table, he drew out two golden bracers and snapped them over his forearms. A faint burst of pink light covered him for a second and winked out.

He held out his left hand. "Staff of Power," he barked.

From the corner of the room, a black staff topped with a dark red sphere shot to his hand.

He eyed his trembling servant for a second and sniffed. "Go change your clothes. You stink of piss."

Without another word, he shoved the man into the hall, stalked out of his chamber and reapplied the door seals with a snap of his fingers. His boots echoed through the black marble receiving hall with measured and unhurried steps. Guards snapped to attention and slaves knelt. Three Sorcerers of the Ninth Circle halted in mid-conversation and bowed low, avoiding his eyes. He ignored them.

He said "she". But which one is it?

None of the available options held any promise. Golvadu gritted his teeth. He willed his pace to remain businesslike all the way down a mirrored hallway.

Is she here to investigate? Take charge? Punish?

He bit his lip, trying to come up with a contingency plan.

A High Priestess of Gudarta in a revealing chainmail outfit and long cloak swept into a curtsey as he passed.

"My Lord Golvadu—" she began.

"Not now." He glared at her momentarily.

"But —"

"I said not now!" he snapped. "We'll talk later."

His mood fouled more the closer he got to the summoning chamber and he forced himself to breathe evenly. To focus his mind, he reviewed possible approaches to the situation. He didn't want to involve the other Archons; calling in the cavalry for support would imply weakness and lack of confidence that could prove deadly later.

He stopped at a pair of towering, dark wooden doors nearly three times his height. He smoothed his robes and nodded.

Two Elven women clad in black-enameled plate mail glimmered into being. Open-faced steel helmets framed exquisitely beautiful features and glowing red eyes. They bowed, crossing their hands before their faces. The doors swung open.

"Make sure no one comes in unless I call for them," Golvadu growled.

"As you command, Archon," whispered one of the women in a dusky voice. Both guards drew bastard swords in unison and set them point-down on the marble tiles. The blades shimmered with red runes.

Golvadu prepared a few escape spells and entered. Before he could make a motion, the doors slammed shut behind him.

A Skull Gate loomed at the far end of the immense chamber. Green witch-fires in braziers cast weird shadows on its massive frame. The structure stood fully twenty feet tall. Two wagons could have fit easily within it at its base. Metal columns festooned with bones arched upward to a point, where a fanged skull leered at him. Wisps of black fog curled up from the archway's interior and he smelled ozone and brimstone.

A tall woman casually leaned against one side of the Gate, watching him.

His mouth went dry and he felt suddenly light-headed.

Shit. It's her. Hold it together, damn it!

"Archon Golvadu," the woman said in a sultry alto. "So pleased to finally meet you."

She glided forward into the light, barefoot and wearing a sheer robe of pale blue that left nothing to the imagination. At first glance, she looked like a very tall and beautiful human woman with dark green eyes — until ruby red lips parted and fangs glinted. He stared at the deep black horns peeking up from her forehead through raven tresses.

A wave of oppressive power pulsed out from her and it took all of his impressive dwarven reserves not to fall to his knees and grovel. He fought to keep his hands from shaking.

"High Majesty Arachnia," he said with a deep bow. "You do me an immense honor."

"Yes, I do," she replied. He straightened and gave a little jump. She stood directly in front of him now. She had covered a distance of twenty feet in under a second.

"To be perfectly honest," she purred, "I'm impressed that a dwarven wizard could attain such a lofty position. I'm sure you came by your lordly title and responsibilities through merit and skill." A mildly intoxicating perfume emanated from her, almost sickly-sweet, an aroma of honey sugar, cinnamon and wine.

She extended her hand and he took it, glad for his gloves. A ring with a carved amethyst in the shape of a sundered heart glowed on her index finger.

Golvadu bowed over her hand, careful not to let the ring touch him. He wasn't that stupid.

The ring pulsed. A wave of wild, dark magic flowed over him and he instantly regretted his decision to come alone.

"Perhaps I should call the other Archons to conference, Mistress of Venom and Treachery," he said, straightening. "They will be flattered to meet you."

"Not now," Arachnia said with a faint smile. "In due time. I wanted to get someone's unvarnished opinion and, naturally, thought of you."

He knew she thought nothing of the kind but he beamed anyway. "I give great thanks to your Serene Majesty."

Her eyes roved over him and he felt as if spiders crawled through his undergarments.

The corner of her mouth rose. "A Librarian's Robe and a Staff of Power... and Vortex Bracers! Impressive. Ah, but the Darkfire Beads are in your left pocket and you're right-handed. So, maybe you've been putting in some practice with your off-hand, yes?"

How does she know...? He gave no response but inclined his head.

"I must compliment you." Arachnia swept back towards the gate, giving him a spectacular view of her body in the flickering lights. "The Skull Gate is an impressive device and a smooth ride from Hades to this world."

She shot him a glance over her shoulder. "I do love a smooth ride, you know."

Golvadu bowed again. "I am honored."

She stroked one of the skulls gently. "Still, I have to wonder at the efficiency of the Gates."

"Efficiency?"

She spun around. "Yes. I understand that they have a limitation on how quickly they can transport our troops."

"Well, yes, Majesty," he admitted. "They tend to overheat if used too often. Three summonings in a row stresses their internal structure and we have to avoid the hazard of breakdown. But it is of no consequence. After letting them cool down for a while, they function normally. Your daemons have been transferring at regular intervals, morning and night."

The Hadean goddess leaned back against the gate. "I see. But I also understand that the war is going slowly."

Golvadu licked his lips. "I am not sure what you mean. We have made great inroads into the —"

"How many kingdoms have you conquered?" she interrupted.

"Well, Your —"

"Don't toy with me," she snapped, eyes narrowing. "How many?"

He took a deep breath. "The kingdom of Naeton on the island of Derelia is entirely in our control, as are Morlan, Jered and Torosc on this continent. Rinad among the lands across the Great Sea has joined the Movement and Rokon to the north is ready to fall."

Arachnia sniffed. "Really? I expected more by now with all these Skull Gates and your combined armies. You owned Morlan, Jered and Torosc before the war began." She patted a thighbone on the structure. "I thought the Gates would have made a big difference."

He nodded. "Of course, but many of the Gates within enemy territories were destroyed, so our forces now have to travel miles in order to get to population centers. Even in Astarel and Eldir, where a couple of Gates survived, it takes time to muster our forces and march."

"Excuses, excuses. And wasn't there a program of insurgency started not long ago to weaken the kingdoms and aid our cause?" Dark green eyes bored into him.

"Yes, but Your Worship must understand that the enemies of the Great Remaking would not take it lying down. The so-called Churches of the Light have been combating our attempts at internal dissension for months now."

"Not so mighty as you thought you were," she mused.." She reminded him of a cobra about to strike.

"No battle plan survives combat, Great Queen," Golvadu replied, stiffly, bracing himself for the first blast of magic.

Instead of attacking, Arachnia clucked her tongue and he felt a wave of relief. "Now, now, don't get testy, Archon. I know that. In your favor, I understand that your magic closed the Celestial Gates, so we can expect no interference from our misguided brethren."

"You are correct, Majesty," he replied, careful to keep his expression neutral. "We estimate that there are no more than two dozen Elohir on Damora at present. They are scattered and trying to be everywhere at once. It is only a matter of time before they are tracked down and destroyed."

"Ah, well, that is easier said than done. I know from experience." She languidly strolled along the side of the chamber. "All their gates were shut?"

"Yes."

She must have detected some hesitation because she stopped in mid-stride. "You don't sound confident."

"It is nothing."

She placed an elegant foot on a red alabaster bench and leaned an elbow on her knee. "I'll be the judge of that. What aren't you telling me?"

Golvadu's mind raced for something to say.

Her eyes flared. Another wave of oppressive power washed over him. "You know, I can just compel it out of you. I don't like to waste magic on supposed allies, but if you insist — ."

"No." He gulped and sweat beaded on his forehead. "Tales tell of an ancient Celestial portal called the Gate of Stars. Its location is lost in the mists of time, but it is also said that your allies on this world hid it behind something called the Dome of Glass. To be honest, Majesty, it is only a legend."

Arachnia looked thoughtful. "All legends have an element of truth. I trust our enemies are also aware of this and have sent someone to find it."

"Your Worship is most insightful."

"Ah. Who did they send?"

"We are not sure, but the Grey Riders cannot be found and our intelligence service suspects they may be the ones."

She lowered herself to lounge on the bench, making no attempt at modesty. "Who are these Grey Riders?"

"One-time free-lance sellswords who serve the unenlightened and backward rulers of the enemy nations. They are of no consequence."

"Really, Archon, your temerity is annoying me. Not once, but twice, you have presumed to reach a conclusion for me." Her eyes glowed and a lurid green fog surrounded her, swirling with forms of scorpions and spiders. "Would you care to rephrase your response?"

The smoky forms began to attain solidity. Golvadu's sweating increased. "Of course, Majesty. As I said, they were once mercenaries but were given knighthoods and honors. They ride winged horses – pegasi – and have been a thorn in our side on more than one occasion."

She nodded. "Such as?" The fog dissipated.

He forced himself to loosen his grip on his staff. "Well, over a year ago, they defeated one of our commanders in order to secure the pegasi. The pegasi were held in temporal stasis from the Esten Imperial Age and guarded by a dragon. Then, the Riders allegedly found a relic of the Christian church and destroyed Zhinia Margoth, a lich-princess from the age of the Paragon Kings. That was when they were honored and given titles. Later, one of their number led them on a quest to destroy the Crossed Swords Assassins Guild, which, as you recall, was led by one of your adherents."

"They destroyed the Crossed Swords Guild, did they?" She sat up, eyes narrowing. "What were they trying to do, piss me off?"

"Our thoughts exactly, Mistress of Venom. Their crimes against our cause continue to mount. Our spies believe they slew one of our High Council wizards recently. But we will have our vengeance after the Remaking is complete, of that you can be sure."

Arachnia's expression changed from angry to thoughtful. "Hmm… a Lich and a High Council wizard. They have some abilities then. How many are there?"

"The number varies between six and eight. We confirmed the slaying of one of them in Gorostol, a gnome named Handor Lervion. Our forces captured two others, the sisters Brandawyn and Megan Alenar. They escaped but we believe them to also be dead, though that has not been independently verified."

"And now?"

"There are six at last count."

Arachnia pursed her lips. "And you don't know where they are, you say?"

"They were last seen in Terenai. But your Worship need not worry. Pegasus riders are rare enough to warrant easy detection."

The Hadean goddess remained lost in thought. "I want you to make sure that this angle is covered," she said finally, rising. "We can't risk them finding any Celestial Gate, legendary or not. Kelson of Celestia with an army at his back would be the ruin of everything. We would be hard-pressed to fight him on equal terms without the added nuisance of the Damoran military. We *apparently* have our hands full right now."

This last phrase she emphasized with a pointed look at him.

"I will stress this most urgently to the Council."

"I'm sure you will." She clasped her hands at her waist and sighed. "Well, I suppose this will have to do. See that your best chambers are prepared for us."

The blood drained from his face. "Us?"

"Of course," she gave him a sweet, maidenly smile. "Didn't I mention it? Silly of me. My most beloved Lords Torvu and Selaan will be joining me presently. We require privileges befitting our rank."

A steady stream of vile profanities surged in Golvadu's mind. He wisely kept them there. "I don't understand, Dread Mistress," he managed.

She waved at him. "We will be taking charge of the Dark Wave. Go. Gather the Archons for your council or whatever, and see that the appropriate accommodations are made ready."

She turned her back on him. "Don't keep me waiting, Golvadu."

He bowed low, his knees trembling. "As you command, Majesty."

His brain churned frantically as he hurried out of the chamber and down the halls.

Three Hadean gods here? In the Archon Palace of Highpoint? This is a disaster!

Who among the Archons could he confide in? Not long in trust of each other, they would have to band together somehow. If Arachnia, Selaan and Torvu took over, everything would be lost.

His mind reeled. Despite his relief at leaving her presence in one piece, his anger rose. All their careful plans crumbled under the prospect of three Hadean monarchs wielding their impressive magical arsenals to drive him and the other Archons from power.

He would be pushed to the sidelines.

"Not if I have anything to say about it," he growled as he headed towards the Council chambers…

Chapter Two – The Better Part of Valor

Buckminster Bydecy hefted his shield and strode to his pegasus. "I know, Shadowbane," he murmured, patting the animal's neck. "I want to get going too."

Drooping willow branches formed a curtain around him but late afternoon sunshine managed to filter through anyway. In the dimness beneath the leafy boughs, his mount's mottled green and grey leather barding melded in with the surroundings.

His right hand reflexively went to the grip of a golden-hilted broadsword at his hip and he ran his thumb over the raised Dwarven runes on the guard. The sword remained still and dark.

He peered into the forest. *I don't know why I bother to watch for them. I won't be able to see them until they're on top of us anyway.*

"Have a seat," said a soft alto voice behind him. "We have a long way to go and we need every bit of rest."

He cast a glance over his shoulder. Andyn Eleandir reclined against a fallen log, reading a scroll. A jumble of saddlebags lay piled next to her. Five other pegasi, armored like Shadowbane, placidly cropped grass near the bole of the willow.

He said nothing and she looked up. A blonde brow arched over bright amber eyes. "I set the wards myself, you know," she said, tapping a smooth black stone by her hip. The rock glittered at her touch. "Nothing can sneak up on us, not even our stealthy companions."

He frowned, then joined her. "I hate the waiting," he groused, easing himself to sit on the log. He would have preferred to stretch out on the ground but his banded mail didn't allow for quick motion and he never knew when he might have to move fast.

"You and Khyron have a lot in common then," she replied. "I don't know how he managed five years in the Guards. He must have driven his commanders crazy."

He gave her a droll look. "Well, you'll have plenty of time to teach him to take it slow, then, won't you?"

Her right hand went from the scroll to a gold ring on the first finger of her left hand. She traced a twining band of emerald, a soft smile curving her lips.

"When is the ceremony?" Buck asked.

She shook her head, brushing a strand of honey blonde hair over one of her pointed ears. "We haven't set a date yet. Seems ridiculous with the War going on. We have to survive first."

"But you've told Khyron's parents."

"Oh yes. Mine too. They can't wait. But, of course, they will have to."

He nodded, eyes drifting to the forest nearby. Talk of marriage and engagements made him think of Carine, thoughts that quickly turned to anxiety. He shoved his apprehensions to the back of his mind.

She's in a big city with a professional army. She and my family are in good hands. They'll be fine.

A mild ping sounded from the black stone. Buck shot a look at Andyn. They stood.

Seconds later, a bird trilled in the woods. Andyn returned a low whistle, sounding like a thrush. The birdsong repeated and she nodded. "That's Khyron and Dar."

She waved a hand and the willow branches straightened, raising the curtain of foliage. Two figures in camouflaged cloaks slipped through the bushes.

One of them swept back his hood, revealing handsome Elven features, slightly pointed ears and short-cropped blonde hair. Sea-green eyes twinkled mischievously as he stepped into Andyn's embrace and gave her a quick kiss.

"Your wards are working to perfection, as usual," he noted.

"Thank you, dearest," she replied.

The other newcomer slipped back his own hood. A human, he stood a little taller than Khyron but had short dark hair and dark eyes. "And they're subtle, too," Dar Cabot added. "If I didn't know where you set them, I wouldn't even have noticed."

Andyn smiled. "Why, thank you, gallant sir. Anything to report?"

Khyron shook his head. "Nothing. It looks like we gave them the slip. The north way is clear."

"Good. We can keep moving then."

Andyn and Khyron sauntered towards the center of camp, arms around each other, speaking softly. Dar averted his eyes and slung his saddlebags over the withers of his pegasus. He began fastening the straps, seemingly intent on his task.

Buck's eyes shot to Andyn and Khyron, then back to Dar. He felt a pang of sympathy. An image of another half-Elven woman filled his mind. Instead of Andyn's honey-blonde locks, this one had hair of reddish-gold and lay on a bed underneath a glowing web of light.

I don't blame Dar for not wanting to look. He probably thinks of Megan all the time, and we don't even know if she's dead or alive. I guess we'll find out when they remove the Preservation Net… whenever that is.

Like all the Riders, he hoped for the best outcome but prepared for the worst. It was entirely possible that Megan had died before they had managed to freeze her in time with the Net.

"Time will tell and Nature will run its course," Buck whispered. He returned to his perch on the log, leaning back on his hands.

His mind wandered. Sometimes he felt a sense of amazement that they were all still alive. A little more than a year and a half ago, they were all neophyte free-lance sellswords slogging through the woods on the northern border of Deran, seeking a secret weapon from a bygone age — only to find that the 'weapon' was a herd of war-pegasi, frozen in time by mighty spells. Unfortunately, the cult of the Ja'al had designs on the pegasi and objected violently to the idea of anyone else obtaining them. When the dust had settled, Buck and his friends prevailed, but this had also earned them the undying enmity of the cult.

He watched Shadowbane clop over to the other mounts and join them in grazing. The winged horses were the reason for their current — and very urgent — assignment: thwart the plans of the Ja'al and their daemonic allies by finding the legendary Gate of Stars. Only a small group of pegasus riders had the stealth and speed to slip past the Armies of the Dark Wave.

Another ping sounded. Buck joined Khyron and Dar in the shadows, bows at the ready, while Andyn repeated her magic spells. A different bird-song drifted back to them.

"That's Eric and Connor," she reported. Two more figures entered the camp with only a few disturbed branches to mark their passage.

The shorter of the two pulled back his hood. "All clear. No Ja'al within a league of here to the east. Let's break camp." Connor Lomin bent to pick up his own saddlebags. Despite the fact that his head only reached to Buck's stomach, the Halfling lifted the gear easily.

The half-elven man next to Connor set a spear against the tree trunk and stretched. Except for his more rounded features and taller height, he could have passed for Khyron's relative. "Agreed. At our current pace, we'll reach the eastern border by tomorrow afternoon," Eric Indidarc offered. His violet eyes rested briefly on Andyn and Khyron, then swept over the camp. "I don't want to try finding a camping spot in the dark in that territory."

"No arguments from me," Khyron said. "I'll breathe easier when we reach the Pass of Eagles."

Eric nodded and set to readying his mount.

Buck suppressed a sigh, watching him. *So much sorrow for Eric too.* Megan's sister, Brandawyn, rested on an identical bed in a hidden place, a golden web of light covering her form as well. The only difference was the stake of wood in her heart.

Hell, thought Buck. *What chance do either of them have?*

Megan had fallen to a poison encoded by an evil archwizard and Brandi was transformed into a vampire slave by the Ja'al cult. Eric himself had to drive the stake into her chest. Only the Preservation Nets gave the Riders the slimmest of hopes that the souls of both sisters remained in the living world, frozen in time mere fractions of a second from their apparent demise.

"Hey, stop daydreaming," Connor slapped Buck on the hip. "Let's get moving."

Buck looked down his nose at him. "Me? Daydreaming? I'm not the one who's been mooning over a twist of brown hair in that silver locket."

Connor reddened and turned away, muttering something Buck couldn't hear.

Buck grinned but didn't follow up. With all the dread tidings of late, a little teasing lightened the mood. Besides, Hannah Lervion, the giver of the lock of brown hair, was in the fortified town of Sentinel, far to the southwest. She, like Carine, was well-guarded.

Buck prepared his equipment and hoisted himself into the saddle. He set his round shield on a hook next to his left leg and shot a look at the cloudy sky.

He rode up next to Eric. "I don't dispute your scouting skills," he announced, "but you should probably deploy your favorite toy. No telling what's up there." Shadowbane tossed his head.

Eric vaulted into the saddle. "You read my mind. After our last tangle with the enemy, I don't want to get surprised again."

Dar likewise mounted up and patted his pegasus on the neck. "I'll be in the first rank this time," he announced. "We follow Eric's lead. He can see for miles through Stealth's eyes. If he turns, we turn."

Khyron rode next to them. "We'll watch your back."

Eric touched a brooch on his cloak and whispered something under his breath. The brooch flared with light and coalesced into the form of a small brown hawk with black-tipped feathers, sitting on Eric's saddlebow.

Eric inspected the bird minutely. "I'll have to oil the wing gears soon, but it should be good for the rest of the day at least."

If Buck didn't know better, he could have sworn that the little golem was a real hawk.

Eric motioned to the sky and Stealth winged up into the air. Eric raised a hand and cantered out from under the trees, leading them to a nearby meadow. In seconds, the Riders raced across the grassy plain and lifted off with the powerful beat of pegasus wings.

When this is all over, Buck promised himself, *I'll take the time to just ride Shadowbane around for fun instead of having to save the world every two weeks.*

He stayed in the third rank next to Connor, behind Andyn and Khyron, trying to keep Dar and Eric in view. The day was extremely cloudy and only occasional shafts of sunlight burst through the grey. Eric led them up higher and higher. In all the murk, Buck soon lost all sense of direction but trusted the rangers to lead them.

Privately, he wondered if even Stealth's superior vision would help.

They soared through the air. Buck heard only the wind and felt the misty wet of cloud vapor. He relaxed, hoping that they could at least find their way to the Pass without further trouble.

He rested his hand on the pommel of his sword. It took him a few seconds to realize that Khelios buzzed with energy. Heart in his throat, he drew the blade partway out of the scabbard. It blazed with golden light.

Eric threw up his left hand and swept it to the side. Without thinking, Buck banked Shadowbane to that direction just as a massive form ripped through the cloud cover below him. He caught a glimpse of a giant lizard-like creature with blue-black scales and huge bat wings. Worse yet, he saw other forms flying with it: two hulking things with orange flesh and two smaller ones wearing metal armor.

The Riders winged away at top speed. Buck bent low in the saddle and concentrated on not losing his fellows, praying that blasts of dragon fire would be hard to aim in the clouds.

The lead Riders swooped left and right, then dove. Buck barely missed getting hit in the head by a stout tree branch before dipping under a canopy of moss-laden trees. Their leaders landed with a splash of water in a marshy, wet morass surrounded by brooding, leafy willows and banban trees.

"This isn't exactly —" Connor started.

"Shh!" Eric said, raising a hand.

A heavy whooshing sounded above them in the murk. A rumbling voice echoed and a flash of green fire lit up the air to the south.

"Down," whispered Andyn. "Off the pegasi."

She landed in swampy water up to her knees and clasped the symbol of a silver tree on a chain around her neck. Her eyes closed in prayer and she murmured under her breath.

Buck started to draw Khelios, but Khyron's hand stopped him. The Elf shook his head, eyes flicking up to the sky.

The trees above and around them curved and twisted, covering them in a convenient dome of leaves, branches and drooping moss. The humid and foul air pressed in on them. Buck covered his mouth and nose with the edge of his cloak.

Andyn beckoned to Dar and Eric. They joined hands with her and she went into a trance. A mild, barely perceptible glow surrounded the Riders, then faded into the swamp.

A heavy thud shook the earth nearby and voices reached them. Buck couldn't make out any words but they were certainly distinct. One held the unmistakable rumble of a True Dragon. Two others sounded deep and guttural while another pair were feminine, filled with malice.

Another flash of green fire lit the swamp. Deep thumps and splashing echoed through the bog and Buck held perfectly still, hand over Shadowbane's eyes. Now he could hear the voices clearly.

"I know what I saw," said the Dragon's voice, sounding waspish.

"Of course," replied one of the females. "We aren't doubting you."

"Though we should," muttered one of the deeper voices.

The group paused and now Buck got a good look at them through a tiny gap in the leaves. His skin crawled.

An immense True Dragon with striped blue and black scales glared at two massive, piggish daemons with orange flesh and dead-black eyes. Each daemon stood taller than Buck by about two feet. Fangs gleamed white against purple lips. Ruffs of white horns protruded from hairless skulls. They wore black scale mail and carried two war hammers each.

"At least I'm paying attention, instead of gathering wool," the Dragon retorted.

One of the huge daemons shrugged, ruffling deep purple wings in the moist air. "Obviously we weren't needed since you were doing such a good job watching for Alliance spies in the clouds."

The Dragon's eyes narrowed.

"Peace," said a sleek female figure in blue-black chainmail. Red eyes glowed from behind a chainmail veil attached to her black spired helmet. She laid a mailed hand on the Dragon's massive shoulder. "Quite frankly, I'm amazed that you managed to see anything in that miasma."

Another female daemon sidled up next to the first, her double-bat wings of green and black spreading out behind her. "Describe it again, if you please," she asked in a conciliatory tone.

The Dragon frowned. "It looked like a pegasus or a hippogriff, but with strange coloration, mottled, almost like a camouflage cloak."

The pig-brute daemons exchanged a quick glance.

"Did it have a rider?" asked the first female daemon, putting hands to the pommels of her scimitars.

The Dragon made a face. "It was too fast. I couldn't see. Possibly. Maybe a human-sized figure in metal armor."

"We should scan the woods nearby," one of the female daemons announced. "Just to be sure."

A finger tapped Buck on the shoulder and only years of experience with his companions prevented him from jumping. Khyron beckoned him further into the copse of trees and Buck gingerly followed. Khyron pointed at Andyn and wiggled his fingers.

Buck's eyes went to Andyn, clasping hands with Dar and Eric. Though not as powerful spellcasters as she, they could lend her what power they had.

Andyn's lips moved, but he heard no sound. Dar and Eric bowed their heads, eyes closed. An ephemeral green mist grew up around them, almost like a morning fog lit by the dawn. A pleasant aroma accompanied the glow. It reminded Buck of peaceful, sunlit meadows. In a heartbeat, both faded away.

He heard a loud sniff from the Dragon. A low chant started up from the daemons, harsh and cruel. Despite not being much attuned to magic, even Buck could feel a pulse of raw power sweep over the forest.

The Riders held absolutely still. A trickle of sweat rolled down the side of Buck's face and his heart pounded. He kept his hand on the hilt of his sword, eyes locked on the protective greenery all around them. Something slithery brushed past his legs in the muck but he held rock steady.

"Anything?" asked one of the pig-daemons.

"Nothing I can detect," replied one of the women. "And I did a complete turn."

"Bah!" the Dragon spat. "Nothing but rotten plants, bog stink and fairy-feather reeds. And I think I smelled crimson water lily. Disgusting."

"Maybe we should search some more," offered the other female daemon. "His Lordship was quite certain that Alliance assassins would try to sneak into the main camp and kill off some of the high officers."

A pig-daemon snorted. "That's just him jumping at shadows."

"Shadows or not, he's the commander," chided a female voice. "At least, until one of the High Lords does away with him. For now, we continue on and report this. I have marked it on the map jewel so we can return later with a larger force if we need to."

Buck heard a scrabble and splashing of movement, then a great driving wind surged over their hiding place. He didn't dare breathe.

After long moments, Eric held up a hand. He focused his eyes on something in the distance, then nodded and dropped his hand.

"They're gone."

Buck's knees felt weak and he realized he had a cramp in his hand from gripping his sword so tightly. He flexed his fingers.

Andyn motioned to the trees and they swept back to their normal shape. Soon, the figure of a brown hawk shot towards them out of the grey and landed on Eric's saddlebow.

"That's the second time," Dar growled, casting a baleful eye at the clouds overhead. "And way too close for my comfort."

Buck leaned against Shadowbane. "No argument here."

"Andyn, why didn't you use a silence spell or one of those wind-wall things that hides us?" Connor asked.

Andyn shook her head. "Too powerful and noticeable, especially for daemons to detect. I went with something more subtle and quiet."

"Which was?"

"A spell called Calming Glade. It puts out a very mild aura of inoffensiveness, pleasantness and complete normalcy."

Eric sighed. "Well, it worked, but now we have a different problem."

He and Dar and Khyron exchanged a look.

"We shouldn't fly anymore," Eric announced.

Buck started. "What? It will take days to get to the Pass of Eagles from here. And we don't have days to spare! The Dark Wave is sweeping over our lands. How much longer can they last?"

Dar held up a hand. "I understand, Buck, but I get what he's driving at. The daemons said they were searching for assassins and it's obvious that they're patrolling. A group as large as ours, flying across the sky, is a dead giveaway. We were lucky the day was so overcast."

Connor bit his lip. "The Pass of Eagle's isn't the only way to get to the Titan's Crown, though. Can't we take another route?"

Eric shook his head. "We've been over this. The Pass is our best course. Coming at Rainbow Valley from the north takes us too close to areas where we know there's open combat and going directly east takes us to mountain ranges too high for us to go over. The air would be too thin and we'd likely freeze."

"There is the Harrowing," commented Khyron.

"No," Dar said. "We know nothing about that area and the legends are dire. I don't even want to fly over it. Besides, it's out of our way."

Buck cursed under his breath. Andyn put a hand on his shoulder. "I don't see any other option."

Khyron stroked his chin. "We could split up into two groups."

Dar shook his head. "If they're patrolling like we think they are, each group would be underpowered and in more danger."

"We do have magical resources," Khyron pointed out. "You and Eric can cast spells of obscuring, just like Andyn. You could use them on each group and make us less noticeable. I'm not generally in favor of dividing a force, but in this case, stealth wins out over strength."

Dar bit his lip, considering, then shook his head again. "No, I don't think so. Our spells don't last very long, even Andyn's. Even if we renewed them periodically, eventually we'll fall victim to mage-exhaustion and then we'd need to rest earlier than planned. It could end up taking longer than even travelling on the ground."

Khyron shot a look at Eric and Andyn. Both of them nodded.

"We have a long way to go," Andyn said. "That much spell-casting will drain the three of us quickly and ultimately end up slowing us down."

"Plus, we'd have no way of communicating with each other," Eric added, "and if something delays one group, we're in a bind. If what we suspect about the Dome of Glass is true, we'll need all of us on hand at the same time."

Buck could almost feel Khyron's resistance. *I have to hand it to him. He's not trying to take over even though he's used to being in command.*

Khyron pressed his lips together, then gave a firm nod. "Very well. I am out-voted. But I share Buck's sense of urgency. We should look for the earliest opportunity to take to the air again."

"Agreed," said Dar.

Buck looked to Connor for support. Fear for Carine and his family clenched his stomach.

Connor's jaw worked. "I know, Buck. And we have to find the Dome of Glass and the Gate of Stars even after we get to the mountain. But we don't have much choice. We can't be seen."

At Connor's expression, Buck paused. At least Carine and his family were deep within Alliance-held lands, in a fortified city.

Connor's family lived in Evendale, a small Halfling country near the Wilderness, close to possible invasion routes. In addition, Sentinel was very close to the evil-dominated land of Torosc, stronghold of the Ja'al cult. With every delay, danger crept closer to both Hannah and to Connor's family.

Dar laid a hand on the Halfling's shoulder and one on Buck's. "Let's move. The sooner we start, the sooner we finish."

Buck swung into the saddle and gripped the reins, following the other Riders through the woods.

Images of daemons rampaging through his hometown haunted him.

Chapter Three – Dark Wave Rising

Of all the forms she could adopt, Druidess Carine Del Rio liked being an owl the best. She knew how Buck Bydecy felt when riding his pegasus.

She banked over the dark hills, low above the treetops, her owl-eyes scanning the campfires and pavilions stretched out below. The wind ruffled through her wings with barely a whisper of sound.

In her mind she kept a careful tally, counting each tent, each siege machine, ogre, dragon and, especially, each daemon. Thankfully, the two moons, Kaliri and Diometrius, waned in the sky above her, leaving mostly starlight for illumination. However, she knew many of the enemy didn't necessarily need light to see her — and an owl as tall as a Dwarf would get anyone's attention. She swooped down onto a bough of a giant pine and latched on with her talons.

Seconds later, the greenery parted on the other side of a meadow. A four-armed, satyr-like daemon stalked out. Three Dark Elves in chainmail accompanied him, riding horse-sized spiders. They moved through the meadow, only the waving motion of tall grass betraying their presence.

Damn it.

Carine would have ground her teeth if she had any. She didn't dare take wing again.

The daemon halted. It held up a claw. A gemstone on its armband flashed crimson fire in the night. Carine's magical senses tingled. She held as still as possible behind a screen of branches.

The daemon turned red-glowing eyes in her direction and her heart leaped in her throat. The Dark Elves charged, one of them reaching into a bag at his hip. Carine launched herself off the branch and swooped down among the trees, diving between massive trunks. The rapid clacking of spider legs and crunch of branches followed. She pulled up.

The daemon chanted a harsh spell. The air crackled with electricity and a bolt of lightning shot past her, blasting away the top of a nearby tree. Sharp splinters cut her and a piece of flaming wood hit her in the side, spinning away into the darkness. She banked into a gap between two more pines.

Carine's heart hammered in her chest. She doubled back and dove into the shadows, heading back towards the Dark Elves at full speed. She burst through the vegetation, scattering leaves and twigs. They scrabbled to a halt, clawing for swords or axes, but she knocked one of them spinning from the saddle as she flashed past on silent wings.

The daemon cursed. A whistling sound made her risk a glance over her shoulder. One of the Elves whirled a sling and shot a glittering black bullet at her.

Carine dodged left and up. A dull thud sounded in the forest and tree branches snapped. Unwilling to risk the daemon, she dove down and doubled back again. She shot past a stand of trees covered with misty black webs.

She soared past the Elves and daemon and waved a claw at a knot of nearby raspberry bushes. They animated, waving thorny branches wildly, entangling elves, spiders and daemon alike. The resulting bellow of rage from the daemon was gratifying.

Now Carine pushed herself to full speed and burst up through the tree canopy, soaring off to the southwest. Sizzling bolts of purple fire lanced past her and an arrow narrowly missed a wing, but she pulled away. A sharp pain hit her back and she smelled singed feathers.

She dared another look back. The daemon and his escorts had cleared the woods, but their arrows and magic spells fell short. Still, Carine sped on, trying to put as much distance between them as she could. Soon, every muscle in her transformed body complained. She pushed herself to her limits, desperately seeking the cover of another dense arm of the forest a half mile away.

She finally alighted on a tree, chest heaving with exertion. Her owl-sight showed no pursuit and she allowed herself to relax. After letting her pulse slow to something more normal, she set off again, aiming for the lights of the Astarellian metropolis of Tyler, twinkling in the distance. She kept to the woods until certain that several miles separated her from the Ja'al army, then flew for the city's north gate. After passing over abandoned villages on the outskirts, she dove into an empty corral. She metamorphosed back into her natural human self as she landed, reaching out for a fence as her transformation took hold. Her feathers melded into a dark grey robe and cloak, singed and torn in three places.

She leaned on the fence rail, panting, eyes closed. *By the Earth Mother, that was close.*

Her head spun dizzily and nausea roiled her stomach. Transformations were hard enough without getting the life scared out of her. She forced her hands to stop trembling, then combed her fingers through her dark brown hair and tied it into a ponytail. Taking a deep breath, she strode towards the gate with her head held high.

The massive Northgate was shut, its steel-banded doors barred. Figures in armor moved around on the battlements in the glitter of magical lights. Two squads of troops guarded outside the towers.

The soldiers raised crossbows and halberds at her approach, but a dwarven officer stopped them.

He measured her with a flinty eye. "State your choice."

"Lux."

He nodded and his men lowered their weapons. "Name?"

"Carine Del Rio."

The Dwarf's eyebrows rose. "Ah. Well, then. Welcome back, Druidess. We were told to watch for you, but Colonel McDonald wasn't sure which gate you'd use."

A sudden weariness came over her and Carine gave him a wan smile. "Thank you, Lieutenant. It is good to be back."

He measured her with his gaze for a moment. "Private Dulor," he said without turning his head, "Go to the outer bailey and find a wineskin and a horse for the Druidess."

She opened her mouth but he held up a hand. "No excuses. You look like you've seen a ghost. I don't know what you were doing out there and I don't want to know. But I *do* know that Sir Buckminster will have my head if you pass out at my gate."

Carine graciously accepted the wine flask and the horse without further protest. To her surprise, the wine tasted fruity and light with a hint of cherries.

"Thank you again, Lieutenant," she said, wiping her mouth. "Not the usual fare they give you at the gate."

The corner of his mouth curved up. "Well, we sometimes have important visitors, do we not?"

She smiled back at him and handed back the flask. He nodded. "Kurental's protection on you."

She rode into the city through the gates, heading for the North Barracks. Despite the late hour, Tyler bustled like a village on market day. Platoons of soldiers marched down boulevards, couriers hurried along the sidewalks, and wagons plodded through the streets. An old woman poked her face between the curtains of a window, brow creased in worry, then just as quickly disappeared. Carine calmly wended her way through the traffic to the inner gate, then gave a different password and her name at the command center.

Colonel Fiona MacDonald met her personally in her office. Her black eyes glinted in the magical lamplight as she gestured to a seat.

"Please, Druidess, don't stand on ceremony."

For the tenth time, Carine's eyes followed the scar on the Colonel's face — a pale line that traced from her hairline above her left eye down to her jaw. For the tenth time, Carine didn't ask.

"Thank you, Colonel," she said instead. "It has been quite a night."

"Hmm. Do tell."

Carine did tell, relating her assessment of the enemy force and her encounter with the patrol. Colonel MacDonald noted it all down on a pad of paper, nodding occasionally. Finally, she dropped the pencil and steepled her fingers in front of her face.

"It's worse than I feared."

Carine caught herself twisting the front of her robe in her hands and forced herself to stop. "That bad?"

MacDonald sighed, leaning back in her chair. "Based on your figures and the information from other scouts, we have a good accounting of the enemy force."

"How many?"

"Almost fifty thousand."

Carine felt faint and closed her eyes. She pinched the bridge of her nose against a sudden headache. "That's... that's impossible. I think the entire military of Rokon is that large."

The colonel shook her head. "The size of the enemy force doesn't worry me. The walls of Tyler are strong, the stockpile has literally tons of magically preserved provisions, we have deep wells within the city, and there are plenty of magical reserves to counter any devilry the Ja'al can cook up. Besides, we've already transferred a lot of the more infirm and vulnerable people south. They're probably in Seacrest by now."

She paused and Carine waited.

"But?" she asked finally.

MacDonald tapped her fingers on the arm of her chair. "What are they waiting for? They've looted, raped and pillaged their way through the countryside, won three pitched battles, and now they suddenly stop."

"Maybe they know the city is too strong for them."

"Indeed. Then why head in this direction at all if they can't conquer it?"

Carine's mind raced for an explanation.

MacDonald nodded, her eyes distant. "Exactly. They're waiting for something. What?"

Carine shook her head and dropped her hands in her lap. "I have no answers, Colonel. Not yet."

The Colonel stood. "Neither do I."

Carine also rose. "If there is anything else I can do to assist you..."

"I will contact you. I know it is hard to wait for orders or a change in situation, but you have already been a great help."

"But surely —"

"You have had a hard night and I am keeping you from taking your rest. I will contact you tomorrow."

Carine opened her mouth to protest again, but a sharp look from Mac-Donald stopped her. "You are staying with the Bydecy family?"

"Yes."

"Who else is guarding them?"

"Two Sword Knights of Astarel, and two Shield Knights. I think I can be spared if you need me."

The officer shook her head. "No. I think you are needed there. Your healing and magic skills are a great advantage if the worst happens."

A chill raced down Carine's spine. "And that is?"

The colonel's dark eyes transfixed hers. "Whatever the Ja'al army is waiting for."

Chapter Four – From A Darkening Sea

The sound of metal on ceramic awakened her. Carine opened her eyes and stretched.

Summer sunlight streamed in around the edges of the shutters. The aroma of pancakes and tea wafted in from the kitchen. She heard Alfred and Jack Bydecy say something she didn't quite catch. A woman's voice answered in the background, too faint for her to make out words.

What a night.

Carine flipped the covers off and sat on the edge of the bed. Though the room had sparse furnishings, she could tell it was Buck's: a practice sword and worn shield hung on a wall, framing a faded map of the Northern Alliance nations. A pair of trophies sat on a nearby bureau, one depicting armored knights fighting with swords and another of a mounted warrior with a sword and shield.

Her eyes flitted to his name on a trophy.

Never in a million years did I think I'd lose my heart to a warrior. Another druid maybe, or a wizard.

Carine sighed. This home, with its aromas of comfort and its welcoming people, reminded her of her own before her parents died. She smiled, remembering her mother's cheerful wisdom and her father's quiet tutelage in the woods, showing her herbs and wildlife.

What would Mother and Father say now?

Remembering her parents' untimely death made her stomach tighten. She clenched her fists, willing the anxieties to dissipate.

Earth Mother, don't let the same happen to Buck.

Sometimes, just before drifting off to sleep at night, a sudden fear for him would surge to the surface and she would have to exercise mind-centering techniques to calm herself. The thought of him taking on such horrors as she'd seen in the Ja'al army jangled her nerves.

Stop it, woman. She scolded in her mind. *He can take care of himself.*

She tried to focus on her mission in Tyler instead, but her brain wouldn't cooperate. Standing, she brushed her fingers on the handle of Buck's practice sword.

Have you found the Gate of Stars yet, Buck? Is there a way to bring the Celestials to turn aside the Dark Wave?

Her eyes drifted to a small portrait hung over the bureau. It depicted a younger Alfred Bydecy, two boys, a girl, and a plain woman with sandy hair. The woman's grey eyes reminded her of Buck.

Carine sighed, then opened a drawer of the bureau and removed a robe. She slipped it on and fastened the ties at the neck and waist before heading out to the dining room.

Alfred smiled at her, his black eyes warm. "Ah, Carine. Good to see you up. Sir Torin and Lady Elise tell me you came home rather late."

Carine nodded. "That's an understatement."

A burly human man in chain mail rose from his seat at the table. A sturdy blonde woman joined him and both bowed.

"Good morning," the man said.

"Good morning, Sir Torin, Lady Elise. Where are Sir Alvin and Lady Marta?"

"Checking in at the guardhouse," replied Lady Elise with a smile. "Nothing to worry about. We told them that Jack was making pancakes. That should bring them around."

"I think pancakes are a small price to pay for the level of attention we're getting," announced Jack, backing through the kitchen door with a heavily laden platter.

He set it down and Carine's stomach rumbled. Pecan-raisin pancakes steamed next to slices of crisp bacon and grilled tomatoes, reminding her of her mother's kitchen.

She shook her head. "Jack, I don't know why you settle for being a ship's cook instead of setting up a café here in town. You'd earn a comfortable living."

Jack wiped his hands in a towel and shrugged. "Cities are boring compared to the sea — and I get to travel as much as I want."

Alfred motioned to the seats at the table. Carine joined them as the guards also sat.

"I hope they pay you enough," she said.

He grinned at her. "They do, or else I sign on with someone else."

Alfred raised an eyebrow but said nothing. Carine hid a smile.

Jack brought in a bowl of fruit salad of peaches, plums, grapes and berries. She detected the aroma of currant wine.

How does he know? She wondered, then dismissed the thought. Her mother wasn't the only one who knew that recipe, for certain.

"What were you working on so late?" asked Alfred around a mouthful of pancake.

Carine shot a look at the knights, who shook their heads almost imperceptibly.

"Just some assessments of our readiness and surveys of the land nearby," she replied with a disarming smile. "I have an attunement to the forest and it tells me much."

"Rumors have it that the Ja'al army is roaming the countryside," Jack said, sipping his tea. "More refugees come in every day."

"Aye," replied Alfred, brushing at his grey mustache. "But I also hear the bastards ran into the 7th Regiment and a company of Crown Knights at Silver Crossing two days ago and had their heads handed to them."

Happy to give them some good news, Carine nodded. "I can confirm that. I'm not sure about the size of the enemy force, but it wasn't a raiding party."

The knights said nothing and no one spoke for a while. Despite the ominous events of the previous evening, she had no problem doing justice to Jack's handiwork.

Finally, Jack leaned back in his chair. He fixed her with lazy grey eyes. At such times, he looked like a shorter, stockier version of Buck. "Will they evacuate Tyler?"

Before Carine could reply, Lady Elise nodded. "Complete evacuation is one of the options. I think the Duke would only do that if he were convinced that there was no hope of holding the city. We are obviously not at that stage."

Alfred frowned and his mustache bristled. "Damned if I'm going to let some rotten devil-worshippers take my home from me!"

"You're worth more than the house, Da'," Jack said with a frown of his own.

Alfred shook his head and sat back, glowering. "This is all I have left of your mother. Everyone will go their separate ways after this is all over and I'll be alone with nothing but memories."

Carine hesitated. She wanted desperately to tell Jack and Alfred to leave immediately, to escape before the daemon army descended on Tyler, but she would have to explain why. Knowing Alfred and his tendency to gab, that might be risky. If word got out and everyone decided to leave at once, the ensuing panic would endanger everyone – and provide the Ja'al a big, fat target of civilians that the army would have to protect. She had to trust the Duke and his advisors to pick the right moment, if it happened.

Who am I kidding? There's an army of fifty-thousand lurking out there, just waiting for something. They will attack. Tyler is too strategic to leave alone. It's only a matter of time.

No one spoke. She measured Alfred with her eyes, seeing only a lonely father separated from his children by distance and necessity.

"I don't blame you, Alfred," she said, laying her hand on his arm and giving it a squeeze. "I would feel the same way."

Alfred blinked and patted her hand. "You're a good lass, Carine. Buck has chosen well."

She felt her face grow warm and released him.

"Well," said Jack, rising. "I have to go down to the waterfront to see about the morning's catch."

"Don't worry about the kitchen," Sir Torin rumbled. "We'll clean it up."

Jack's frown returned. "I can't ask you to do that! Sword Knights as kitchen knaves? What would people say?"

"You're not asking," Lady Elise said with a smile. "We're volunteering.

Besides, I see Sir Alvin and Lady Marta heading this way along the avenue."

Carine considered staying too, but her musings about Buck, daemons, and evacuations made her edgy. She stood.

"I'd like to go with you, Jack," she said. "It will do me some good to get down by the sea. If you wait a moment for me to clean up a little, I'll join you."

Jack nodded. "I'll meet you in the sitting room."

She snatched a towel from her room and headed out the back door of the house. Striding to a wooden enclosure with an open roof, she slipped inside and latched the door, then peeled off her robe. A firm tug on a nearby chain brought down a bracing stream of cool water from a cistern overhead. She gasped from the chill but washed quickly, toweling off in seconds. She scooted to her room and dressed in a shift, new robe and sandals, then buckled on her dagger and took up her staff.

Jack's mouth curved in a grin. "My sister would still be picking out a wardrobe for the day."

She tossed her head. "Your sister and I run in completely different professional circles."

Jack's grin widened as he stood, a covered basket in his hands. "Ready?"

Without waiting for an answer, he headed out the door. Carine followed him down the sloping cobblestone street towards the main boulevard. By now, the sun had burned off most of the morning's low clouds and many people bustled about. Seagulls wheeled overhead, their raucous calls punctuating the murmur of voices and creaking of cart wheels. People cast glances at them with nervous eyes, then turned back to their work.

She breathed in deeply of the salty air and kept pace with Jack. "Have your sister and her family gotten settled?"

Jack nodded. "Summer, Weston and the children are at my place while I stay at Dad's. I thought it would be too much to try to fit them in. My niece and nephew would love to be around the knights, but they can get underfoot very easily."

Carine smiled. She met Buck's sister and her family the previous day. Despite the long and harrowing escape from the now-ruined town of Greenglade, to the east, both of the children peppered her with questions about their famous uncle the whole time.

Summer and Weston have their hands full…

She accompanied Jack downhill towards the marina, where the street leveled out. He jerked a thumb at a wharf.

"The best catch is there, but I'll have to do a bit of haggling. No offense if you're otherwise inclined."

Still wrestling with a feeling of unease, she nodded. "I'll go over to the beach park. Join me there when you're ready."

With a wave, he headed off. A young man in the livery of the city messenger service tended to his steed at a hitching post. Jack paused and clapped a hand on the lad's shoulder, saying something Carine couldn't hear. The messenger grinned broadly, then returned to brushing his horse's mane.

Carine shielded her eyes against the sunlight. After Jack disappeared among the fishmonger stalls, she strolled south along the boardwalk until she reached the beach area.

A few families with young children waded into the shallows but she continued on to the tide pools. Stepping carefully along the rocks, she reached the edge. Waves crashed below her, spraying her with salty mist.

Again, she lifted her hand to her brow, squinting against the sunlight dancing on the water. After a while, she sat on a rock, contemplating the ocean. Several attempts to center her mind and listen to the sea ended in only more worries about Buck, the war and the Ja'al plot.

Earth Mother, why am I so uneasy?

She closed her eyes and waited a few minutes, listening to the sounds of the ocean, the wind and the sea birds. She breathed slowly and deeply of the air, laden with the aroma of salt, sand and ocean plants. Slowly a measure of peace settled on her.

She was just starting to relax when her arcane senses tingled. A sudden sense of urgency struck her and she opened her eyes.

A motion in the water below caught her attention. A dolphin's head broke the surface. It bobbed up and chittered at her. Its side bore the marks of heavy bruising and one flipper lay limp in the water.

"By the Mighty Oaks!" she breathed. She laid her staff on the rocks and clambered down, scraping her calf twice in the process. She tried to reach the dolphin but it was too far away.

Throwing caution to the winds, she whipped off her robe and jumped in, clad only in her shift. The dolphin floated towards her and she swam to it, whispering a spell as her hands touched its skin. In her mind's eye, she saw broken bones, internal injuries and shock.

"Steady, fellow," she murmured.

Healing energy flowed through her. Bones knitted together, bruised organs regenerated and micro-hemorrhages sealed. Next, she gave the dolphin a jolt of energy. The expenditure of magical power made her dizzy, but she kept treading water, catching her breath.

The creature nosed her and nestled closer.

Following an instinct, she placed both hands on its head and simply floated with it.

"What happened, friend?" she whispered. "Who did this to you?"

The sunny sky, clouds, ocean waves and rocks disappeared. She drifted through deep water in the dolphin's memory, following others of its pod through a forest of kelp. The pod circled around a group of creatures arrayed in a neat company.

She recognized them instantly. Some had the lower bodies of fish and the torsos of humans. Other, human-like figures accompanied them. They were nude, with webbed fingers and toes. Everyone carried tridents, spears, daggers or oddly-shaped crossbows. Equal numbers of males and females floated side by side.

Merfolk and Sirines…

A blonde female Sirine nodded to a nearby Mermaid and motioned to the troop. As one, the Merfolk, Sirines and dolphins glided through the deep blue in a tight, cohesive formation.

Presently, a crimson light glowed in the distance. It shimmered as if through a screen of heat or bubbles. As they approached, her heart clenched.

Unextinguishable mage-fires of lurid red boiled in a vast circle around a massive structure of skulls and bones. Carine recognized it instantly.

Skull Gate! Her mind shrieked.

Lights flared near the sea-folk and a magical gong thrummed through the water. A horde of dark figures swarmed at them from the area around the Gate. Some looked like fish with arms and legs while others were sharks with spiny ridges down their backs and black horns on their heads. She felt the dolphin's anger and fear as it charged into battle. The ocean swirled. Magic spells lanced out from the ranks of the sea-folk. The two forces clashed and Carine's dolphin slammed down two of the shark-beasts in quick succession. Spears and daggers stabbed. Crossbow bolts sizzled past, propelled by magical charges. Figures of the dead and wounded spiraled away into misty, bloody water. She felt a heavy, vicious blow in her side, then another. Carine's dolphin spun away from two shark beasts. A pair of male Sirines skewered the enemies with spears and the creatures thrashed violently in a cloud of black ichor, fouling the water even further.

A merman put his arm around her and turned the dolphin towards the Skull Gate. The fanged skull at the apex flashed. In horror, she saw a half-octopus, half-crab creature emerge from the Gate, purple eyes blazing.

"Fly!" a voice echoed in her head. "Warn the land-people! The Hordes of Satan have arrived!"

The vision snapped off like a lamp extinguished. A heavy splash of water hit Carine and she swallowed a big gulp of it, nearly choking. The dolphin bore her up as she coughed and sputtered. It pulled her away from the tide pools and towards the beach. When she could stand, she did so.

The dolphin tossed its head twice at her and chirped, then spun away into the water.

"No!" she screamed. "You know what's out there. Don't go! They'll kill you!"

With a flip of its tail, the dolphin raced off.

Tears of desperation and fear flowed down her cheeks. "No! Come back!"

"Miss?"

She whirled. A young man with two little girls stared at her. "What's the matter? Who's going to kill the dolphin?"

She looked past him without seeing him, then splashed up to the beach. "Go home!" she ordered. "Quickly!"

Muttering a magic phrase under her breath, she held out her hand. From the rocks, her staff vibrated, then flew to her palm.

Heedless of the fact that she wore only a shift and sandals, she raced along the beach towards the boardwalk.

"Jack!" She screamed at the top of her lungs. "Jack Bydecy!"

He came around the corner at a dead run, eyes wide. She staggered from the soft sand to the wood of the boardwalk.

"A horse, quick! I need to get to Colonel MacDonald!"

He met her eyes and she saw the sudden recognition. He gritted his teeth.

"Braden! I need to borrow your horse!" he shouted over his shoulder.

***

Carine gathered her grey owl-robe around her, staring down at the detailed map laid out on the massive table. Conversation echoed in the meeting room but her thoughts were elsewhere. Her eyes flitted all over the giant parchment, taking in the fine detail of woods, villages, the city of Tyler and coastline.

Blue pins with flags showed the location of allied forces. Red pins marked known enemy camps and strongholds. Her eyes drifted to the ocean area, where four markers indicated sea-folk communities. She tapped her fingers on her staff.

Far too many red pins and not enough blue...

"Well, I think we have our answer, Your Grace," said Colonel MacDonald. The other conversations in the room ceased. She inserted six red pins out near the sea-folk markers.

Carine surveyed the other people in the room. The Duke of Tyler gazed at the map, arms crossed. He stroked a black beard peppered with grey, nodding slowly. He towered over the blonde woman by his side, attired in the same tabard of sea-green and grey as he.

Next to them, two dwarven men leaned on the table, dark eyes hooded. A Christian bishop, an Elven Matriarch of Verian, and a Halfling high priest of Irial crowded around. All wore armor and bore weapons.

"I understand, Colonel," the Duke said. "Druidess Del Rio's news certainly fits in the last pieces of the puzzle."

The Duchess nodded. "Vodyanoi and fell sharks carry the assault from the ocean with daemonic support while the land army presses in from the east. We're caught between two forces."

The bishop shook his head. "Who would have thought that the Dark Wave would come from the sea? We've been concentrating our efforts on Skull Gates on land."

The Verian matriarch frowned. "For once, the Ja'al were literally telling the truth: part of the Dark Wave is from the ocean."

"Your Grace?" Carine asked. All eyes turned to her.

She cleared her throat. "I realize that many civilians have already been evacuated to Deran. Wouldn't this be the time to move out the remainder?"

The Duke of Tyler nodded again. "Yes, we have already started. What you saw in your vision is but a small part of the attack. This means that the enemy has only to reach the coast and then the hammer will strike. We don't have much time."

He shot a glance at the Dwarves. "You know what to do. Prepare the Coast Passage for the final departure and set countermeasures." They bowed and departed.

"Colonel MacDonald," the Duke continued, "Tell General Matson to mobilize the militia and prepare for an all-out assault. Also, contact all the sea-folk. Let them know that we appreciate their valor, but I don't want them to sacrifice their communities in vain. Advise them to retreat to deeper waters to the south immediately."

"At once, my lord," The Colonel gave Carine a grim smile before she left.

The Duke regarded the remainder of his Council. "I will need all your help to carry this off. Our priority will be to get as many civilians out into the Coast Passage as we can. If it comes to it, we will seal the entrances to cut off pursuit. I will remain as long as possible."

"As will I," said the Duchess with a toss of her head.

"My dear —"

"This is not open for debate, my lord," she replied, eyes flashing. "I would not have it said that the Duchess of Tyler departed for safety when her people were in peril."

He glowered at her. She took his arm. "Your children are in other lands, lord. Your legacy is safe. I would honor Marissa's memory by staying at your side, as she would have done."

He opened his mouth as if to speak, then clamped it shut and nodded.

Carine regarded the Duchess in undisguised admiration.

She faces certain death if she stays but insists on remaining with her husband. Is that what marriage is?

The remaining Council members bowed. "Then we will stand with you," the Halfling priest announced. "We all have capable subordinates who can help guide the evacuation. The daemon hordes will feel the might of our gods if they dare set foot inside the city."

A vision of the enemy camp flashed in Carine's brain and her heart skipped a beat. "As soon as I see to it that Sir Buckminster's family is safe," she said, "I will help defend the city."

The Duke regarded her thoughtfully and the Duchess smiled.

"You need not, Druidess," the Duchess said. "We know your solemn charge to the Papal Nuncio. As soon as you can, accompany the Bydecy's to safety."

Carine opened her mouth to protest but the Duke shook his head. "Tyler is not your home, yet you would sacrifice yourself to save it. For this, we are all grateful. But you have another task. See that Sir Buckminster's family are sent through the Coast Passage to safety. That is my command."

Carine swallowed her protest and bowed instead. "I will do so, then."

"Good," the duke replied as she straightened. His mouth quirked up in a wry grin. "At least I can command someone in this room." His eyes twinkled.

Despite the dire situation, Carine found herself smiling.

The Duchess rolled her eyes and pinched his shoulder. "God speed you all," she said, not looking at him. "And may the morrow find us victorious…"

Chapter Five – Hammer and Anvil

Carine pulled on the reins of her horse. "Don't run and don't push," she called out over the line of citizens. "There are guards in the passage to guide you."

The refugees nearest her seemed to calm and she smiled down at them, trying to project an aura of confidence that she had trouble feeling.

Something boomed in the distance, out by the city walls. She glanced that way. Already, black tendrils of smoke lifted skyward near the city gates. She smelled woodsmoke and other, unsettling odors on the wind.

The defenses are holding so far, she thought. So far.

The huge column of people surged past her, carrying bundles on their backs or pushing wheeled carts laden with supplies or less mobile refugees. She scanned the crowd, looking for Buck's family.

Where are they? She twisted the reins in her hands and bit her lip. *They should be here by now.*

Her eyes followed the crowd towards the great fountain in the middle of the market square. The entire structure, some eighty feet in diameter, had been tilted up on one edge like some massive trap door. Indeed, she saw enormous hinges on one side. Gigantic, thick metal pistons held up the structure along the edges. The fountain turned out to be hollow, a structure of wood, metal and cut stone constructed to make it appear as if it were one solid piece of marble. A ramp led down into a tunnel lit by magical glow-lamps: the entrance to the Coastal Passage.

Early that morning, she had caught a glimpse of the opening sequence. Using a set of mechanical devices set into fittings on one side of the fountain, engineers lifted up one edge, then did the same to others on the opposite side. While teams of oxen pulled ropes, dwarven mages applied lifting spells. Then, as smoothly as a kitchen cupboard door, the entire fountain swiveled up, revealing the hidden passage underneath. Then, sturdy pistons had been inserted into other fittings to keep the fountain in place. The whole exercise had taken less than a half hour.

Even the fountain itself was amazing. The pipes that brought water to the top of the fountain had flexible metal-and-rubber sections that made the pivoting action easy to accomplish.

I never would have guessed any of this if I hadn't seen it with my own eyes.

She watched a trio of engineers install detonation charges near the pistons. The rectangular devices crackled with magical energy.

A Dwarf stumped by next to her and set down a charge on the street, mopping his brow. She eyed the object warily and he smirked.

"Ah, lass, you have nothing to worry about," he said, patting the charge as refugees hurried past him. "We only arm them after they're installed and they're for emergencies anyway. We can close the passage just fine by using the mechanisms."

"I'm glad of that," she said. "I wouldn't want to be around when you set them off."

He clucked his tongue at her. "That would be wise. One could blow you fifty feet in the air — if you remain in one piece, that is. And worse yet if there's a very hot fire nearby. But you don't have to worry. We have it well in hand."

"Good," she commented, scanning the crowd. The engineer moved off.

"Torin, where are you?" she muttered under her breath, anxious yet unwilling to leave her post. "We're running out of time."

From the other side of the city square, a guard in splint mail cantered up.

Seeing her chance, she pointed at the line of refugees. "Keep them moving."

He nodded. She trotted her horse back towards the harbor, heading towards the Bydecy home. She rode through avenues empty of all except formations of troops hustling towards the city walls, accompanied by mages and priests.

She turned onto a wide boulevard but a shout from a nearby alleyway alerted her.

The four Knights hustled towards her with Jack, Alfred, Summer and her family in tow. Her eyes widened. Jack carried a bloodied cutlass and Alfred bore an ancient sword that glittered blue. Even Summer and her husband carried daggers; their two children clung to them, trembling.

"What happened?" she asked, pulling up. *And where did Alfred get a magic sword?*

Sir Torin rested his bloodstained greatsword on his shoulder pauldron. "Hobgoblins and Kaftu came up through the sewers in the hilltop districts and headed straight for the Bydecy house," he reported. "We were cut off and had to take the roundabout route, past the East Gate."

"Damn it! How many?"

"More than a dozen. They were there specifically for Buck's family."

Carine's heart fell. *And I wasn't there…*

Sir Torin nodded to her. "Don't blame yourself, Druidess. We miscalculated. We should have sent them all out days ago."

"Is anyone else left in the neighborhood?" Carine asked, submerging her guilt.

Lady Elise glanced back the way they had come. "Not that we know of."

Carine turned in the saddle. "We can't cut across to the plaza?"

Lady Marta shook her head. "The enemy swarms over the gate like ants. We took a chance coming this way at all."

Carine's stomach clenched. *This isn't supposed to be happening. I wish I knew the city better.*

Jack pointed down a side street. "We can save time by crossing down by the harbor and turning left to get to the square."

Sir Alvin nodded. "Great idea. Druidess, if you can get Summer and the children on your horse, we could move faster."

She nodded and quickly swapped places, giving the reins to Summer's husband, Weston.

"Are we going to be okay?" asked one of the children.

Weston patted her arm. "We'll be fine. We just have to get to the plaza and into the escape tunnel."

Thank the Earth Mother I found them at least.

They hurried away with Jack in the lead. He guided them through smaller avenues past deserted homes and businesses. Clothes, empty baskets and scattered papers littered the street, mute testimony to the haste of the evacuation.

Carine shot a look towards the East Gate as they went. Plumes of smoke spiraled up into the air and bat-winged creatures floated above the walls. A shaft of light stabbed down, then another and she heard several booms. Then came a sound from the East Gate that froze her blood in her veins: the roar of a dragon, then another.

She exchanged a glance with Lady Marta, trotting at her side. The knight shook her head, face grim.

She doesn't think they'll hold...

Carine shifted her staff in sweaty palms, her heartbeat accelerating.

At the next major street, Jack turned left and they saw the seaport. Carine's eyes locked on the scene and she slowed, heart in her throat.

Dark green, finned fish-men stormed ashore along the boardwalk and the wharfs. Arrows, fire darts, lightning, and fireballs arced out at them from defenders behind barricades. Dozens of invaders dropped, were immolated in thunderous blasts, or had holes blown in them, but they came on, more taking the place of the fallen.

Astarellian navy ships circled in the bay. Sailors dropped melon-sized, glowing metal spheres into the water while marines stood guard. Dull, heavy thuds sounded and bloody disks of froth formed under the surface, followed immediately by fountains geysering up out of the water. Dark figures swarmed up the sides of the vessels. The marines met them head-on, slashing with cutlasses while archers in the upper works shot down the attackers.

Carine's eyes widened. Slimy tentacles grappled a battleship and a hideous kraken emerged from the water, red eyes blazing. Crewmen hacked at the monster's arms with axes as enemy fish-men clambered aboard.

Six pegasi with riders took off from the deck of a nearby carrier and dove at the beast, hitting it repeatedly with arrows and spells. The kraken roared and slapped a pegasus out of the sky. Mount and rider careened madly into the ocean, slamming into the water with a tremendous splash. The kraken's tentacles flexed. With a massive cracking sound, one side of the battleship caved in.

From the harbor towers, flaming catapult rocks splashed, steaming, into the ocean near the kraken. Then one scored a direct hit, detonating in a ball of flame. When the smoke cleared, half the kraken's head was gone and it slid back into the water as the battleship began to sink.

Sweet Earth Mother!

"Druidess!" Sir Alvin's firm hand pulled on her arm and jolted her from her state of shock. She followed them into the square.

Few civilians remained. The Knights ushered the Bydecy's to the rear of the line, then faced the square, weapons at the ready.

"At least we're here," Carine said, letting out a deep breath. "They'll be safe now."

Lady Marta nodded. "We just need to hold long enough to close the tunnel. Then we follow."

Chanting and drums sounded from the city. She distinctly heard snarling.

"What do you want me to do?" Carine asked Marta in a whisper. "I've fought Hobgoblins and Ogres from time to time but I'm no soldier."

"We're armored," she replied. "Stay behind us and use your magic to help. Don't fight hand to hand unless you absolutely have to."

Carine licked dry lips and gripped her staff, eyes darting in all directions.

"Just about done!" called out one of the dwarven engineers.

How can he be so calm at a time like this?

Carine heard a shout from a nearby street. Three city guards raced towards them.

"Daemons!" one shouted. "And goblins! They're heading this way!"

The evacuees let out a collective scream of terror.

"Let them come!" roared Alfred.

"Keep moving into the passage!" Carine screamed. "We'll hold them off!"

"You heard the lady!" the dwarven engineer bellowed. "Move it! And don't trample anyone or I'll knock your heads together!"

The city guards stopped near them and turned, aiming bows down the street. Carine's eyes flickered around the square, counting the number of trees and shrubs she could call upon to help her.

Then a swarm of goblins in black scale mail surged down the lane at them, hooting and brandishing spears and axes. The guards loosed, killing three of them. Lady Marta and Lady Elise stepped forward, their shields up. Sir Torin and Sir Alvin stood beside them, greatswords at the ready.

The goblins hurled their spears; some struck the ladies' shields and cracked in two. Other missiles clashed harmlessly off the Knights' plate mail. The balance of the goblin horde hit the Knights' line.

Carine called to the trees. To her immense satisfaction, they bowed to the ground, plucking goblins from the pavement. They hurled the screaming Ja'al through the air to smash into nearby buildings.

The Knights amazed her. Outnumbered more than ten to one, the four of them worked together like a finely-tuned clock. The women bashed aside attackers, slammed them down with maces and opened holes in their front line. The men stepped through, slashed goblins, then drew back behind the shields. As soon as the enemy counterattacked, the women repeated their maneuver, felling goblins with shield and mace while the men stepped through and cut down the enemy, two or three at a time.

Javelins landed near her and Carine backed up, casting flashes of light to blind enemy warriors. There were too many. A dozen howling goblins got past the Knights. The dwarven engineers stepped in front of her, hammers and axes raised. She readied her staff as the attackers hit.

Then all was a swirling riot of blades, armor, blood and screams. She smashed down two enemies, her staff flashing silver light each time. She ducked under a spear thrust aimed at her eye and kicked its owner into a nearby flowerbed. With a quick spell, she entangled it in the plants while two dwarven engineers smashed it with hammers.

Suddenly, the plaza fell quiet. Carine stood amid the carnage, trembling. The city guards lay still, the victim of goblin axes, but scores of enemy dead lay in piles. The Knights trotted back to join her.

She shot a look back at the escape route. Alfred grudgingly backed into the tunnel, his glittering sword out and Jack at his side. The last of the terrified refugees hurried down the ramp. Carine saw the frightened faces of Alfred's grandchildren among them.

"Don't wait!" she yelled.

A cackling laugh made her turn. She felt the blood drain from her face.

A dozen daemons hovered near the fountain, dark red bat wings flapping. They stood only a little taller than the goblins, but their legs ended in cloven hooves. They looked like a cross between a Dwarf and a wolf: bearded and sporting fanged snouts. They carried red-glowing short swords.

"Oh shit," swore the dwarven engineer. "Dwerrolves…"

The daemons chanted in unison, a vile, harsh song ringing with pure malice. Carine squeezed her eyes shut as a splitting headache hit her.

Sir Alvin and Sir Torin shouted something in response. The song cut off and the headache vanished, but the daemons swooped down at them. Carine called to the trees again and they entangled two of the Fallen Ones, pulling them down in a thrashing melee of arms and legs and branches as they strangled them. The daemons detonated as they died, blowing limbs off the trees.

What? They explode when they die?

Two Fallen Ones charged her. She deflected a sword strike. The other daemon bowled her over and she tumbled backwards towards the Coast Passage, losing her staff.

"No!" yelled Alfred.

She rolled out of the way of one red blade but the other stabbed her in the side and she gasped. She dove away, clawing for her dagger. She pressed her other hand on her wound, trying to use healing magic to banish the searing pain. Buck's father descended on the two daemons like an avenging angel.

"You'll not take her!" he bellowed. The glittering blade arced and a daemon head spun off into the plaza.

"No, Alfred! They ex —"

With a dull boom, the daemon corpse detonated, spraying Carine with bone fragments. Alfred jerked backwards like a rag doll, impaled by shards. His head hit a stone.

No! Alfred!

"Da!" Jack shouted, leaping to his side. He swept up Alfred's blade and stood over his father, cutlass and sword at the ready.

The remaining daemon cackled, eyes blazing, and darted in at him.

Carine called to nature. A swarm of gnats and flies burst up out of the nearby bushes, surrounding the daemon's head. The Fallen One shrieked and backpedaled.

Carine unleashed another spell. Her dagger blade burst into flame and she charged, stabbing. The daemon shrieked, slashing wildly. A fiery blade cut into her leg. She screamed and fell, gasping. This injury burned worse than the first one.

The daemon held a hand in front of its face and screeched. A cloud of flame immolated the insects. The Fallen One whirled on her, blade held high.

Its red-glowing sword arced towards her face but a cutlass deflected it to clang into the cobblestones.

"No, you don't," growled Jack Bydecy, eyes hard.

"Oh, a feisty one," the daemon replied in a high-pitched voice, like that of a young girl.

Carine's skin crawled. She struggled to stand.

The daemon's eyes flicked to her then back to Jack. "I kill her first," it simpered. "Then you."

It lunged at her and she twisted out of the way. Jack swung his cutlass again. The daemon parried and Jack thrust his father's blade through the daemon's eye.

Carine cast a pushing spell and the daemon jerked backwards, then exploded. This time, sharp fragments cut into her chest and legs and she gasped in pain, falling to the cobblestones.

She pulled herself up onto a nearby stone bench. "Come on, Jack! Into the tunnel!"

"Dad!" Jack knelt by his father.

She limped to his side, healing spell ready.

"Save them…" Alfred whispered.

She released the spell and a mild green light covered him, but Alfred's eyes flickered and faded.

This can't be happening!

She bit back a sob. Jack sat back on his heels and stared at his father.

I was supposed to protect them! Carine gritted her teeth and hauled Jack to his feet. "Into the tunnel!"

"But Dad —"

She stared into his eyes through vision gone misty with tears. "If you want to honor him, escape to live another day! Get out of here!"

"What about you?" Jack said, hesitating.

She blinked away tears. "I have to make sure the enemy can't follow. Don't worry about me. There are other ways out of the city. Join Summer and Weston and the children. You have to leave, now!"

With one last stricken look at his father, Jack darted into the tunnel. Carine drew a deep, shuddering breath. Her head hurt at the temples, her ribs ached and blood ran down one side of her head.

"Druidess!" called Sir Alvin. He stumbled towards her, his armor scorched. He tossed aside his ruined helm and blood trickled down the side of his face. "Are they all through?"

Carine nodded and looked around, feeling numb. No daemons remained but all the dwarven engineers lay dead. The Knights somehow managed to remain standing, their smoking armor covered in daemon ichor.

"What about you?" she asked.

A dragon roar sounded from the lane.

Sir Alvin's jaw worked. "We have to hold the line. You'll need to close the Coast Passage."

She shook her head mutely. He stood tall and saluted her with his bloody sword and returned to his fellows.

Close the tunnel? I don't know how to work the mechanism! The engineers didn't tell me!

Then she remembered the charges. Her eyes shot to the supports, where six of the blocky devices nestled next to the pistons.

A nearby house burst apart in a shower of flame and stone. A sixty-foot-long drake with scales of blue and green slithered through the wreckage. Its purple eyes blazed.

Carine's heart froze.

"Not so fast," it chuckled. "You'll miss all the fun."

Lady Marta and Lady Elise immediately leaped towards it, shields up and maces ready. Sir Torin and Sir Alvin rushed to join them. Carine barely had time to throw up a fire-shield spell before the drake breathed a jet of flame. The blast curled up and over her and she gasped from the amount of energy it took to deflect it. Likewise, the fire curled around Marta and Elise's shields.

The Knights laid into the drake and it lashed out. Greatswords cut great slashes in dragon hide and maces crushed bones, but the dragon bit off Lady Marta's mace-arm. She screamed in agony and smashed the drake in the face with her shield. The dragon slammed her into a building and breathed again, this time catching the other Knights unguarded. Carine watched in horror as the three warriors, engulfed in flames, drove their blades into the creature's heart and smashed it in the skull with a mace.

The dragon let out a gurgle and writhed, then lay still. The three remaining knights slowly dropped to their knees, then fell face-down on the gore-soaked avenue.

Carine tore her eyes away and fired a jet of flame at the detonators on one side of the fountain. With an earsplitting boom, they went off. She ducked behind a bench as rock and metal showered the plaza. The fountain tipped on one side and slammed down.

Dizzy, her ears ringing, Carine aimed a spell at the last three charges but a drake with tiger-striped black and yellow scales landed next to the fountain. With a look of disdain, it swept the munitions away with its claws.

The three charges tumbled towards her. She barely got out of the way of one of them and blinked to clear her vision.

The drake leered at her. "Tsk, tsk," it said, wagging a claw. "It's rude to close the door just when the most important guests arrive, little bitch."

An indescribable rage surged through her. "I'll have your head, Dark One!"

It laughed. "How, puny druid? You're practically dead yourself."

She scrambled backwards and her spine hit something smooth and hard. Her hand touched a detonator and a slow smile crept over her face.

"I have a surprise for you," she said through bloodied lips.

The drake laughed, then opened its maw. Hellfire raged.

She threw magical power into a lifting spell and hurled the charge into its gullet. She remembered the nearby trees.

"Catch me," she whispered. She heard them answer on the wind.

The world exploded and incredible pain surged through her. She sailed through the air and a basket of branches caught her. Then darkness hit.

***

Slowly, consciousness returned. Her entire body was a mass of ache. *Curing spell,* she thought foggily. *Curing spell. I have to get out of here…*

It seemed like it took hours for her to remember but she managed to whisper the right combination of magic words.

Pleasant coolness flowed through her. Able to think more clearly, she used a scanning spell. Shocked at the number of bruises, lacerations and broken bones, she realized she didn't have enough energy left to repair everything. Panting, she used the last of her magic to knit broken hand, foot and rib bones together.

Whispering a spell to put herself into a restorative trance, she lay back and darkness returned.

After what seemed like ages, she opened her eyes to a night sky, foul odors and the light of flickering flames. Soreness wracked her body but at least she could move. Loud voices chanted somewhere and a rasping growl echoed among the ruined buildings. She heard an agonized scream that cut off suddenly. Wild, raucous music broke out towards the east accompanied by a chorus of laughter and breaking glass.

Now rested, she applied more healing spells and much of her pain receded. She sat up and realized that she lay on a pile of wooden fragments and leaves that had once been one of the trees in the plaza. Rubble surrounded her in massive piles.

Then her eyes alighted on the Coast Passage, or more precisely, where it should have been. Only a massive pile of stone, melted metal and dragon pieces remained. The drake's head sat off to one side, a single eye staring at nothing.

Soldiers and mages gathered as Dwarves in the livery of the Skullhead Legion dug with picks and shovels. Many held torches or lanterns. A babble of animated discussion filled the air.

"Damn your hides!" roared a voice. The crowd turned and a creature out of a nightmare thumped into the plaza. He stood as tall as a troll, with deep red bat wings growing from his back. A bestial visage with four eyes glared out at the assembly, horns and fangs gleaming black. Shoulders rippling with muscle connected to four arms that ended in clawed hands. Massive legs thudded into the ground, grinding small stones under taloned feet.

Carine's mind gibbered and she crept back into the rubble, trying to make herself as small as possible.

"Do I have to do everything myself?" the daemon snapped. The assembled Ja'al recoiled.

A priestess with the symbol of Gudarta on her chestplate bowed low. "We just arrived ourselves, Battle Lord. There is much damage and the dragon's flame has made matters worse. Some of the metal pieces and stonework have fused together. It will take some time."

"Curse you incompetents!" the daemon growled. "I have to feed my legions. The civilians were supposed to supply them."

The priestess looked confused. "But… your Power, there are many dead all about."

"Dead?" He sneered. "Yes, mangled and roasted and mixed in with wood and stone and all other manner of contaminants. Disgusting! We need fresh kills. We've already used up all the captured defenders of this miserable city."

The priestess bowed again. "A thousand pardons, Great One. I will confer with my colleagues and devise a solution."

She backed away from the daemon, bowing as she went, and a few officers went with her.

The daemon glared after her. "You had better. And we claim a third of the treasures of this place as well! Don't forget that."

His eyes glittered in the torchlight as he swept them over the plaza. Finally, his gaze alighted on the trembling warriors and engineers near the ruined fountain. "Well, what are you imbeciles staring at? Get to work and clear out that mess!"

With a huff of disgust, the daemon took wing and soared off towards the port.

Carine waited until her thundering heartbeat had slowed to something approximating normal. She willed her hands to stop shaking and summoned up strength in her weak legs to stand.

Her throat constricted as she remembered Alfred. "I am so sorry, Buck," she whispered, her eyes stinging. "I couldn't save him."

With a shuddering breath, she closed her eyes. *I will honor him by not dying,* she decided. *It's what Alfred would have wanted.*

Keeping an eye out for patrols, she slipped back towards one of the intact buildings and entered. Finding a set of stairs, she ascended to a rooftop door and emerged, dagger at the ready. The area was deserted.

With a sigh, she sheathed her weapon and appraised the nearby neighborhood. The East Gate lay in ruins and hundreds of enemy troops gathered near it.

Her eyes sought darkened areas, searching for a neglected point she could exploit. One of the sections of the city near her was not in flames. She watched for a while, extending her senses.

Yes, she felt two malignant presences there, but she had a way for handling that.

Murmuring a phrase under her breath, she pointed in the direction of the east gate. The sound of rushing feet and scrabbling rock echoed in that quadrant. Two lithe shadows with burning eyes slithered off towards the sound.

Carine pulled her robe around her and prayed that it still worked. A surge of power flowed into her bones and soon she saw with owl-sight and felt her wings again.

Without waiting another second, she launched herself into the air and shot through the night, soaring over the wall without even a whisper of sound, heading towards Deran to the south.

Chapter Six – The Cost of Conquest

Your Highness," the Battle Lord rumbled.

Tarvener, Prince of Hades and Captain-General of the Dark Wave, spun away from the balcony, his cloak billowing in the night air. He raised an eyebrow.

"I trust there is a good reason for this interruption."

"The officers from the Subversion Directorate are here, Your Highness." The Battle Lord retained his posture: bowed with his arms spread, massive indigo bat wings furled, all four eyes downcast at the cracked marble tiles. "They say they are expected for a discussion about resources."

The daemon towered over Tarvener by a good six feet when standing upright and outweighed him by three hundred pounds. Despite the difference in size, the Battle Lord kept his hands away from the long daggers strapped to his thighs.

He has good discipline, at least, Tarvener mused. "Rise," he commanded.

The daemon straightened. His horns almost touched the tiled ceiling.

Tarvener smiled briefly. "I admit I had quite forgotten."

The Battle Lord inclined his head. "Shall I send them away?"

Tarvener waved a hand. "No. Bring them in. And make sure we aren't disturbed."

He clasped his hands behind his back and swept the ruined bedchamber with his eyes. Ripped velvet curtains hung down in rags, the floor bore wide scorch marks and only the massive bed remained unbroken. Two steel cages leaned in opposite corners of the room.

"We have guests, Your Graces." He gave a mocking bow to the piles of bones and skulls in the cages. "Oh, you needn't trouble yourselves. I will take care of it."

A tall, potted plant next to the balcony doors shook slightly, almost as if laughing. Tarvener pretended not to notice. He returned to the balcony and gazed out over the ruins of the city of Tyler. At night, it looked almost pleasing. Figures capered wildly around blazing bonfires and raucous, bawdy song echoed in the otherwise empty streets. Occasionally, a fight broke out: a short interval of violence and magic flashes until the military police could restore order.

He knew he would have to move to the next city soon. Supplies were running low, and they couldn't very well use their own allies as delicacies for daemon consumption — at least, not yet.

Even with over fifty-thousand troops at Tarvener's disposal, plus the marine invasion force, the city of Tyler had been a tough nut to crack. Losses had been significant.

The Ja'al better work those Skull Gates night and day, or there will be Hell to pay… literally.

Tarvener detected the presence of creatures entering the room behind him but remained where he was. He waited until the door latched before turning around.

A succubus and an incubus knelt before him, eyes downcast. The male was sleek and muscular, with dark skin, red-gold hair and short curved horns. His golden-haired, fair female counterpart matched him for attractiveness: curvaceous and supple, bat-winged and sporting a cat's tail. Neither of them wore very much: a grey embroidered breechclout for the man and a sheer, thigh-length black tunic for the woman.

Tarvener sighed. "Rise."

"Your Highness," the daemons said in unison. They straightened, meeting his gaze. The female's golden cat eyes flicked to the skeletons, then back to Tarvener.

"I understand you have a matter of resources to discuss." The daemon prince clasped his hands behind his back and paced towards the cages. The sound of his cloven hooves echoed in the chamber.

"Yes, Highness," began the succubus in a husky and low alto. "Rather, it is a matter of the misuse of resources."

Tarvener paused and inspected the skull and bones of the Duke of Tyler. "You surprise me. Resource management is the Quartermaster's job. If you are running low on something, use the requisition system. You are all officers in a special unit. You have authority."

"If you forgive me, Highness," said the incubus, "There was an agreement that we would receive an allocation of prisoners from this city for the Subversion Project. As of yet, we have received none."

"Worse yet, Highness," the succubus added, "we now find that all the prisoners have been killed and eaten by the common daemons and there are none left for us."

The branches of the potted plant shifted. Tarvener's eyes shot towards it. The plant stilled.

"How does that concern me?" Tarvener asked. "It is understandable that our Hadean warriors have tired of the other fare available on this world. I myself like a bit of Elf or human flesh now and again. Take, for example, the former Duke and Duchess. Very tasty when prepared correctly."

The male daemon inclined his head. "Of course, Highness. However, the agreement with the High Command was that our unit would be given sufficient numbers to breed half-daemons for counter-insurgency efforts in the future. As our mission is a long-term solution to the inevitable rebellions that will result from our occupation of this world, we have to get started as soon as possible. This is the second major city in Astarel that has fallen to the Dark Wave but we have yet to be given an allocation."

"I see," Tarvener mused. He strolled to the other cage and poked at the Duchess' skull. "I am not inclined to disagree, but there are priorities for the captives. The prospect of feeding on mortal flesh is a great motivator and our field troops need that motivation, especially after a costly battle such as this one. Projects with long time horizons will have to wait."

"We understand, Highness, but —" began the male.

Tarvener spun around. "Am I or am I not commander of this army?" The daemons started and the incubus cursed under his breath.

The succubus regained her composure first and bowed. "Yes, Highness.

We will, of course, have to advise Her Serene Majesty, Queen Arachnia, that her instructions cannot be followed due to other priorities." The emphasis she put on the last two words left little doubt as to the subtle hints that she drop about Tarvener's ability to honor agreements.

Prince Tarvener pressed his lips together. "You presume too much, Commander. I am well aware of Her Serene Majesty's long-term plans. Do not mistake my inaction for inattentiveness."

With a snap of his fingers, he covered himself with four different repulsion screens and protective shields. He channeled energy into his horns, making them glow red-hot.

The daemons had the good grace to blanch.

He clasped his hands behind his back. "Plenty of prisoners will be available for your special unit. Our next target is the Deranese city of Seacrest, which has many humans and elves to satisfy you."

The succubus bowed again. "We hope that Your Highness' promise will be given."

They demand guarantees? From me?

Tarvener's temper surged but he checked it. It would do no more good to splatter the Ducal apartments with their innards than it would if he did the same with the Battle Lord for his inability to control his troops. Besides, Arachnia was not someone to be trifled with. A display of uncontrolled temper would not go over well.

Managing this phase of the Dark Wave was giving him a headache.

He smiled. "I readily give it. If you require, I will issue written orders to that effect: no further prisoners are to be eaten without first consulting the Subversion Directorate, upon pain of dismemberment. Satisfied?"

Two pairs of daemon eyes glittered and the officers nodded. "We are honored by your indulgence, Highness," replied the male.

The delegation backed out of the room, bowing as they went.

Tarvener waited until the doors shut to let out an explosive sigh.

The potted plant chuckled. "I can hear the curses in your head from here."

"Not now, please, Majesty."

The plant warped and transformed. A naked, seven-foot-tall man with blonde hair sauntered over to the remnants of the bed and lounged on it.

One purple eye and one green one followed Tarvener.

He grinned impishly. "Now, now, Prince. A little thing like resource allocation shouldn't bother you that much. You have several victories under your belt already."

"It's not the military effort that drains me, Great Majesty. It's the politics. This Subversion Project seems ill-advised."

"On the contrary, Prince," replied Selaan. The Hadean god of Deception, Lies and Trickery flicked a bit of blood-matted golden hair from the bed. "If we have lots of half-breeds of our own on this world, it will be easier to manage than by continually sending units here via the Skull Gates. Eventually, all will be like us, at least in part. Conquest will be complete."

"Understood, Majesty."

"Therefore, long-range plans or no, I am confident you are up to the challenge. That's why you're here."

Tarvener didn't answer, trying to figure out onto which of his subordinates to foist the Subversion Project.

"Or we can find a replacement," Selaan shrugged. "I'm sure there are others who will be amenable."

Tarvener's ability to control his temper was getting quite the workout. "I will not disappoint Your Majesty."

"I am thrilled to hear it. Now, what do you think of this?" Selaan asked. He rolled onto his stomach, his skin tone changing from tan to dark and his hair color to white. He winked at Tarvener.

"An interesting palette."

"Isn't it?" Selaan laughed and bounced off the bed, changing into a slender Elven maiden with white horns on her forehead and golden eyes. "I do love the wide range of inspirations at my disposal on this world. I tire of the bat wings, horns, cloven hooves and all that on Hades. This is so refreshing."

Selaan sashayed over to the balcony and breathed deeply of the smoky air, standing up on tiptoes. "Ah, the smell of charred cities and roasting flesh. You don't know how long I've waited to see this, on the world that has rejected me repeatedly."

"That was their loss."

"Quite right. The fools." Selaan leaned on the balustrade.

Tarvener remained silent.

"They don't know the power of being able to make and unmake one's own reality," the Hadean god mused. "Such a heady tonic. All I have to do is say whatever I want and it becomes. Likewise, my willing servants will be able to make themselves into whatever they wish, as long as they do my bidding."

He transformed into a Dwarf, then a human woman, then finally returned to the form of the tall man, this time clothed in a snow-white robe with black trim.

"I will show them all my blessings and advantages," he continued. "They will see in time. I can change anything I want."

Tarvener didn't answer. He knew from past experience that a rambling, quixotic discussion with Selaan could last for hours and he didn't have the energy. He needed to think and that would not be possible with a Hadean Royal — especially Selaan — gadding about mouthing inanities.

Selaan spun around in a circle, arms spread out, singing a song in Elven, then threw up his hands. Amethysts sprang from his fingertips. The jewels glittered and sparkled as they bounced on the marble and then evaporated.

He pouted. "I can never make them stay. Fickle things."

With a bright smile, he put an arm around Tarvener's shoulders. "Speaking of fickle, how is that granddaughter of yours? You know, the one that married the lord down in Deran… Siren or something like that."

Tarvener's headache intensified. "Oh, you mean Saren," he offered.

"Yes!" Selaan exulted. He warped into a dark-haired succubus. "Ziniva's child! What plans do you have for her? I understand she practically served up your bounty hunter on a platter years ago."

"To be honest, Great Majesty, I hadn't thought about it. She lives near Oakmoor, to the south. We have much ground to cover before we get there."

"Of course, of course," replied Selaan. "However, you and I both know that she didn't listen to reason before, so she will need to be persuaded. So how will you do it? Kidnapping? Hostages?"

Tarvener smiled. "She values the lives of others over her own. I have a few ideas."

Selaan clapped her hands. "Oh really! Come, tell me. I do love a good scheme!"

"The plans are not complete and I would not bore you, sire. And I have to clear everything with Her Majesty Arachnia and His Majesty Torvu."

Selaan changed into male form again and slapped a fist into his palm, changing his hair to red and eyes to pale green. "Arachnia! Damn it! I knew I forgot something. She's waiting for me in the main camp. Thank you for reminding me."

Tarvener bowed as Selaan grew snow-white eagle's wings from his upper back. The god's horns took on a golden sheen.

"How do I look?"

"Splendid, Majesty."

"Thank you. I haven't used this form in quite a while." Selaan leaped to the top of the balcony railing and extended his wings. "Well, I can't keep her waiting. She's probably finished with Torvu by now so it will be my turn. Until tomorrow, Prince."

Tarvener watched the receding form of the Hadean King as he winged away towards the woods north of the city. Singing ended as Selaan soared overhead.

Tarvener remained at the balustrade, relieved to have some quiet.

He'll probably blight the forest with his presence. Have to make sure I keep him away from any farmland. We can't do anything if our non-daemon allies starve to death.

Seeing Selaan's white wings reminded him of Saren; rumor had it that her wings had changed to white through some Christian ceremony or other. He wondered. He had never seen her.

He shrugged. He had many granddaughters, and most of them more obedient than she. She would turn to the side of Hades, to the side of the victors, or perish. The blight on his family name would be removed, one way or the other.

He would see to it.

Chapter Seven – A Final Vengeance

"Well, Kili, you apparently will get your wish," said Arlene Summervale, former Countess of Harlinsville, Deran. She tilted her head to the side, eyeing her companion.

A sturdy, brown-haired Halfling man shrugged. "Which one? I have many."

Arlene stepped to the entrance of her pavilion and regarded the regiment of goblins and humans encamped outside. Early morning sunlight sifted in through the trees, just enough to let the humans see but not enough to hurt sensitive goblin eyes.

"You remember the Lomin family? The ones related to the Grey Rider, Connor Lomin?"

Kili Mikman's black eyes sparked with interest. "How could I forget?"

"Well, apparently the leadership feels that it would aid the cause of the Great Remaking if you would eliminate said family. Their continued existence is an affront to our cause, particularly their connection with the Riders."

"I thought you didn't want me going after them."

She sniffed. "There is a time and a place for everything. Now is the time."

"Then I am at your service. How is this to be done?"

Arlene waved at the forest. "Twelve leagues beyond, the Republic of Evendale waits to be harvested like a ripe peach on the bough. We will harvest it. The tumult from that conquest will be your opportunity to slip in unnoticed and end the Lomins."

Kili inclined his head. "I am gratified that my lady has come around to my way of thinking. However, as you pointed out previously, Connor Lomin's mother is a High Priestess of Irial and her family is well-guarded. Even I can't overcome that alone."

"You won't have to," she replied. "Our forces have breached the eastern borders of Terenai and Evendale in four different locations. You will travel with the invasion force marching for the city of Glen and detach at the right time, posing as a refugee. Your targets are Brendan and Cerys Lomin and their children, Darren and Deena. A separate team will attack the High Priestess and her husband. They will have their hands full and will not be able to intervene when you strike."

A crooked smile broke out over Kili's face. "That's better. When do I leave?"

"Immediately. But I have something for you."

She opened a coffer on a nearby table. "Here," she said, handing him a patch of black lace.

Kili took it with a skeptical look. "Why do I need a black doily? Will I be entertaining royalty?"

"Don't be cheeky. This is a Web of Snaring. You may need it to capture your prey. Don't ruin it. I want it back."

"I will endeavor to return it to Your Ladyship in the same condition as when it was given to me." He bowed and turned to go.

She eyed him as he approached the exit. "And Kili?"

He paused.

"I want them dead. Not captured for ransom or for some Ja'al rites.

Dead. Understand?"

His smile broadened. "Your wish is my command, milady."

Chapter Eight – An Unscheduled Vacation

Halfling soldiers, servants and underpriests bustled around in a swarming crowd. Miriam Lomin pushed a lock of hair off her forehead and took a deep breath, trying to focus amid the bedlam.

"Miri?" asked Seamus. He approached, dodging scurrying attendants. "The inventory is complete, but there's a young man at the door. He has a letter addressed to you. He won't let me have it. He keeps pointing to your name and nodding. I don't think he can talk."

Well, sending a mute messenger means he can't be tortured to give up information easily, I suppose. Miriam thought.

She patted her husband's arm. "I'll see to it. Keep an eye out for Cerys and Brendan and the children. They should be here soon."

He gave her a firm kiss and strode off into the swirl, shouting orders to a knot of soldiers clustered around a stack of crates.

Miriam took a moment to watch the bustle of activity in the main temple of Irial.

So different from Worship Days and Festivals, she mused. *Then, the commotion means happiness and joy — and there are smiles and laughter and music.*

With a short sigh, she marched to the main double doors, where the messenger stood next to two temple guards in silvery scale mail.

"Yes?" she asked.

A young man bowed to her, hand on his heart, and extended a letter.

She took it and saw the seal — and froze.

With a sharp glance at him, she opened it. The paper was blank, only showing the symbol of a wheat sheaf and scythe at the top center. Miriam pulled her holy medallion from her blouse and touched it to the symbol. A faint bell rang in her head and the symbol sparked.

She pressed her lips together and beckoned to the messenger. "Come with me."

He followed her to her vesting room and she shut the door. She laid the paper down on a table and passed her medallion over it, murmuring holy verses as she did so. The messenger watched her every move with bright black eyes.

Glittering letters in Humana flowed across the page in a golden wave.

Hail and High Greeting,

Matriarch Lomin, I have it on good authority and intelligence that a Ja'al assassin team will be dispatched to slay you and your family. Your connection with the Grey Riders is well known and, now that the War has begun, the Manipulator Church will take the opportunity to exact vengeance. Please, by our mutual reverence for the One Creator, retreat to Mil-Tereth in Terenai. That city has the means to protect you for some time, and Andyn Eleandir's family will be there to assist you.

This messenger is one of my most trusted servants. He has knowledge of many secret paths and can spirit you away to safety. Please keep this in mind when he speaks to you. Do not be deceived by appearances. Trust me.

Most respectfully,

Thomas Cardinal Williams

Papal Nuncio to Damora

She regarded the young Halfling man with a raised eyebrow. "This letter says you can speak. Why pretend to be mute all this time?"

The man bowed again. "The magic disguises appearance, not voice," he said in rough, guttural tones.

That's not a Halfling…

He removed a medallion from around his neck. His visage changed, as did his physique. Now, instead of a burly Halfling servant, a wiry goblin with black eyes faced her.

Miriam's reaction came unbidden, lightning-quick. She leaped back in a crouch, hand thrust forth. A white light pulsed out and struck him, folding around until he stood imprisoned in a globe of radiance.

"A goblin! How is it that you bear a message from the Nuncio?"

Instead of protesting, he merely smiled. "I serve Father Thomas, as I served Father Edward before him."

She looked into his eyes, and to her surprise saw neither devious cunning nor oily deception but genuine honesty — and admiration.

Her eyes narrowed. Was he telling the truth? Or was this a very cleverly disguised attempt to get into her good graces? Could they have forged the letter? Her mind whirled.

She murmured a spell of finding and one of true-reading, but neither of them revealed any kind of trickery. Still, if the Ja'al were after Connor, they would spare no expense and the Ja'al had ample magical resources to deceive even experienced wizards.

The goblin remained still, smiling. "If I be bold, High Priestess, you look like him. Eyes the same."

Miriam blinked. "Like who?"

"Connor."

She straightened. For long seconds she gauged him. "If you know Connor, you know the Grey Riders," she said. "Very well then. One of them has a pet animal. Tell me the name of the beast and its owner."

The goblin grinned. "That an easy one. Buck Bydecy has pigeon named Puup. But Puup retired now. He lives at Chancery gardens, with lady pigeons. Very happy there."

Miriam relaxed. She dispelled the globe holding the goblin in place. "My apologies. With the invasion from the Wilderness, things are a little tense. Thank you for bringing the message, Mister…"

"Gorlak."

Gorlak… "Sky Flash" — the Goblin word for lightning. Interesting.

She tapped the letter in her palm. "Your message comes at a critical time."

"It seem so, High Priestess. What does Nuncio's letter tell you?"

Though she suspected he already knew, she told him. He smiled again. "I will take you by hidden paths to safety, Priestess. You and family."

"I appreciate the Nuncio's concern," she said briskly, smoothing the front of her blouse, "but that's quite out of the question."

Gorlak's eyes widened. "But High Priestess —"

She held up a hand. "My responsibility is to our people, here, in Glen. We have withstood other invasions from the wild lands from all manner of wild tribes and we will again be victorious. My family and I cannot desert them in their time of need."

Gorlak shook his head. "Many, many enemies come to Evendale nation. All must leave this town and get to places of safety. Largest cities with stone walls best for now."

"How so? Any invaders would have to take on the Republican Guards in Lakeview and the First Dragon Legion. Besides, the centaurs have agreed to help and even now they ride to the capital. No horde can stand against our united forces."

Gorlak's eyes widened and he held up his hands. "No, please, High Priestess. You not understand. This not mob of goblins and ogres from Wilderness. These are Ja'al soldiers, with hyena-folk and Dark Elves and griffon-riders and even some evil dragons. Worse yet, daemons come with them."

She set her mouth in a firm line. "Daemons? Well, I have dealt with their kind before, make no mistake. No grues or grims can frighten me."

"These not grues or grims. These stronger daemons."

"Like what?"

"Skreets are their scouts. Tiger daemons come with them, and blood satyrs and others, much worse."

Her heart skipped a beat. "How do you know this?"

The goblin's eyes flicked to the letter. "I serve the Nuncio," he said.

Miriam folded the letter and put it in her belt purse. He watched without blinking. Then she strode to the door and put her hand on the doorknob. "I must think on it. For now, you are our guest. For obvious reasons, you will have to reactivate your magic disguise. You can stay at my home, but it is probably best to keep this between us for now."

"Well… I thank you with humbleness, High Priestess."

Miriam smiled suddenly. "You're a friend of Connor. That is enough for me."

***

In her dream, Deena Lomin ran through the city of Glen, trying to warn everyone of a terrible danger. People smiled at her indulgently, as if watching her play an adventure game with her friends. No matter how much she shouted, only a whisper came out.

She heard faint voices and struggled unsuccessfully to wake up.

"A courier just arrived from the eastern districts. It doesn't look good."

Other people talked at once and she lost track of their words, lapsing back into a fog of sleep.

Voices roused her again. "We need to make a decision, Miri." That sounded like Grandpa. "The situation has changed."

"Call everyone to the living room," said her Grandma's faint voice.

Deena flipped over in bed, trying to fight her drowsiness. I have to wake up and warn them… wake up… wake up.

"Deena! Wake up!"

Deena sat up, rubbing her eyes. "What is it, Mama?"

Her mother pulled Deena out of bed. "Get dressed. We have to go."

"Right now?" Deena blinked in the dimness. She couldn't see very much of her mother besides a dark shadow and the faint reflection of candlelight in her eyes.

"Please, Deena!" Her mother sounded worried, very worried. "Just do as I say. Travel clothes – trousers, blouse, boots. Bring your school backpack, empty, and wear the magic medallion Grandmother gave you. Then go to the kitchen to get supplies."

Deena's stomach clenched. Why did they had to go this early in the morning and, more importantly, where? Did this have to do with Uncle Connor? She had overheard his name during whispered discussions among her parents and grandparents but no one told her anything.

Deena quickly dressed, snatched her school pack and emptied it onto the bed. Briefly, she considered bringing her favorite doll or a book but shook her head. Mama had told her to hurry. She was nearly to the door before she remembered the medallion and darted back to snatch it from her nightstand.

She stared at the tiny golden shield with a spinning wheel embossed on the surface. Her fingers touched the proverb of the Worldmaker etched on the back.

"Speak My Name in the darkness, and I will bring you Light," Deena quoted in a whisper.

She kissed the symbol of her god and looped the medallion over her head, then rushed out of the room. On the way, she passed Calder, the young Halfling courier who had been staying with them for the last few days. He gave her a kind smile as he hurried in the opposite direction and she smiled back.

She liked Calder. Too bad he couldn't speak.

Deena entered the vast kitchen. "There you are," said Carisa, one of the acolytes from the temple. Carisa wore a chainmail tunic and carried an axe and dagger at her belt.

Why is she here in the house? And why does she have armor and weapons? Deena's heart beat faster.

"Here." Carisa handed over a stack of wrapped packets, two full water skins and a small wooden box.

"What are these?" Deena asked, slipping them into her pack and pulling the drawstrings shut. The pack felt heavy, much heavier than when full of schoolbooks.

"Preserved food, water and a camp kit for making fire," Carisa replied, shooing her towards the front of the house. "Quickly now. Your family is waiting."

Deena scurried to the living room and paused, her mouth agape. All the magical lamps in the place shone with white radiance. The place fairly gleamed with the reflection of light on metal.

Grandma Miri leaned on her hands over a map on a table. She was clad in a peculiar armor made of horizontal metal bands. A steely mace with a glittering head hung from her belt. A helmet and shield sat on a nearby couch and a spear leaned in a corner.

The others with her were similarly attired. Grandpa Seamus wore armor of metal plates and carried a sword at his hip. Two Temple Guardians waited nearby in armor that looked like fish scales, carrying shields. Even her parents had chainmail and swords.

Darren bumped into Deena from behind and she winced. Her brother started to say something but she put her hand over his mouth. She wanted to hear what the grownups had to say and knew they would stop if they noticed the two of them.

"How many?" her mother asked.

Grandpa's brow furrowed. "We heard that two regiments broke through the lines at Darcy's Wood."

Papa pointed at something on the map. "What about here?" he asked in his mild, whispering voice. "There's a regiment posted in Orl's Haven. Can't they cut them off?"

Grandma inspected a letter on the table and shook her head. "This says the Citadel at Orl's Haven is already besieged, and another two thousand Ja'al are marching from Shadow Lake towards Dwarfshire."

"The centaurs?" asked Mama hopefully.

Again, Grandma shook her head after scanning another dispatch. "Half of them went to gather up their people and evacuate the villages. The others are heading to Lakeview but it won't help. An army of five thousand has already razed Wildford and is heading towards the capital."

All of the adults stared at Grandma Miri.

"Wait. Another five thousand?" asked Papa, fist clenching at his side. "There are ten thousand coming from the northern borders? And how many from the east?"

"Counting the action at Darcy's Wood and the Citadel, probably another brigade or two," Grandma replied, face grim.

"Too many," Mama murmured.

"We will be all right, Cerys," Grandfather said, laying a hand on her shoulder. "However, we have to leave Evendale."

"This isn't happening," Mama whispered, face pale.

Papa slammed a fist on the table and Deena jumped. She had rarely seen a fit of temper from him.

"Only a couple of days ago, it was just a matter of leaving the area," he said. "Now we're evacuating out of the country."

Grandpa Seamus put a hand on his arm. "The situation is changing rapidly. Thank Irial the couriers made it through or we would have no word. The last dispatch just arrived less than an hour ago."

Papa nodded. He let out a deep breath and put his arm over Mama's shoulder.

Grandpa reached for his spear and nodded to the Guardians. "Captains, get everyone moving. Rear-guard action only to harass the invasion force. Don't defend property. We have to get on the south road to Terenai."

A sudden surge of terror coursed through Deena and she clasped her medallion. Terenai? That was the Elven Empire, many miles to the southwest. That meant…

"When will we come back?" Darren asked in a plaintive voice.

The adults whirled, then relaxed.

"Mama?" Deena asked.

The adults exchanged a look but no one spoke.

A horrid thought struck her and Deena glanced wildly around the living room. Her eyes rested on a rocking chair, where she had listened to Grandmother read many stories of heroes and adventure. A couple of her favorite books sat on the side table.

No! This is our home! We have to come back!

Grandma Miri's stern expression softened. She knelt down by Deena and Darren. "We have to get to a safer place, for now. I need you to follow our directions exactly. If we don't have to worry about you, we'll be able to do our jobs all the better."

Darren clutched the straps of his backpack, looking doubtful.

"We'll return when the danger is past," Papa soothed. "Until then, we'll be in a different place, kind of like a surprise vacation."

"You're sure?" Darren asked.

Papa nodded.

"Okay." Darren looked at his shoes.

He's too young to understand, Deena mused.

She opened her mouth but Father shot her a look. "Deena, we need you to help your brother. You're the eldest."

Deena nodded back, butterflies in her stomach.

"Grandma?" Mama suggested. "I suggest that our new friend Calder go with Deena and Darren." She patted Deena on the shoulder.

"Ah yes! Excellent choice." Grandma strode out to the hallway and beckoned. Calder followed her into the living room. He wore a leather jerkin with metal studs and had two daggers in his belt. A silky black cloak draped over his shoulders and Deena glimpsed a silver clasp in the shape of a bat.

"Calder will look after you," Grandmother announced. "Make sure you stay with him."

Calder smiled at them. He had a nice smile.

Papa nodded. "Off you go then."

Calder bowed to him and motioned towards the front door. He hustled Deena and her brother into a covered wagon driven by two Temple Guardians. Deena tried to find a good place to sit among all the boxes, barrels and crates and peered out at the morning sky.

Darren, characteristically, found a box with nut pastries and snatched two of them, handing one to Deena. They munched their impromptu breakfast, watching as Halflings filled wagons and climbed aboard. By the time they had finished their snack, several other conveyances joined them, escorted by Halfling soldiers on armored ponies. Mama and Papa rode by, beckoning to the drivers. With a lurch, they surged forward.

The sunrise came up in the east, where it always did, but she saw a faint red glow among the hills off to the north, among a lot of dark clouds. It looked like fire.

Deena felt a shiver.

Chapter Nine – By Secret Paths

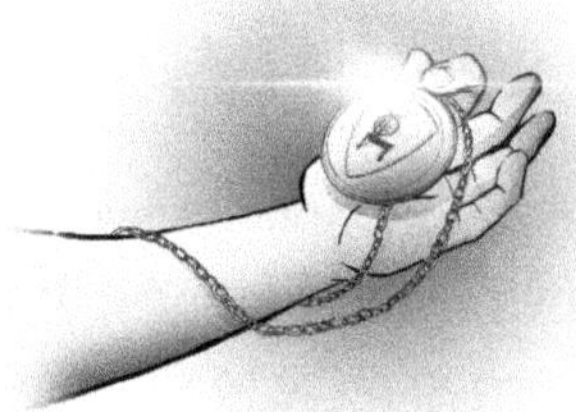

Deena held onto her seat in the wagon. The caravan rumbled down the street, turned through the town square and headed along the boulevard towards the highway out of Glen. Ranks of Halfling soldiers assembled in plazas and open fields, accompanied by Irial priests and wizards. More pony cavalry trotted down the avenues.

"Wow," said Darren. "The whole army's here!"

"Not the whole army, but a lot of it," Deena replied. *Surely, with that many to protect us, we'll be safe.*

"Maybe we'll get to see the centaurs," Darren said.

"Maybe." She began to relax. They were going to Terenai. She had never been there and had heard many stories of wondrous Elf magic and their glittering cities among the green trees.

It might not be so bad after all, even if we have to leave home for a while.

Their caravan continued along the highway, passing more troops and some ponies pulling wooden and steel contraptions. Deena recognized them from school as some kind of military throwing machines. She wished she had paid more attention to that part of her studies.

The sight of the machines made her nervous. She had never seen any of them this close to town.

Families hurriedly packed carts or coaches along the road. Parents frantically gathered children, their voices tight with worry and tension. Other carts and wagons joined their exodus and the caravan grew. Everyone looked and sounded frightened.

A group of soldiers marched past, now close enough for her to see their faces. They looked grim.

Why are the soldiers scared? Grandma and Mama told me of an invasion that happened when I was only two, but it was over quickly. This will be the same. Won't it?

Thoughts of a pleasant holiday began to fade from her mind. She sat back, holding her medallion.

The cavalcade turned out of the city onto the main highway and headed out into farmland. After watching endless fields of grain and vegetables go past without so much as a goblin whelp to menace them, Deena let out a sigh of relief and hunkered down next to a crate. All the tension of the morning was making her tired.

Darren grinned wickedly and reached behind his back. He pulled out a dagger from a sheath.

"Darren! Where did you get that?"

"Swiped it," he replied. "There were a bunch of them on one of the tables and no one was looking, so I took it."

"Brat! Mom's going to be sore."

"Hey, everyone else has weapons. Why not me? I know how to fight."

Deena made a face at him. He knew how to fight, all right — fight for extra helpings at the dinner table.

"Don't blame me when you get punished," she retorted. This was going to be a long trip if Darren was already this annoying.

Darren shrugged, aggravating her even more. She turned her back on him and watched the road behind. Still, no enemies attacked.

Her hometown receded into a shadowy dark lump among the hills and fields as the sky lightened to the east. After a while, the early-morning departure took its toll and she dozed off.

The wheels hit a bump, jerking her awake, blinking and groggy. Darren rubbed his eyes, trying to pretend he hadn't fallen asleep too. She smirked.

The sun shone brilliantly in a summer sky of blue with puffy clouds. Her eyes wandered towards the fields, watching for anything interesting. Far past the tall, waving grain, forestlands brooded.

A great flock of birds suddenly took wing at the edge of the woods. They winged away to the south, calling raucously.

For some reason, Deena felt apprehensive. The grain in the fields near the woods continued waving, as if a crowd of people walked through them.

She watched the rhythmic pattern, her nervousness increasing. She clambered to the front cab of the wagon.

"Guard," she asked one of the temple soldiers. "Do you see the waving grain over there? It looks funny."

The Guardian smiled at her and cast a glance that way. "That's nothing but the wind, miss, and —"

He stopped in mid-sentence, sitting bolt upright. "Get back!" he hissed, reaching for a horn at his belt.

Fearful now, Deena rejoined Darren as three horn blasts echoed out over the still morning. Then she heard something else that made her heart skip a beat: the pounding of drums and many guttural voices chanting.

No, no, no! Please Lord Irial! Protect us!

Officers called out orders. Horses pounded past and the wagon surged forwards. Soon, they raced and jolted along the road, Deena and Darren holding on for dear life. The load shifted and they clambered on top of the heavier crates, trying to avoid getting bumped and bruised in the jostling and rolling.

The roar of many voices erupted from the fields and Deena held onto her brother, trembling. She heard the whistling hiss of arrows and several thumped into the wagon walls.

"Great Creator, please protect Mama and Papa," she prayed under her breath.

Halfling voices shouted and metal clashed. Now she heard the unmistakable sizzle of magic, and horrible screams. Deena squeezed her eyes shut.

The wagon turned, then stopped. A dull thud sounded nearby and their conveyance lurched. Deena grabbed for a nearby crate. Acrid smoke drifted across the road and into the compartment.

A Halfling man appeared at the back of the wagon and she gave a short scream, but it was only Calder. He beckoned to them, eyes animated. Deena remembered Grandma Miri's orders. She snatched up her backpack and led Darren out of the wagon.

Mayhem greeted her eyes. Arrows sang past and bright flashes of magic exploded. Shouts rang out from all quarters. Armored Halflings formed shield-walls against triple-horned chimpanzee warriors surging at them like a wave.

Goblins! Her throat clenched.

The goblins leaped, snarling, their spears and swords stabbing. Halflings hacked at them with axes and maces and blood flew in all directions. Many figures lay unmoving on the road or nearby fields in dark puddles. Deena's eyes alighted on one of them and she couldn't tear her gaze away. It was the guard she had just talked to, lying face up on the road. Three arrows were stuck in his chest, his sightless eyes open to the morning sky.

Her mind gibbered in panic. *Where are Mama and Papa?*

A spitting, sizzling firedart shot past her head and exploded into the side of the wagon with a crack. Deena reflexively ducked. A knot of goblins charged the flank of the shield wall. Halfling pony cavalry galloped towards them. A priestess at the head of the formation thrust a hand at the goblins. A sun-bright burst of light dazzled Deena and she staggered back into the wagon. Goblins screeched in agony and rage.

A strong hand gripped her wrist. Calder dragged her and her brother away. Feeling numb, blinking to restore her eyesight, Deena followed, stumbling over clumps of reeds. After racing through brush and skirting a pond, Calder led them to a small barn.

He pushed them into a nearby stall and motioned for them to hide. Placing a finger to his lips, he drew his blades and rushed back out again.

Deena huddled with her brother in the old straw and hay, listening to the horrible sounds of battle beyond. Her heart thundered in her chest. Terrible, unbidden images of her parents and grandparents lying dead on the ground haunted her and she forced herself to take a deep breath.

"We'll be okay, Darren," she whispered. "Irial will protect us."

Darren nodded, clutching his dagger in trembling hands.

After a while, the sounds of war lessened and she heard a great cheer from somewhere far away. Halfling voices called in the distance but she couldn't make out any words.

Is it safe now? She wondered. *Did they drive off the goblins?*

Unsure of what to do, she waited, hoping Calder or one of her family would come for them.

"Hello?" called a male Halfling voice. "It's okay to come out now."

Darren looked up at her. "That's not Calder. He can't talk," he whispered.

Deena nodded, holding her medallion in one hand. "It's one of our people though."

"Your parents are waiting," the man called. "They sent me to get you. Come on out."

The children didn't answer.

"We have to keep moving," the man said. "More goblins are on the way. Quickly now!"

Indecisive, Deena hesitated. She wasn't sure about all this but it was a Halfling, not a goblin, and she knew they couldn't stay here. Taking Darren by the hand, she stood and peeked out.

"Ah, there you are!" A sturdy Halfling man with dark hair and eyes beamed at them. He wore a leather jerkin like Calder and carried a sword in a black sheath.

"Let's be off," he said, putting his hands on his hips. "No time to lose."

Deena's medallion tingled and she stopped.

Something isn't right...

"Where are Mama and Papa?" she asked.

The man waved a hand behind him. "Back there by the road."

"You know our parents?" Darren asked.

The man's eyes glittered. "Of course! I know your whole family."

The medallion tingled again. Deena clamped her hand on Darren's shoulder, holding him back. For once, he obeyed her.

The man cocked his head to the side. "Come now, I even know your uncle Connor and the Grey Riders."

Deena and Darren exchanged a look. "You do?" Darren asked.

"Of course. Eric and Dar and Andyn and Buck are his friends. Am I right?"

Well, if he knows the Grey Riders… Deena started to relax.

Her pendant tingled, more strongly this time. The man's eyes flicked to it. One of his hands moved an inch closer to his sword.

Deena nodded. "You're one of their friends?"

"Why, yes!"

Deena lifted her chin. "What's the name of Buck's pet?"

The man started. "What?"

Darren put his hand to the pommel of his dagger. "Buck has a pet. If you're their friend, you'll know its name. What's the name of Buck's pet?"

The man's smile faded and he nodded. His eyes glinted like those of a snake. "Well, well. Very clever, children. Your uncle would be proud of you. Too bad you'll never see him again."

He drew his sword and the blade burst into purple flame. "I'll make this quick," he murmured, "but that doesn't mean I won't enjoy it."

Deena's heart froze. The man stalked forward like a hunting cat, his other hand holding what looked like a tiny net made of ink.

Deena held forth her medallion. "Irial!"

The pendant flashed bright white and the menacing Halfling stepped back, arms up and blinking. Something moved behind him and Deena gaped. An enormous bat fluttered through the open barn doors, soaring over their assailant and alighting next to her. Now she saw it was Calder, except that his silky cloak had turned into bat wings. He lifted his shoulders and the wings became a cloak again. His two daggers glowed with silver light.

"No," he said in a rough, guttural voice, a tiny smile on his face. Deena's eyes widened. He didn't sound like any Halfling man she had ever heard.

He can talk!

The evil Halfling rubbed his eyes and his face warped into a snarl. "Really? And who are you?"

Calder's smile widened. "Gorlak." He danced lightly on his feet, blades making tiny circles in the air. "You are?"

"Me?" their assailant asked. A warped smile twisted his features. "They call me the Death Adder, or Kili Mikman, if you must know. But Gorlak, now, that's a goblin name. Are you as weak as a goblin?"

Gorlak's eyes flashed. "Come and see."

With that, the two leaped at each other. Deena pulled Darren back. She called Irial's name again. Her medallion flared. With a curse, Kili threw himself to the side as Gorlak's daggers swished through empty air.

The two men moved so quickly that she had a hard time following them. They slashed, stabbed, dodged, leaped and rolled, one motion following after another in a fluid dance that looked like it was choreographed. She drew back into a stall, afraid for Gorlak but unsure of what to do.

Twice, Gorlak used his cloak to flutter up out of the way of the assassin's attack but never let him have a clear line at the children.

Kili plied his little black net, flicking it at Gorlak. The net became a web of darkness and stuck fast to anything it touched, releasing itself upon a short word from the assassin. He managed to snag one of Gorlak's daggers and hurl it into a corner, but Gorlak called to the blade in a strange language and the weapon leaped back to his hand again.

The deadly net arced out, clamping onto Gorlak's leg. Deena gave out a short scream as Kili jerked Gorlak towards himself, sword slashing.

Instead of trying to get away, Gorlak swooped down at his enemy, parrying with his daggers. He landed and kicked the assassin's legs out from under him. Kili fell backward into a roll, losing his grip on the magic net. Gorlak retreated. He sliced into the net on his leg. His daggers flared blue and the net parted, bursting into purple flame. He cast it into a corner.

Both men bled from several minor wounds and they panted with exertion.

"That's not nice." The Death Adder stalked forward, his sword pulsing with a hypnotic flame. "Lady Arlene is going to be mad when she finds out you broke her toy."

Gorlak hesitated and Kili kicked a pile of straw into his face and charged, slashing. Deena screamed. Gorlak tumbled to the side and Kili's blow cut a wooden post into two flaming pieces.

Gorlak rolled to his feet, darted in, ducked a swing at his head, and hurled himself at Kili, bright blades stabbing. Both men hurtled into a water trough, shattering it in a shower of water and wood.

Darren leaped forward but she grabbed him. "No, Darren!"

Two dark shapes lay among the wreckage of the trough. Finally, one of them stood and turned.

A goblin in Calder's clothes and cloak faced them, his weapons red with blood. A pendant and a broken necklace lay at his feet. Kili sprawled on planks of wood, his sword's purple flame guttering in a water puddle. The goblin scooped up the pendant and stuffed it into his belt pouch.

Deena held up her medallion but it didn't tingle. Gorlak didn't flinch, instead sketching a short bow to her.

"I not enemy," he said in accented Humana. "I true friend of Grey Riders."

"What is Buck's pet's name?" Darren challenged.

Gorlak smiled. "Buck has pet pigeon named Puup."

Deena relaxed. "And what is the name of Dar Cabot's pegasus?"

"Virasi. It mean 'white star' in Elf-tongue."

A wave of relief surged through her. "Thank you, Gorlak!" She and Darren rushed to his side. He smiled and put his arms over their shoulders.

They heard a gurgle. Kili struggled to rise and fell against a stall. Gorlak brandished his daggers, but the Death Adder collapsed against a post, his clothes dark with blood.

"You… you really are a goblin!" he gasped, grimacing. "What does this mean?"

In a gentle voice that Deena had a hard time equating to a goblin, Gorlak said, "No one forced to be evil. I choose good."

His eyes going glassy, Kili shook his head. "No. That's impossible…"

Gorlak nodded. "Is possible. I serve Christ now. You can too, Kili Mikman, if you turn from evil ways."

Kili's eyes rolled back in his head and he keeled over.

Gorlak sighed. "Hope he had a chance to say he sorry."

"Are Mama and Papa okay?" Darren asked.

Gorlak nodded. "Yes. After I hide you, I go to find them. They in big fight; not hurt bad but too many enemies in the way, so I return. Good thing, too!"

Deena spared a glance at Kili. "Who was he?"

"Killer sent by Ja'al. Evil cult seeks revenge on all enemies — and you are family of Grey Rider, their worst enemy of all." He squared his shoulders. "He speak one thing true. More foes sure to come and your parents wait on road. Hurry now. You follow me. Gorlak take you to safe places by secret paths..."

Chapter Ten – En Garde

aptain Lervion? The Council is ready, ma'am."

Hannah Lervion blinked her eyes open and turned her head. Slowly, she stretched on the cot, trying to work the soreness out of tired limbs.

A blond young human in ring mail waited beside a table in the barracks. She smiled at him. "Thank you, Sergeant Adrian. Where are they?"

"In the Manor Library. Colonel Meraloy instructed me to fetch you."

Reluctantly, she sat up and swung her legs off the edge of the cot. The scar under the bandage on her upper arm itched and her ribs still felt sore, but broken bones still needed time, even with the assistance of healing magic. She stood and smoothed her tunic over scale mail, settling her brother's sword firmly in her belt.

"Lead on then."

She followed the soldier through sleeping areas and the mess hall. When they reached the infirmary, her pace slackened. She watched Christian nuns, Irial monks and Verian auxiliaries tend to wounded laid out on beds. The light of curing spells flared briefly here and there. On a few cots in a corner, exhausted healers slept. The smell of healing herbs, alcohol, wine and blood suffused the air.

Hannah's eyes followed the line of injured to a few tables where cloth-covered forms lay unmoving. As she watched, attendants reverently lifted them onto wheeled carts. She paused, remembering those forms as living, breathing people with dreams and aspirations of their own. Her eyes stung and she gritted her teeth.

We can't save everyone.

Her thoughts wandered to Connor, travelling to parts unknown on some secret mission. She fervently prayed he would finish quickly and return to her. She missed his kindness and his strength.

Where is he now? O Holy Irial, please watch over him.

Sergeant Adrian led her across a courtyard bustling with horses, troops and civilians to the great double doors of the city manor. Guards in chainmail saluted her with their halberds as she passed through the portal.

The interior of the manor house looked as crowded as the courtyard, minus the livestock. The sergeant stopped at another set of double doors carved with the figures of a man and woman in armor holding spears. Two Elven guards opened the doors at her approach.

Sergeant Adrian came to attention and she nodded to him. "Thank you, Sergeant. Carry on."

She entered and took a deep breath at the sight. Lord Justin and Lady Cassandra Martin stood with Sister Lynne Ambrose around a large table in the center of the Baron's receiving chamber. The nun motioned to something on the map and Lord Justin nodded.

Footsteps made Hannah turn and look up. An Elven couple approached.

"Did you rest, Hannah?" asked Lady Caria Meraloy. Her amber eyes showed concern.

"A little, thanks," she lied.

Colonel Sir Caridan Meraloy gave Hannah sidelong glance. "Hmm… I believe the 'little' part. You're looking a bit pale." Forest green eyes measured her as if to gauge her health by sight alone.

Hannah shrugged. Caria bent down and laid a hand on her shoulder. "I recommend spending as little time at the council as possible then. And don't mind Caridan. He fusses over me too."

Caridan kissed the top of Caria's head. "And with good reason."

Hannah nodded at the others at the table. "What is the latest?" The Elves at her side followed her gaze.

Caridan's demeanor became more serious. "Lord Justin and Lady Cassandra have done well since the Baron's death, though we are still in dire straits."

Caria nodded. "Lord Justin's decision to send the hill sprites out under cover of darkness to sabotage the enemy's siege engines was inspired. I don't think the Ja'al will ever find all the missing pinions and gears."

"Yes," Caridan agreed. "Now we won't have to worry about the walls getting battered down, at least until the enemy makes repairs."

Hannah's thoughts flew to the heartbreak of the previous day. "Any word about the Baron's children?" she asked in a quiet voice. "Did they make it to Ryker's Shoal?"

"Yes," Caridan replied. "We received a messenger pigeon today. They'll be in the city tomorrow."

"From there, they'll be sent on up the Moon River to Meridian," Caria added. "They'll be safe there."

"And orphans," Hannah finished, a bitter anger welling up in her. She squeezed her hand into a fist and pressed it into her leg, hoping the pain would disrupt her memories.

Caria sighed. "Yes, but the Baroness' dying wish will be fulfilled. Her children will live and heal under her sister's care."

Hannah felt the sting of tears and angrily brushed them away. "I wasn't fast enough."

Caridan bent down to meet her eyes. "None of us were. No one suspected that disloyal servants had hidden Ja'al assassins in the manor. Remember, Hannah, the children are alive because of you."

The images of the Baron of Sentinel, his Baroness and the Colonel of Guards lying dead in the Grand Hall burned in Hannah's brain. She tried to banish them with thoughts of the Baron's three children, wounded but alive, heading towards safety, guarded by a squad of the city's best troops.

"Damned Ja'al," Hannah hissed under her breath. *I'll make them pay if it's the last thing I do.*

"Yes, they are," Caria murmured, voice cold.

"Let's go see Lord Justin and Lady Cassandra," Caridan offered. "I still have to give my report. We had quite the time this morning."

Lord Justin Martin looked up at their approach. Tall and burly, he wore plate armor under a white tunic. A greatsword leaned against the table. Lady Cassandra smiled at Hannah. Black leather armor gleamed under her ivory tabard and she bore a longsword and war hammer at her belt. Her hair was gathered in a tight bun on top of her head. Hannah bowed alongside Caria and Caridan.

"None of that," said Cassandra. "We are comrades-in-arms now. No formalities."

Hannah shook her head. "But —"

Justin raised a hand. "You killed an assassin who was taking aim at me. No titles. I mean it."

She smiled back at him. "Thank you, Lor… I mean, Justin."

"That's better. Caridan, what news from the field?"

Caridan smiled. "The plan worked very well. We were able to confuse the enemy in the fog and misdirected two companies to crash into two others. It didn't hurt that one group was Kaftu and the other Ogres. We all know how much Ogres love a Kaftu steak."

Caria's mouth quirked up in a grin. "We helped them along with a few well-placed arrows and magic spells, then headed back inside the walls."

"Enemy casualties?"

Caridan considered. "Based on the re-arrangement of the enemy formations, it must have been significant. The enemy commanders have dispersed the Kaftu to the far eastern side of town and the Ogres to the west. We only lost five."

"Good. That will make them think twice. We've bought some time." Justin replied.

Cassandra tapped a finger on the huge map on the table. "Is the northern road still clear?"

Caria nodded. "We've routed Kaftu scouts and raiders who have tried to set up roadblocks and ambushes, so we're not cut off from the rest of the country — yet."

Hannah clambered up on top of a chair so she could see the whole map. With a finger, she traced the roads out of Sentinel: one to the east to Duarvar, one to the west to Starpoint, and the third, and most important, to the interior of Gorostol.

If Sentinel falls, the invaders have a clear path all the way to Meridian.

"Any word from any of the other cities?" she asked.

Cassandra made a wry face. "Well, about that. There is a mix of bad news and good news. First, the bad. Starpoint has fallen."

Hannah's heart sank.

Caria sighed. "Wonderful."

"A Ja'al invasion fleet fought its way past a naval blockade," Cassandra continued. "It landed two battalions of marines while a full division invaded from the south on the land route. Refugees escaped up the coast and are in Ryker's Shoal by now."

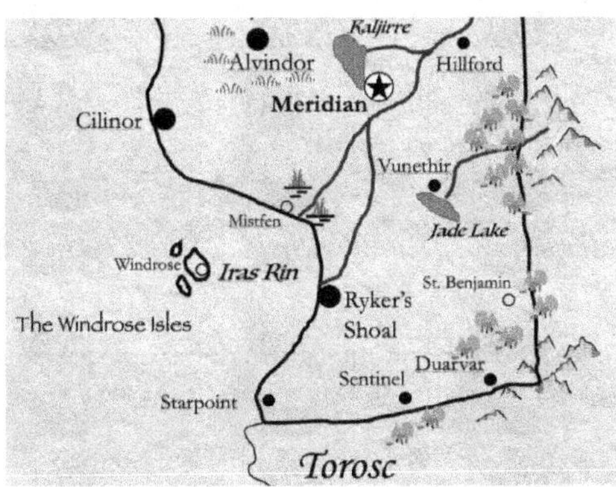

Hannah's eyes followed the coastline on the big map. With Starpoint and its harbor lost, the Ja'al could transport and land troops much faster. Worse, the situation forced the Gorostoli High Command to divert resources from helping Sentinel to Ryker's Shoal.

"What else?" she asked.

Cassandra sighed. "The towns to the west between here and Starpoint have also fallen. Knightbrand and Willow Glen are leveled."

"I thought you said there was good news," Caridan said with a wry expression.

Justin smiled. "There is. The navy turned back an invasion force headed for the Windrose Islands. A pitched battle was fought near Jade Lake and the Ja'al lost badly. Best of all, the 4th Division is headed our way, making for Duarvar."

Finally! Some help…Hannah nodded. "When can we expect a relief column?"

Justin shook his head. "I don't know. 4th Division's priority is to reinforce

Duarvar since they are faced with a large Torosci army. So far, we've only been attacked by a couple of regiments in Sentinel, so the greater danger is to the east."

Hannah stared at the map. She understood why the 4th headed to Duarvar. If that city fell, Sentinel could be easily surrounded. Then the way to the center of Gorostol would be clear. "We have to hold on here."

"For now. The Torosci haven't sent a massive force here like they did at Starpoint." Justin stroked his chin. "We've mauled them pretty badly and they haven't been able to get more than a few dozen troops over the walls despite several attacks, so we're doing pretty well. However, I'm not sure why they don't just bypass us and head north."

His mouth set in a grim line. Cassandra eyed him.

Sister Lynne spoke for the first time. "Were there any daemons at Starpoint?"

Cassandra brushed a hand through her nut-brown hair. "Yes, unfortunately."

"There's your answer," the nun said.

The others looked at her in confusion.

She stared at the map as if to burn a hole in it with her eyes. "They don't want to bypass us because they need us, all of us."

"Why?" asked Hannah. "As hostages? Slaves?"

Sister Lynne's eyes met hers. "Food. The Fallen Ones consider us a delicacy."

Hannah's heart skipped a beat and she fought to control her stomach.

The others stared at Sister Lynne. She slowly nodded. The silence dragged on.

Justin's jaw worked. "Then we will have to maintain the north highway as an escape route, no matter what else happens here, with priority to saving the civilians. If it appears we cannot hold, we have to evacuate."

"Agreed," Caridan said. "We'll have to make sure we're ready to go at a moment's notice."

"We should see to the stores and water supply," Cassandra noted. "We'll need every ounce in the event we make the trek to Ryker's Shoal, or beyond."

Justin appeared lost in thought and Hannah watched him carefully. A veteran of several large-scale engagements, he knew far more than any of them.

He stared down at the map. "If we're just a larder for the daemons, then where are they? We know there are Skull Gates in Torosc. The border is less than ten miles away. Why haven't they brought them?"

The other commanders stared at the map silently.

Justin tapped the markers depicting the enemy force. "My thought is that they want to pin us down inside Sentinel so we can't escape. I'll lay you ten to one odds there is an even bigger army out there. It's what I would do if I were in their place."

"Have you seen more enemy nearby?" asked Sister Lynne.

He shrugged. "No, but with the hill sprites busy sabotaging siege engines and scouting for Kaftu on the North Highway, our usual eyes and ears aren't where they should be. The Torosci probably mustered far beyond the border to keep from tipping us off. They'll be here in due time."

Where will the attack come from? Hannah's eyes followed the border of Torosc and Gorostol on the map, just southeast of the city. The Eastern Highway led through thick forests along the border towards the neighboring city of Duarvar, perched on the slopes of the Rampart Mountains.

"What news from Duarvar?" she asked, tracing the road with her finger.

Caridan shrugged. "Last we heard, they had beaten off an attack by two regiments of Ja'al and dark elves. Their city is bigger than Sentinel by half, and its fortifications are Dwarven designs — very tough to overcome."

"But that was four days ago, just before the assassination of the Baron and Baroness," Cassandra noted. "We've heard nothing since."

Hannah pointed at the dark grey symbols of the mountains. "We don't know what's under those peaks."

Caria smiled at her. "The Dwarves do. They've mined that area near Duarvar for generations."

"I see what Hannah is driving at," Justin added. "The Dwarves know what is on the Gorostol side of the border. But what about the Torosc side? It would be the perfect place to hide a Skull Gate."

No one said anything, lost in their own thoughts.

A Skull Gate! If there's one near Duarvar, could there be one near us? Dear Irial, I hope not.

Hannah shivered. The Ja'al had constructed the Skull Gates as magical space-time portals to the hellish world of Hades to summon their infernal allies. Several had been destroyed in the months leading up to the start of the war, but if daemons now roamed the land, others doubtless remained.

"Maybe we should send the sprites to find out," Cassandra offered.

"The sprites?" Caridan interrupted. "Lady Cassandra, I need them for situational awareness. I can't be blinded."

"But we have to know what's going on in Duarvar," she said in a measured tone. "They've been silent for too long. Something has happened."

Caridan shook his head. "That won't do us any good if the Torosci launch a surprise attack while the expedition is away."

"Do we need to send them all?" Caria asked. "Maybe just a few."

"That's a better option," Justin agreed. "We can ask Lady Tinira and Lord Esdan to take a small team."

Caridan looked doubtful but he gave in. "If you're sure about this, Lady Cassandra."

She sighed. "I hope I'm *wrong* about this."

Hannah's eyes returned to the map.

Starpoint is lost, the Ja'al have daemons helping them, an invasion fleet is lurking by the Windrose Isles, and now a pitched battle at Jade Lake…

If Duarvar fell, a vast dark wave threatened to engulf all of Gorostol.

The noose tightens.

Images of daemons boiling up out of a Skull Gate just beyond the Torosc border made her break out in a cold sweat.

She clenched her fists. *I won't give in to despair. We have to hold.*

"We *all* hope you're wrong," concluded Justin.

Chapter Eleven – The Arts of Massed Warfare

Remember, there and right back," Hannah said.

Esdan and Tinira grinned at her from the nightstand. No more than a foot tall, the hill sprite couple wore no clothing but carried tiny bows on their backs and swords strapped to their thighs. Their iridescent dragonfly wings fluttered, sparkling with rainbow colors in the lantern-light.

"Are you actually fretting about us, young Captain?" Esdan asked, his eyes twinkling.

Hannah gave a sheepish grin of her own. "No. Well, yes. I just wouldn't want anything to happen to you. I mean, Connor would never forgive me if I sent you heedlessly into danger."

Tinira stepped to the edge of the nightstand and put one of her tiny hands to Hannah's cheek. "None of this is heedless. My lord and I are taking every precaution. Besides, the Grey Riders didn't save us from a Hell Wisp months ago for us to get smashed by some stinking Ja'al."

Esdan put his arm around his wife's shoulders. "Hannah, we know these woods like our own home. And the sprites who live near the Rampart Mountains are kin. We'll be fine."

Hannah nodded. "I'm being silly."

"No," Tinira replied with a kiss on her cheek. "You're being a dear, like always. We'll be back before you know it."

Hannah opened the library window. Esdan and Tinira landed on the sill and beckoned to four other sprite warriors waiting outside. With a final wave, they zipped out into the night.

She stared after them. A faint unease clawed at her and she gave her head an irritated shake.

"What's the matter with me?" she groused. "They'll be fine."

To clear her head and give herself time to think, she strode out of the manor and climbed up the steps to the nearest parapet.

Three guards came to attention. She nodded to them.

She gestured at the enemy campfires blazing five hundred yards away. "Anything happening?"

A young corporal shook her head. "Not much. Lord Caridan gave them quite a bloody nose this morning, Captain. Maybe they don't have the stomach for another pummeling."

Hannah drummed the stone wall with her fingers. "They're Ja'al. They always have something else up their sleeve."

"Ma'am?" asked another private. "Is the Army coming soon? Will we get reinforcements?"

Hannah hesitated for a moment. "They are on the move. I know that for certain. At least one division is heading in our direction but there are battles all over the country. I'm not sure when we'll get any reinforcements. We have to hold here as best we can."

She leaned on the parapet, staring at the tents and bonfires. Their sheer numbers daunted her.

We have to hold. And I have to lead them.

"Carry on, Corporal," she said. The troops came to attention and saluted.

She continued along the wall. She climbed to the top of a tower, examined the catapult, then proceeded to another station to check on a ballista crew. Everything looked ready: troops alert and watching the enemy camp, magical ammunition in good supply, pots of boiling oil ready, equipment in working order. She made sure the water barrels were full — the last time the Ja'al attacked, they had used incendiary ammunition and flaming arrows and only the heroic efforts of the citizen firefighters managed to avert a disaster.

She descended the stairs to the parapet, pausing at a crenellation. She stepped up onto a platform and peered out at the Ja'al fires blazing in the nigh.

Why am I so nervous?

The two crescent moons in the sky above cast a pale light. The air felt warm and a bit humid, normal for early summer. Nothing seemed out of place.

Her eyes wandered to the woods outside the city walls, seeking anything unusual. About a master sharpshooter's bowshot away, the trees loomed dark and shadowy. Nothing moved in the cleared expanse of land between the trees and the walls.

With a start, she realized the forest wasn't supposed to be so close to the city. Hannah's eyes locked on the trees, waving in the breeze. Her heart froze.

Breeze? What breeze? There's no wind!

She whirled to the nearest private. "Raise the alarm! We're under attack!" He saluted and darted off.

Racing back to the ballista crew, she pointed at the forest. "There! The attack is coming from there! Load a fire bolt!"

The sergeant ordered his crew into action immediately. They cranked the gears and inserted a bolt crackling with red sparks. The bell of the citadel rang and troops raced to their stations.

The trees dissolved into a black mist. In place of the phantom woods, a massive throng of skeletons and walking corpses advanced. In their wake, orderly ranks of Elves clad in dark chainmail followed.

"Attack!" Hannah shouted. "Dark Elves and undead! Eastern Gate!"

A horn blasted from the Dark Elven ranks and the revenant horde broke into a shuffling run. Two sizzling ballista bolts and two sparking catapult stones from the city walls flew past and struck the undead ranks. The catapult shots burst, releasing a storm of lightning bolts that fried zombies and shattered skeletons. The ballista missiles detonated, immolating some of the undead and hurling Dark Elves into the air. The majority of the formation continued on.

"No, no, no!" Hannah cursed, snatching a round shield from a nearby stack.

She charged along the parapet towards the East Gate, dodging soldiers. A low-voiced chant sounded from the enemy force and she heard slavering growls and howling. The animalistic snarls made her skin crawl.

Those aren't zombies!

She slid to a stop near a crenelation and stood on tiptoe. One of the garrison mages joined her. Nearby ranks of archers loosed, but she couldn't tell if they hit anything. A ballista bolt sizzled in from one of the towers and slammed into the ground, exploding in a blast of flame. Hannah saw the enemy illuminated briefly in the flash.

"Wait!" She ordered. "We need more light."

The wizard chanted, raising his hands over his head. With a final syllable, four bright balls of white light arced out from his fingers to hover over the attackers.

Hannah gasped. Dark figures loped at the sides of the Elven ranks. They looked like Kaftu, but these versions of the hyena-folk had eyes that glowed blue-white and a grey fog rolled at their feet.

Dolmide's Beard! What are those things?

The enemy advanced into the teeth of a volley from the Sentinel defenders. Dozens dropped, but the undead surged ahead. Many of them carried ladders or battering rams.

"We need clerics here now!" she screamed, heading for a portion of the wall where the undead would show up first.

"Here, Captain!"

She whirled. Sister Lynne slid to a stop next to her, clad in a leather brigandine and carrying a flail in her hand.

"Right on time, Sister," Hannah said. She pointed at the foul Kaftu. "What are those?"

The nun crossed herself. "Darkspawn! The Ja'al must have a potent necromancer among their ranks to create greater undead."

More catapult shot and ballista bolts exploded near the enemy, thinning their numbers but many had reached the walls by that point. Supporting fire from the fortress slackened.

"That's all the help we'll get," Hannah muttered. "The firing angle is all wrong now – the enemy are too close to the walls."

"But it will trim them down a bit." said Sister Lynne.

Hannah shook her head, drawing Shriek from its scabbard. Her brother's sword shimmered and then burst into silver light.

"What about the boiling oil?" asked a sergeant, nodding to a nearby kettle.

Sister Lynne shook her head. "Undead don't care about that. Save it for other opponents."

Sentinel archers leaned over the parapets, launching volleys of arrows into the advancing horde. A few guards were hit by return arrows and dropped, but the others kept up the rate of fire.

Hannah stood on tiptoe again to peer through the crenelation. Despite the arrows and occasional magic spells from the defenders, some of the enemy had managed to hoist ladders against the walls. The Darkspawn Kaftu leaped into action, scampering up the ladders like cockroaches.

Hannah hefted Shriek. "Get ready, Sister."

"As always, Captain."

The archers drew back. Soldiers in chainmail and shield replaced them, armed with mace, axe and sword.

The top rungs of a ladder slammed into the wall in front of Hannah. Her heart hammered in her chest.

"Irial, guide my hand," she whispered, hefting her blade.

A Darkspawn vaulted over the parapet, wielding a battle axe. Hannah leaped and struck the thing's head from its shoulders. Shriek emitted a high-pitched whistle and flared white light as the undead burst into flame and pitched back into the darkness. Another Darkspawn leaped over the wall and lashed out at her with a pair of hooked swords. She ducked under both blows.

A foul, stinking cloud pulsed out from the Darkspawn and Hannah fought to keep from retching. It was so strong she could almost taste it. She drew back, eyes watering. Three Sentinel guards fell under Darkspawn daggers.

At Hannah's side, Sister Lynne clutched her crucifix. Her holy symbol flared even brighter than Shriek.

"Begone, in the name of the Christ!" The nun marched at the

Darkspawn, her crucifix held before her. The undead wailed and threw their hands in front of their faces, backing away. The miasma of rot dissipated like mist blown away by the wind. With a shout of triumph, the Sentinel guards charged, shields up, hacking. Two Darkspawn tripped and fell over the wall. Their howls echoed in the night.

Good. They make a very nice crunch when they hit the ground, Hannah thought with satisfaction.

A team of soldiers pushed the ladders away from the wall. Again, Hannah strained to see over the parapet. The ladders, complete with Darkspawn clinging to the rungs, slammed into a mass of zombies and skeletons, scattering bones and bodies.

A trio of Darkspawn vaulted over the wall from another ladder. Hannah fought side-by-side with her troops. Darkspawn blades struck sparks off stone as she darted and dodged. Undead Kaftu snarled with rage and redoubled their efforts to bring her down, but Hannah whirled like a miniature dust devil. She slashed through Darkspawn legs or leaped to impale rotted skulls. Shriek let out its triumphant cry each time an undead fell.

Three more defenders fell by her side but her troops held. Sister Lynne was everywhere, slamming down undead, healing soldiers she could help and praying for those she couldn't. The troops rallied around her and Hannah, shouting battle cries.

Hannah scanned left and right, panting to catch her breath. Despite some of the attackers making it over the walls, the defenders held. So far, the East Gate stood against the mob of zombies hammering away with battering rams.

A tall figure in plate mail took the steps two at a time to join them.

"Lord Justin!" said Sister Lynne. "Thank God."

"Sorry I'm late, Sister Lynne." Justin Martin hefted his greatsword. "Had a bit of an incident at the gate."

"We're just glad you're here, milord."

An arrow missed Justin by less than a foot but he didn't even flinch. He grinned down at Hannah. "We're doing well, thanks to you, Captain."

"Me?" she retorted. "I think it was Sister Lynne and our troops."

A fire dart sizzled past Justin and cracked on a nearby tower. "We live in interesting times, yes?" he mused, as if surveying the weather on market day.

"That sounds like an Elven curse," Hannah replied, making a face at him.

"I'll tell you what else is interesting," he said over the clash and clangor of battle. "The dark Elves are hanging back. They seem to be content in commanding the undead but not expending too much energy."

Hannah's eyes narrowed. Sure enough, the Elven Ja'al directed the masses of undead in the attack. Some of their archers sniped at defenders on the walls and an occasional magic spell arced out from their ranks, but they didn't wade into the fray.

They're not attacking in force, like last time. Why? Hannah's thoughts winged back to the Council meeting. Something nagged at her. Her eyes darted all around.

What am I missing? It's like they're just trying to get our attention.

Another ladder rattled against the walls and Justin leaped to help two other warriors push it away. One of them stumbled against a nearby water barrel.

Water! Oh no! The supplies! The well! This is a diversion!

She went cold. Sheathing her sword, she scurried down the stairs.

"Where are you going?" yelled Justin and Lynne.

"The supplies and the well!" she shouted back.

They shouted something else she couldn't hear over the racket. She beckoned to two archers and an Elven mage who had just helped a wounded soldier descend the stairs.

"You three, with me!"

The soldiers raced to follow her. She ran as fast as she could, cutting corners and jumping over debris in the street.

Panting, she slowed to a trot near the twin warehouses and the town well by the barracks. Pale faint moonlight shone on the massive well, fully ten feet across. She noticed its protective cover was removed.

She halted, drawing Shriek again. Her impromptu squad caught up to her.

"Looks quiet," one of the archers said. Hannah nodded. She heard only the distant sounds of combat behind her.

"Where are the guards?" asked the mage. She flicked her hand and a small ball of light floated out over the plaza.

Something shimmered in the well and Shriek flared white. Two hulking, dripping nightmares hoisted themselves out of the water. They looked like misshapen human corpses enrobed in weeds and creepers. Eyes glowed a ghostly white. An unmistakable stench of rotting vegetation and putrid flesh assaulted her.

Holy Irial! They found a way into the city!

The mage chanted. A trio of firedarts hissed past Hannah's ear and detonated on one of the beasts, knocking it off its feet.

Hannah leaped forward. "See to the storeroom!" she ordered. Visions of the slain Baron and Baroness hovered in her memory, along with a bitter anger.

"But Captain! You can't hold them on your own!"

"There are only two. We have no idea how many are in the warehouse! Make sure they don't destroy all the supplies!" she screamed, hefting her shield. Not even waiting to see if they obeyed, she leaped at the injured creature as it struggled to its feet. She severed its head and Shriek let out its ghostly scream as the thing burst into flames.

The second one lurched towards her, dead hands reaching. Creepers and weeds writhed and slapped against her shield. Hannah dodged a ham-fisted haymaker and lopped off a leg at the knee. The shambling corpse tilted to the side and fell but kept flailing at her. One blow hit her shield dead-center and she staggered.

She took a deep breath, stepping back.

Hannah timed its next swing, then darted in and split its skull down the middle. Shriek let out its exultant screech again and the creature fell into a burning heap.

Two more undead heaved themselves out of the well and joined the fray. They shuffled at her, arms and tendrils reaching.

Great. How many are there?

Hannah gave ground, then sidestepped, putting them in line with each other. She hacked weeds and arms and hands until one zombie lumbered around its fellow. She dodged again to put them in line and attacked the lead undeaed. It overextended itself and she jammed her blade into its midsection, then ripped sideways, nearly cutting it in half. Shriek wailed in triumph as the blazing corpse toppled over.

She didn't even notice her blade's call this time. Her breath came in gasps. Yet another corpse wrapped in weeds climbed out of the well.

This might not have been such a smart idea.

Dodging yet again, she put her opponents in line, but her fatigue caught up with her and one managed to get around its fellow. Faced with two at once, she backed into the side of a peddler's stall. A rotting arm slammed her to one side and she gasped at the force of the blow. She tried to avoid another haymaker and caught it in the shoulder instead, crying out as she felt muscles tear. She ducked and dodged, but vines wrapped around her hands and legs and rotting hands grasped her by the throat and lifted her up. With a shriek of fury, she drove her brother's sword up through the enemy's jaw. The creature dropped her and burst into flame. She slammed into the side of the stall, eyes watering from the overpowering stench.

Then a bright light exploded and the undead recoiled. She dropped to her knees, fighting for air as the odious fog dissipated.

Justin Martin caught her by the collar and hauled her behind him with one hand, his greatsword in the other. She landed heavily, dropping Shriek, but strong arms caught her.

"We're here, Captain," Sister Lynne said.

Hannah nodded blearily. Her wounds seared with a raw, maddening pain. Through tear-streaked vision, she saw Justin slash two undead in half with powerful blows, kick another into a pile of wood, then split another from crown to navel.

Sister Lynne's gentle hands settled on her and soothing warmth flowed into Hannah's body. She sighed with relief as the burning receded to a dull ache. Now all the fatigue and residual pain hit her. She rested her forehead on her knees, breathing deeply.

"Stay here," Sister Lynne said. Hannah nodded, too tired to look any more. The pop of metal splitting undead skulls rang in the courtyard, punctuated by an occasional blast of magic. Then all fell silent.

Boots clumped on the cobblestones but Hannah left her head down. The Elven mage's voice echoed in the square. "We found the guards, all dead," she reported. "They must have been surprised by the attack from the well, though they did destroy three of those things. We found three others in the warehouse. We got them all, but some of the boxes and crates are smashed. We'll have to do an inventory."

"How is the captain?" asked an archer.

"She'll mend," replied Sister Lynne. "Why did you leave her here by herself?"

"We wanted to stay but she was worried about more of them ruining the stores, so she ordered us into the warehouse."

"Not the brightest idea," sniffed Sister Lynne, "but brave."

Hannah shook her head to clear it and dragged herself to her feet.

"How did they get into the well?" asked Justin.

Hannah sheathed her brother's sword and limped over to join the others.

"Could they have found the water source?" Sister Lynne asked.

"That's impossible," said one of the archers. "They'd have to go hundreds of feet underground."

The Elven mage frowned. "Dark Elves were commanding the attack. They know the underground."

Justin shook his head. "We'll need all available clerics here to try to purify the well now. The water is probably undrinkable as it is."

Hannah nodded. "I'll get back to the walls."

"You most certainly will not!" retorted Sister Lynne, taking hold of her arm. "To the infirmary with you. No telling what kind of disease those things managed to infect you with."

"But—"

Justin shook his head. "The attack is broken. I applaud your bravery, Captain, but perhaps it wasn't a prudent choice to take on those undead by yourself, was it? Do as Sister Lynne says." He raised an eyebrow and she closed her mouth.

Hannah knew when to let matters lie.

Chapter Twelve – First Command

Hannah spent two days in the infirmary, submitting to scans and tests and getting more impatient all the time. Finally, on the third morning, she tried to slip out the back door but Sister Lynne corralled her.

"No, you don't." The nun fixed her with an exasperated look. Hannah paused. From past experience, a clash of wills with Sister Lynne usually did not have the desired results.

"I'm fine," Hannah protested, backing towards her bed, eyes flitting around for another escape route. "The tests all came back negative for Corpse Rot and Crypt Fever. I have to get back to Lord Justin."

"Well, he's busy right now," Sister Lynne announced. "Besides, you're not going to go see the Lords and Ladies in a flimsy shift. It isn't decent."

"I was just going to get my gear from the next room," Hannah replied.

Sister Lynne raised an eyebrow, her arms crossed over her chest.

Hannah tried a different tack. "Can someone bring me a uniform in case anyone comes looking for me?"

Sister Lynne tried not to smile. "Very well. But don't try to slip out again, or I'll have to take sterner measures."

Hannah sighed. She did feel better but really wanted to find out what else had happened. More than that, she fretted about Tinira and Esdan. The journey to Duarvar, for a band of sprites, was a three-day round trip at most. They were late.

They're probably fine. I'm turning into such a worry-wart.

A female soldier brought her uniform and, surprisingly, her brother's sword and a war hammer. Feeling more like herself, Hannah changed and was just stamping into her boots when Sister Lynne returned.

"You're in luck. Lord Justin needs you in the Council chambers," she announced.

"Did he say why?"

The nun shrugged. "No, but doctors and medics aren't required so I think it's a military strategy session. Go on now. I can see you're itching to get out of here."

Hannah paused at the door, then returned to Sister Lynne. She impulsively hugged her.

"Thank you," she whispered, before darting off.

"Get off with you," replied Sister Lynne, but Hannah could hear the smile in her voice.

She hustled to the manor. Justin and Cassandra were already there, as were Caridan, Caria, and, much to her delight, Esdan and Tinira.

"You're a little late," Hannah said, beaming as she hopped up on a chair.

Tinira gave her a wan smile and Hannah's joy at seeing the sprites evaporated.

"What's wrong?" she asked.

Justin held up his hand. "They were just about to tell us. Go on, Lord Esdan."

Esdan took a deep breath. "There is no easy way to put this. There is a large column of refugees heading our way from Duarvar. The city has fallen."

Stunned, Hannah leaned on the table. "What… how?"

In her mind's eye, she saw the city of Duarvar from her last visit, years ago: a sturdy, prosperous town with ten towers and outer and inner walls of stone.

"Two Torosci divisions attacked, almost ten thousand strong, with artillery and air support," Esdan continued. "Dark Elves and Dwarves in the service of the Ja'al attacked from underground. The people of Duarvar fought hard and the Dwarven Iron Legion held the tunnels for days, but eventually the artillery bombardment and the attack from below were too much."

Hannah's gaze fell immediately to a map on the table. With Duarvar conquered, there was nothing to protect Sentinel's eastern flank.

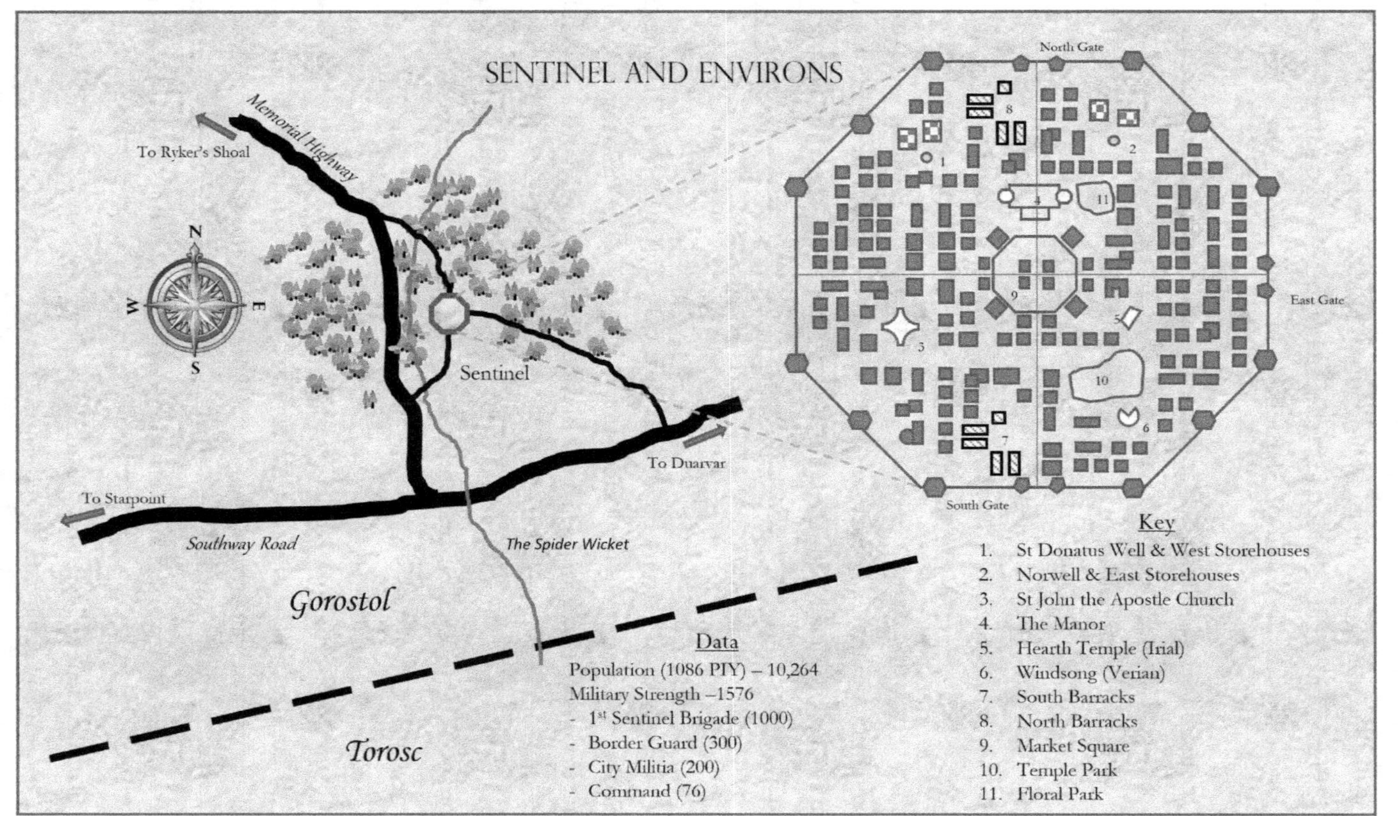
SENTINEL AND ENVIRONS
North Gate
East Gate
South Gate
To Ryker's Shoal
Memorial Highway
To Starpoint
Southway Road
Sentinel
To Duarvar
The Spider Wicket
Gorostol
Torosc
N
E
S
W
Data
Population (1086 PIY) – 10,264
Military Strength –1576
- 1st Sentinel Brigade (1000)
- Border Guard (300)
- City Militia (200)
- Command (76)
Key
1. St Donatus Well & West Storehouses
2. Norwell & East Storehouses
3. St John the Apostle Church
4. The Manor
5. Hearth Temple (Irial)
6. Windsong (Verian)
7. South Barracks
8. North Barracks
9. Market Square
10. Temple Park
11. Floral Park

"We'll be surrounded," she whispered.

Caria laid a hand on her shoulder with a gentle squeeze.

"Worse yet," Tinira continued, "The enemy force also had daemons with them, just like at the Battle of Starpoint. This time there were more than ninety of them."

Stunned silence followed. Hannah felt the blood drain from her face.

"Sweet Jesus help us," Caria breathed.

"Wait." Caridan held up a hand. "Are you sure?"

Esdan nodded. "I spoke to the Lord of Duarvar himself."

Caridan ran a hand through his hair. "There were forty of them at Starpoint and they almost wiped out a company of two hundred men by themselves. Ninety…" He stared down at the map.

Tinira held up a hand. "Granted, many of the ones at Duarvar were small, not much bigger than a Dwarf, but they were dangerous. And the large ones were even more deadly. The defenders were able to kill some, but many remain."

"What do we know about them?" Caria asked.

Hannah barely heard her. *First Starpoint, now Duarvar… we're trapped.*

"The clerics of Kurental identified four types," Esdan replied. "They're using Skreets as light reconnaissance units – they look like winged boars. The shock troops are Dwerrolves, a cross between Dwarves and wolves. The subunit commanders appeared to be War Fiends. These are very dangerous. They are as tall as a human and can fly. They wear chainmail and use fiery scimitars. Worse yet, their bracers shoot iron spikes that cause flesh to turn into hot lava rock where they hit."

Dearest Irial! How do we fight those things?

"And the fourth?" asked Caridan.

"Bone Knights," whispered Tinira with a shudder. "Taller than Lord Justin. They wear hellish armor of enchanted human bones that is stronger than steel. They can't fly but fight with halberds and blast out waves of hellfire that scorches and sears. They turn the dead into skeletons and zombies at will."

Hannah clenched a fist on the tabletop. *Fear is useless. I have to help somehow.*

"How many refugees?" asked Caria.

"Anywhere from ten to twelve thousand," answered Esdan. "There were about two thousand military in that mix, including wounded."

Hannah's mind reeled. The entire population of Duarvar was sixteen thousand or eighteen thousand… or had been. She couldn't believe that more than a third of the population had died, nor that only four of Duarvar's six regiments remained.

"We have to escort them to safety," she offered, hoping that she could have some role in that task. "We owe them that much."

"You have that right," Justin said, resting his fist on the tabletop. "But more importantly, we can't hold Sentinel against a force that large, not with daemons."

"Are you saying we should evacuate?" asked Cassandra. "Surely that's more dangerous than remaining here. We'd be exposed on the road. God only knows what's lurking out there in the wilds now."

Justin shook his head. "If we stay in the city, we're trapped. With the force from the east and the current one besieging us here, there's no way we could hold out. Even if reinforcements arrive, against a horde of tens of thousands, we don't stand a chance."

"I'm not so sure," Caridan said. "We're in a fortified position."

Tinira hummed into the air over the map and landed on the diagram of Duarvar. She tapped the drawing with her little foot. "This city was almost twice the size of Sentinel and better fortified. It fell. It's only a matter of time."

"Lady Tinira is right." Justin's gaze roamed over them all. "We have to get the civilians out, and quickly. The sooner they're on the way to Ryker's Shoal, the better chance they have for avoiding contact with Torosci units."

Caria sighed. "Some of our people won't make it. The old and infirm and some of the wounded are in no shape to travel."

Caridan put his arm around her shoulders. "Whatever small chance they have, it's better than facing certain death here."

Hannah racked her brain, trying to think of another solution. Her eyes flitted all over the map, but she saw only danger everywhere, a dark wave surging inexorably upon them.

Justin shook his head. "There is little alternative. We will empty Sentinel and install traps in the town. Our engineers will see to it that the Ja'al pay for every cobblestone. The civilians will leave at dawn, accompanied by the remainder of the town militia. Citizens will travel light; nothing more than what is absolutely necessary for survival. We will empty the remaining provisions and use that for the trip to Ryker's Shoal. We can get boats from there to go up the Moon River to Meridian."

"Lord Justin," Hannah began, "I volunteer to escort —"

He held up a hand. "I already have it worked out. I will send Captains Topping and Colletti with two companies to join the refugees from Duarvar and link up with our own people on the way to Ryker's Shoal."

"What about us?" asked Hannah. Her eyes met Justin's.

"The remaining regulars will fight a rear-guard action to slow the enemy after the engineers are done setting traps in the town. It will be a challenge, to say the least."

The rear guard? Hannah hesitated. She knew the risks of such an assignment. It would take all their skill and cunning to both harass the enemy long enough to delay them and make it out alive.

She thought of the citizens of Sentinel, particularly the children, and she clenched her fists. "I will do what I can," she said, looking up at Justin.

Despite the situation, he gave her a little smile. "I'd like you to take command of a company of your own, Captain. What do you say to that?"

My first command! Yes! Her trepidation about the assignment faded and her heart surged with a sudden, fierce bravery. "Sir, yes sir!"

Now I can strike back at those bastards…

"Good. We're going to be very busy."

***

It's been two days since the townspeople left… feels like it was two hours.

Hannah ran through her preparations in her mind, trying to see if she had forgotten anything. Her company hid among the trees and brush. About two hundred mixed medium infantry and light cavalry, they wore mottled colors to blend into the woods. Cloth sacks around their horses' hooves muffled the sound of their passage.

She shot a look to the northeast. There, Justin, Cassandra, Caria and Caridan commanded almost two full regiments, blocking the northern route out of Sentinel. Against the massive Ja'al army barreling towards them, their force seemed pitifully small.

Hannah comforted herself in knowing the civilians and militia had a head start, heading northwest as fast as possible. It would take them almost four days to reach the large port city of Ryker's Shoal but, with a head start on the Ja'al, their chances were good.

"Now, we just have to survive long enough to get there ourselves," she murmured. Warm winds blew through the trees, rustling the leaves and branches and carrying familiar woodland scents to her.

"We only need to hold out until the 4th Division gets here," noted the dark-haired woman at her side, mounted on a courser. "They have a lot of resources, including air cavalry and magical support units. That will make a big difference."

"I understand, Lieutenant Hunt," Hannah replied, gathering her war pony's reins in a gloved hand. "But it won't make much of a difference if none of us are alive to greet them."

Her officer nodded, a distracted look on her face as she scanned the forest beyond them. She ran a hand through her curly locks, dark eyes distant.

Doubt still gnawed at Hannah. What if the Ja'al did something unexpected and she wasn't quick enough to counteract them?

"Is there a chance that the Ja'al would try to outflank Lord Justin's force through the forest, or bypass the road altogether?" she asked.

Silence reigned. Hannah shot a look up at Lieutenant Hunt. Hunt remained lost in thought, eyes fixed on the distant city of Sentinel.

"Lieutenant?"

"Oh, sorry. No, ma'am, I don't think they will. They have siege engines they probably want for the attack on Ryker's Shoal, and they can't very well drag those through the woods. And they have scouts, too, so they likely know that 4th Division is very close. They don't want to risk us linking up."

Hannah nodded. Despite looking like she was daydreaming half the time, Lieutenant Hunt had served in the Sentinel regiment for almost ten years and seemed to have good ideas.

Hannah remembered well Lord Justin's latest orders: Hide in the woods west of town. When the Ja'al advance, perform a flanking maneuver and hit them in the side. Retreat and repeat. Stealth and surprise are of the essence.

A triple boom sounded from the direction of the city, followed by a high-pitched whine and a deep rumble. A few heartbeats later, more explosions and crackling sizzles echoed from Sentinel, accompanied by faint screams and daemonic shrieks.

"And that would be our engineers' handiwork," Hannah noted with satisfaction. *And good riddance to you.*

She didn't miss the smiles on the faces of her soldiers.

A few seconds later, a light whirring sounded above Hannah. Four hill sprites drifted into the woods.

One of the males landed on her saddlebow. "All done, Captain Lervion," he said, patting his tiny bow. "The Ja'al pickets on the east side of the Spider Wicket are sleeping like babies. We took their boots and weapons and scattered them in the woods. It will take days to find it all."

Hannah smiled. "Excellent, Ambrose. Please lead the way. Lieutenant Hunt?"

Lieutenant Hunt gathered up her jet-black hair and fitted her helm over her head. "Ready to go, Captain."

"Excellent. We move out immediately."

Hannah led the company south, following the glimmer of hill sprite wings. Not long after, she glimpsed a massive column of enemy infantry through the trees, marching north along the highway. Their black armor and steely weapons gleamed in the sun. The air filled with the tramp of many boots and the thump and rattle of drums, accompanied by a low chanting. Overhead, Skreets and Dwerrolves soared and swooped.

Hannah listened, straining to hear the words of the chant. Ambrose landed on Hannah's shoulder.

"Rise together with bloody blade!" the invaders thundered. "Together Ja'al will rule the Age!"

"Like Hell!" Hannah snarled under her breath. Her hand itched to draw her blade and charge them head-on, before they reached Lord Justin and the defenders on the highway. Remembering her near-failure at the well in Sentinel, she gritted her teeth and let out a deep breath.

I can't get overconfident. Just delay the enemy long enough for Fourth Division to get here.

From Lord Justin's position, the trumpets of the Sentinel Guards blared. Arrows hissed out at the enemy. Magical fire blazed and heavy thuds shook the ground. The Torosci infantry charged with blood-curdling yells and the daemons dove, shrieking. The Ja'al lines hit the defenders and soon a maelstrom of battle swirled on the highway.

Hannah tore her eyes away and focused on her mission. Her company proceeded south through the woods with skirmishers and rangers fanning out ahead of them. Hannah held her bow in one hand, arrow at the ready. Her heart thudded in her chest.

A cloud of black smoke rose from the southeast, a sign that the Torosc army had begun looting and pillaging the town. Hannah smelled burning wood and cloth on the air.

Her scouts reported the Spider Wicket in sight and she slowed the company. Sure enough, Ja'al guards lay in heaps along the east bank. After trussing and gagging them securely, Hannah's company crept through the woods on the opposite side, angling for the rear of the enemy formations. She saw the Ja'al battle flags through the trees and her heart beat faster.

She looked up at Lieutenant Hunt. "Prepare the company. We advance to the attack."

"Yes, ma'am, I —"

"Captain!"

One of the scouts raced back to her, leaping over fallen logs. "Hide! An enemy force of undead marches north from the city. They're not two hundred yards east of our position!"

That close?

"Everyone down!" Hannah hissed. She induced her pony to lie on her side in the brush and she laid her bow across the animal's belly, arrow pointed towards the east. A rock pressed painfully into her side but she ignored it.

She heard no voices in chant nor the sound of horses, yet something in the air made her skin crawl. She felt a vibration at her hip. Shriek glowed brightly in its scabbard and she threw her cloak over it.

Her mount stirred, unsettled. Hannah covered the pony's eyes with her hand and whispered to it. The animal calmed.

True to the scout's words, a mass of walking corpses with battle axes shuffled through the woods, accompanied by skeletons bearing spears and clubs. A cloying mist curled at their feet, rising knee-high. A few black-garbed Ja'al priests marched at their sides, amulets shimmering against their armored chests. The stench of rot and sulfur wafted out over the forest. Hannah estimated there were more than five hundred zombies and skeletons.

Then she saw their masters.

Dearest Irial defend us…

Three tall forms clad in bone armor swaggered in the center of the enemy formation. They wore helmets crafted from the horned skulls of some nightmare beasts. Each daemon glared with four burning crimson eyes and they bore massive halberds of crimson steel. Flanged maces with flaming heads hung from their hips and they wore medallions of Torvu, the Ja'al god of the undead. The mist around their ankles boiled greyish black and all nearby vegetation withered.

Hannah forced herself to remain still. Her palms felt slick but she dared not move even to wipe them on her hauberk. She prayed that her troops wouldn't bolt and run.

The enemy column continued its deathly parade towards the battle and were soon obscured by brush and trees.

Hannah took a deep breath and coaxed her mount to rise.

The expressions on the faces of her troops gave her pause. Even the Elven chaplains looked unnerved and pale.

She set her jaw. "Bring the company to me," she told Lieutenant Hunt.

She took advantage of the time to compose herself.

"I know you're scared," she said, keeping her voice just loud enough to reach them. "I am too. Those things would take the heart of the bravest of us. But we have a job to do. They are bent on destroying Lord Justin's force at the highway crossing and catching up with the townsfolk. It is our duty to prevent it."

She sat up straighter in the saddle. "This new Ja'al force has a disadvantage: they have no idea we exist. We will shadow the Bone Knights and their undead horde and when they attack Lord Justin's main force, we will hit them from behind. For now, all hinges on stealth and discipline. I commend your amazing bravery in remaining silent in the face of such evil."

She patted her sword. "This is Shriek, Bane of the Undead. With this blade in my hand, I will lead you. Follow me, follow the orders of your commanders, and we will live to see the next dawn. Are you with me?"

"To the death, Captain," a sergeant-major growled. The more senior troops nodded grimly.

She smiled at them through her own fear. "Good. Ambrose and Meadow, we need your help again."

Ambrose and a red-haired female sprite landed on a nearby branch.

"Shadow them and get back to us the instant they deploy."

"Yes Captain." The two sprites whirred off.

Hannah motioned to Lieutenant Hunt. "Send scouts to follow the sprites."

As silently as possible, Hannah's company stalked the Bone Knights and their shuffling regiment, hanging back to avoid giving away their position.

She forced herself to take a breath and calm her nerves. *I hate the waiting worse than battle.*

With a darting flash of rainbow colors, the sprites returned.

"The daemons and the undead gather in battle array on the highway about a hundred yards from Lord Justin," Meadow panted. "The Bone Knights are animating the bodies of the dead on the road. Zombies join the attacking force by the dozens."

"As I feared," Lieutenant Hunt said with a grim look.

"We have to attack now," Hannah replied. "We can't let them get close to Lord Justin's barricades. There are enough dead there for the daemons to summon up several platoons, at least."

"Captain, if we take them on too early, they'll just detach two companies to deal with us and continue on," the lieutenant cautioned. "We would be overwhelmed. We should wait until the Bone Knights are actively engaged with Lord Justin's regiment."

"Damn it." Hannah gripped Shriek's pommel. "There's no good option! If I let them get too close, they gain undead allies. If I strike too soon, we could all be overrun instead."

The lieutenant paused and chewed her lip momentarily, twisting the reins in her hands. "Our best advantage is being a hammer to Lord Justin's anvil. If we're too far away, it won't work."

Hannah didn't answer, thinking of all manner of catastrophic scenarios with hordes of undead swarming over Justin's force.

As if reading her mind, Lieutenant Hunt sighed. "We all know the risks, Captain, and we accept them. Our best chance lies in waiting until the right moment."

Hannah's mind whirled and her eyes lit on one of the Veriani priestesses. *That's it.*

She snapped her fingers. "We have seven clerics of Verian. If we charge and induce the undead to follow, the clerics can use their priestly magic to make the skeletons and zombies flee. That should throw enough confusion into them to buy time. Any suggestions on tactics?"

Hunt nodded. "We can use the light cavalry to hit them and withdraw, then employ the archers and infantry to guard the clerics."

"Good. Have the priests and priestesses follow in the back rank."

Her stomach knotted by apprehension, Hannah kicked her pony forward. *If this doesn't work...*

The company formed up and followed according to the new plan.

She recited the prayer of Dolmide, Hero of Irial, as she led her troops forward. *"I go now into the Heart of Shadow. May the power and might of the Holy God be with me. Destruction to the enemies of the Light. Life for the Faithful."*

They saw the swirl of dust and cloying mist before they heard the clank of armor and weapons.

"Ambrose, Meadow, be my eyes," she ordered. "Tell me the instant they charge."

Before the sprites could even take wing, the undead battalions surged forwards. Justin's force counterattacked. The air hummed with arrows and the crackle of electricity. Magical light flared and the earth churned in front of the attacking horde, opening up pits. Skeletons and zombies tumbled in but their fellows simply trod on them to get to the other side. Beyond them, the defenders spread across the road behind upturned wagons. They looked pitifully few against the advancing horde.

Memories of the swamp zombies in Sentinel intruded on her mind but she shoved them aside.

She set her jaw. *This is different. I'm in command now.*

"Cavalry to me!" she commanded, bow up and at the ready. Her mounted troops arrayed next to her.

Justin's troops continued to hammer the undead advance. Explosions hurled zombies into the air and sling bullets shattered skeleton skulls. One of the daemons raised a fist over the battlefield and corpses of Ja'al warriors and

Sentinel defenders lurched to their feet, vacant eyes staring.

The Bone Knights raised their halberds overhead and shouted a foul word. A wave of black smoke curled out from them and rolled over the barricades. Hannah snarled as she saw Sentinel Guards drop, clutching their throats.

Two bright lights cut through the dark fog. Caria and Cassandra held staves overhead and spheres of blue energy surrounded them. The fog dissipated into wisps of grey. Next to the women, Caridan plied his bow, planting two sizzling arrows in the skull of a swooping War Fiend. The creature shrieked and slammed into a tree, detonating in a cloud of flame.

Justin cut down two Ja'al Legionaries with his greatsword in a shower of blood. A Dwerrolf shot at him. He dodged and he slashed it in half, ducking as the daemon exploded, scattering bone shards everywhere.

The Bone Knights headed straight for Justin and the other leaders. Caria and Cassandra unleashed roaring fans of magical flame from their staves, immolating living and undead enemy alike.

The Ja'al arrived at the barricades in a seething throng.

"Now!" Hannah spurred her pony, loosing arrows at zombies. A volley from her cavalry dropped several undead.

"From the rear!" bellowed one of the Ja'al priests. He thrust forth a hand and a purple light flashed.

Hannah averted her eyes in time, but she heard some of her men cry out.

"Back!" she yelled, levering an arrow at the Ja'al priest. She spun her pony to lead the retreat back into the woods.

"After them!" shrieked a Ja'al priestess. Scores of undead turned away from the barricades and pursued.

Hannah spotted Lieutenant Hunt and the rest of the company hiding behind trees and bushes. She passed them and wheeled her mount around.

"At the ready!" yelled the lieutenant. "Loose!"

A flight of arrows and crossbow bolts hissed out at the undead, felling dozens. Behind them, more surged towards Hannah and her force.

"Now!" Hannah called.

The Verian clerics stepped out from behind the shields of their protecting swordsmen and raised their holy symbols, chanting.

Bright light flared. The entire front rank of the undead halted, hands up and faces averted.

The clerics sang a verse in Elven and the undead retreated, cowering.

Hannah felt a surge of elation. *It's working!*

"Drive them back!" she ordered.

Her company followed, loosing arrows and bolts, dropping enemy left and right. They emerged from the woods, cutting down the undead not fast enough to escape.

"Counterattack!" roared a Bone Knight, waving his halberd at Hannah. "Reclaim the undead, you fools!"

With cries of rage, the Ja'al clerics turned away from the swirling melee at the barricades, raising their own symbols. The undead spun in their tracks and advanced back at Hannah's force.

The Verian clerics chanted. White light burst forth and for a few heartbeats, the undead froze in place, pinned between the Ja'al and Hannah's clerics. Then, the Bone Knight held a fist in front of its face and cursed.

A wave of shimmering blackness broke over the undead. The light from the Verian clerics winked out. The enemy charged.

Hannah drew Shriek and set her shield on her left arm. *Well, it worked for a little while.*

Undead swarmed at her. She danced her pony left and right, laying about her with her brother's sword. Shriek snapped skeleton bones and hacked off zombie heads, wailing its triumphant refrain each time.

An enemy cleric swung a flail at her head and she jumped her pony closer, inside the arc of his strike. The chain wrapped around her shield. The weapon head hit her shoulder and back, but her blade found a gap in the man's armor. He gave out a choking cry and staggered backward. She followed, driving him with rapid slashes, preventing him from bringing his flail into action again.

He cursed and brought up his hand, but two arrows hit him in the side and he dropped.

Hannah turned in her saddle. Lieutenant Hunt lowered her bow and galloped to her, bowling over three skeletons on the way.

"Any sign of Fourth Division?" Hannah asked, reining in her pony. An arrow whistled past and she ducked.

The lieutenant shook her head. "We need to buy more time."

Fighting swirled around them. By now, hundreds of Ja'al warriors and undead had detached from the main body and wheeled into her charging force. Her troops struggled to hold their own, fighting in disciplined teams, but the press of the enemy drove them slowly backward. She watched as two of the clerics and their shield-men fell under the onslaught of ten zombies and skeletons. Two of her archers dropped, transfixed by spears from Ja'al infantry.

Hunt wheeled her horse around, lifting her shield and drawing her sword. "I don't know how long we'll last at this rate! There are too many undead."

A Bone Knight waved a hand over a knot of fallen Sentinel Guards and Skullhead Legionaries. The dead staggered to their feet, lifted weapons and turned dead eyes towards Hannah and her troops.

We're losing, Hannah thought in despair. *I have to do something!*

"We need to break their control!" Hannah's eyes alighted on the Bone Knight. Without another thought, she charged.

"No, Captain!"

Four red eyes swiveled in her direction. The daemon raised its halberd overhead and slammed it butt-down into the earth. A searing blast of red light blew her off her mount, shattered her shield and tumbled her in a heap.

Her ears ringing, Hannah stumbled to her feet. Somehow, she had managed to keep her grip on Shriek, now blazing sun-bright.

Wait… what was that? Where am I?

Her pony lay dead not ten feet away.

Towering behind its troops, the Bone Knight sneered at her. It turned its back, marching towards Caria and Cassandra.

"For the Grand Remaking!" the daemon thundered. "Together, Ja'al will rule the Age!"

Zombies and skeletons advanced toward Hannah, brandishing weapons. She staggered backwards, lashing with her blade at any undead within range. She chopped skeleton femurs in twain and dodged a battleaxe that would have split her in two. Her breath came in gasps.

We have to hold out! Where is Fourth Division?

A zombie thrust a spear at her. She sidestepped and darted in, hacking the undead in the midsection. It folded and toppled to the side. A mace slammed into her thigh and her leg buckled. A zombie bent low to finish her off, but she jammed her blade into the bottom of the zombie's jaw, ripping its rotting skull in two.

A club hit her in the shoulder and she reeled, then tripped and turned it into a backwards roll. A poleaxe bit into the earth where she had been.

Not enough time…We failed…

She retreated until her back hit a tree. A sea of undead closed in and her limbs felt like they were made of lead.

"Hang on, Captain!" cried Lieutenant Hunt.

Two zombies dropped with arrows in the eye and sling bullets shattered three skeletal crania.

Hannah tripped on a tree root and a sword descended at her face. Another blade intercepted it and then whirled around to sever the neck of the offending skeleton.

Lieutenant Hunt and two wounded troopers hauled her to her feet.

The enemy surrounded them, bristling with weapons.

Her vision swam and she struggled to focus against pain and fatigue. She kissed the hilt of Shriek.

"Dear Handor, I will join you soon," she murmured, heart strangely calm. "I'm sorry, Connor…"

A Verian priest ran to join them, his hand raised. A beam of pure white light lanced out, searing a hole through a pair of zombies. Two others replaced it.

There are so many…

"Maybe you should have left me and led the retreat into the woods, Lieutenant," she managed through bloodied lips.

"I'm sorry ma'am," said the Lieutenant cheerfully, hefting her sword. "I didn't quite hear that."

Then Hannah heard a strange, howling whistle. Three dark globes the size of melons dropped down out of the sky into the back ranks of the attacking undead. The spheres detonated with dull booms, hurling bones and zombie parts in all directions.

Hannah stared at the blue sky as three griffons swept by overhead. She saw the symbols on their barding: a white sword on a blue field with the number four beneath it.

Finally!

Another trio of bombs hit the enemy, closer this time. Fragments of undead showered them and the concussion knocked Hannah back into the tree. Her head hit the trunk and she saw stars.

Her knees buckled. Strong hands clamped on her collar and dragged her backwards. A great weariness overtook her and her vision became grey, then black.

"Captain?" Lieutenant Hunt's voice sounded tinny and distant, as if she were speaking to her from the top of a well.

Someone set her down on a firm surface with some sort of padding beneath her. She reached for Shriek, but a gentle hand took hers.

"I'm here, Hannah." That was Caria.

Thank Irial! She survived.

"My troops…" Hannah began. She fought to open her eyes.

"Are departing with us up the highway," Caria interrupted. "The enemy has retreated to Sentinel. Your attack worked. We have linked up with the 4th Division."

Hannah had a hard time making her out, but Caria's skin was pale and several cuts marred her cheeks, a burn along one side of her jaw.

"But the Bone Knights —"

"Destroyed. They had no defense against the aerial attack. The griffon riders pummeled them repeatedly until they died and exploded. We are safe."

Hannah tried to sit up but her arms and legs wouldn't work. "My troops? How many survived?"

"More than one hundred fifty."

I lost fifty men? Hannah tried to focus but her fatigue and pain made her wince and drop back down.

Caria gently laid a hand on her brow. "Leave all that for later. Your part in this battle is over, Hannah. Rest now. All will be well."

Hannah formed words of protest in her mind but they never made it to her mouth. Blissful darkness beckoned and she succumbed to it.

Chapter Thirteen – News from Home

A familiar, strong arm encircled Andyn's shoulders and gave her a squeeze.

"How are you holding up?" asked Khyron.

She rested her forearms against Medianox's saddle and let out a breath. "As well as anyone else, I suppose. This isn't my idea of an ideal camping trip."

Her fiancé kissed her on the cheek, then returned to his task of breaking down their camp. Andyn gazed at the landscape looming before them. The dense forest marched into the distance, eventually thinning and fading out into a jumble of rock-strewn hills and short, stubby trees a few miles away. And beyond…

Andyn shaded her eyes and regarded a wide, vast expanse of thick mist, rolling hills, and tall grass under a restless sky in the distance. Through occasional breaks in the greyness, she glimpsed the reflection of light on water. Gigantic, isolated trees loomed above the fog like brooding tyrants. Two large, winged creatures soared high above, making lazy circles like hawks searching for prey.

The Harrowing. I can see how it got its name — it sure looks like an ordeal. I'm glad we're going around it.

Dar drifted past her, his camouflage cloak blending with the nearby bushes. "Someone's coming," he whispered.

Instantly, she broke from her reverie and flipped up the hood of her cloak, leading her pegasus back to the others.

They gathered near the campsite as Eric scattered branches and leaves over the cold remnants of their fire.

"Who is it?" Buck asked, leading Shadowbane and Virasi.

"Connor and I think they're Dwarves," Dar whispered, taking the reins of his pegasus. "We also heard horsemen. They're a quarter of a mile off, heading our way. This glade is a good campsite and I'll wager that they know of it."

"There's equal chances of friends or foes," noted Eric.

"Let's get back among the doriff trees," Khyron suggested, heading back farther in the trees with his pegasus. "Lots of cover and underbrush there. Hopefully they'll just pass us by."

They followed him, leading their mounts with great care among the leafy boughs and thick undergrowth. Dar and Eric hid their tracks with tossed dirt and leaves.

Andyn removed a glove and laid a bare hand on the bole of a tree, reaching out with her senses. The forest seemed normal — quiet even. Birds chirped and squirrels scrabbled in the underbrush. Andyn smelled only earth, leaves and flowers. She detected no hint of the otherworldly. This comforted her. She had seen enough of daemons to last a lifetime.

The Riders hid behind screens of tree branches and large shrubs. She peered between the leaves as the sound of hoofbeats and the clink of metal grew louder. Eventually, four creatures emerged from the woods.

Her eyes widened. They had the lower bodies of horses and the torsos of humans. They wore leather jerkins and carried bows in their hands; their braided tails matched their long, braided hair. Each bore a large saddlebag extending from withers to croup and had two swords belted to their waists. Sharp black eyes flitted around the area.

Centaurs! Why are they here?

Khyron stared at one of the centaur women. "No. It can't be."

"Khy?" Andyn asked. To her alarm, he dropped Zasural's reins and strode forward.

"What the hell?" Buck hissed.

Khyron sauntered into the campsite. "Well, this part of the forest is obviously reserved for outcasts and mental incompetents," he announced, casually flicking a twig off his armor.

Wait a second... he knows them?

Four bows trained on him immediately, but one of the women held up a fist. The bows lowered.

The centaur woman's lip curled in a sardonic grin and her eyes danced. "Clearly, if you're in it."

Khyron bowed. "As charming as ever, Chieftain's daughter."

"Likewise," she answered. "But what are you doing out here, Khyron Demaris? I'm sure your questionable talents are needed elsewhere, especially in these times."

He straightened. "Our mission, unfortunately, is classified."

"Hmm. When have I heard that before? And your fellows skulking in the stand of doriffs?"

"Ah, yes. Some introductions then."

He beckoned to the other Riders. The female centaur motioned to one of the male centaurs and he cantered back the way they had come.

"Let's go," Andyn said to the others, stepping around a bush. "Let's see what this is about. And leave the pegasi here for now."

"Grey Riders," Khyron announced as they approached, "I introduce to you Kelaire, daughter of Olduvar of the Ivory Clan of the Equinae. Kelaire, these are the Grey Riders: Dar Cabot, Eric Indidarc, Connor Lomin, Andyn Eleandir and Buck Bydecy."

Kelaire inclined her head. "My condolences if you have to travel with Major Demaris."

The centaur's demeanor made Andyn relax. She smiled and took Khyron's hand, lifting it to her shoulder. "It is obvious that you and Khyron are old friends."

Kelaire nodded. "Yes, from some other, er, classified activities in the past. But, come, Lady, I see you have a betrothal ring and this misfit before me has an identical one. Is it possible that someone managed to make Khyron stand still long enough to consider matrimony?"

Andyn gave Khyron a coy look. "Am I to be considered fortunate or foolish, Lady Kelaire?"

"Neither. Saintly is a term that comes to mind."

Andyn laughed.

"I like this Kelaire already," muttered Dar.

The sound of more hoofbeats, armor and marching boots filled the air. A veritable cavalcade of centaurs entered the glade. On their heels, amazingly, trooped dozens and dozens of Dwarves.

Andyn felt her jaw drop and snapped it shut. *What is this? Dwarves and centaurs travelling together?*

The Dwarves wore chainmail or scale mail. Each carried a bow or crossbow as well as a battle axe or mace. Several wore deep grey tabards with the symbol of an anvil and hammer: priests or priestesses of Kurental. There were no small number of younger Dwarves and even children among them. The adults and teens bore backpacks and Andyn glimpsed an occasional handcart, laden with packages and bags pulled by a pair of young Dwarven men.

Andyn blinked as the glade filled with even more people. She now saw that some of the centaurs were very old or very young, some even barely out of the foal stage. Many of them also carried packs or goods.

"You're all refugees," she said.

"Correct," announced a deep male voice. An older, bearded centaur male came to the front of the formation and nodded to Khyron. "Major Demaris, I did not think to see you here."

"Nor I you, Lord Olduvar," Khyron replied with a bow.

A Dwarven man in plate mail stepped up next to Olduvar. "Sounds like we're in court," he observed with a wry look. "I can guess that you're not enemies or Kelaire's arrows would be in your heart."

"Indeed, sir." Khyron inclined his head. "I am Khyron Demaris, lately of the 1st Imperial Terenai Light Infantry. These are the Grey Riders. And whom do I have the honor of addressing?"

The Dwarf brushed at his beard. "Delvos, most recently First Alderman of the city of Sommvik. Excuse me. The former city of Sommvik."

Eric shot a glance at Khyron. "Former city?"

Delvos smiled, but his eyes did not. "Aye. Our town is no more. A Ja'al army of twenty thousand saw to that. While fleeing the wreck, we came across Lord Olduvar's band, also fleeing. We decided to join forces."

Stunned, Andyn swept her gaze over the refugee column. Sommvik had at least nine thousand inhabitants and she doubted that there were more than two hundred Dwarves here.

I can't believe it… they've practically been annihilated.

"I…" she swallowed with difficulty. "I am sorry beyond words, Lord Delvos. Are you all who remain?"

"No, praise Kurental. Other groups took off in different directions, to foil pursuit and ensure they couldn't get all of us at once."

Andyn let out a deep breath.

"Well, that's a relief," Eric said.

Olduvar turned to his people. "Rest here a while," he announced. "Captain, make sure everyone gets a ration of water."

Delvos nodded to one of his officers. "Set up guards with the centaurs. And see if there's any way to lighten the load a bit."

A Dwarven soldier bowed and headed off. Andyn watched the refugees drop their packs and bags and collapse on the grass. They stared at the forest with haunted eyes and bleak expressions. Some of the Dwarven clergy and centaurs moved among them, handing out waterskins and words of encouragement.

Olduvar led Delvos and the Riders to a place near the edge of the trees.

"As you can see, we're caught between the dragon's flame and the daemon's sword… literally," Lord Delvos continued.

Khyron shook his head. "But twenty thousand Ja'al! Was it the same army that chased you, Lord Olduvar?"

The centaur chief shook his head. "Our clan was attacked by a different, and smaller, army. Many Fallen Ones marched with them. After a few battles, we realized we could not hold our lands and decided to evacuate."

"Is this all who remain?" Connor asked.

"No. Like Lord Delvos' people, we broke up into smaller groups and departed by multiple routes. Our fields and hills are lost to us but our people survive. We will return."

Something in Olduvar's expression made Andyn wonder exactly how many of them had survived.

"Forgive me, but it is unusual to see Dwarves and the Equinae so allied," Eric said. "My impression is that your communities have little, if any, inter-action."

Olduvar and Delvos exchanged a look and shrugged. "In times, past, yes. We've been more inclined to ignore each other and go our separate ways. But this war makes new alliances," replied Delvos. "To be perfectly honest, we probably should have been on better terms to begin with."

"Misplaced pride, in my estimation, on both our parts," Olduvar added. "That will change in the future if I have anything to say about it."

"Where are you headed?" Eric asked.

Delvos waved at the forest. "We thought to make for Marolpeth."

Andyn went over a map of Terenai in her head and frowned.

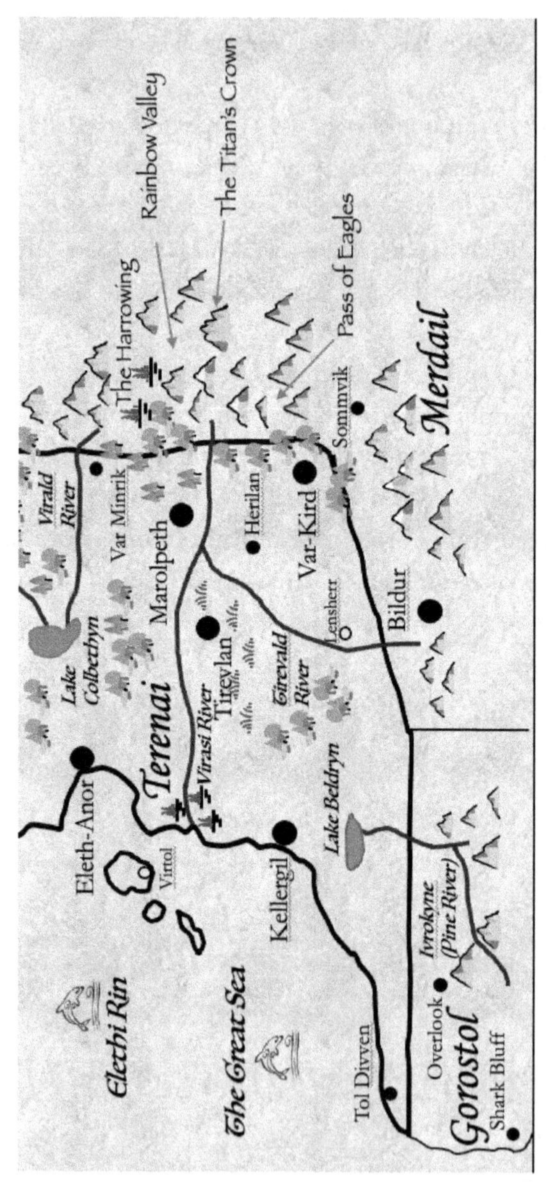
Rainbow Valley
The Titan's Crown
Pass of Eagles
The Harrowing
Merdail
Sommvik
Var Minrik
Virald River
Marolpeth
Herilan
Var-Kird
Lensherr
Bildur
Lake Colbethyn
Terenai
Virasi River
Tirevlan
Girevald River
Eleth-Anor
Virtol
Lake Beldryn
Kellergil
Elethi Rin
The Great Sea
Ivrokyne (Pine River)
Gorostol
Overlook
Tol Divven
Shark Bluff

"Not a good idea," she said. "Marolpeth was conquered a few days ago and the Ja'al hold that area."

Olduvar frowned. "Damn it! What way is open?"

Now it was Buck's turn to shrug. "We don't know. When we passed the refugees from Marolpeth, they were headed for Tirevlan, which we assume is still viable."

"I suggest going north along the border to Var-Minrik," Eric suggested. "Your peoples have complimentary skills and you stand a good chance of making it. We would accompany you, but our path leads in the opposite direction."

"You mean to go south?" Delvos pulled at his beard. "I'd advise against it. Not only was Sommvik razed to the ground, but we saw an enemy army encircling Var Kird. It is under siege for sure."

Andyn's heart sank. With a Ja'al army surrounding Var-Kird, the Riders couldn't go anywhere near the city.

She met Khyron's eyes. He looked grim. "This changes things," he said. "The area was supposed to be clear. If Var Kird and Sommvik aren't safe, we can't get to the Pass of Eagles. The path to the Titan's Crown from the south isn't an option anymore."

Eric bit his lip and shook his head. "I hate to say it but it looks like we might have to try the Harrowing after all. We should check in with Father Thomas. He'll need to know."

Delvos, Olduvar and Kelaire stared at them in confusion. Eric opened one of his saddlebags and removed a flat wooden box with steel bands. He withdrew a small oval mirror. Four aquamarines glittered around the mirror frame, equally spaced.

The Riders crowded around.

"Servite Deo tantum," Eric intoned. *"Sancta Maria, Mater Dei, ora pro nobis."*

The four gems glowed and transformed into blue eyes that stared back at them.

Andyn felt a keen sense of envy. *I would love to have one of these for myself… or better yet, learn how to make one.*

After a few heartbeats, a mild ping sounded. The mirror glass rippled like the surface of a pond. It resolved into an image of the head and shoulders of a dark-skinned human male with intent green eyes. He wore a black cassock with a tab collar. A burgundy skullcap edged with white sat on his short-cropped, curly hair.

"Your Eminence," Dar said. The Riders bowed.

Father Thomas shook his head. "None of that. It is very good to see you."

Andyn smiled back at him. "Likewise, Father Thomas."

"I trust there is some great need for you to use the mirror."

Andyn nodded. "It appears our intended path to the Titan's Crown is blocked. We can't go to the Pass of Eagles."

Dar explained and Father Thomas frowned.

"We also met some refugees." Eric turned the mirror and introduced Olduvar, Kelaire and Delvos.

"From what they said, it looks like we're boxed in," he concluded. "Do you know of any other way?"

"Not unless you try going over the mountains," Father Thomas said. "From what I understand, that is a very harsh environment. Even the passes that are low enough are hazardous. Have you considered the Harrowing? I know it is not the preferred route, but…" he spread his hands.

Eric exchanged a look with Dar. "Yes, but that way is guarded. We've seen flying creatures there, probably Drakes or Balar, and if they're in the Harrowing, they serve the Ja'al."

Father Thomas shook his head, eyes anxious. "Time is slipping away even as we speak, Riders. You have to get to the Titan's Crown as quickly as possible."

Something in his voice made Andyn look at him sharply. "What do you mean, Eminence?"

Father Thomas hesitated. "I have to make this quick. If we maintain the connection for too long, the Ja'al may be able to track it to your location. Rokon is lost. Most of Eldir has been conquered and only a few large cities in Astarel remain free. Buckminster, I regret to say that Tyler has fallen, but many civilians and some of the military were able to escape to Seacrest in Deran. Two of the remaining Elohir are in that city with two divisions, covering the retreat towards Alrihan." He gave Buck a sympathetic look. "I have no news of your family yet, but there is much turmoil and communications are sporadic at best. They could be on their way to Oakmoor and I wouldn't know about it. I'm sorry I don't have better news."

Andyn's stomach clenched.

The Dark Wave is overtaking everything…

She looked up at Buck's face. The tall warrior nodded, his face a mask of stoicism, but she saw the shine of tears in his eyes.

"We understand," Andyn said, laying a hand on Buck's shoulder. "Any news you can give us is welcome."

"I am sorry it cannot be better. Your father and mother, Andyn, sent word that they are safe in Mil-Tereth helping with the defense. Connor's family has joined them but there is no word of Hannah Lervion. Darius, your family is here in Oakmoor with me, as is Lord Melinor and his family. Beyond that, I have nothing to add. The situation is dire. Nations across the Great Sea are also hard-pressed. We are running out of time."

Connor nodded slowly, the knuckles of his hand white against his sword handle.

What do we do? Andyn saw the looks on her companions' faces: tired, downcast, afraid, worried. They mirrored the dread and apprehension in her heart. Her hand touched the emblem of Verian resting between her breasts and she set her jaw.

I know what I do. Hold to my faith for starters. Be strong, for all of us…

"We will find a way, Eminence," Andyn said, lifting her chin. "The Ja'al know nothing of our quest and have no idea where we are. With the help of the Highest Lord, we will win through or die trying."

Father Thomas smiled at her. "That's the spirit, Andyn. I have no doubt of the outcome. I'm sorry I don't have any better advice to give you."

Andyn nodded, thinking of her family. What hardships faced them? Had the Ja'al already attacked? What happened to their homes?

She bowed. "Thank you, Father Thomas. We know you are doing your best."

The Papal Nuncio to Damora gave them a little smile. "I do what I can. Soon, I will be sternly tested and I pray that I will be up to the challenge. For now, we must cease communications. Contact me again when you reach the Titan's Crown."

His image faded.

Delvos, Olduvar and Kelaire exchanged impressed glances. "You are in the service of the High Priest of the Christians?" mused Olduvar. "Well done, Grey Riders. He has a good reputation."

Andyn nodded distractedly, mind whirring. *There has to be another way.*

Buck surveyed the mountains. "Do we have to go through the Harrowing at all? Maybe we can move through another path if Lord Delvos' people know of one."

"You're heading for the Titan's Crown?" The Dwarf tugged at his beard. "We know of some underground ways in the Wilderness, but they are perilous, even for our folk. We don't go there unless at great need."

Olduvar grunted. "Aye, and moving above ground is just as bad. Even the lowest passes are ten thousand feet high and snowy, even at this time of year. There are many creatures in the wilds who would attack you for food or your gear, including troll and ogre tribes. There are even harpies, griffons and dragons lurking in the caves."

"Can we fly over it?" Eric asked.

Khyron shook his head. "Not those peaks. Father Thomas is right and I've seen the maps. To get over them, we'd have to go so high that the thin air and extreme cold would freeze us, and the mounts."

"Fly? You mean you can fly?" Olduvar asked, brow furrowed.

Andyn whistled and Medianox minced out of the trees and brush towards her, followed by the other pegasi.

"You have *pegasi*?" Kelaire blurted. "What have you been doing, Khyron Demaris?"

"Not enough, it seems." Khyron said in a distracted voice. He reached out for Zasural's bridle. "In our current situation, they won't help us. Our original plan was to go through the Pass of Eagles, which is only two thousand feet. From what you're saying, we can't take the mountain passes near here."

"So you're convinced the Harrowing is the way," said Kelaire.

"We have little choice," said Eric, eyes flitting to his companions. "We can't go over the mountains or go too close to Var Kird. It's the only remaining path. But we'll have to go on the ground. Those dragons patrolling the Harrowing would see us for sure if we try to fly."

Connor found his voice. "I don't see how going on foot will help. The dragons can detect us just as well if we're on the ground."

Kelaire held up a hand. "Not necessarily. It's difficult to see anything in the mist from above. If you stay on the ground, in the fog, you can make it."

Olduvar nodded. "True enough."

Dar spread his hands. "We would be handicapped, though. We don't know the paths. Eric and I are good, but even at our best, we're not that good. We'd end up feeling our way through and losing time."

"Not if I go with you," said Kelaire, putting her hands to her swords. "I know the way."

"Kelaire, I cannot spare you," Olduvar rumbled. "Besides, the Harrowing is no place for our folk."

"I am no mere filly-girl to be coddled, Father," Kelaire said with an arched eyebrow. "Or did you train me to lead our people into battle only to recoil when the danger is great?"

Olduvar glared at her. "Your place is *with* your people."

"Who will have no home unless something is done! I do not know what mission Major Demaris seeks to complete, but if the High Priest of the New Faith speaks to them, then Khyron has indeed risen in the service of the Light."

"If I may, Lord Olduvar," Delvos offered. "Perhaps Kelaire can lead the Riders to a place where they can continue on their own, then return to us. Maybe she can take some of your folk and mine with her."

"Can we spare any?" Olduvar asked.

Delvos shrugged. "Maybe two of my rangers. You?"

Olduvar chewed his mustache. "Two scouts, I suppose."

He whirled on Kelaire. "To the entrance to Rainbow Valley and no farther. You must promise me!"

The hint of a smile curved her lip. "I promise."

Olduvar stared at her as if to determine whether she was toying with him. She returned his gaze steadily, unflinching.

"All right, all right," her father sighed, throwing up his hands. "I never could refuse your mother either."

"Well, you certainly don't take on small tasks, do you, Grey Riders?" Delvos opined, stroking his beard.

"No, we don't," Andyn answered. She squeezed Khyron's hand and received a squeeze in return.

"Well," Olduvar said brusquely, "Flying horses or no, you need to move quickly. We will follow your advice and make for Var-Minrik. You will have such aid as we can give you. Verian grant his blessings and protection to you all."

Andyn's gaze drifted to the misty expanse of the Harrowing.

"We will need every bit of it," she whispered.

Chapter Fourteen – The Noose Tightens

A sizzling bolt of lightning shot past Nolan Hanford and blew a limb off a tree. He wheeled his horse and raised a shield glowing with energy. A Ja'al sorcerer popped out from behind a boulder and shot another bolt at him.

Nolan ducked behind the shield and spoke an arcane word. A blue-white globe of light surrounded him. The electric jolt struck the globe and dissipated into a cloud of sparks.

Nolan spurred his horse and brandished a longsword burning with red flame. The Ja'al mage scrambled away, casting firedarts as he went. Nolan's blade flared golden and absorbed the missiles like water going down a drain.

The mage tripped over the corpse of a Kaftu warrior and tumbled in a heap. Nolan pursued.

The wizard spat an oath at him and struggled to his feet, a flaming ball growing in his fist. Nolan danced his mount to the side and thrust, impaling him through the neck. The man's eyes widened in shock and he folded in a spurt of blood.

"My lord!"

Nolan whirled his steed, lifting the visor of his helm. Sir Colin Parker cantered to him and reined in his mount.

"The enemy is driven from the field," Colin said. Blue eyes gleamed.

Nolan regarded the nearby woods. Soldiers from his Forester regiment clambered over the nearby rocks and roots, some of them loosing arrows at the retreating enemy. Dark forms of Ja'al attackers withdrew, uncorking the occasional spell or crossbow bolt as they did so. The air reeked of ozone, blood, ogre-stench, and burning wood.

"Yes, for now, Sir Colin," he replied. "Confer with the scouts and see if we can get an idea of the enemy rally point and their relative strength. We will have to evacuate the Dwarves quickly."

Colin bowed in the saddle and rode off.

Nolan's eyes wandered over the glade towards twin gate towers set into the cliff face. One of the steel-braced wooden doors of Dorn's Hall hung from one hinge, flaming and smoking.

A platoon of Dwarves advanced towards him, checking the fallen. Ku-rental medics followed, their hands flaring with healing light when the touched the wounded. Nolan made out the figures of Jalek and Riti Dorn.

Nolan counted scores of dead littering the forest floor: humans, goblins, Ogres, and a few Trolls. His jaw tightened at the sight of Forester livery among them.

He felt a twinge of guilt and suppressed it. No battle ever went perfectly and losses were expected. Even more, he knew that his troops went into battle knowing the risks and would be ashamed if he held back to avoid injury to them. Still, seeing his people lying dead in the woods…

When will it end?

With a sigh, he swept his gaze over the trees to the mountains looming in the background. His eyes lingered on the towering bulk of Whitehorse Peak. In his memory, he saw again Dar Cabot and the other Grey Riders, eager and bright-eyed, accepting their first commission from him. That had been almost a year and a half ago.

Was that really the beginning? He wondered. The prophecy of the Grey Riders, the finding of the pegasi, the Ja'al plot… is it all leading up to this?

He wasn't even sure where the Riders were. What little he had been told indicated that they were on a quest to find something that could bring the Ja'al plans crashing down into ruin. He had no idea if Dar would ever return to his home town.

Another horse cantered next to him. "Are you alright?" Ellen Hanford asked, resting the end of her ghostwood staff in her stirrup.

He tried to smile. "As well as can be expected — and not injured, if that's what you're getting at."

"I am." His wife's brown eyes flicked to the battlefield. "We've seen enough casualties."

"How many?"

"Last count was twelve dead and eighteen wounded."

"And the Dwarves?"

"I'm not sure," she said, "Jalek will tell us."

Nolan leaned over, snagged an enemy cloak with his blade, and wiped off his sword. "At least we got here quickly this time." He sheathed his weapon.

Ellen gave a wry little smile, white teeth gleaming against dark skin. "You coordinated well."

"Thank God. We didn't want a repeat of what happened last time. Zhinia Margoth almost trapped the Dwarves in the Hall."

She turned her mount. "I'm going to go talk to the healers. Let me know when everyone is ready to move."

Nolan walked his stallion towards Jalek and Riti Dorn.

"Hail, Lord and Lady of Dorn's Hall," he said, swinging down out of the saddle. Both Dwarves bowed.

"Well met, my lord Baron of Forester," Jalek replied, setting his battle axe against a nearby ogre corpse. "Your arrival is timely and well-appreciated."

Nolan bowed. "Considering how much your people sacrificed to defend us from Zhinia Margoth, we would be remiss if we did not come to your aid."

Riti sheathed her sword. "There are no debts among friends, my lord." She removed her helmet, releasing her jet-black braids.

"We dealt them a stiff clout to the head this time," Jalek said. "I'll wager there are three score dead on the field, and more in the entryway to the Hall."

"They'll not try that again soon," Riti opined.

Nolan wasn't so sure but he inclined his head. "Let us hope not. How did your people fare?"

Jalek stroked his beard, now stained with troll blood. "The advance warning let us bring our farmers and tradesmen into the Hall and lock the doors before those bastards could get started. We have eight dead and a dozen wounded, plus another twenty-one injured after the Ja'al breached the outer gate. It is better than last time."

Nolan nodded. "I am sorry for your loss."

"It is war, my lord." Riti waved a hand at the battlefield. "It seems that you took the brunt of it. The Hall is safe and we humbly thank you. Our condolences to your people."

"You are very kind."

Pounding hoofbeats cut off further discussion. Sir Colin halted near the three leaders. He inclined his head.

"Lord Nolan, Lord Jalek, Lady Riti."

"What news?" Nolan asked.

"The enemy regroups near a cluster of four hills about two miles north of here. They cleared a path through the forest."

Riti scowled at the remains of four Ja'al battering rams in flames. "Do they bring more siege equipment?"

Colin nodded. "Yes. And they're setting up a camp instead of regrouping for a counterattack. It looks with a field hospital and some sort of wooden structure. They're also moving a lot of stones around."

Nolan's brow furrowed. It didn't make sense. The enemy force outnumbered the combined alliance of Dorn's Hall and Forester. So why would their commander wait? The Ja'al's inability to break into Dorn's Hall was a setback, certainly, but Nolan thought the Ja'al commander would at least deploy scouts and skirmishers to harry and harass until the bulk of the enemy brigade could be brought to bear again.

Ellen rode up and dismounted. "Good news, my lord," she announced. "The medics were able to save three of those we thought would die. We have already sent them on to Forester in a wagon."

"That is excellent, my lady, but we now have a conundrum." He related Colin's account.

Ellen shook her head. "You are the military mind in our household. I cannot guess the intentions of a Ja'al commander."

Nolan bit his lip. He shot a look at Jalek, who shrugged.

They have the advantage. Why are they waiting? Nolan's sense of agitation increased.

He swung back into the saddle. "Lord and Lady Dorn," he said, gathering the reins, "I recommend you immediately evacuate your people to Forester. We can make a better stand there. Sir Colin and I will observe the enemy and see if can determine their purpose."

The Dwarven couple nodded and headed back towards the gates.

Ellen took Nolan's hand. He leaned down and kissed her.

"Be careful, love," she admonished, eyes warm.

"Always."

Nolan followed Colin into the forest down a hunter's path until they eventually emerged at the edge of a meadow atop a plateau. About a mile away, the Ja'al camp sprawled over a group of four hills. True to Colin's word, campfires burned and profusion of tents in neat rows marched among fallen trees and burned brush. A black flag emblazoned with a white, helmeted skull fluttered in the breeze near the largest tent. Nolan spied pickets and guards but his eyes alighted on a sort of stockade. Ja'al soldiers swarmed around, constructing what appeared to be a massive cage.

A dark track of burned vegetation and blasted trees led back into the Wilderness like an infernal highway.

Nolan made a face of disgust. *I'll have to get the Church of Verian out here. That's a forest in need of healing if ever I've seen one.*

"Have you seen that flag before, milord?" Colin pointed.

Nolan nodded. "Ja'al Army of Death, dedicated to their god, Torvu. Their presence here doesn't bode well."

"Why?"

"The main garrison is in eastern Torosc. If they're this far north, that means no one detected them moving to Deran's borders. They must have come up via the Wilderness, which means alliances with goblins and Kaftu tribes, at the very least. I wonder what else we missed."

The pair watched in silence as the Ja'al continued setting up their camp. Nolan's eyes lingered on the stockade. Death Army troops stacked stones outside the cage, forming a sort of blocky table. A nearby Ja'al priestess held up her hands and light flashed from the seams between stones, welding them together.

A stockade for holding creatures or animals... and a stone table?

The priestess gestured and the screaming daemon-head symbol of the Ja'al cult sizzled into being on the top surface of the table. Nolan gasped.

"What is it, milord?"

He pointed. "That's a sacrificial altar."

A flurry of movement in the forested shadows on the other side of the Ja'al camp drew their eyes. Nolan's magical and spiritual senses went wild. A formation of creatures tramped along the track of destruction from the Wilderness. The first rank looked like deer with serpent tails that crackled with electricity. The creatures strode on their hind legs, carrying red-glittering spears in human-like hands. Their eyes glowed pink. Wicked steel capped their antlers.

Another rank of tall satyrs with four arms and red-striped hide followed the deer-creatures. These carried two bows and four maces each.

Finally, six heavy beasts like giant cattle lumbered over the scorched forest floor, but they were travesties of the normal animal. These had the tentacles, eyes and snapping beaks of squid where cow heads should have been, and claws gripped the earth. Bone spines ran down their backs to club tails.

Colin turned white as a sheet. "Daemons!"

God help us. "Yes. Shock Hind, Blood Satyrs and Curbolgs."

"Is the stockade for them?"

"No. It's for daemon fodder, the sacrifices to the Ja'al gods that the daemons will feast upon."

Colin's wide eyes met his.

Nolan nodded. "Yes. Us. Humans and Dwarves."

Colin crossed himself.

Nolan turned his horse, heading into the forest. "There are at least forty daemons there, probably more. They won't waste any time after the sacrificial area is finished. We have to get to Hillton as fast as possible."

"Hillton? But that means —"

"Yes, Hillton." Nolan set his jaw. "Forester isn't safe."

"But what there that can save us against those monstrosities?"

Nolan set his jaw. "A fortified city with double walls and thousands of Count DeGrance's troops. Let's move. The Ja'al will not wait long."

His mind raced as they cantered back towards Dorn's Hall. *Grey Riders, you were here at the start. I pray to God that you'll finish it.*

***

Saren DeMey shaded her eyes against the bright sunshine. Long lines of refugees approached Hillton via the northern highway. Squads of light cavalry galloped off to escort them through the North Gate.

"Can you see Lord Nolan's standard?" she asked.

Terenil swept his spyglass to the left and right. "Ah, yes. There it is, and the flag of Dorn's Hall, too, so it looks like they managed to evacuate the Dwarves as well."

"Those poor people," she sighed, resting her hands on the battlements. *Zhinia Margoth destroyed their towns last year, now this…They rebuild just to lose their homes again.*

"The retreat is well-organized," Terenil offered. "It looks like they travelled light. The able-bodied are walking while the wagons and carts carry the wounded or infirm."

Overhead, pennons snapped in the summer breeze and the air brought with it an incongruously clean scent of grass and wildflowers. Far in the distance, plumes of smoke billowed skyward from the communities of Forester, Athor and Sun Plains. Massive brigades of troops marched with multicolored banners towards Hillton, a creeping carpet of black doom glinting with flashes of steel. The blocky forms of siege artillery followed behind them like massive beetles.

"What's the strength of the Ja'al force?" she asked.

"Our guess is near seventy thousand," Terenil replied.

God save us! "Seventy thousand? That's the size of some national armies!"

"But we will meet them nonetheless. Our cause is just," rumbled Count Marcel Degrance as he joined them at the parapet.

She shot a glance at him. Degrance wore his High Wizard's battle kit: a heavy tabard over grey robes, black boots, silver bracers at his wrists and a mage's war helmet on his head. Her eyes flicked to the coat of arms of Hillton prominently displayed on his tabard: on a green background, a black tower under a yellow sun with the motto "Fidelis Ad Mortem" emblazoned below.

Faithful Unto Death. Well, that motto will be tested soon… "Where did they all come from?" she mused, turning her eyes back to the scene outside the walls.

Degrance shrugged, brushing at his grey mustache. "They've probably been recruiting from the goblin, Kaftu and ogre tribes far beyond the borders in the Wilderness. They have an axe to grind after what we did to them last summer. And there are several dark Elven city-states who stand to profit by joining in. Beyond that, based on what we know now, we think the Ja'al have been pre-positioning forces in the wilds from before the time of Zhinia Margoth's invasion. Ultimately, we think she was just another deception, a tool to cover their buildup."

He lapsed into silence.

"So Zhinia Margoth herself was only a ruse," Saren concluded, "Even when we think we defeated them, the Ja'al had something even more menacing waiting in the shadows. How could we have been so blind?"

Terenil put his arm around her. "The leaders of the Free Lands have had their hands full with the recent social unrest and we've been busy rebuilding from Margoth's War. It's a miracle we're as ready as we are."

A miracle? Saren thought.

Victory against such a vast army would be a miracle indeed. Even with all the militia, levies and help from the capital, the enemy still outnumbered the defenders more than six to one. Even if they could manage to hold off a force that large, the Fallen Ones added a lethal dimension that would surely tip the scales in favor of the invaders.

Saren, Terenil and Lord Degrance watched the stream of civilians and soldiers heading towards the outer walls of Hillton. The city perched on a hill on the shore of Sun Lake. It controlled traffic on three major highways, so it was well-fortified and defensible, but could it hold out against the Dark Wave?

The enemy bring daemons: my mother's people… and, strictly speaking, mine too.

Terenil's arm tightened around her. She relaxed into him, willing herself to let go of her anxiety. Her gratitude for his support warred with a lingering fear about how she would measure up. It had been so many years since she had contended against any creature from Hades.

And that was not an easy encounter. Her hand tightened on the rough stone of the wall and Terenil covered it with his own.

Count Degrance slapped the wall. "Well, they are refugees, but there are fighters among them, so they will bolster our force."

"How many can we expect, Excellency?" Terenil asked.

"I'd say more than two thousand between Hanford's Forester Regiment, the forces from Athor and Sun Plains, and Jalek Dorn's Dwarven contingent. That, of course, doesn't count casualties they have taken."

Still too few…

Degrance continued. "Also, don't forget these are border folk; most of the civilians are military veterans or former free-lance mercenaries and can put up a stiff fight on their own. We will give the Ja'al something to think about! What does the King send from Oakmoor?"

Terenil released Saren and collapsed his spyglass. "Third Deranese Division arrives tonight."

"Who's in command?"

"Arfax Ironhand."

Degrance brushed at his mustache. "Good. He's an excellent officer and brings that Dwarven common sense with him. How many did you bring? Roughly a brigade, correct?"

"Yes," Terenil responded. "Two full-strength regiments from First Division, all that the King could spare. Heavy infantry, heavy cavalry, artillery, air cavalry, magical support units, medical — everything we need. I brought my personal guard as well."

Marcel Degrance nodded his head, his mane of grey hair flowing in the wind. "Excellent, and well-appreciated. Now we need the beneficence of Irial's favor to win through. But win through we must."

"We have our work cut out for us, and that's an understatement." Terenil put his spyglass into the case at his belt.

"Beg pardon, my lords." One of Degrance's orderlies sketched a bow. "There are two freelancers in the audience chamber with a message from the Papal Nuncio."

Degrance's eyebrows rose. "Interesting. Well, hand it over."

"Forgive me, Your Excellency, but they say they were instructed to give it to no one but you."

Lord Degrance made a face. "I'm not sure why people don't just use Tele-post these days. It's certainly secure." He dismissed the servant and ushered Terenil and Saren down the stairs from the battlements and to his waiting coach. They piled in and the conveyance set off.

"I'm sure His Eminence had a reason," Terenil offered.

Degrance shrugged. "We will find out soon enough."

They arrived at the manor and Degrance led them into the grand audience hall.

A golden-haired man and woman conversed with Bishop Velucci near the dais. Attired in simple white robes, the pair towered over the portly form of the bishop. The male carried a halberd while the female wore a sword at her hip.

Bishop Velucci inclined his head, trying to hide a smile.

Now, what is he grinning about? Saren opened her mouth to ask but the bishop gave her a quick head-shake.

The newcomers bowed. "Lord Degrance."

Degrance nodded to them, motioning for the servants to clear the room. "I understand you have a message from the Nuncio."

"We do," said the woman, fixing him with bright blue eyes.

Degrance held out his hand. The messengers remained still until the doors closed behind the servants.

The woman transformed. She grew taller and stronger. Great white wings tipped with tan unfurled from her back. Her eyes changed to gem-like blue orbs that glittered from within. The man with her likewise changed form, but his eyes were like garnets.

Oh my God! Elohir! Saren dropped to one knee, eyes closed. She sensed Terenil and Lord Degrance kneeling next to her.

"Hail Great Ones!" Degrance exclaimed. "This is a most welcome surprise!"

Saren remained where she was, eyes shut.

"Thank you for your kind greeting, Lord Degrance, but please rise and do not call us great," replied the male in a mellow baritone. "There is only One who is Great. We kneel only to Him."

Saren rose and took Terenil's hand. Her heartbeat pounded in her chest. *What will they think of me?*

In her natural form, the Elohir woman took Saren's breath away. A heart-shaped face with a flawless complexion regarded her. Shiny blonde hair cascaded down her shoulders.

"I am Melissa," she said in a musical soprano, gesturing to the male Elohir at her side. "This scoundrel is my brother, Simon."

Degrance bowed. "These are Lord Terenil and Lady Saren of Tallemar."

"Splendid!" Melissa exclaimed. "So, you are the famous White Demon?"

Saren's throat tightened and she tensed.

Simon raised an eyebrow. "Have you two met?"

"No, but I know of her, Simon," Melissa answered with a coy smile. "This is Saren DeMey, a half-daemon and follower of the Christ. I met her half-brother, Eric Indidarc, near Shadow Lake last summer, when I gave him the holy spear, Fidelis. Saren is our kinswoman returned to the fold."

"Excellent!" said Simon, beaming.

A wave of relief hit Saren. She felt her cheeks grow warm. "I do not know if I am your kinswoman, Lady."

"Nonsense," replied Melissa. "In eons past, daemons and Elohir were one people, before the Sundering and the Great War. Now, let's have a look at you, in your natural form."

Saren hesitated. Melissa nodded, keeping her radiant smile. Gentle kindness and warmth flowed from her.

Terenil squeezed Saren's hand.

Here it goes… Saren let out a breath, then closed her eyes and transformed. A ripple of otherworldly power surged through her as bat wings extended from her upper back. With a familiar, sharp motion, her horns and fangs emerged. She opened her eyes.

"Oh, Simon!" Melissa exclaimed, taking Saren's hands and slowly turning her in a circle. "Is she not lovely? She reminds me a little of Great-Aunt Dora, don't you think? Dark hair and eyes?"

"Yes, I see the resemblance."

"Thank you, Lord Simon, Lady Melissa." Saren said, out of other words to say.

"You are indeed blessed by the Most High, Lord Terenil," Melissa said, with a roguish look at Saren.

"As I remind myself every day," Terenil replied, wrapping a comforting arm over Saren's shoulders.

Degrance frowned at Bishop Velucci. "You don't seem surprised, Denis."

The prelate's cherubic face creased in a broad grin. "Of course not. I detected them for their true selves when they entered the manor. But they swore me to secrecy. I can't go back on my word, you know."

Degrance harrumphed but he turned to the Elohir. "How did Your Excellencies come to arrive at Hillton? I had heard that the few Elohir on

Damora were helping defend the largest cities."

"Father Thomas thought we would be best used in Hillton," Simon replied. "This city is a major crossroads in the center of the country and controls multiple highways. If we delay the Ja'al here, we buy time for other areas, including the capital. We have no doubts that we will need to move quickly somewhere else after our time here is complete."

"I see," Lord Degrance said. "And I trust that you do not want your identities revealed until the proper time."

Simon and Melissa exchanged a glance. "We think the Ja'al already suspect we are in the area," the male Elohir said. "We can reveal our true natures to other trusted individuals, such as the commanders of allied forces, but we don't want it known generally. At least not until it won't matter."

"Fine then," the Count said. "In that case, we can meet with the other lords and ladies tonight in Council. They are trustworthy. Come, let me introduce them to you."

Melissa and Simon reverted to their disguised forms and he led them out.

Two Elohir, Saren mused as she followed the Count and the Celestials. *Maybe we stand a chance, if for no other reason than to buy for time the Grey Riders …*

Chapter Fifteen – A Family Feud

That night, after all the refugees settled in private homes, inn courtyards or city parks, Saren accompanied Terenil to a meeting in the Manor's Council chamber. She knew many of the other attendees by reputation if not by sight: the dwarven lord and lady of Dorn's Hall as well as the human rulers from Forester, Athor and Sun Plains. She and Terenil took their seats next to Bishop Velucci.

Now attired in full plate armor, Simon and Melissa stood on either side of Count Degrance's throne.

Degrance stood and inclined his head to the assembly. "Thank you all for coming, especially my lords and ladies of Dorn's Hall, Forester, Athor and Sun Plains. I know it is asking a lot since you narrowly escaped disaster but we need to establish a strategy."

"We understand, my lord," replied Ellen Hanford. "We are all in this together."

"Indeed. Setting up the order of battle is difficult enough in normal circumstances," the Count rumbled. "It is doubly hard when daemons are in the mix."

"Perhaps the new arrivals can tell us what they've seen," Terenil suggested.

Saren listened intently as Lord Nolan told of the large daemonic contingent he had seen in the Wilderness.

More than two score daemons? She nodded, trying to keep the shock from her face.

"The force that attacked Sun Plains also brought the Fallen with them, around two dozen," added Mary Sarith of Sun Plains. "These were flying daemons, pig-like, with bat wings, and they breathed fire."

"Skreets," Saren said before she could stop herself. All eyes turned to her.

She forged ahead. "Scout daemons. Not very powerful individually, but very alert and dangerous in large numbers."

"Bravo, Lady Saren!" said Melissa. Her eyes gleamed. "You have been studying. Soon, you will be an expert."

"My lady is too kind. I think you and Lord Simon are the experts on the Fallen."

"Perhaps." Melissa answered. "As much as anyone who isn't part of their culture. In any event, their numbers are formidable. If you add up the ones that Lord Nolan saw, plus the Skreets that attacked Sun Plains and the force Simon and I spotted on the way here — which includes War Fiends and Bone Knights following the force that overran Athor — there are probably close to two hundred of the Fallen Ones approaching Hillton."

A murmur of dismay ran around the room. Saren's heart sank and she took Terenil's hand.

Two hundred daemons? God help us…

"All is not lost," proclaimed Bishop Velucci. "We have clergy from three faiths in abundance, we are in a city with not one, but two fortified ring walls, and General Ironhand arrives this evening with the Third Deran Division, five thousand strong. With Lady Saren, Lady Melissa and Lord Simon, we can hold off even a daemonic contingent."

Simon held up a hand. "We may indeed be able to stymie the enemy —
for a time. You should know that there is another force advancing on us from
the north, past the ruins of Wit's End."

"Do they have daemons with them?" asked Lady Ellen of Forester.

Melissa nodded. "Unfortunately, yes, but more significantly, they have a
Battle Lord."

Saren felt dizzy. Lord Jalek Dorn's lips moved. She thought he was praying but then realized he unleashed a stream of Dwarven profanities under his
breath.

"What does that mean?" asked Lord Dellingdale of Athor.

"Battle Lords are daemonic generals," Melissa explained, "The lesser
daemons are very prideful and difficult to control once they smell blood. A
Battle Lord is one of the few creatures who can intimidate a daemon horde
into fighting in good order."

Bishop Velucci drummed the tabletop with his fingers. "Even with such
a commander, we have two Elohir."

Simon smiled. "That is true, Excellency, but Melissa and I can't be in two
places at once, no matter how fast we fly. It will not take the Dark Wave
commanders very long to figure out how to keep us occupied long enough
to force a breach in the walls somewhere."

"Why not just swoop in and destroy the Battle Lord before it gets here?"
asked Lord Dellingdale.

"If it were on its own, we might," Melissa replied. "However, this one
comes with an army and a contingent of daemons. The Battle Lord would
simply wait within his horde. We would have to plow our way through the
entire force in order to get to him — not a very good strategy. We are neither
immortal nor invincible."

The leaders exchanged glances in the silence that followed.

"Even if we defeat the force currently on our doorstep and wipe out all
the daemons, the Battle Lord will arrive eventually." Simon said. "With apologies to Lord Degrance, we cannot hold Hillton against such an army. It is
only a matter of time at that point. They will break through the outer walls,
then to the inner city."

Degrance's hands balled into fists. "What do you recommend?"

"Delay the enemy as long as possible while evacuating to Oakmoor and Darlon. Set up a rally point for the rearguard to regroup, preferably somewhere on the way to the capital."

"The refugees have only just arrived!" Bishop Velucci protested. "We can't make them travel again! The aged and infirm will die if they have to make another forced march."

"We have little choice," Lady Riti announced. "It's either make the trip or remain here and perish."

"We can send a guard with them," Degrance mused. "But it will be a perilous journey. They will not have any assistance from us once they depart."

"If Your Excellency will permit," Melissa suggested, "I recommend that the forces from Sun Plains, Athor, and Dorn's Hall, plus a company of militia, escort the refugees and any other people of Hillton who cannot stay."

Degrance nodded slowly. "Yes, that would increase their chances considerably, though we would lose some of our capability. But it is the least I can do."

"Many of your folk will not want to leave, Excellency," Terenil noted.

Degrance sighed. "I am proud that they are so dedicated, but I will not command them to a likely death. I will issue a proclamation to allow them the option and make it clear that anyone remaining must do their part. Then it will be their choice."

Lady Mary Sarith of Sun Plains straightened in her seat and her husband gripped her hand. "We cannot abandon you, Lord Degrance," she declared.

"It is not abandonment if it is my order that you leave," Degrance replied with a tiny smile. "Athor, Sun Plains and Dorn's Hall, technically, are all vassals to the County of Hillton. Your people are your charge. I command that you take them to safety."

The lords and ladies exchanged rueful looks, but eventually all of them nodded— even Jalek Dorn, though Saren thought he would rather swallow his own beard.

Count Degrance rose and the other leaders did likewise.

"As the liege of Hillton and authority in the county, I will take command here. My team will consist of General Ironhand, Lord Terenil, Lady Saren, Lord Nolan, Lady Ellen, Lady Melissa and Lord Simon. My lords and ladies of Athor, Sun Plains and Dorns Hall: my adjutant will accompany you to the quartermaster to set aside provisions."

The nobles bowed to the Count, though Saren felt certain that at least a couple of them would have preferred to argue further. An officer in dark green and silver escorted them out.

Degrance clapped his hands together. "Now, to the order of battle."

He gestured and an image of a map of Hillton coalesced in the air above the table. Saren marveled the detail: it showed the double ring of walls, the farms on the plains, the manor house on the tall hill by the lake. She even saw birds swirl in the air above the water.

The Count touched the outer wall. "We will have to use defense-in-depth since we will not have the capacity to repel them for long. With the Fallen Ones, they simply have too many options. We will delay them as long as possible, then set traps in the city and retreat to Oakmoor."

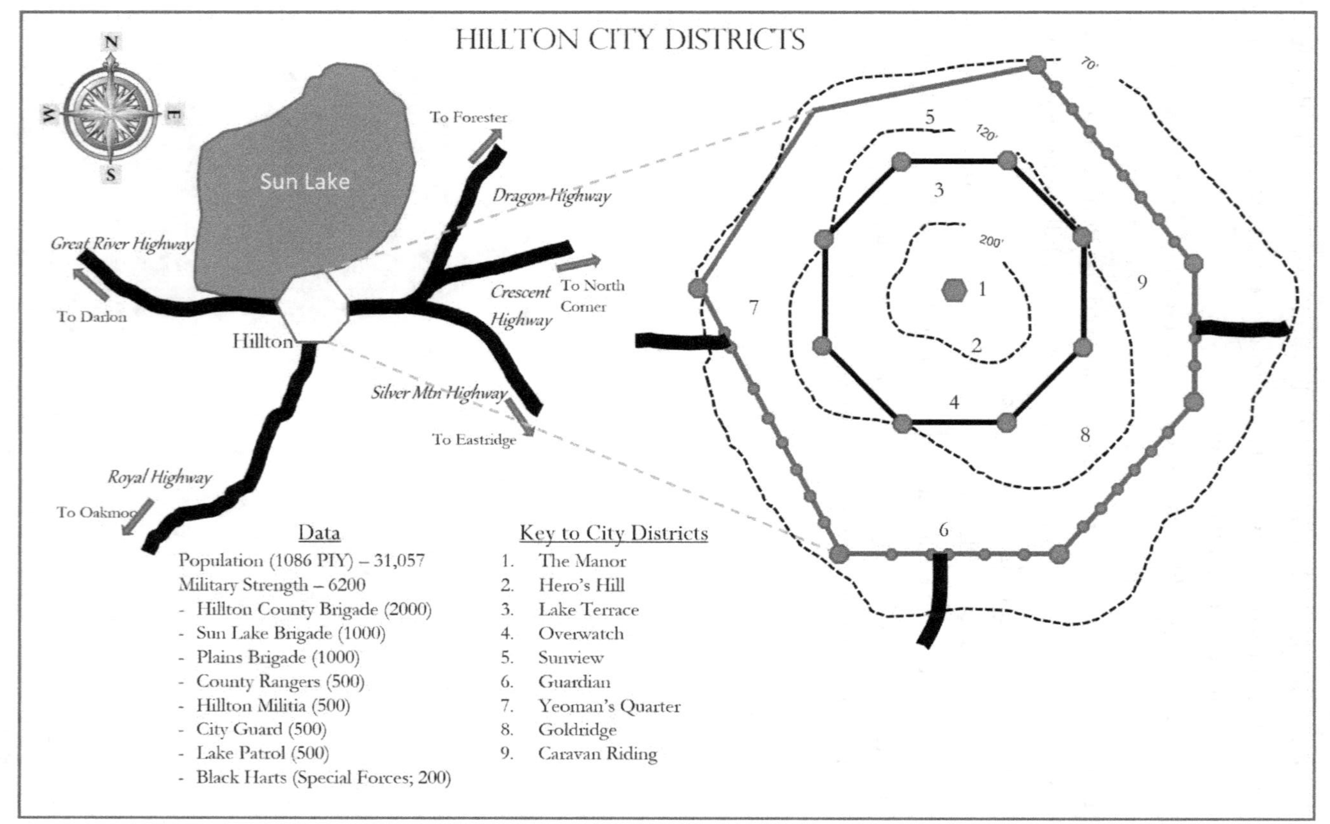
HILLTON CITY DISTRICTS
N
E
S
W
Sun Lake
Great River Highway
To Darlon
Hillton
To Forester
Dragon Highway
Crescent Highway
To North Corner
Silver Mtn Highway
To Eastridge
Royal Highway
To Oakmoor
70'
120'
200'
1
2
3
4
5
6
7
8
9
Data
Population (1086 PIY) – 31,057
Military Strength – 6200
- Hillton County Brigade (2000)
- Sun Lake Brigade (1000)
- Plains Brigade (1000)
- County Rangers (500)
- Hillton Militia (500)
- City Guard (500)
- Lake Patrol (500)
- Black Harts (Special Forces; 200)
Key to City Districts
1. The Manor
2. Hero's Hill
3. Lake Terrace
4. Overwatch
5. Sunview
6. Guardian
7. Yeoman's Quarter
8. Goldridge
9. Caravan Riding

He pointed at the eastern side of the city. "This is the closest point of entry for them and I have no doubts they will attempt an immediate attack."

"Why not just encircle the city and starve us out?" Lord Nolan asked.

Degrance smirked. "Our intelligence indicates that Berek Lordwain, a High Wizard of the Ja'al, is in command. He is known to be vain and ambitious. With a Battle Lord on the way, the last thing he wants is to get bogged down in a siege and have to depend on a daemonic general to help him. No, he wants to present Hillton as a captured prize of his own."

"What else do we know about Lord Berek?" Nolan Hanford asked.

"He is a powerful mage and has many contacts in the hierarchy of the Ja'al cult, including Adina Tenspire and the late, unlamented George Oxbridge."

"Adina…" Saren hissed. She forced herself to unclench her fists.

"You know this Adina?" Lady Ellen asked.

Saren didn't trust herself to speak. Terenil answered for her. "She is Berek's lover. She captured Brandawyn Alenar and warped her into a vampire thrall. The Grey Riders managed to rescue her but there were, er, complications."

He fell silent.

Saren cleared her throat. "When the Riders found her, Brandi was still under the effects of the Ja'al curse," she finished. "She knew she would destroy them all, so she insisted the Riders put a stake through her heart. Eric had to do it."

Ellen's eyes met Saren's, full of sympathy. "I am so sorry."

"Thank you." Saren smiled and blinked rapidly.

Come on, woman, focus, she chided herself. *Honor Brandi.*

Lord Degrance paused for a moment before continuing. "It is fitting then, that we will spend our efforts to thwart Miss Alenar's tormentors."

He pointed at sections of the city in turn. "We will focus our defense here at first. The air cavalry, Lady Melissa and Lord Simon will be a quick-reaction force to oppose the Ja'al air units as well as provide counterattack options if there is trouble. I will have Lord Terenil's Brigade defend the South Gate and provide a blocking force to prevent the Ja'al from cutting us off. As the Ja'al breach the walls, as they will inevitably do, we will draw back to the Inner City. Lord Terenil and Lady Saren will hold the South Gate while

General Ironhand delays the enemy through Hero's Hill, then we retreat to the West Gate. I will bring the remainder of the center defense with Lord Nolan and Lady Ellen to the South Gate. We will retreat separately and scatter into the plains."

"Why, milord?" asked Lady Ellen, her brow furrowed.

Degrance smiled again. "We have noticed that the bulk of the Ja'al invasion force is infantry, archery and artillery. Aside from the Kaftu and some Dark Elf cavalry, they have no units with high mobility — and even the high elves are limited because the giant spiders and scorpions they ride cannot match horses for stamina. They will be unable to effectively pursue and overtake us. I will provide each commander with coordinates of eight separate rally points. After gathering our remaining force, we will unite along the Royal Highway and proceed to Oakmoor to assist with the defense."

Terenil frowned. "The daemons will not allow that. They will try to trap us, hold us up until the Kaftu can entangle us long enough for their other units to catch up."

Simon nodded. "We are counting on it. That's why His Excellency and I have devised a plan to foil the daemons."

Saren shot a look at the two Elohir but they merely returned her gaze, though she thought Melissa's eyes twinkled for a second.

Degrance snapped his fingers and the image disappeared. "Do not worry about the Fallen. Lady Melissa and Lord Simon will handle that part of the defense. Is the plan clear to everyone?"

They all nodded. He let his gaze roam over the assembly. "Then may Irial bless us all with courage and steadfast dedication."

The meeting broke up. Saren turned to go with Terenil but a gentle hand on her shoulder stopped her.

"A word, if you please," Melissa suggested.

Saren joined her, Terenil and Simon in a corner as the room cleared.

"I take it this is about Lord Degrance's special plan," Saren said.

"I knew you would catch on," Melissa answered.

"I take it you have something already in mind," Terenil noted with a sidelong glance at her.

Simon's lip curved in a wry smile. "The daemons will find it very difficult to resist attacking an apostate, one of their 'own' who has rejected the allure of Darkness, don't you think?"

Saren's pulse quickened. "I'm to be bait?"

Melissa nodded and put an arm around her. "Let's call you an 'irresistible target.' But don't worry, it's all worked out. And Simon and I will have a hand in the proceedings…"

***

I must be insane.

Saren gripped the handles of her sword and dagger, trying not to fidget. She crouched in the shadow of one of the towers on the outer wall of Hillton.

What are they waiting for?

She peeked around the corner. The banners of the Ja'al host waved in the wind over serried columns of infantry that wound towards her like a gargantuan metal snake. Siege engines rolled at their sides, guarded by skeletal Bone Knights, Shock Hind and the Blood Satyrs. Bulky forms of the horrid Curbolgs lumbered alongside. Metal cannisters, slung over their backs like odd steel saddle-bags, held goblin warriors and witch doctors.

She remembered Melissa's words: *Stay hidden. Wait until the daemons have made their move. We are fairly certain the enemy knows you are in the city. They just don't know where and they don't know what you can do… yet. You need to strike at just the right time.*

Her fingers traced the cross emblem on the dagger scabbard and her palm cupped the little crystal in the weapon's pommel. Unbidden, her eyes rested on the minute figure of an archer suspended in the glass ball. It pointed north, as always.

"Well, Demonspike," she mused aloud. "I'm going to need you to live up to your name. Again."

"You cannot hope to hold out against us, Lord Degrance of Hillton!" thundered a man's magically amplified voice from the Ja'al ranks. She jumped in surprise.

"If you surrender now," the voice continued, "I will guarantee safe passage to all within your fortress. I, Berek Lordwain of the Ja'al High Command, pledge it!"

Saren peeked around the wall. Down below, she made out the figure of a human male in plate armor. A red-enameled symbol of a whip and pincers on his breastplate glittered and pulsed. His blond hair fairly shone in the hot sun and he raised proud blue eyes to the ramparts.

Berek Lordwain… I'm sure Eric would like a crack at him…and Adina.

Marcel Degrance's likewise augmented voice replied. "Forgive me if I have no faith in the pledge of a High Lord of the Manipulator Church, Purveyors of Lies and Deception. Your history of treachery and carnage contradicts your words."

"But you are few and we are many, Your Excellency. Take the chance while you may!"

Though she couldn't see Count Degrance's face, she could sense a sardonic smile. "I will take my chances with the great god Irial and his beneficent mercy."

"Then let it not be said that I failed to give you a fair opportunity!" Berek retorted. "Now meet your doom!"

She now heard the sound she had waited for and dreaded: the blaring of horns, the rolling of drums, the chanting of the Ja'al troops and, behind it all, the howls of dozens of Skreets and screamed challenges of the War Fiends.

Deranese officers on the battlements shouted orders and bows sang. Wizards chanted. Fireballs, lightning, fire-darts and ice globes shot out at the enemy. Catapults and ballistae on the walls and towers flung their magical ammunition down at the attackers. The walls shook with the thump of counter-fire from the Dark Wave.

Wait…

Then a dark squadron of winged figures arose from the Ja'al ranks. Half of them soared upwards to engage Third Division pegasus-riders in aerial dogfights while the others swooped low over the walls.

Still, she waited, clutching her weapons. The edges of her vision tinted red and she fought down her rising daemonic battle-rage.

Not yet!

War Fiends laughed as they hurled glowing spikes of white-hot metal at the defenders, turning siege artillery into flaming pyres and soldiers into piles of ash. The Skreets breathed clouds of fire and swung their halberds, felling warriors and mages. Return fire from archers skewered three of them. The scout-daemons crashed into the walls and battlements in sharp explosions.

One War Fiend got caught in a crossfire from two Elven clerics and a pair of wizards. Lightning bolts and beams of pure light burned through it. The daemon gave an echoing shriek and simply detonated in mid-air, scattering hot fragments of armor, bone and meat in all directions.

The main body of the daemons attacking the fortress flew past her position and Saren leaped into action. She drew her sword and Demonspike, transforming as she did so. Her ivory wings spread out behind her and she sprang into the air.

She screamed as loud as she could. "Where do you think you're going, Spawn of Hades?"

She hovered, away from the walls. The daemon flight banked around towards her. To her immense satisfaction, the entire squadron halted, wings flapping. The daemons gaped at her.

"What means this?" snapped one of the War Fiends, eyes blazing behind her chainmail veil. "You are some illusionary artifice of the weaklings in the castle, I'll warrant!"

A joyful surge of energy raced through Saren, filling her with confidence and power. Here, she would fight against the Fallen Ones once again, her mother's people, and prove on Whose side she stood. The daemon-rage swirled in her chest and she captured its power, transforming it into focused intensity.

"If you do not leave this place immediately, I will show you just how real I am!" she called, her voice almost singing, "The Elves name me Kired-Azen, or half-daemon, yet, behold! I serve the Church of Christ Jesus! What say you? Am I too much for you or have you lost your wits as well as your courage? For you fight not against me, but against the Emperor of Heaven!"

The faces of the Skreets contorted in savage rage and the War Fiends shrieked as one. Saren clashed her weapons together and shot out over the battlefield, away from the Ja'al and the city. Arrows, fire darts and Lightning Spears lanced out at her from below, but she banked left and right, avoiding them easily. She peeked over her shoulder.

"No! You idiots!" Berek's augmented voice roared from below. "Get back to your assignments! Ignore the bitch!"

The daemons still raced after her, but she saw some of them falter at Berek's words.

She flipped onto her back in mid-air and blew them a kiss. "I knew you didn't have it in you!" she shouted.

The screams of anger echoed once again, followed by a vicious curse from Berek. She arrowed out over Sun Lake.

Now just watch for the flash of light…

She dipped and soared and flew in wide circles. The daemons hurled magic spells and the deadly War Fiend spikes at her, but her maneuverability gave her the upper hand. Even when they split into two groups to try to pin her down, she dove into the water and then out again, causing both flights of daemons to slam into each other.

If it were possible for them to be more infuriated, that did it.

Her eyes darted around the shore of the lake near the city, looking for a signal. Nothing showed on the still waters. She looped over towards what she thought was a flare of light, but it was only a reflection of the sun.

Nope, not that one…

Fire darts hummed at her like angry wasps. Six of them cracked on her magic shields.

Saren wheeled around towards another glint, but it was only a rock among the waves.

I guess it's hard to find a rally point in unfamiliar territory while being chased by raging daemons.

A Lightning Spear sizzled just under her.

Her back muscles ached and her breath came in gasps. Despite the euphoria of contending against the Fallen, she began to tire.

I can't keep this up forever…

More firedarts penetrated her shields and exploded on her armor. She winced in pain. She banked left and then right. A Nightshade Dart hissed past, burning her right wing and jolting her sword arm. She gasped.

Then she saw a glint of pale blue beneath the waves and made a beeline for it. She skimmed the top of the water and cast another look over her shoulder. The daemons followed, frothing in rage. She flashed past the azure light.

When the daemons passed over the glint, the water fountained up. Melissa and Simon shot out of the lake like porpoises, weapons slashing. Four Skreets perished in clouds of flame.

Saren hovered over the water, panting, her dagger glowing with sun-bright radiance. Her jaw dropped.

The Elohir swirled through the daemon ranks as if in some kind of elegant dance, dispatching two War Fiends before they even had a chance to shriek. Brother and sister dodged attacks in the nick of time or arrived with halberd or sword at just the right moment. She winced each time one of them got hit, but they didn't slow. Daemons whirled all around them like a cyclone, hurling magic and hacking.

Damn it! Don't just hover here, gawking, woman! She charged into the fray.

A strange combination of holy power and daemon rage burned through her. She slashed, cut and blasted the Fallen with an efficiency and deadliness that she never knew she had. Demonspike punctured War Fiend helmets and cut through Skreet armor alike, their owners perishing in fiery explosions. Her sword severed daemon limbs and shattered spear hafts. She unleashed Storm Force spells, hurling daemons away from her. Her firedarts battered through daemonic energy shields and one of her Lightning Spears skewered a Skreet. She was dimly aware of being hit several times but didn't care.

Caught between the anvil of the Celestials and the hammer that was Saren, the daemons began to waver. Finally, they retreated under cover of black clouds of stinging smoke, many of them fluttering unsteadily in the air as they flew back towards the Ja'al host.

Saren drifted down towards the lake, chest heaving with exertion. Melissa and Simon flew over to her and took her by the arms.

Saren tried to shake them off. "Wait, why don't we pursue? We can finish them off —"

"You're bleeding all over the lake," Melissa chided, belying the fact that she flew far slower now and was covered in daemon ichor and some of her own blood.

Intense pain hit Saren like a boulder and her vision grew misty. Her limbs felt three times as heavy as normal and she fought to keep her eyes open.

The trio landed at a spot along the city's west parapet. The Elohir propped her up against a wall as troops crowded around. One sergeant called for a healer.

Saren's head spun and she dropped her weapons onto the stones, nausea roiling her innards. Melissa's gentle hands rested on her head and power flooded into her. After what seemed like an eternity, the worst of the pain receded.

"I think I'm going to throw up," she croaked, leaning her head on her knees.

"Don't do that just yet," Melissa said. "Listen."

Saren raised her head.

The roar of thousands of voices reached them from every direction. A chill ran down her spine. Hillton defenders crowded the fortifications, waving at them and cheering.

"It seems we had quite the audience." Simon smiled as he laid back against the wall. Melissa leaned into him to reset a separated shoulder and he winced.

Saren struggled to her feet but her husband pushed his way through the crowd. He swept her into his arms and gave her a bear hug.

"You were marvelous!" he exulted. "Amazing!"

She winced. "Gently dearest. I'm still a bit sore."

He soundly kissed her lips. "There. That part of you isn't sore."

The nearby troops burst into laughter and she felt her cheeks flush.

"Yes, we did well," Simon said. "They will think twice about using the Fallen in an outright assault. It might give us the extra advantage we need."

Melissa nodded slowly. "Yes, it will make them pause, but they won't stop. We have two days at most. As soon as they can figure out another approach, they'll try again."

The euphoria of victory faded and Saren ran a hand through her hair, watching the Ja'al regroup outside the walls. "Just two days? And then?"

Melissa's eyes narrowed. "The Battle Lord. And we had better be gone before it gets here."

Chapter Sixteen – Bend, But Don't Break

M *elissa was right.* It really was two days… only two days.
Saren came to her feet and stretched. Every muscle ached and she felt numb inside. Her heart ached worse.

"The scouts are back," whispered Terenil. The light of the two moons illuminated his handsome features. The figures of other soldiers moved behind him in the shadows. He gathered his saddlebag and hefted it onto his mount. "General Ironhand is waiting at the rally point. No sign of Ja'al patrols."

She swung into the saddle, determined not to dwell on matters. "Any news of Melissa and Simon?"

He mounted up and gathered the reins. "Apparently there's something big going on in Madrigal, in Eldir. They flew off to help after the Ja'al stopped pursuing us."

Saren said no more but her mind whirred. *Why would they leave so suddenly? Whatever it is must be more important than the Eastern Front…*

"Quick and quiet," Terenil said to the remainder of his company of knights. "Follow us and the scouts."

He and Saren led a column of thirty-eight troops through the tall grass and boulders of the Deranese plains in the summer night. Even if she didn't know their bedraggled and exhausted state from experiencing it herself, she would have detected it from their body language. Soldiers rubbed their eyes and cast furtive glances at the nearby terrain.

The formation moved at half speed through the moonlit night. Summer winds brought her a familiar aroma of wildflowers, prairie grass and warm earth. She also detected other, more unsettling scents from the direction of Hillton: woodsmoke and a sickly-sweet odor of burning dead.

She gritted her teeth, remembering the flames leaping high over the inner city.

If we want to truly honor them, we survive to fight another day…

She kept a wary eye on her surroundings and occasionally cast a magic spell of detection, despite knowing that professional rangers led them.

Nothing assailed them and they passed through the plains with only an occasional jangle of harness or clink of armor.

A rider trotted up to Terenil, whispered something, and rode off.

"Just around the jumble of big rocks there," Terenil said in a voice just audible to those nearby. "Sergeants, pass the word."

They rounded a pile of massive boulders to be greeted by a forty-foot long Sarkany, its grey and black scales reflected dully in the moonlight. The dragon regarded them with calm golden eyes and nodded her four-horned head.

"You're late," announced Arfax Ironhand from his saddle atop the dragon's back. His stout figure looked miniature in comparison to the Sarkany. Three knights rode horses at his side. Behind them soldiers moving quietly and slowly in an orderly camp devoid of firelight.

Saren's eyebrows rose. "Greetings, General. And friend."

She caught the gleam of General Ironhand's smile. "This is Kaeleristianeas, or Moonflash in Humana. She was good enough to meet us with a few of her kin."

The dragon smiled, showing teeth as long as daggers and just as sharp. "I was glad to come," she hissed in a sibilant voice.

"Where are Count Degrance and Bishop Velucci?" the general asked. Saren noticed he hadn't bothered to clean the bloodstains off his plate mail.

Saren let out a deep breath, feeling the sorrow anew. "We will confer on that separately, General."

His smile evaporated. "I see. Well, then, please join me." He beckoned to a knight next to Moonflash. General Ironhand clambered down off the Sarkany's back and onto the knight's saddle, then vaulted down to the ground. With a wave of his hand, he led the DeMey's to a low tent set next to a looming boulder.

She and Terenil dismounted. General Ironhand spoke quietly to Moonflash. She nodded in understanding as he spoke, then shot a glance at Saren and Terenil. With a final word to the general that Saren couldn't make out, the dragon slithered into the plains, then launched herself skyward with barely a whisper of sound.

Saren and Terenil stowed their saddlebags and sat on a large cot inside the tent. General Ironhand followed them in. He regarded them for a moment, then plucked a flask out of a small pouch at his belt. "Here. You need this. No arguing."

The fiery hot fumes of the Dwarven brandy served to jolt her more than she thought. They also made it harder to keep a handle on her emotions and she fought against tears.

"What happened?" General Ironhand asked, settling himself on a camp chair. "When we saw you last, you were holding the South Gate."

Terenil nodded, taking a swig of the brandy. He shook his head. "We were, but the Ja'al had another trick up their sleeve. While you were fighting off most of their infantry and the Elohir and air cavalry were otherwise occupied, they brought Curbolg and Shock Hind to the southeastern wall. While we were fighting the daemons, goblin sappers installed charges. They collapsed the walls at the gate, blocking the exit. We had no way out."

Arfax blinked. "What?"

"Yes," Saren added, feeling numb at the memory. "We were trapped. Kaftu swarmed over the rubble and we struggled to keep from being overwhelmed. That was when the Count and Bishop Velucci led us to the southwestern wall. The Bishop used a stone-shaping spell to open a hole in the fortifications so we could escape. He and the Count were cut off and isolated while covering the retreat."

The general nodded. "I take it they didn't make it."

Saren bit back a sob and squeezed her eyes shut, feeling the tears leak out.

Terenil clasped her hand. "They used every bit of magic and martial skill at their disposal, but the Ja'al threw everything they had at them."

"I tried to go back to get them," Saren managed. "But —"

"It wasn't your fault," Terenil murmured. He addressed General Ironhand. "The Ja'al sensed she would come to help so they laid in wait for her. If she even showed her face, they riddled the area with arrows and magic spells."

Saren gritted her teeth at the memory and the feeling of desperation and helplessness, pinned down in the rubble only yards away from Degrance and Velucci.

Why wasn't I braver?

The general nodded slowly. "They figured out a way to neutralize you, milady."

"For now," Terenil said, kissing her head. "For now…"

"We couldn't even recover their bodies," Saren choked out. "Those vile, horrid, disgusting daemons —"

Terenil pulled her close and she buried her head into the crook of his neck. "Dwelling on what we couldn't do isn't going to help us now," he soothed. "We did the best we could. Their sacrifice enabled the rest of us to get away."

General Ironhand sighed, replacing his flask. "Well, the Count had a good plan, and it worked for a time. The booby traps and pitfalls did their job. Our troops fought well and never broke, not even when fighting daemons. But the first casualty of a battle is always the plan."

"You're right," she whispered. "It's just so…"

She trailed off into dejected silence.

"If I may be so bold, Countess," the Dwarf said finally, straightening his hauberk. "You can comfort yourself with knowing they didn't give their lives in vain. Even in death, both of them will be happy to know that we escaped with the balance of our troops alive and that the Ja'al failed to trap you. We survived to fight another day."

Saren said nothing, staring into the darkness.

The Dwarf bowed. "I take my leave of you and suggest you get some rest. We leave at dawn."

"Thank you, General," Terenil said.

Saren closed her eyes and took a deep breath, forcing herself to relax. Now, in the midst of over five hundred troops, her mind turned from survival to memory.

Once again, she saw Count Degrance standing tall, his fingertips sizzling with magic, searing the enemy with bolts of lightning or pummeling them with icy hailstones, his mantle glittering as it shunted aside crossbow bolts. Bishop Velucci stood by his side, as immovable as a Dwarven Royal Guard, using healing spells on himself and the Count. His silvery, glowing mace hammered down enemies foolish enough to get close. Enchanted sling bullets exploded on the magic screens of the Bishop and Count, firedarts rained down on them and enemy blades slashed but the pair didn't budge. Only when two Curbolgs and four Shock Hind attacked them at once did they falter. The Ja'al kept coming in waves, heedless of how many fell.

Her hands balled into fists.

"The Ja'al knew I was going to leap in and help," she whispered. "That's the reason they tried so hard to isolate the Bishop and the Count. It was all to make me try to save them."

"Well, I'm glad it didn't work, even if I had to pull four arrows out of you and use up most of my healing."

"The Ja'al used them to try to get revenge on me and they paid the price. It's all my fault!" she spat before she could stop herself.

"Saren, you know that's not fair. The Ja'al had more in mind than just you, and they had a score to settle with the Count for defying them."

She sighed. "I couldn't save them."

"Correct me if I'm wrong, dearest, but there were two Elohir fighting the Ja'al, and Lord Degrance and Bishop Velucci were powerful practitioners and able combatants, and I was there. Does the blame also fall on us? Or were you expected to defeat the entire Ja'al army yourself?"

She had no response to that. Despite her sorrow, weariness and despair, anger still burned hot as an ember.

The Ja'al won't win. Degrance and Velucci's deaths won't be in vain. I'll see to it.

His arms held her tightly. "I know, love. It hurts me too." He pulled her down onto the cot next to him.

She lay in his arms, praying for peace and drawing comfort from his presence. Slowly, her storm of emotions faded.

Holy matrimony…

"When will it all end, Tren? When will we have peace?"

"When Jesus returns, Saren, on the Last Day. That's the only time we will have true peace."

"But —"

"That's enough. Rest, or I'll put a sleeping spell on you."

She fell silent. The faint sounds of their camp reached them through the tent fabric. No matter what she tried, she couldn't banish the swirl of her thoughts.

What if, what if, what if…

"Tren?"

"Yes?"

"I think I'll take that sleeping spell now."

"Of course."

The spell worked.

Chapter Seventeen – Behold the Liberators

Elven cities burn just as well as any other, thought Lady Arlene.
Her eyes took in the view beyond the glass window: sundered walls, smoldering ruins of buildings and a vast camp of survivors in the wide city plaza and college commons.

The door opened behind her and she observed a dark Elf soldier in the window's reflection. "Yes?"

"High Priestess Adina Tenspire of Gudarta has arrived," The soldier announced.

"Ah yes," she replied. "Tell Her Excellency I will attend her immediately."

Arlene settled a gold circlet on her head and patted her long brown hair, shot through with grey. She settled her daggers at her hips, then examined her reflection for any stains on her black leather jerkin. Satisfied, she gestured to a nearby rack. A dark purple cloak floated up to her hand and she swirled it around her shoulders, affixing the screaming daemon-head clasp.

With another pleased glance at the broken city, she exited the bedchamber and descended the curving staircase of the baronial manor house. In the grand ballroom, a squad of dark Elves and humans in purple livery lined the hall at attention. At the far end, a golden-haired woman in a skimpy chainmail outfit slouched in the baron's throne. A human man with short blond hair waited behind her.

Arlene sidestepped the corpse of the former Baron of Eldirian sprawled on the marble tiles. She bowed.

"High Priestess," Arlene said, touching fingertips to her forehead as she straightened. "You do me great honor."

"Yes, I do," replied Adina. She draped one shapely leg over an arm of the throne. Her bright eyes transfixed Arlene like a javelin. "But it is deserved, of course. To capture a city of fifteen thousand— excuse me, thirteen thousand now, I think— is a substantial victory for the cause. You are to be commended."

"Your Excellency is most generous. I am only a brigade commander."

Adina said nothing for a few heartbeats. She flipped her blonde braid over her shoulder, watching Arlene with amused eyes. "I'm glad you know your place. A rare quality these days. So many people try to reach beyond their station, don't you think?" A palpable wave of energy wafted out from her.

Arlene smiled. "Some do, Excellency."

"You yourself reached somewhat high in your former life, did you not?" Adina raised an eyebrow. "A countess, according to my information."

"Yes," Arlene replied, readying herself for an interrogation. "In Harlinsville, a suburb of the Deranese capital of Oakmoor."

"But no longer." Adina examined the fingernails of one hand. "I understand the King of Deran takes a dim view of courtiers who assassinate their elderly husbands before abruptly vanishing in the night."

Her spies are accurate, at least, Arlene noted. "He does indeed," she answered instead.

"Why did you do it?"

Arlene shrugged. "My unlamented husband had reached the limit of his usefulness and the Grey Riders were on my trail. Besides, Lord Dunstan knew some otherwise innocuous tidbits that, in the right hands, could have been used to reach conclusions about my activities in service of the Grand Remaking. Colonel Benitez of His Majesty's Intelligence Service is no fool. I had to leave and make sure I tied up loose ends."

Adina eyed her for a long moment. "Yes, we all need to make sure there are none of those. I'm sure you want to avoid being a loose end in the future, Lady Arlene." She made a flicking gesture with one hand.

Arlene's skin began to warm and itch at the same time. The discomfort changed to pain and she fought the urge to flee the room. For long moments, Arlene battled the invisible affliction while the High Priestess simply observed her.

"Yes, milady," Arlene managed.

Finally, Adina smiled and the tormenting feelings faded. "Well, enough banter for now. This is a great day for the cause. I do not know if you have heard the news, but the Deranese city of Hillton has fallen and its Count and Bishop are both dead, and good riddance."

Arlene swallowed, relieved that the torture had ceased. "Indeed, Fortune smiles on us," she managed. "I had wondered about the war effort to the north."

Adina ran the fingers of one hand on the lion's head carving on the throne arm, caressing it like a pet cat. "My beloved Lord Berek drove the infidels from the city. Even now they retreat to Oakmoor in disarray. But that is not all. Marolpeth is ours as well. Fenbluff and Eastridge are besieged and the bulk of our Northern Army descends on Oakmoor. Saint Martin's Town has been razed to the ground and we expect Var Kird to fall any day now."

Arlene's mind whirred, calculating the probable value of those prizes. The smallest of those cities would eclipse her winnings in Eldirian seven times over and she felt a pang of envy.

Patience, she counseled herself. *Queens are not made in a day.*

Instead, she inclined her head. "Good news on all fronts then."

"Yes, and, even better, I am summoned to join with Berek as he marches to the capital, so my sojourn here will be brief." Adina waved a casual hand at the blond man. "This is Arless Octavio. He is my… assistant in the cause.

His talents will be of great use to you, I think."

Octavio's smile revealed short fangs. Arlene only now noticed the paleness of his skin and the purple medallion against his tunic. His eyes glinted red. "Lady Arlene, a pleasure," he said.

Arlene favored him with a nod. *Great. A vampire, no doubt enthralled to Adina.*

"Mister Octavio will assist you here to maintain Eldirian, as it is a significant farming community and source of supply to the war effort," Adina continued. "Second Archon Golvadu impressed upon me the importance of maintaining logistics to forward-deployed units, especially those that have diets similar to ours."

Octavio smirked.

Arlene ignored him. "You have spoken to His Grace the Second Archon lately?" she asked Adina.

"Oh yes. Golvadu travels northwards with a battle fleet to meet High Majesty Arachnia at the siege of Oakmoor. I believe he should be there by now."

Arlene's heart skipped a beat. "High Majesty Arachnia?" she managed.

"Why so shocked, Lady Arlene? You did know that Arachnia, Torvu and Selaan had arrived on this world, did you not?"

Arlene struggled to regain her self-control. "I — I was not informed, Excellency, but then, I am not a Great Lord."

"Just so. Their High Majesties decided to assist in the conquest of Oakmoor to demoralize the remaining resistance since the Papal Nuncio is there. The Grand Remaking will proceed as planned."

Adina rose and sashayed down the steps of the dais, running the fingers of one hand along Arlene's sleeve. It took all of Arlene's control to avoid shivering from the untamed, wild savagery emanating from Adina's touch.

"For now, my dear," Adina whispered. "Carry out your duties here. If you do well you will be awarded greater responsibilities. Who knows how high you could rise?"

"I am only here to serve the cause," Arlene replied.

"I am overjoyed to hear it." Adina caressed Arlene's waist and bottom in the same way as she had stroked the lion carving. Arlene resisted the urge to cringe.

Adina sauntered past her. "In my absence, make sure that the survivors of this town understand the rules for living in the New Order. I will see that you are rewarded upon my return. Oh, and I will be leaving some of the Fallen Ones to help you."

Damn it! Daemons too?

Arlene spun to follow her. "I… Your Excellency's generosity knows no bounds."

"Naturally." Adina continued towards the ballroom door and her troops filed into formation to follow her. "See that they are fed well, Arlene, but be economical, yes?"

"Yes, Excellency."

"Well, come along. We mustn't keep our new subjects waiting."

Mind whirling, Arlene followed, accompanied by Arless Octavio.

Keep the daemons fed? And maintain the population? How the hell am I supposed to do that?

The procession descended the wide steps outside the manor and marched towards the town square. There, Adina led them to a large wooden platform erected next to the now-shattered fountain. Ogres and human Skull-head Legionnaires guarded six Elves in chains on one side of the platform.

Dark Elven officers saluted. Adina and her retinue ascended the steps. Arlene lifted her chin and scanned the throng of citizens gathered in the massive square and on the sward. Encircled by a ring of Ja'al warriors, they crowded next to each other, almost elbow-to-elbow. The more able-bodied supported the wounded and sick.

A few coughs echoed in the plaza but otherwise, the citizens made no sound. Though they were mostly Elves, Arlene spotted a substantial number of humans and a few Dwarves and Halflings. They all looked dirty, exhausted and defeated. Some still raised defiant eyes to Adina and her crew, but many just stared without expression.

Arlene felt a cold satisfaction. *Good. A discouraged populace is easier to control.*

Adina beckoned to a guard and he brought her a two-headed Cerberus Hound on a gold chain. The Hound's silver eyes darted this way and that and a faint blue mist drifted from its mouths.

Adina tapped a symbol of Gudarta resting between her breasts. The medallion flared.

"Hear and attend, citizens of Eldirian!" she announced in a voice that boomed over the assembly. People closest to the platform winced.

Adina swept the crowd with her gaze. "A New Order has arrived. You are fortunate indeed to be freed from the outdated strictures of your old masters. Gone are the days of adhering to the rules and so-called ethics of Verian, Christ and Irial. Henceforth, you may only select from three options with respect to religion: swear fealty to the gods of the Ja'al, join in the cult of Gariil, god of Chance and Luck, or foreswear any religion whatsoever. This is your new reality."

She stepped to the edge of the platform. "To those with the wit to perceive it, opportunity beckons. You have the promise of a new life of plenty and security and stability within the Grand Remaking. In return, the Great Ones of the Ja'al require your obedience and allegiance. It is well-known that this town and its dependencies produce much in the way of agricultural products and finished goods and we generously allow you to continue in this endeavor, for the greater glory of the cause. Serve well and you will be apportioned resources in proportion to your loyalty."

She beckoned Arlene forward.

"This is Lady Arlene, formerly of the backward nation of Deran. She will be your overlord. Obedience to her is equated as obedience to me and the Ja'al. She has the power of life and death over you."

The people remained sullen and quiet.

Adina's eyes narrowed. "Know this: there are likewise only three options forevermore on the world of Damora. One, join with us in the Great Remaking. Two, submit to serve as slaves for the rest of your miserable lives. Or three, die and become food."

She snapped her fingers and pointed to the sky. A dark purple spark of light shot up and burst above the treetops. The rush of wind and flapping of wings echoed in the square.

"As proof of this," she continued, "I will conduct a demonstration."

It took all of Arlene's discipline not to turn around as heavy thuds behind her shook the platform.

Large forms moved up next to her and she clenched her fists at the malice emanating from them in waves. Adina motioned her to step back and Arlene gratefully but regally did so.

Those are daemons all right, she thought, hoping no one could see the perspiration on her brow. She got a good look at the one nearest her.

It looked like a cross between a man and a tiger. Taller than the nearby Skullhead Legionnaires, it wore red enameled scale mail and carried a scimitar at its belt. A ruff of black horns surmounted a black and white striped feline face. Burning green cat-eyes glared at the captive citizens. It flexed its shoulders and deep purple bat wings ruffled in the breeze. Two others just like it stood nearby.

On the other side of the Ja'al High Priestess, three bigger daemons lurked, each at least eight feet tall. Dead-black, pig-like eyes stared out from fleshy, dark orange faces. Fangs gleamed white against purple lips and ruffs of white horns protruded from hairless skulls. They wore black brigandine with iron studs and carried two war hammers apiece. Black and purple striped bat wings lay against their upper backs.

Adina smiled kindly and waved an elegant hand at the six Elven prisoners. "You see before you some of the former leadership of this town who have refused to see reason and join with the cause. Let their fate be confirmation of our steadfastness in our rules and regulations."

The prisoners raised their heads, eyes flashing in defiance.

"You will never win," spat a woman in the tattered robes of a Verian priestess.

Adina shrugged and nodded to the Skullheads nearest the prisoners. The Ja'al warriors drew swords as one and plunged them into the backs of the Elves. With only a gasp or gurgle, the Elves fell face-forward in growing pools of blood.

"Feed," Adina said to the daemons.

With deafening howls, the Fallen Ones pounced on the dead Elves, tearing off armor, clothes and boots. Soon, they ripped them limb from limb, gorging themselves.

The captured population screamed, wailed aloud or retched. Several fainted and fell. Arlene's stomach lurched and she struggled to keep a disinterested look on her face.

Amid horrible slobbering and crunching behind her, Adina spoke again in her magically augmented voice. "Remember well what you see here, else you meet the same fate."

She nodded to a waiting guard, who brought her an armored warhorse. A phalanx of Skullheads formed behind her as she mounted up.

Adina snapped her fingers and the Cerberus Hound bounded down from the platform to her side, eyes blazing.

Adina's eyes bored into Arlene's. "The Fallen Ones will obey you until and unless I tell them otherwise." She flicked her eyes back at the daemons and their ghastly feast.

"Don't disappoint me, Lady Arlene," she finished.

Arlene bowed, glad she had maintained a stoic face. Adina rode off with her retinue trailing her.

"Congratulations on your new assignment, my lady," said Octavio.

"Thank you," she replied. Setting her jaw, she turned to the Skullhead commander nearest her. "Colonel, see that the people are dispersed from the square to their hovels. Make sure that regular patrols are set up and send the Quartermaster to the manor house within the hour. I want a production schedule by nightfall."

"Yes, milady," the soldier saluted and turned to his troops.

Without a backward glance, Arlene marched back to the manor, glad for the activity to hide her jangled nerves.

Once in the receiving hall, she ordered guards to heave the former baron's corpse into the woods and summoned an orderly.

"Blackflame Whisky," she said, removing her cloak from her shoulders and settling into the throne on the dais.

Arless slid up next to her, silent as the tomb.

The orderly brought a decanter and a shot glass. She downed the first in one gulp, not even noticing the vaporous fumes. After her second shot, she began to relax.

"Well," she said, staring straight at the sundered doors on the other end of the hall. "We all know what the daemons want. What do you require, vampire, other than pay?"

He inclined his head. "Just a virgin maiden every couple of months or so, my lady. Other than that, I will do just fine on regular food as long as a few quarts of animal blood are available every day."

"Only just? Well, I will endeavor to make sure you get what is coming to you."

She lapsed into silence again, mind whirring. A surly population she could handle with spies and intimidation. Daemons, on the other hand, were an entirely different matter. She wondered how in the world she was supposed to use them. Raiders? Reconnaissance? Enforcers?

She made a face. This would require some thought and careful planning. She had over two thousand troops at her disposal, including wizards and priests of the various Ja'al deities, more than a match for the Fallen in case they decided to test her. However, the daemons could fly and she had no illusions that they considered her any more than a puppet. At the slightest excuse, they would take off to alert Adina and then Arlene would have to move very quickly indeed.

She spoke to Octavio without turning her head. "What news of the Ja'al High Command? We already know where Second Archon Golvadu is."

"First Archon Clanut remains in Torosc for now with the Third Archon, but I understand that the Fourth, Fifth and Sixth Archons have been sent to the Western Continent, Erleth and Derelia, respectively."

"Why? I did not know that those areas needed assistance."

"Your Ladyship will doubtless make of it more than I can. I am only a humble servant of Lady Adina and not versed in the arts of international intrigue."

"Of course." She gave him a sidelong glance. "Were you aware of the arrival of the Hadean royalty?"

Octavio's eyes glinted. "I only learned of it a few days ago myself, Lady Arlene."

Wondering if he were lying and resolving to make sure she kept an eye on him, she nodded. "That will certainly tip the balance in our favor."

"Yes, Milady. With the fall of Oakmoor, a major obstacle will be removed. It will only be a matter of time until Madrigal, Mil-Tereth, Highmountain and the Dukes of Kortos are also conquered. It is inevitable."

She sipped her drink in silence.

"It will be glorious," Arless Octavio concluded.

Remembering the feasting daemons, Arlene wasn't so sure anymore…

Chapter Eighteen – Hope Amidst the Darkness

W ell, we knew it would be bad."

"Yes." Thomas Williams leaned his hands on the balustrade. "Yes, we did."

Just not this bad, he finished in his mind.

King Phillip Tremane joined him at the railing, the summer wind whipping the pennons overhead.

The cityscape of Oakmoor spread out before them. Glittering towers soared from castles and citadels on three massive hills that straddled the confluence of the Deor and East Rivers. Grey-white walls with a multitude of towers surrounded each strongpoint in turn: first, the fortresses and palaces, then the communities around them, then each hill, then the urban areas and beyond to the suburbs stretched out for ten miles in all directions. Streets and boulevards curved between the various districts and graceful bridges arced over the waterways, connecting each community with its nearest neighbors. Even the poorer sections looked orderly.

Except…

The Papal Nuncio sighed. The great highways, usually full of commercial traffic and travelers, were empty.

"Well, at least we can see firsthand what we're up against," he noted, eyes reaching to the horizon.

Beyond the thoroughfares heading west, north and south, beyond green farmland and forest, great dark blotches crawled towards them like a vast carpet of ants, leaving flames and clouds of smoke in their wake.

"The Dark Wave is aptly named," said King Phillip.

"What's the estimate?"

"Do you really want to know?"

"I know I'll regret it, but yes." Thomas braced himself.

"Estimates are two hundred thousand, in six major groups consisting of anywhere from six to seven divisions each, all well-equipped with artillery, magical support, healers, and even some airborne units. That doesn't count the forces we know are streaming in from the Wilderness."

"What's the force composition?"

The king shrugged. "The usual suspects: goblins, Kaftu, ogres, trolls, Dark Elves, renegade dragonkind."

Father Thomas tried to remember what a Kaftu was. *I know I saw it in the briefing before I came here.*

He frowned. "Refresh my memory. What is a Kaftu?"

"Hyena-folk. Most of a typical tribe is female, but the larger males are seen when they take the field of battle. Don't they have them where you come from?"

The Nuncio shook his head with a little smile. "Only in books and legends. No goblins or ogres either, not to mention dragons." Father Thomas felt the king's eyes on him but he didn't elaborate.

"You've doubtless assumed there are daemons," the king continued. "We've detected hundreds. Everything from the small scout daemons to Battle Lords."

Dear Jesus... "Any word from Saren and Terenil?"

"Nothing lately. I have no doubt that the attack has come upon them by now."

Thomas let out a deep breath and nodded at the approaching Ja'al force. "How long until they get here?"

Phillip shrugged, eliciting a mild clink from his plate mail. "At their pace? A day at most. We should see skirmishers and sappers fairly early, disguised and hidden by magic, but we have ways for dealing with those. We've already intercepted Ja'al agents posing as refugees, so we know there are spies already within the city."

The wind blew and pennons snapped overhead as the leaders

contemplated the scene before them.

"Have you heard from the Riders?" asked the king.

"They contacted me from eastern Terenai yesterday. They are on their way, but, due to circumstances, they cannot fly. They'll have to make it through on the ground through some inhospitable territory."

"They'll find a way through," King Phillip noted with more confidence than Father Thomas felt. "Cabot and Indidarc are good rangers."

"Indeed. They found some unexpected allies: refugee Dwarves and centaurs from the area who volunteered to help."

"Well, that evens the odds a bit."

The door to the balcony behind them opened. A young blond man wearing the white-and-gold tabard of the Nuncio's House bowed.

"Begging your pardon, Your Eminence, Your Majesty."

Thomas smiled. "It's quite all right, Detlef. What is it?"

"The Black Star mercenary company has arrived. The Bydecys, the Cabots, and Lord Melinor's family are with them."

Thomas felt a wave of relief. "Praise God. Some good news."

"Where are they?" asked Phillip.

"Captain Volan brought them around to the visitor's quarters as the Lord Chamberlain had directed. Did you want to speak to them, Majesty?"

Phillip shook his head. "No, they've travelled far. They need their rest. I can speak to them later."

"Captain Volan has a young Irial priestess named Varienne Walker with him," Detlef added. "She has asked about Megan Alenar."

Father Thomas exchanged a glance with King Phillip. "Oh. Does she know Miss Alenar?"

"Yes, Eminence. Apparently, they were both enslaved to a Ja'al High Wizard named George Oxbridge before the Grey Riders freed them… and Miss Alenar was…" Detlef looked at the stone floor and stopped.

"Ah. I understand." Father Thomas smiled. "After we are finished, Detlef, tell Priestess Walker that I will speak to her tomorrow. Please assure her that Miss Alenar is in good hands."

"Yes, Eminence."

"On that note, I take my leave of you, Eminence." King Phillip inclined his head to Father Thomas. "Queen Ahlana has arranged a conference with the other Alliance heads of state."

"Of course, Majesty. Contact me if there is a need."

"There will be eventually. Until then."

Detlef bowed as Phillip departed.

"We need stern measures," Thomas muttered, glowering at the Dark Wave spreading across the countryside.

"I beg pardon, Eminence?"

"Nothing Detlef. I would actually like to see the vaults before you speak with Priestess Walker."

"Of course, Eminence. Please follow me."

With one more look at the forces of evil inexorably approaching the capital city, Father Thomas strode to the doors and followed. He eyed the ballistae and catapults arrayed at each level of the palace. Guards came to attention as they passed. They descended the stairs from Heavenspire Tower to the Cloud Courtyard, then to a wide set of doors at one end of the plaza. Two guards swung them open at their approach and Detlef walked into a boxy chamber with a crystal pedestal in the center.

Detlef placed his palm on the hand-pattern etched into the top of the pedestal. The doors closed and the room descended.

The Nuncio smiled. *Remarkable. They managed to make elevators that run on magic. Resourceful people...*

A mild pinging announced the various floors of the palace, then the conveyance halted and the doors slid aside.

Father Thomas trailed along in Detlef's wake, smiling genially at the many people who bowed at his approach. After traversing more stairs and hallways than he could count, they stopped at a pair of tall, arched doors guarded by two knights attired in white and gold hauberks over sparkling plate mail. They bowed and swung the doors open.

"Please wait for me here, Detlef," the Nuncio whispered. "If I tried to get back on my own, I'd be lost for a week."

Detlef tried not to grin and failed.

A surprisingly small chamber awaited and the doors shut behind him.

The Nuncio held up his left hand. "*Deus vult,*" he said and his signet ring flashed. The outline of a door flared on the opposite wall, then slid aside. He stepped beyond.

Twelve magical lights glowed to brilliant life in corners of the room and he paused, surveying the room. Glass cases marched along the walls from the doorway, breaking their shiny, reflective monotony at a desk directly across from the door.

The treasures of three thousand years of history, he mused.

The magic lamps flashed silver, then gold, then copper. Father Thomas stood still. Arcane energy flowed over him and he felt a feathery, tingling itch over his mind and body. A faint bell rang and he stepped inside.

He strolled along the glass cases, inspecting the items therein: coronation regalia, ancient heirlooms, serviceable-looking but unremarkable weapons, coats of mail and elaborately decorated scroll-cases. He stopped before one particular cabinet. Delicate symbols etched in the glass walls of the case shimmered at his approach.

A crown sat on an oblong mannequin head. Crafted of platinum, it reminded Father Thomas of a soaring cathedral with stained glass windows, rainbows, and the sparkle of sunlight on a baptismal font. Seven points surmounted it with a cross capping the center point. Two chains of platinum hung from the left and right temples, as long as his thumb, ending in rubies. A single diamond in a triangle-shaped setting glittered from the center, where the wearer's forehead would be.

Four crosses carved of a solid sapphire, ruby, emerald and diamond lay on the shelf below the crown at the points of the compass. A gold nameplate drew his eyes.

Coronam de Regina Sanctus Alyssa, Servi Dei Martyris, qui, Regina Alenariensis, he read.

"The Crown of Saint Alyssa, Servant of God, Martyr and Queen of Alenar," he whispered.

Father Thomas touched the symbols on the glass in a particular order. They sang under his fingertips, then quieted. He reached in and gently drew out the crown on its holder and brushed a finger over the cross at the top.

"So much mystery…"

He remembered a conversation with Queen Ahlana and Sister Karen Mercato three days ago.

"The Crown of Saint Alyssa is in the vaults," the Queen had murmured to him in the drawing room after dinner one night. "We all know how powerful it is.”

"I'm afraid I don't follow you."

"Andyn Eleandir used it to destroy the lich-princess Zhinia Margoth," Sister Karen had added. At his blank look, she explained how the Grey Riders had been given the Crown by an Elohir for the express purpose of defeating Margoth. She related how Margoth invaded eastern Deran with a formidable army. At the Battle of Hillton, she had killed all of the Riders with dark eldritch wizardry — all except Andyn. She stood alone before the fearsome power of an undead sorceress-queen from a bygone age and, with the aid of the Crown, crushed Zhinia Margoth in a magical duel. The lich's demise broke the back of her military coalition and the invasion disintegrated. Then, incredibly, Andyn used the Crown to raise her friends back to life.

Queen Ahlana had taken his arm. "You should use it. A siege is coming. We need to blunt any advance of the Dark Wave long enough for the Riders to find the Gate of Stars."

He had shaken his head. "I wouldn't have the slightest idea of how to use it. Maybe one of you should try."

Both women had exchanged doubtful glances.

"If it was meant for either me the Queen," Sister Karen stated, "We would know it by now."

"Well, I don't think I'm the right person either," he replied. "The Elohir could have awarded the crown to whomever she pleased. She selected Andyn Eleandir, the only woman member of the Grey Riders present at the time. And don't forget there were two Christians there: Dar and Eric. One would think that a Celestial Knight would give a Christian relic to them, but no. It was a Verian priestess."

Ahlana had sighed. "Well, that makes sense for that time, but the prophecy has been fulfilled, so maybe things have changed."

He shook his head, not understanding. She explained that the Song of the Grey Riders, an ancient prophecy, had predicted all the events leading up the Margoth's destruction.

"The Song says "Holy relic, giver of life, meant for tresses of carpenter's wife"", she concluded. "We figured that meant Andyn Eleandir, since her deceased spouse was a carpenter."

"There, you see? It's obvious that it's not meant for a man," he had replied. "Both of you are more qualified than I."

"I'm not a carpenter's wife," Sister Karen had noted dryly.

"Neither am I," Ahlana added. "Then who shall wear it?"

Her last words echoed in his memory as his thoughts returned to the present. "Indeed, who?" he murmured, breaking his reverie.

He brushed his fingers against the triangular diamond on the Crown. *Holy Father in Heaven, give me a sign. Or at least give me an idea of what to do next.*

Not receiving any heavenly inspiration, Father Thomas sighed and replaced the Crown. He reactivated the safeguards, then exited the room. At the antechamber, Detlef met him, an excited look on his face.

"Eminence!"

"What's the matter?"

"Visitors in the main courtyard! The King and Queen asked me to come get you immediately!"

"What kind of visitors?"

"There's no time, Eminence! Come quickly!" Detlef darted off. Father Thomas had to trot to keep up with him.

"Blast it, boy," he muttered. *How am I supposed to keep up a dignified demeanor if I'm chasing around after you like I'm at a track meet?*

That thought brought a grin to his face.

It turned out that a lot of other people were heading the same way so they emerged in the midst of a crowd from a pair of double doors into the main palace courtyard. Father Thomas halted in his tracks, blinking from the bright sunshine and the scene before him.

Melinor Indidarc conversed with a dragon. Not a picture from a fairy tale book or some kind of theater show, but a real dragon.

And there isn't just one. He counted nine.

Three of them towered over the throng of people crowding into the courtyard, their heads topping out some thirty feet above the ground. Their wingspans would have easily measured fifty feet.

Father Thomas had seen smaller aircraft.

"I never thought I'd see even one dragon…" Detlef breathed.

The biggest had scales of tawny, tannish gold. Two small dragons, also tawny gold, kept close to his side, their shining eyes taking in the scene. Two other large dragons stood nearby, one deep black with white tiger-stripes and the other a bluish-white.

Four other dragons, fifteen feet tall, talked to King Phillip and Queen Ahlana and several courtiers. Their scale colors were more muted but ran the gamut from lavender blue to deep grey.

"What does this mean?" asked an astonished guard next to him.

"It means we have some help," said Sister Karen, appearing at Father Thomas' side and taking his elbow. "Come along, Your Eminence. It's not very courteous to keep them waiting."

"Er, yes," he replied as she hustled him through the increasing crowd. He had no idea what to say to a dragon.

"Ah! Your Eminence!" Melinor beamed as he approached. He bowed formally and swept a hand at the largest dragon.

"May I introduce Donnervassilianelikilandra of the Sunfire Clan, or, Iron Thunder as he is known to us non-draconian folk."

Iron Thunder inclined his head low to the ground and his companions followed suit. "I am honored to meet you, Servant of the High God."

Father Thomas gaped, then decided that a Papal Nuncio had to do something other than gawk. He bowed in return. "The honor is all mine, Iron Thunder of the Sunfire Clan. To what do we owe this great privilege?"

A glittering light shone around the dragon's form. The light warped and twisted until he transformed into a white-bearded old man in a grey robe. He regarded Father Thomas with golden cat-eyes. "The Dragonkind have decided that we cannot stand idly by and let the Accursed have their way in the world. We have come to offer whatever aid we can."

The King and Queen joined them. "We are especially grateful since we know that conflict rages in your clan territories," the Queen said. "We hope that your help here does not expose your people to greater peril."

Iron Thunder inclined his head. "There is much risk in war, Majesty, but we are confident that our brethren will defeat those who have taken the Blood Sign and are now allied with the Great Serpent, cursed be his name. We are confident."

He addressed King Phillip. "Zeligar of the Ebonheart Clan and Dargelana of the Ice-Star Clan agreed to accompany me. In addition, members of the Azure Court, the Dawn Concordia and the Verdant Order volunteered. Even now, there are Sarkany and Balar taking up positions within the city."

"And we're here to help too!" interjected the smallest of the golden drag-ons.

"Tholi! It's rude to interrupt!" retorted the larger one, batting him in the head with a wing.

"Ow, Kindri!"

With an indulgent smile on his face, Iron Thunder put his arm around the necks of each of the small gold dragons. "These are my daughter's chil-dren, Kindriana and Tholerios. Their parents passed away to the Spirit Realm years ago and these two have been in my charge ever since. They have just recently come of age."

"That is indeed an added blessing," Father Thomas said, smiling at the young dragons, each of whom was as long as an ox-cart and taller than he by a foot. Iron Thunder's grandchildren beamed happily. "We are glad to have you with us."

"You have come far," King Phillip announced. "Colonel Wayland will see to your accommodations. All are invited to our council tonight."

Iron Thunder bowed. "We will be there, Majesty."

All of the assembled dragons — except Iron Thunder's grandchildren — likewise transformed into human form and followed a female officer in the grey and burgundy of the Royal Guard. Father Thomas shook his head, watching them go. "Okay, God. Message received."

"What was that, Eminence?" Sister Karen asked.

"Nothing, Sister. Let's get ready for the Council meeting, shall we?"

Chapter Nineteen – A Surprising Strength

"Courage, Detlef," Father Thomas said.

Detlef gripped his longbow with white-knuckled hands. The hot summer wind whipped the royal flags of Deran and Oakmoor overhead. It brought them the scent of wildflowers and woodsmoke.

Now that the Dark Wave occupied the fields outside the city, it seemed even more invincible. Their front lines arced around the city walls half a mile away and their camps and tents stretched into the distance. Even from their vantage point on the battlements of Saint Michael's Bastion, a hundred feet above the enemy, Father Thomas clearly made out the forms of dragons, ogres and trolls.

He sighed, surveying the city defenses. *And we are as ready as we'll ever be.*

The lower walls of the outer city loomed fifty feet above the fields. Divisional pennons fluttered in the wind. Arcane protective symbols glittered

"

on smooth stone surfaces. Archers and infantry formed orderly units of their own near catapults and mangonels on towers or broad stone walkways. Healers and wizards of the Faiths of the Light held discussions in knots of three or four, then broke apart to consult with other practitioners.

Father Thomas cast his gaze up at the sky. Above the Dark Wave, winged daemons, enemy pegasus- and griffon-riders and dragons swirled. Deranese air units patrolled above the city limits, accompanied by Iron Thunder and his allies. Yet the evil air force made no move to attack.

The Nuncio wondered. Never much of a military tactician, he nevertheless sensed what they were up against. The sheer bulk of the enemy army ensured that they would eventually get past the walls and assault the second ring. Worse yet, though the hills and plains east of Oakmoor were empty of Ja'al units, he held no illusions that they would remain that way. Word had reached them of the fall of Hillton.

The welfare of the many civilians housed in every nook and cranny of the vast metropolis remained his most pressing concern. Every available yard of space, including inns, taverns and hotels as well as city parks and private yards had been commandeered for the refugees. Upon arriving in Oakmoor, some of the more able-bodied had decided to strike out to the north towards Darlon before the arrival of the enemy. King Phillip had counseled them to remain, but many decided to leave. Loathe to prevent them from a possible safer destination, he let them go.

No one knew if they had made it or not. There was no word from Darlon, a vast city of more than two hundred thousand.

Despite the impressive stores and protected resources and meticulous planning of the King and Queen, Thomas knew it was only a matter of time. If the siege dragged on long enough, eventually hunger and stress and battle would wear down the defenders to the point where they could no longer defend the city.

Then the horror would begin. Father Thomas struggled against a knot of fear in his stomach.

Standing around worrying won't help, he chided himself. "You remain here, Detlef," he said.

Detlef shot him a startled look. "Where are you going, Eminence?"

"If this goes the way it usually does, there will be a parley. In that case, my place is at the front, with the King and Queen."

"But Your Eminence —"

"No arguments, Detlef. I know what I'm about. Trust me."

His aide opened his mouth, then clamped it shut.

"Good man." Father Thomas descended the stairs to the second level of the wall, then to the ground floor and a waiting horse. Seven mounted Knights of the Chalice awaited him, resplendent in their snow-white hauberks embroidered with a golden cup. Their commander nodded to him as he mounted up.

"Take me to the King, Captain," Thomas said.

The entourage trotted off through the suburb of Tallemar in a jangle of harness and clank of plate armor. The Nuncio nodded as people called greetings to him. He raised his hand in benediction. Many knelt for his blessing and he was heartened to see the absence of panic on their faces.

It helped forestall the misgivings in his own heart.

They neared the Angel's Gate with its thirty-foot high towers. He dismounted, eyes roaming over the graceful silver overlay on top of steel-reinforced oak. Father Thomas' grasp of Elven improved daily and he felt satisfaction at being able to read the topmost inscription: *Humans and Elves are family, whether in feast or battle.*

An officer met him and ushered him up to the top of the wall, where the Royal Couple awaited.

"Good to see you, Eminence." King Phillip bowed. He wore a glittering suit of plate mail under an ivory hauberk and carried a pair of swords at his belt.

Queen Ahlana curtseyed and kissed Father Thomas' ring.

He laid a hand on her head. "I am glad to be here."

"Liar." Ahlana's lip curved in a little smile. Silvery chainmail that looked like metal lacework sparkled under her battle robes. She carried a staff of pure silver with a disk of clear crystal at the top.

He smiled back. "No, really. This is my place. What is the situation?"

Phillip gestured towards the horde beyond the gate. "The Dark Wave has increased since yesterday. We now estimate more than a quarter million enemy, all told, including thousands of daemons. There are Goblins, Kaftu, Ogres, Trolls, Dark Elves, humans, Dwarves, even Halflings seduced by the call of greed and envy and revenge. We're not sure who leads them, but our scouts report that a dwarven wizard is in attendance. I suspect it's Golvadu Fellhammer, one of the Archons of Torosc. There is one pavilion that no one is permitted to enter, and I'm willing to bet my crown that some other devilry hides within. Literally."

Ahlana's eyes flashed. "The Dark Angel of Hell has recruited well, it seems."

Father Thomas clasped his hands behind his back. "Or badly. With that many disparate elements, they must spend a lot of energy to keep them from each other's throats."

"Agreed," said Phillip. "But with Battle Lords, I doubt if the Ja'al have to make too many threats."

A raucous horn blared on the field outside and drums rolled. A contingent of riders trotted towards the city. One carried a white pennon and the other a purple flag with a bone-white, screaming daemon-head. Behind them marched a squad of armored trolls, then a full platoon of troops guarding a bedraggled assortment of prisoners.

"It begins," said the King. "If you would care to accompany me?" He led the way down to the ground level.

"I frankly don't know why they even go through with the charade," hissed Ahlana. "We can expect only brutality, deceit and sadism from them. Those prisoners are just bargaining chips — if the Ja'al have any intentions of actually releasing them, which I doubt."

"So, the poor things are doomed?" Father Thomas asked. He saw women and children among them.

"The Ja'al rarely negotiate in good faith, Eminence. Fortunately, they also rarely take the field in open warfare, so they don't often have prisoners to offer."

Father Thomas paused and took a good look at the enemy cavalcade as he followed behind the King and Queen, mind whirring. The spacing of the ogres, prisoners and guards with respect to the parley delegation particularly struck him. The germ of an idea formed in his brain.

Yes! It's risky, to be sure. But it might work and gain a major victory at the outset.

He formulated a plan as they mounted up and his heartbeat accelerated in anticipation. He joined the Royals and their personal guard platoon, their officers, and his own knights at the gate.

"I have an idea," he said quietly as gate wardens marshalled their engineers to swing the massive doors wide. "But I don't have time to explain it in detail. I just ask that Your Majesties follow my lead and get the prisoners to safety as a first priority. They will be more focused on me once I put my plan in motion."

Phillip frowned. "What does that mean? Surely you're not going to take all of them by yourself?"

"If my idea works, I won't have to."

Queen Ahlana looked askance at him. "If your idea works? Forgive me, but that doesn't fill me with confidence."

Father Thomas smiled. "Trust me. I'm an unknown quantity to them and once I get going, they'll be more than willing to forget everything else."

The massive gates shuddered open.

"Alright," replied Phillip. "But I reserve the right to ride in and drag you back to Oakmoor if I think it necessary."

"Agreed."

King Phillip spurred his horse and the delegation rode out. When they reached a point about a hundred feet from the Ja'al, King Phillip's hand went up and his entourage halted.

The Ja'al likewise stopped. The guards dragged the prisoners to a point about a hundred feet behind their masters. As expected, the Skullhead Legion was well-represented, as were dark Elven troops riding giant scorpions and representative clergy of the Ja'al pantheon. Thomas tried to make out distinct figures among the contingent in the back rank but the banners and the hulking, armored trolls blocked his view.

Hmm…should be just enough spacing, thought Thomas, surveying the delegation now that they were close. *Now, if only the enemy will cooperate.*

A handsome, horned male daemon with a goat's lower body strode to the front of the formation, armored in red scale mail. He flexed his shoulders and black-striped purple wings unfurled, lifting him into the air.

Father Thomas' eyes widened. "So that's what a daemon looks like up close," he whispered.

King Phillip and Queen Ahlana placed their hands on their saddle horns and simply waited.

The daemon raised an eyebrow. "Well? Don't you have anything to say?"

Queen Ahlana smiled, her eyes like ice. "Get out."

The daemon laughed. "Well-said! I take it you are Ahlana and the lout at your side is Phillip."

She nodded.

"Can't he speak for himself?"

She smiled. "When he finds someone worth speaking to."

"As you wish," the daemon replied, his eyes amused. "I, Prince Tarvener of Hades, make this declaration in the name of the gods of the Ja'al. Surrender and lay down your arms. Phillip and Ahlana of Deran. Know that you stand no chance against the might of the Dark Wave. It is only a matter of time before our forces blast through the thin walls of your pitiful garrison and take what is rightfully ours: the due that has been denied us."

Now Phillip inclined his head. "Well, then Your Highness, it appears that we are at an impasse. We will not cede our lands to the likes of you or your vile crew. Know that your doom approaches from places unseen. Escape now while you are able."

Tarvener's confident expression flickered to confusion and one eye twitched. "Escape? Escape from what? You are the ones under siege. It is obvious that you do not realize the extent of your peril."

I wonder what he suspects... Thomas mused.

"We will withstand you," said Phillip in a calm voice. "The battle is the Lord's."

"Hmm. No doubt you actually believe that." Tarvener waved a hand at the trolls. "Perhaps you will be convinced by other means. Allow me to introduce Torvu, God of Death and King of Hades."

The form of a particularly large troll shimmered and warped, then faded away. A seven-foot-tall man encased in dead-black armor made of bones emerged from a twisting cloud of grey and white fog. Glowing red eyes peered out from the visor of a daemon-skull helmet. A knobbed mace and curved sword swung from his hips and knife-like spikes gleamed on his metal gauntlets. A swirl of dark energy preceded him, wilting nearby grass and flowers into blackened mulch.

Torvu strolled forward. When he was a stone's throw away, he removed the helm.

Surprisingly, he didn't look as vile as the Nuncio would have expected. The daemon King's striking, rounded features looked almost normal — if one could ignore the pallor under his skin and the burning red eyes. A single stripe of white hair ran through otherwise dark locks from his forehead to the nape of his neck. Short horns of dark red curved upwards at his temples.

His eyes flashed and a wave of pure cold swept the area. A combination of odors drifted towards King Phillip's parts: a mix of the musty smell of tombs, the stink of corruption and a sickly-sweet aroma of embalming herbs.

Father Thomas felt perspiration on his brow and amended his earlier musings. *Did I say this was risky? Maybe foolish is better. I might just end up very, very dead.*

He felt dizzy and sick and he struggled to master a sudden terror. The horses snorted and backed up, eyes wild.

"Fear is useless," he quoted to himself desperately. *"What is needed is trust."*

"Peace. Be still," he whispered, raising a hand. The steeds quieted. Thomas felt the limbs of his mount trembling. He patted the horse's neck and it relaxed.

I have to focus. I know how to deal with this…

Torvu raised an elegant eyebrow and frowned. "Is this it? There aren't any others?" His voice was deep, like the depths of a grave.

Tarvener sounded almost disappointed. "Pitiful, aren't they, High Majesty?"

"Yes. Not very impressive," Torvu agreed. He sniffed, eyes flitting over the Deranese until they came to rest on Thomas. "Although that one is a little unusual."

The Lord is My Shepherd, Father Thomas prayed. *Though I walk through the valley of the shadow of death, I will fear no evil.* He focused on the words of the prayer and met the gaze of the behemoth steadily. His fear abated, receding until a quiet calm remained.

Torvu frowned deeper. "I am having trouble reading him. What is he, one of those priests of the Thorn-Crowned God?"

Thomas opened his mouth but King Phillip answered first. "That is the Papal Nuncio to Damora, Thomas Cardinal Williams."

Tarvener's eyes widened and he grinned. "Well, then. You did find a replacement for the last one."

Thomas merely inclined his head and Torvu smiled, showing fangs. "And he is mute as well?"

"When I speak," Thomas replied. "You will know it."

The Hadean god's smile remained. "We will see. In the meantime, you have heard the Prince's message. If you do not surrender, we will slay you all as a celebration of my dominion over death. We will start with the captives."

"If I may, High Majesty, I believe we can offer an alternative," Tarvener said. He smiled. "We, of course, are entirely honorable. We will consent to an exchange of these prisoners for a single member of your community."

King Phillip's eyes narrowed. "And who would that be?"

"My granddaughter, Saren of Tallemar."

Father Thomas shot a look at the King and Queen. They looked a bit paler.

Queen Ahlana answered first. "That is out of the question. We do not bargain with kidnappers and terrorists."

"Come now," soothed Tarvener, placing his hands on twin scimitars at his belt. "It's just one person, traded for all of these. Besides, she is one of our people after all. It won't be that much of a sacrifice."

King Phillip shook his head. "We do not have the authority to command such an exchange. That is a matter for her and Lord Terenil. In any case, they are not here."

Tarvener made a face. "You're not a good liar." He aimed his gaze at the city.

"Come, Saren!" he shouted. "Would you leave these innocents to die when you could save them? I will not harm you, daughter of my daughter. I only wish to give you your birthright. Leave this sorry excuse for a life and receive the glory that is due to you!"

Silence reigned in the breeze, broken only by the flapping of pennons and banners.

"Saren, hiding won't help you!" Tarvener's eyes raked the battlements of Oakmoor.

Father Thomas stepped his horse closer. "They are not lying. While you may not trust the King and Queen for political reasons, I have no such bias. The DeMey's are not in Oakmoor."

Tarvener's lip curled. "As if I would take the word of a —"

"Peace, Prince Tarvener," Torvu held up a hand. "I take him at his word. It is unfortunate then. Our original demand still stands. Surrender or the prisoners die slowly and painfully."

The King and Queen shook their heads.

"Well then, it is a pity Gudarta couldn't come," Torvu said, brushing at his hair. "She could devise some mighty and long-lasting tortures. I suppose her clergy will have to do."

From the Ja'al contingent, women attired in skimpy outfits of leather and mail emerged, bearing a stomach-turning assortment of devices. Even if Thomas didn't know what the vile tools were for, he would have guessed from the leering anticipation in the eyes of the priestesses.

"We will not surrender the city to you," answered the King, face grim and eyes pained.

Tarvener shrugged. "Suit yourself." He waved a hand and the priestesses leaped forward with shrieks of glee. The prisoners screamed in terror and struggled in the grip of their laughing captors.

Now!

Thomas moved, casting both hands over his head. *"Perturbare et obscurare!"*

A pulse of pure light blasted out from his hands. Wherever the light touched, it covered the enemy in a heavy white mist. Tarvener, Torvu and the ogres staggered backwards. The guards and priestesses recoiled, cursing and raising their hands to cover their faces.

Thomas leaped from his horse and ran towards the guards and priestesses, energy tingling in his throat. "Quickly!" he called in a voice not his own. "The prisoners are escaping to the south!"

With screams of rage, the Ja'al troops and executioners pelted off over the plains in that direction with the ogres lumbering in their wake. The prisoners froze in amazement.

Thomas beckoned to the captives frantically, waving them towards the city. After a moment's hesitation, they ran as one towards Oakmoor's gates. The King's guard spurred forward to escort them.

"What? Escaping?" roared Tarvener. Magic flashed from within the white mist and it thinned. Thomas gestured and it became a thick cloud again. "After them, you idiots!"

Torvu shouted and the mist bulged like a balloon. Thomas gritted his teeth. He concentrated on the mist and it resumed its shape.

"Bah, damn it!" the Hadean god cursed.

The ground rumbled and a wave of power surged from within the cloud. The white mist warped, twisted and then burst asunder.

The Hadean god glared after the retreating forms of the captives and their protective escort. With a wave of his hand, the misty cloud covering the guards and torturers dissipated.

"Not that way, you morons!" Tarvener thundered, leaping into the air, wings flapping. "There!" He pointed at the retreating prisoners. His forces skidded to a halt, then altered course to intercept.

Torvu turned his gaze to Thomas. "Well-played indeed, Nuncio to Damora. What do you have in reserve, I wonder?"

His eyes flashed and Thomas sprang to the side as a beam of blistering heat lanced past, setting the green grass ablaze. His foot hit a rock and he tumbled, avoiding a blast of purest cold that turned the ground into permafrost.

"Father Thomas!" came Queen Ahlana's cry.

"Get the prisoners back to the city!" he shouted. "I'll join you!"

He scrambled to his feet and held his palm forward, his other hand clutching his crucifix. "*Reverbare!*"

Another pulse of energy shot out from his hand. Torvu staggered backwards several feet. Tarvener pinwheeled wildly in the air and came to a hard landing, tumbling in a heap. He rose to his feet, shaking his head.

Torvu stared at Thomas, eyes wide. "What the fuck was that?"

Thomas didn't answer, setting his lips in a firm line.

Tarvener clenched a fist in front of his face and hissing tentacles of darkness shot out at Father Thomas. He twisted out of the way, moving his hands in circular motions. His palms flashed red and destroyed the tendrils but one wrapped around his left ankle. An intense cold burned through his trousers and he cried out in pain, falling to one knee.

"*Deus adiuva me,*" he gasped, clamping his hand on the tentacle. It dissipated and he focused his mind on his injury, willing it to health and wholeness. The icy cold pain vanished.

Torvu drew his weapons. The blades flared to life, burning with a sickly green luminance.

"So, you can be hurt!" Tarvener exulted. "Now we'll see who is the stronger." He pointed a finger at Thomas. Electricity crackled.

"*Dominus increpat te*," Father Thomas recited, clapping his hands together. The sound of the clap thundered over the plain. Tarvener staggered backwards and fell, his triple-forked lightning bolt shooting off harmlessly into the sky. Torvu grimaced in pain and staggered.

The Papal Nuncio shot a glance over his shoulder. A sally force from the city met the escaping prisoners as the King and Queen's party laid into the pursuing Ja'al. Father Thomas caught the flash of the King's twin swords and the flare of magic from the Queen's silver staff.

"You have more ability than I realized," Torvu announced, stalking forward. "I won't make that mistake again."

Thomas straightened, a hymn resounding in his head. *Salve Regina, Mater misericordie. Ora pro nobis pecatoribus.*

A hemisphere of golden light surrounded him. Torvu leaped and swung both weapons with blinding speed. Thomas backpedaled, thrusting his hands at Torvu's attacks. The screen of light shifted towards the deadly sword and mace, deflecting them. Torvu's attacks sliced into the ground, turning it to rock or molten lava depending on which weapon hit.

A motion drew Father Thomas' eye. Tarvener swooped down at him. Thomas ducked, casting up both hands. Three gouts of black flame pummeled his light-screen and Thomas gritted his teeth against the brutal force. Tarvener looped in midair, hurling a veritable cloud of burning darts of fire at Father Thomas.

Nope. Not going to work. The Nuncio threw himself to the side and rolled. Tarvener's fire darts lanced out at Torvu instead.

"Fool!" Torvu cursed as several cracked on his armor.

Tarvener's visage darkened and he muttered a curse. Spinning towards Father Thomas, he blasted a beam of sickly green at him but it fizzled against the Nuncio's golden dome of light.

"Deathfire, Majesty!" Tarvener growled, landing. Both daemons went to one knee and slammed the ground with their fists. A disk of purest blackness shot out at Thomas.

"The Lord is my Light," the Nuncio said quickly. A shield of blue light shimmered into being on his left arm and he ducked behind it. The black disk slammed into his shield, shoving him backwards twenty feet, his boots cutting a furrow in the green sward. He put his hands on his knees as the black disk dispersed into a faint mist.

"Can't take another one of those," Father Thomas gasped, feeling lightheaded.

Tarvener drew his scimitars. He and Torvu charged. Thomas maneuvered left and right, leaping over attacks when he couldn't dodge, trying to get Torvu and Tarvener in each other's way, using his golden screen and shield of light to foil their attacks. He was gratified to see them collide when Torvu missed and jammed his blade into the ground. When he jerked it out, he slammed Tarvener to one side. The daemon prince's fireball arced off into the distance, detonating on an unoccupied hill. Tarvener hit the ground hard.

Panting heavily now, Father Thomas pushed his golden light screen at Torvu. It slammed into him and he tumbled in a heap, losing his grip on his mace.

Torvu clambered to his feet. "He's making us look like a couple of mindless blockheads!" he growled. He gestured and the mace flew to his hand.

Despite the tension, the Nuncio grinned. His breath came in gasps and sweat poured down his body under his cassock. He was sure he had at least one broken rib and a cut on one leg burned like fire.

"Your words, not mine," he replied.

Torvu's face twisted in rage and he slammed his mace into the ground. An earthquake lifted up rocks and earth in a wave, hurling Thomas backwards. He tumbled over the plain, getting roundly bumped and bruised along the way.

Okay, maybe two broken ribs now, he thought as he struggled to his feet.

Some innate sense warned him and he rolled to the side as one of Tarvener's spells burst the ground asunder where he had just been. Rock shards slashed his side and arm. The two daemon royals charged forward, murder in their eyes.

Thomas felt blood trickling down the side of his head and weariness hit him in a wave. "God, I'm going to need a little more help," he panted.

Unbidden, the words of one of his sports coaches from childhood echoed in his mind. "The best defense is a good offense."

Thomas smiled and lifted his hand, palm up. "The Lord is my rock and my salvation," he recited.

Heavy boulders ripped up out of the ground at his motion, smashing into Torvu. The Hadean god flew into the air with a grunt and slammed into Tarvener as the prince dove down at Thomas. Tarvener spun off into the fields, thumping into a hillside. He struggled to rise but could only get to his hands and knees, wavering unsteadily. Torvu crunched into the turf and rolled to his side, shaking his head.

Thomas' legs trembled with fatigue. He wiped sweat and blood from his eyes.

Torvu stared at him, breathing heavily. "This cannot be borne. How can one small human do this?"

Thomas grinned. "Prayer. There is no other answer for miracles." Dizziness hit him and he gritted his teeth against it, determined not to show weakness.

Torvu hauled himself to his feet and grinned back, nodding towards his army. "Then I think you are out of miracles, priest."

Thomas' heart sank at the sight of Ja'al cavalry thundering towards him. *I bought them some time. But not enough for me.*

A rushing wind made him look up. Iron Thunder hurtled down at him. Two shining figures rode his back.

Queen Ahlana waved her silver staff and a hail of fiery comets rained down at Torvu and Tarvener. King Phillip loosed a single arrow from his bow and the shaft instantly multiplied into a volley of more than twenty.

Torvu cursed, clashing his weapons together. A deep grey hemisphere arced over him. The comets exploded and the arrows shattered on it.

"There's a Scripture about eagle's wings," Thomas whispered, his vision going bleary. "Well, a dragon's wings will have to do, I guess."

The dragon landed next to him, unleashing a searing wall of flame at the Hadean god and his deflecting screen. The daemons recoiled.

The last thing Father Thomas remembered was reflecting on how big Iron Thunder's claw was, and how gently it held him.

Dizziness and exhaustion overtook him not long after.

***

"How is he?" Saren asked.

Sister Karen closed the door and laid a hand on her arm. "He's alive and improving but tired. He took quite a beating."

Saren's stomach clenched.

Sister Karen grinned at her. "But you should see what he did to them."

Saren gaped. "Really?"

"Really. I have only seen a few daemons in my time and never one of their High Kings, but Torvu was actually quite aggravated — not to mention alarmed — when he couldn't smash Father Thomas like a bug. You'll be happy to know your grandfather got pummeled too. The Nuncio won't show it but he's actually quite pleased."

Saren considered pressing her for more details but shook her head. "May I see him?"

The nun held up a hand. "You only just arrived from Hillton. You must be exhausted."

"I can rest later. Please, Sister Karen."

The nun measured her with her eyes, then nodded firmly. "Only a few minutes," she admonished, opening the door to the bedroom.

Saren broke stride for a moment at the figure swathed in bandages on the bed but she set her jaw and marched forward. The Papal Nuncio gave her a wan smile. He lay back against the pillows on the bed, a cloth around his head and another one wound around his arm and shoulder.

"Your Eminence, what were you thinking?"

"There wasn't a lot of thinking going on, actually," he replied. "I did, however, engage in a fair amount of dodging and getting battered, if that's what you mean."

She frowned severely, hands on her hips. "It's *not* and you know it."

"Don't you know it's unseemly to upbraid the Papal Nuncio, even if you are a Countess? And besides, Sister Karen already let me have it, so please, spare me another round. I'm surprised she didn't twist my ear like a little boy."

She tried not to smile. "As if that would have helped."

"Probably not. No matter. It will be a little while until I'm up and about. In the meantime, you will have to attend to matters."

"Me? I am no replacement for you. Besides, there are several Cardinals in the city, not to mention Lord Melinor and the King and Queen… and all the generals."

"Military and secular and even ecclesiastical leaders we have aplenty and in good competence. I am not speaking of that. I am speaking of your special gifts, the ones I hear you put to such good use at Hillton."

Oh God, no. Does he want me to take on Torvu? This is madness!

"Come now, don't look so distressed. I have had plenty of time to consider it and my mind is made up. Here. This will aid you." Father Thomas patted a teak wood box on a table next to his bed.

"What is it?"

"Open it and see."

Saren pulled up a chair. She set the box in her lap and he handed her a roughly-cut, mundane-looking stone. She pressed it against the lock and the stone adhered to the surface immediately. The top of the case popped up and back.

Saren froze. The Crown of Saint Alyssa sparkled in the flickering lamplight.

Her heart hammered in her chest. "Father, you can't mean —"

"I do mean," he replied.

The enormity of the situation hit Saren like a tidal wave. Here lay a holy relic over three thousand years old, the very one that she had seen Andyn Eleandir use to vanquish a mighty lich-sorceress — and bring back Saren's half-brother from the dead. Her magical senses went wild at the vast resources of the Crown looming before her like the ocean depths. Her mind reeled. She couldn't breathe.

"I'm not worthy to receive this," she whispered.

He chuckled, closing his eyes. "Says who?"

"Father Thomas," she protested, "this is the crown of a martyr and a holy woman, a hero of the Church. I am…" her voice trailed off.

"The latest in a line of good women to wield it."

"I don't think I'm that good."

"Hogwash."

She shook her head. "You can't mean this. How are you sure?"

"How about a prophecy like the Song of the Grey Riders?"

"The events predicted by the Song have already come to pass. It doesn't apply anymore."

His opened his eyes. "And who says that God cannot use something over and over if it is His will and pleasure?"

"But nothing in the Song applies to me."

"Really?" he said, looking entirely too pleased with himself. "If I recall correctly, one stanza of the Song says 'Holy relic, giver of life, meant for tresses of carpenter's wife'. What was Lord Terenil's profession before he joined the military?"

"Yes, but..." Saren stared at the crown, shaking her head. *Not possible...*

"I'll answer for you, carpenter's wife. I can't believe I didn't think of it sooner. But getting thrashed by otherworldly alien royalty does wonders for the clarity of one's thinking."

Hardly daring to believe it, she gazed at the glittering tiara in her lap. "You think it was meant for me."

"For Andyn and for you, each in your own good time. In God's good time. Maybe it is also meant for another woman in the future. It is your turn."

Abruptly, a memory came to her mind, on a field outside Hillton seemingly ages ago, at the celebration after the defeat of Zhinia Margoth. Andyn had surrendered the Crown to Father Edward, the previous Papal Nuncio — and Father Edward had looked right at Saren with a peculiar glint in his eye.

Did he know even then? She thought as a chill raced up her spine.

Saren reached out with trembling fingers to gently touch the cross at the peak of the crown's arch. A tingle like a mild electric shock rippled through her hand, then through her whole body. Not unpleasant, it revitalized and energized. Then her self-doubt reared its ugly head, replete with old revulsion at her half-daemon heritage, suffused with guilt for her past sins and fear that she couldn't control her mother's evil legacy.

This can't be for me. I'm not worthy. The line in the Song is just a coincidence.

The tingle intensified and her doubt wavered. Then one of Melinor's favorite phrases flashed through her mind: *There are no coincidences — only steps in the plan of God that we finally recognize.*

A warm sense of peace, confidence and strength filled her. Her weariness from travel and sorrow and stress melted away and the self-doubt vanished with it. The Crown pulsed with a gold light once, twice, three times.

"What is happening?" she breathed.

"I imagine Saint Alyssa is identifying you as her next protégé. Put it on."

"I shouldn't," Saren said. Despite her new level of comfort with the Crown, she hesitated. "It doesn't feel right, not yet."

"Well, I defer to your better judgment."

Father Thomas settled back in his pillows, a contented look on his face. "Now, take it with you and let me rest. I've had enough of your lollygagging."

She tried not to smile. He opened one eye and winked, then relaxed.

She kissed his forehead. "Rest then. I will do as you say."

Chapter Twenty – The Harrowing

"Well, if this is the Harrowing, I don't think I've been in a worse location," Dar muttered.

"Sure you have," replied Connor, peering through the brush. "Remember the forest with those Darkwood Drakes near Shadow Lake? And don't forget the Darkhollow."

"I stand corrected."

"You're not standing. You're crouching."

"Which is why we're eye-to-eye," Dar replied, a serene expression on his face.

"Ouch. I'll get you back for that. When you're not looking."

"Counting on it."

The brush and reeds ahead of them parted and the two fell silent. A Dwarf slipped through the vegetation, treading lightly on the moist earth. Behind him, a female centaur followed through the misty air, her spear held at the ready. Both looked like part of the terrain in mottled grey and green hauberks over their armor.

How a large creature like a centaur could move that quietly was beyond Dar. He could do nothing more than admire it.

He gave a low, chirping whistle. The Dwarf and centaur paused, then joined them in the underbrush.

"Anything, Rorlic?"

The Dwarf shook his head. "That way leads to a wide lake with very soft ground at the shore. Lots of dead trees in the shallows."

The centaur frowned. "I sensed something foul. That way lies death."

Dar nodded slowly, eyes following the way Rorlic had come. "I trust Fantine's instincts. Let's get back to the camp and see what everyone else found."

He and Connor followed the pair back towards a rare bit of high ground. Buck and Andyn waited with the pegasi.

"That's not the path." Rorlic jerked a thumb back towards the way he had come. "It's marshy and muddy and Fantine thinks something vile lurks in the water. We have to find another way."

Buck slammed a fist into his palm. "Damn it! This is taking too long! We're running out of time."

"Buck…" Andyn put a hand on his shoulder. He turned away.

Fantine pressed her lips together and her eyes narrowed. "Don't blame Buck too much," Dar said. "He's very worried about his family."

The centaur sighed as Rorlic joined Connor and Andyn at Buck's side. "I understand. But he isn't the only one with loved ones in peril."

Dar felt a pang of guilt, knowing that his own family was safe, for the time being. "He knows that. It's just that we can't seem to get a break. What are the odds of an entire village of lizardkin, squatting right in the middle of our easiest route across the Harrowing?"

Fantine nodded. "That worries me. Kelaire said it wasn't one of their established villages and Lizardfolk don't move without need. What is driving them? Has the Dark Wave reached even to here?"

"I don't know," Dar replied. He gazed out at the Harrowing, brooding under an oppressive grey sky. A faint breeze brought him the odor of decay, brackish water and marsh herbs. The deep grey fog shifted and swirled around them like a quiet, slow-moving storm. He set an arrow to his bow, restless. "One thing is certain: lizardfolk don't take kindly to outsiders and we can't deal with two hundred of them. And you make a good point. They may be fleeing something."

A rustle in the brush had them all reaching for weapons, but it was only Khyron returning with a Dwarven ranger and centaur scout.

Khyron shook his head. "That way is overgrown and tangled. Keldur and Rhianne ranged east and west for a while, but it didn't get any better. Plus, we saw ghost creepers in the underbrush."

"Lovely." Eric noted with a wry expression on his face.

"Any lizardfolk?" Fantine asked.

"Yes. A patrol passed just west of us, but they were heading away and trying to stay hidden."

"They're just as jittery as we are," Dar mused.

"Can you blame them?" Fantine replied with a wary glance at their surroundings. "The entire world has gone mad."

They gathered near a large boulder while Khyron and Fantine compared notes. No one said much; the previous day's trek only halted long enough at nightfall to rest. Dar wondered how much sleep they would get this night.

Dar patted Virasi's flank and the pegasus scraped the ground with a hoof. "I know you want to be up in the air, boy," Dar soothed. "So do I."

"We all do," said Connor. He absently stroked Phantom's nose and the pegasus tossed her head.

The look in Connor's eye made Dar pause. He watched the Halfling for a few moments, then adjusted one of his saddlebag straps. "Hannah is probably just fine, Connor."

Connor gave a little smile to match the faraway look in his eyes. "I'm sure she is. She's one determined lady." His hand went to his hauberk, just above his heart.

"Something she gave you?" Dar nodded at him.

"Her last letter."

The image of Megan lying on a bier under a Preservation Net came unbidden to Dar's mind. "At least you have something."

Connor gripped his arm. "You'll see Megan again."

Before Dar could respond, Andyn strode up to them. "They're back," she said.

Dar felt a wave of relief at the sight of Kelaire with Eric, unhurt. Despite his newfound respect for her abilities in the wilds, he also detected a certain rashness in her, an eagerness to prove herself.

Must be hard to be the chieftain's daughter…

"We think we've found a way," Kelaire said, taking a drink from a water skin.

"Thank Irial," Connor said. "Where?"

She swallowed and waved behind her. "There's a drier pathway. The mist is heavy, but if we take it nice and careful, we should make it to the edge of Rainbow Valley by evening."

"Good," said Buck with a sour look at the drooping trees and jutting rocks nearby. "I don't want to be anywhere near this place at night."

Kelaire chuckled. "Don't worry, Sir Buck. I remember this area. If the lizardfolk are moving west, we should be well clear of them by the time the sun goes down."

"When were you here?" Dar asked.

"Last spring." She looked at him sidelong. "I know what you're thinking. A lot can change in fifteen months. Acknowledged. But the land won't have moved."

Eric shrugged. "There really aren't any other options."

The company formed up with Kelaire, Dar and Khyron in the front rank, followed by both Dwarves, Buck and Connor, then Eric, Andyn and the two centaurs.

Dar set an arrow to his bow and held up his hand. When the rest of the group nodded to him, he waved them forward. With the barest clink of armor and the mild thud of hooves, they set out.

He felt proud of his comrades. Back when they first met, so long ago, he was sure that they made enough noise in the forest to wake the undead, but now? Even Buck managed a semblance of stealth, despite wearing banded mail.

Dar kept his eyes moving and occasionally turned around to take a look at their back trail. No telling when they might have to make a quick retreat.

Kelaire and Khyron led them calmly, not hurrying but not going slowly either. They slipped along a path through massive stands of reeds, then past low marshy areas with little hillocks crowned by tufts of greyish-yellow plants, then over rocky expanses with brooding, leafless trees. Always, the mist limited visibility to a mere hundred feet or so, and the pale sun struggled to burn through the overcast skies.

The air hung close and humid. Dar was thankful that enchanted magic armors had a feature to repel heat. Otherwise, he wasn't sure how he would have managed.

Kelaire halted them near a dead tree on a little knoll. "Here's where it gets interesting," she murmured. "Stay sharp. The mist will thicken."

Dar stared ahead and bit his lip. The landscape transitioned from rough, damp ground with scrubby growth, boulders and occasional ponds to a vast marsh, cloaked in mist like a burial shroud. A few massive trees poked their heads up out of the grey and occasionally he saw a quick motion of a small creature or a ripple of water.

Most importantly, far on the other side of the swamp, mountains loomed under cloudy skies. Dar caught glimpses of green meadows in a broad valley. "We're close," he said, casting his eyes skyward, searching for the Dark dragons. "And no sign of Ja'al patrols yet," he noted.

"Oh, they're out there," Keldur said. The Dwarf scowled at the clouds. "I'm sure of it. But, if we get into the fens quick enough, they'll never see us."

Kelaire got them moving again and they crept into the marsh and its enveloping mist. Dar wiped suddenly sweaty palms on his camouflaged hauberk.

We'll be well-hidden from the dragons. So why am I feeling edgy?

He made sure to keep his bow ready and eyes moving. The farther they advanced, the more the mist thickened. Soon, visibility reduced to a dozen yards. Dar saw no more of the grey sky above.

She said it would get thick, but this is ridiculous.

From places hidden in the fog, he heard an occasional rustle, splash or clack of rock. Once, he felt certain something whispered but he couldn't be sure.

A motion out of the corner of his eye made him whirl in that direction, bow up. Nothing moved. He aimed at small clumps of earth with the remnant twigs of some dead plants, but nothing assailed him.

He cursed under his breath. *Stop jumping at everything! Geez…I even think little clumps of dead plants are monsters…*

"Yeah. I know how you feel," Eric said next to him, his own bow held at the ready. Buck and Connor turned in slow circles.

"Keep within sight of each other. Don't spread out too much," Kelaire hissed. "The Harrowing is well-named for a reason. And I don't like this fog. It's not normal to get this thick so fast."

Their path turned to the right and they approached a clear space with a small pile of rocks. Grateful for a respite from the fog, they stopped for a chance to rest their jangled nerves.

Dar eyed the rocks. "Kelaire," he asked. "Are there sprites out here? This looks like a little cairn."

Kelaire's brow furrowed. "I don't know." She gestured to one of her scouts. "Rhianne? What do you think? You've dealt with moor sprites before."

Rhianne shook her head. "They wouldn't be this far into the Harrowing. And even moor-sprites bury their dead under grassy meadows, not in stone tombs."

"Lizard-folk?" asked Eric.

Kelaire shrugged. "Possibly. I am not an expert in their customs."

One stone reminded Dar of Whitehorse Peak, the mountain near his hometown. Some kind of sparkling white mineral glittered at its top, almost like snow. A plant with yellow-striped green leaves and bright blue flowers grew next to the pile.

Dar leaned in for a closer look. He shook his head. How anything flowered here was beyond him.

"It's different from all the others nearby," said Andyn, crouching down next to the plant. "Very bright colors. Fantine, do you know what it is?"

"No, though I've seen other flowering plants in the fens. I wouldn't touch it, though," the centaur added when Andyn reached out a hand.

Andyn blinked, as if suddenly noticing what she was doing, then nodded and stood. Khyron beckoned to her and she joined him with a puzzled glance back at the bright plant.

Connor joined Dar, chewing a piece of dried, spiced beef. "Kind of weird, a flowering plant and some crystals in all this muck."

Dar shrugged. "Who knows what it is? Even Fantine isn't sure. How are you holding up?"

"Tired. More than a little tense. Hungry, but you probably guessed that. I just want to get through this place." Connor nodded at the blossoms. "That's pretty. Janey's favorite color, though I doubt she would have liked the surroundings."

Something in Dar's brain tingled and he started. "Did you feel that?"

"Hmm?" Connor blinked and looked at Dar. "No. Are you feeling okay?"

Dar marched over to the others. "Did anyone feel some kind of tingling sensation?"

They gave him blank looks and shook their heads.

Andyn held up a hand, murmuring a phrase. Her eyes flashed light blue for a second and she shook her head vexedly. "I can't detect anything." She took off a glove and put her hand to the ground, then closed her eyes for a few moments.

"Nature is restless," she announced, rising. "Something is interfering with my other detection spells so that's all I can find out."

Dar pressed his lips together. "Connor?"

The Halfling didn't respond, gazing out into the Harrowing with a little smile on his face.

"Connor?" Dar repeated. *What's wrong with him?*

Connor chuckled and waved a hand. "I don't know what you're talking about, Dar. Maybe you're having an allergic reaction to some moss or algae out here." He reached for his pack. "We should continue."

"Fair enough," Eric said, trudging off.

Behind him, Dar heard Connor murmur something and he shot a look at him. Connor still smiled to himself as he trudged forward, his bow at the ready.

He sure seems distracted. Probably memories of Janey…

Dar resumed his place. The fen went on and on without end. The mist and phantom sounds made him feel like he was in a tense and endless waking nightmare of uncertainty and dread. Perspiration trickled down his forehead and he had to wipe it away from his eyes several times.

I can do this. Trust Kelaire. She knows what she's doing.

Their path led them towards one of the huge trees. For some reason, this didn't comfort Dar. He knew that the ground near such a large one was likely firm and drier but something made him pause.

He shot a glance at the tree. It towered above the fog in the distance, like some imperious queen surveying her domain.

Something sharp bounced off his chest armor and he jerked his bow up.

"Attack!" hissed Eric.

At first, Dar thought that a mob of tiny balls of fur with miniature spears attached to their backs charged at him. Then he realized they were clumps of turf with spiny branches — just like the ones he had noticed earlier— except that these had red pinpoints for eyes.

Dar plugged one with an arrow. The swarm paused and arched their backs. A flight of spines shot out at them and he ducked behind his cloak. Something flashed with purple light out in the marsh. The pegasi whinnied and backed up, rearing.

One spine penetrated Dar's leg armor and he felt a burning sensation. He managed to get one more shot off before the creatures were among them.

Dar thought to draw his sword, then realized the quarters were too tight. Instead, he drew his handaxe and dagger, hacking and stabbing at the little monstrosities. He struck down so many that he lost count. Still they came, leaping from the muddy water or careening out of the tall reeds, shooting spines. Just at the corner of his vision, another flare of purple light flashed but he couldn't spare any time to look. He hoped it was a new spell Andyn had learned to repel vicious mud-balls.

Virasi reared, beating his wings and casting up dirt and twigs, hurling mudballs away into the reeds. The creatures veered away from him.

More sharp pains hit Dar. The burning sensation increased and his concentration faded. One spiny dart narrowly missed his mouth, glancing off his helmet instead. Then Eric and Andyn spoke arcane words and sheets of flame shot out from their hands, incinerating attackers by the dozens, the monsters giving thin shrieks as they died. The smell of burning grass and wood filled the area.

"Back up!" Andyn hissed. "Rally on me and Eric!"

Dar did as he was told but one leg refused to work. His vision swam. He dropped his dagger and stared at it, not comprehending.

Buck's strong hands latched onto his shoulders and Dar let himself be dragged backwards, blinking through blurred vision. Next to him, two centaur women carried a Dwarf towards them. Medianox struck out with her front hooves, pulverizing two mud-balls. Her barding bristled with tiny darts.

Andyn and Eric chanted again and sheets of flame burst forth.

Dar closed his eyes, trying to regain his faculties. *Why can't I think straight?* More shrieks echoed out in the wetland, then silence, broken only by the sound of heavy breathing.

Andyn's voice cut through his mental daze. "Dar? Hey, sit here for a minute."

A vial met his lips and a liquid tasting of blueberries, tomatoes and salt swirled on his tongue. He grimaced but swallowed.

"Wow," said Buck. "You're a pincushion."

The mental fuzziness faded and Dar opened his eyes. He stared in amazement at the small pile of thorny twigs at his feet.

"How many?" he asked.

"About fifteen," said Eric, pulling a last dart out of his own pauldron. "For some reason, they really liked you… er… hated you."

Dar cast a look at their company.

The three centaur women brushed spines out of their barding. Rorlic administered a healing potion to Keldur, an empty vial on the muddy earth next to him.

"How's everyone else?" Dar asked. "How are the pegasi?"

Andyn straightened her hauberk. "They're fine. Barding and horsehide are great protection. You got the worst of it. Usually, Connor is the one taking the beating. Right, Connor?"

Dar looked over his shoulder, searching for the Halfling.

"Wait," Buck said. "Where is he?"

Everyone froze. Dar stood, his fogginess vanishing. "He was right behind me."

"Connor?" Eric called. He led Niveral to Phantom's side. Connor's pegasus minced aside, obviously agitated.

"What's wrong?" asked Kelaire, dabbing her arm with a bandage.

"Connor's gone."

"Gone? He was right here." The centaur frowned.

Everyone scanned the misty swamp. The pegasi stamped restlessly.

Fantine turned in a circle. "He had to have left under his own power. Those things weren't big enough to kidnap a mouse, much less a Halfling."

"Could something larger have taken him?" asked Khyron. "Lizardkin? Some other horror?"

Kelaire shook her head. "Lizardfolk would just attack and try to take us all at once. And as far as some other creature…" her voice trailed off and her expression remained grim.

"Connor!" Andyn called in a harsh whisper. Her voice echoed out over the swamp. "Connor! Where are you?"

"I saw a flash of purple light," Dar said. "Did any of you see it?"

Eric nodded. "It came from behind us, twice."

Keldur plodded up to them, his face grim. "Recognize this?"

Dar's stomach churned and he nodded, accepting a short sword in an ornate scabbard decorated with filigreed tongues of fire.

"Might he have dropped it?" asked Fantine.

Khyron shook his head. "He would never leave Tiuz behind."

Dar met Eric's eyes. "This was all a set-up. We've been toyed with and led into this place, right into an ambush." His heart sank. *Why didn't I recognize it earlier? Some leader I am…*

Kelaire put a hand on his shoulder. "Don't blame yourself. I missed it too."

Eric set his mouth in a firm line. "Well, blame aside, we had better start tracking and pray to Saint Michael that we find him."

Fantine's eyes swept the mist-shrouded swamp and the leaden sky. "Let's get moving, fast — and keep a wary eye out. We might have just told the dragons where we are."

Chapter Twenty-One – Close to My Heart

When the muck-balls first attacked, Connor saw Dar reach for his sword, then change to dagger and handaxe.

Good idea, Connor thought. He touched the brooch on his cloak and a misty sword of light materialized in mid-air.

Connor dodged a charging muck-ball and slashed it in half, his sword blazing with fire. Two more enemies shot spines at him but he skipped aside and flipped a knife into one.

Damn. There sure are a lot of the buggers.

Five more raced at Connor. His phantom blade slashed two of the attackers in half. Connor crouched, prepared to spring.

A purple light flashed behind him and his tiny attackers stopped. Something tingled in his brain. An odd lethargy set over him and he had a vision of Janey in his mind's eye, just as she had appeared on their wedding day.

He shook his head. *What the hell?*

His eyes flicked to his companions, battling swarms of assailants. Keldur dropped under a fusillade of thorns. Rhianne and Fantine leapt to his side.

I have to help —

The tingle returned, more intense. Purple light flashed again and the image of Janey coalesced in his mind, except now he saw her in his waking vision, as if she were there. The vicious little mudballs in front of him whined and retreated, cowering. Connor's magic sword hovered in mid-air, awaiting his command.

"Connor?" asked a familiar female voice behind him.

He spun and his jaw dropped. There she stood, clad in a dress of her favorite sky blue, her eyes warm and smile welcoming.

"Ja— Janey?" He asked.

His mind wrestled with the unreality of it, but a strange, sickly-sweet aroma now suffused the air. He remembered it. The little blue flowers by the rock had given off the same scent.

"Yes, my love," Janey answered, holding out her hands to him. "I have come back for you."

"But…" he struggled to focus his thoughts but they swirled unsteadily. "I… you died."

She shook her head. "That wasn't real. I lived, as you can see."

"But the Plague! I saw you die!"

She smiled at him again. "No, dear. That was an illusion sent by our enemies to deceive you. Come with me."

How is this possible? He put a hand to his forehead, trying to remember. "But what about Rose?"

"Rose?"

"Yes, Rose," replied Connor, feeling a nagging sense of disquiet. "Our daughter."

Janey laughed. "Of course, dear. She's waiting for you. If you come with me, all will be explained."

She beckoned to him and the sweet aroma wafted over him again. He felt dizzy.

A faint rattle of combat sounded in the distance. He ignored it. *I don't care! To be with her again is worth everything!* With a smile, he walked towards her.

"Wait." He struggled to remember something. "I have a pegasus. I need to bring her with me."

Janey's expression turned unreadable for a second but her smile returned in an eyeblink. "We can come back for her later." Her eyes flicked to his sword. "You won't need that either, love. As long as you're close to my heart, you'll be safe."

Connor stared at Tiuz as if he had never seen it before. "Yes. Yes, of course," he said, sheathing it. He unbuckled his sword belt and laid it down on a nearby rock.

"And you can dismiss that magical… whatever it is."

He touched his brooch. The phantom sword swirled into it and vanished.

Her eyes brightened and he felt a wonderful lightness.

"I am close to your heart," he murmured.

"Follow me, love." She turned away with a coquettish glance over one shoulder.

Connor Lomin followed his wife into the Harrowing.

***

Dar stood, brushing his gloves against his tunic. *Damn it. Why would he go backwards, to our last rest stop? Connor, where are you?* He glared at the blue-flowered plant, now wilted and shriveled.

"Someone is trying to hide his trail," Eric muttered. "Connor's tracks stop right here."

Dar nodded. "I suspect our little muddy friends. Andyn, can you detect anything?"

Andyn's eyes flared blue. "There's latent magic. I think the plant and the rocks were designed to work together. The flowers would lower the victim's defenses and then the rocks would steal a memory." She slapped her thigh vexedly. "And I couldn't even detect it."

"Don't blame yourself," said Kelaire. "There's no way we would have figured that out when we stopped here, even if we had known what to look for. And I've been in the Harrowing before."

Khyron put his arm around Andyn and her aggravated expression softened. "But what's more important now is finding him," he said.

"Can you pick up the trail again?" Buck asked the rangers.

Eric and Dar exchanged a look. Dar nodded. "We will. Even if it takes all day."

He joined Eric in traversing the area in ever-widening circles. Dar's eyes darted from rock to lichen to leaf to twig, searching, but he saw nothing. His fist tightened on the grip of his bow. He prayed that Connor wasn't trying to hide his own trail for some reason; if he chose to go undetected, it might be hours before Dar or Eric would find any sign.

Dar's eyes locked on a lichen-covered stone. *There! The edge of a bootprint.*

"This way," he announced, treading carefully in that direction. The others followed, bringing the pegasi along. He took turns with Eric, sometimes watching their trail ahead, sometimes tracking.

"Dar," Eric whispered as they crossed a rivulet among a stand of reeds. "This is leading to that big tree we saw earlier."

"I know. Look sharp and be ready for trouble."

***

"How much farther, dear?" Connor asked.

"We are close. Our camp is over by that tree."

Connor's heart leapt. To find Janey alive after all this time was a miracle, but now to see his daughter was the stuff of dreams.

"Is Rose well?" he asked, following Janey over a jumble of rocks.

"Quite well," Janey replied. "She talks of you constantly."

"Shouldn't we hold hands?" Connor asked.

"No need, dearest." She glided over the rocks with an agility that amazed him. "Here we are."

Connor stared at the immense tree. Set in a massive clearing surrounded by brush and tall reeds, it towered over him and the swamp. Leafless branches reached towards the sky like the points on a lich's crown and the whole thing looked twisted and dry. An ornate throne of gnarled roots sat at the tree's base. The throne glowed with a purple light.

"Marvelous, isn't it?" Janey asked.

"Yes, it certainly is." Something nagged at Connor's mind, as if he needed to remember something important.

He felt an itch at his chest, near his heart. "Where did you say Rose was?" He slipped his fingers under the neck of his armor to scratch and touched a folded paper.

That's odd. Why do I have a letter? Whose letter is it? A name flickered in his memory.

Hannah! The image of a pretty Halfling girl with nut-brown hair and warm eyes flashed in his mind's eye.

All at once, his memories rushed back to him. He remembered the Grey Riders, Hannah, their mission, War — everything became clear in an instant. He remembered Janey and Rose's caskets being lowered into the earth on a mild spring day, years ago.

A cold chill raced through him. He whirled on Janey. "What is this?"

Janey's smile became a leer. The purple light from the tree leapt to her hand and she flicked her fingers. A net of energy with the heaviness of chains wrapped around him, pinning his arms to his side. To his horror, Janey transformed.

Her body warped and shrank until a sprite hovered before him, bat-wings fluttering as it floated in the stinking air.

Connor's stomach churned. It looked like no sprite he had ever seen. Unlike the pure and innocent forms of the hill sprites near the Blue Mark's home, this one fairly radiated perversity and power. His skeletal features kept the same leer, red eyes blazing. His body was at once perfect and warped.

"You have some strength in you, Halfling," the creature hissed. "It will not avail you."

He beckoned and the reeds parted. Four hulking creatures, as tall as Buck, lumbered into the light. Reptilian heads with a single horn marked them as lizardkin, the swamp folk. They wore armor made from the hide of giant reptiles and carried rock-studded wooden clubs. However, their expressions were vacant and their eyes glowed with the same sickening purple light. Their movements seemed halting.

"Yes," said the misshapen sprite. "Like these, you will be close to my heart, as one of my loyal servants. And you will enjoy it."

***

Dar tapped Eric on the shoulder. "We're getting too close to that giant tree for my comfort."

The half-Elf straightened from his crouch. "Yes. We are." He held up a fist. The others halted.

Dar's eyes narrowed. "This may be the time to use Stealth. Send him above the tree."

Eric gave him a sharp look. "Why?"

Dar bit his lip. "Remember what Megan and Brandi wrote about when they found that ruined Elven village? Remember the Hell Wisp?"

Eric's eyes widened. "Good God! I just made the connection! The little mud-balls, the purple flash of light…"

Buck stared at them as if they had grown a third eyeball. "What are you talking about?"

Eric activated his hawk golem medallion.

"A Hell Wisp captured the entire remnant of an Elven town," Dar explained. "Little creatures called Skitterlings did its bidding and attacked with thorny darts that had a numbing poison."

Andyn stared at him. "One Hell Wisp captured an entire town?"

Dar nodded. "And the only reason Megan and Brandi defeated it was because they found a Celestial plant, a Crown-of-Thorns, in the woods."

"Well, that's comforting," replied Andyn. "And not. I don't see any helpful plants around."

Dar pulled his sword scabbard to the front and drew Rindara. The sword's black blade glittered with stars.

"Great," said Khyron. "We'll have to send the pegasi away until after we free Connor. We can't let them fall into the Wisp's hands."

Buck still looked confused. "Wait. What is a Hell Wisp?"

Eric released Stealth into the misty air and the golem soared high overhead. "An undead faery wizard," he answered. "A sprite lich. Think Zhinia Margoth, but in sprite form. The only saving grace is that they're smaller and not quite as lethal."

"Oh wonderful," Buck muttered. "Well, can we avoid a repeat of the result the last time we faced a lich? We've run out of Christian artifacts that can raise the dead."

Dar faced the Dwarves and centaurs. "I'm sorry to have to put you in this danger —"

"And what exactly did you think we expected when we agreed to come?" Rorlic interrupted him, one eyebrow arched. "Flowers and unicorns? A Halfling feast-day carnival?"

Kelaire chuckled. "Indeed. However, it would help if we knew what we faced. I've only heard of Hell Wisps. Can we destroy it?"

Andyn made a face. "It's likely that the only things that will hurt it will be Eric's spear, Dar's sword, and Khyron's blades, since they're of Celestial origin. Realize that the Wisp will have slave warriors, so it will likely use them as shields."

Kelaire nodded and the troop readied their weapons.

"What do you see, Eric?" Andyn asked.

Eric nodded, his eyes focused on something far away. "It's a Hell Wisp all right, and it has Connor pinned in a net of purple Magicords. There are a few creatures skulking about in the reeds near the tree and I saw something large hunkered down in a big, muddy pond. I'm not sure what else is going on but the Wisp is talking to Connor. He doesn't look too good."

"Let's go get him then," Buck said, hefting his shield and drawing his blade. The sword flared briefly with golden light.

Khyron held up a hand. "Let's don't charge in there without thinking this out. This needs to be executed perfectly, so please let me lay out the plan of attack."

He knelt and began drawing in the dirt with a stick. "This Hell Wisp is a wizard, you say. Well, in my experience, wizards stay at the rear of the battle line, behind infantry and archers. The Wisp will likely do the same thing. Now, it has Connor as a prisoner, so it will probably keep him nearby. Since Eric and Andyn can counter the Wisp's spells and Eric can use his spear from distance, they'll be behind a front line of Rorlic, Keldur, Fantine and Kelaire. When the main group moves forward, they will draw the Wisp's attention. When the Wisp and its thralls attack, Dar and I slip around the sides. One of us keeps the Wisp busy while the other frees Connor."

Dar opened his mouth but closed it. When faced with any military-style situation, the Riders tended to defer to Khyron, but he wasn't so sure this time. The Wisp had managed to spirit away Connor — an experienced agent freelancer with some formidable weaponry —— and none of the Riders had even noticed. It had also stolen Connor's memories, thwarted Andyn's attempts to scan the swamp, summoned a veritable army of muck-ball warriors and hidden Connor's trail from two master trackers.

"I think we might need a different approach," Dar said.

Khyron pressed his lips together. "What did you have in mind? This is a standard hostage rescue, and I've done plenty of those. We just have to keep the Wisp's attention elsewhere while the extraction element rescues Connor."

Andyn shook her head. "I'm not so sure, Khy. Take it from me: I've fought a lich before. They are far from standard, and this Wisp has a lot of tricks up its sleeve."

He shot a look at her. She put her hands on her hips and returned his stare.

Dar caught Kelaire's eyes and flicked his gaze at Khyron. The centaur princess nodded back at Dar.

"I agree with Dar and Andyn," Kelaire said, "Consider that Wisp has a considerable advantage in its own territory and it has already shown a propensity for unconventional tactics. Once we attack it may simply kill Connor outright."

Khyron frowned, then saw the expressions on everyone's faces. "Well, yes, that's a possibility, like in all situations of this kind," he admitted. "Did you have something else in mind?"

Kelaire smiled. "It captured Connor instead of killing him. It likes to capture things? Well, let's give it something to capture. I guarantee it won't like the end result…"

***

Connor expected intense pain and torture, but instead, a warm, enticing oblivion beckoned. It seemed that his every heartbeat made the purple cords of light pulse in response and with each one, his resistance weakened.

He fought to concentrate, bringing up thoughts of Hannah, his family, the Riders, Megan and Brandi — anything to keep the void at bay.

"Now, now," the Hell Wisp clucked. "There's no sense in fighting it. You will only prolong things. I have infinite resources at my disposal and your little friends have no idea where you are. Stop struggling."

"Like Hell!" Connor snapped, using his anger as a focus.

The Hell Wisp chuckled. "A marvelous choice of words, Halfling. Like Hell indeed."

Connor forced himself to look at the lizardkin thralls instead. At least he could survey their trappings and try to figure out if they had any rank in their tribe.

A crackle of energy out in the swamp drew his eyes there instead. The Wisp frowned. "Hmm…What's this?"

Three sharp reports echoed out in the marsh, followed by a double-thump.

"Marvelous!" the Wisp exulted. "I have caught another fly! Go, my pets. Bring me back something interesting."

Two of the lizardkin trudged into the tall reeds and grass, splashing through ankle-deep water.

Please, Irial, don't let it be…

A commotion in the brush presaged the return of the lizardmen, this time manhandling Fantine, Keldur and Khyron. All blinked in confusion and looked around with dulled eyes. The lizardkin shoved them. Khyron and Keldur tumbled into a heap.

"Three of them! Splendid!" The Hell Wisp fluttered closer to the massive tree. He touched one palm with two fingers and pulled his hands apart, drawing out a glowing cable of energy. He gestured and the cord whipped out at Keldur.

"I will have to increase the size of my territory," the Wisp mused as the cords wound around the Dwarven ranger's legs. "It's getting positively crowded around here."

Khyron's eyes met Connor's and he grinned. For the first time, Connor noticed that his sword, Tiuz, hung on its belt from Khyron's shoulder. His heart leapt.

In a motion so smooth that Connor hardly believed he saw it, Khyron rolled to one side, folded himself into a crouch and bounded away from the lizardkin.

"No, no, no," the Wisp chided him, pointing ahead of him. "Running away is not allowed!"

A table-sized section of the earth along Khyron's escape route erupted, showering the area with dirt and opening a five-foot deep pit. Khyron reversed course and tumbled back towards the tree, drawing his sword. The blade burned with a pure white light. With one motion, he slashed through Connor's imprisoning bonds. The lethargy vanished from Connor's mind.

"Get to work," Khyron said with a wink, then tossed Tiuz to him. He jumped and turned a handspring to avoid a blast of purple fire from the Wisp.

Connor drew Tiuz. The weapon's edge immediately burst into bright, hot fire. He touched the brooch on his cloak and his Spectral Sword leaped into being in front of him.

"Damn it! Servants! Kill them!" the Wisp ordered.

All hell broke loose. Little mud-ball assailants swarmed out of the bushes, two more lizardkin lumbered out of the misty shadows, and the Wisp swept backwards in the air, behind his thralls.

With a shout, the Grey Riders and their allies charged out of the reeds and grass. Andyn touched the cords around Keldur's ankles and the restraints dissipated in a cloud of steam. Buck dropped a foe with a well-placed thrust.

"Over here, Connor!" yelled Dar, swinging Rindara at one of the lizard-folk. It backpedaled, hissing and parrying with its club.

"A little busy!" Connor called, cutting two mud-balls in half and dodging a quartet of spines. His Spectral blade skewered a flying dirt-creature in mid-air.

The lizardkin charged his friends, but the Buck, Andyn, the Dwarves and centaurs expertly intercepted them. Dar, Eric and Khyron to raced around the thralls, heading for the Wisp.

"This cannot be borne!" the Wisp hollered, sweeping up into the air. The tree behind him flared purple.

The Wisp spread its fingers and a hail of fire-darts shot out at the Grey Riders. The missiles peppered them, detonating on armor and magical screens. The Riders staggered back and the Wisp's slaves surged forward.

Connor's eyes widened and he narrowly missed a dart in the eye. He rolled behind a fallen log as spines riddled the wood.

Dolmide's Beard! I haven't seen anyone shoot that many firedarts since we fought George Oxbridge!

With a scrabbling noise, four mudballs charged over the top of the log but Connor and his hovering guardian sword cut them down.

"This is an outrage!" screamed the Wisp. He made a fist and thrust it at them. Nearby rocks and stones shivered, then flew at the Grey Riders.

Connor ducked a pair of stones and rolled out of the way of a volley of spines. One rock belted him in the shoulder, spinning him out of the way of a leaping mud-ball. Andyn and Eric blasted lightning at the Wisp but the electric bolts merely dissipated on a globe of reddish energy. Eric threw Fidelis. The sprite lich motioned with a hand and the weapon flew off into the reeds. The Wisp cackled at them as Eric recalled his spear.

Connor spent the next few breathless seconds cutting down enemies, dodging rocks and jagged shafts of wood, and avoiding lightning bolts. To his elation, the Riders kept fighting. Though bruised and battered, they still struggled to close with the fluttering, dancing Hell Wisp. Every time Dar, Khyron or Eric approached within ten feet, the Wisp dodged out of the way, covering his retreat with clouds of stinking fog or fire-darts.

"We're coming!" called Kelaire. She leaped over the collapsing corpse of the last lizardkin. The centaurs and Dwarves followed her.

"No!" shrieked the Hell Wisp. "I will not have it!"

He slammed both fists together and a rumble shook the glade. The tree flashed again and, to the right of it, something massive lurched out of a pond of brackish water.

Connor's jaw dropped.

It was a Drake, fifty feet long, with green-black scales and purple eyes. Its jaw hung slack and rotting weeds trailed from its scales. It lumbered forth, its movements halting and somewhat leaden like the lizardkin, but its wicked fangs and claws gleamed sharp and menacing in the purple light.

"Burn them," the Wisp snarled.

The dragon opened its mouth and a cloud of sizzling green acid shot out. His shield up, Buck leaped forward and deflected some of the blast but a portion got through, striking him, Rorlic and Fantine. They staggered, faces contorted in pain, their armor smoking. Nearby vegetation blackened and wilted in a hiss of steam.

The remaining Riders and their allies whirled on the enslaved Drake, pummeling it with weapon and spell. It retreated under the onslaught, lashing out clumsily with claws and tail, its hide rent and oozing blue ichor. It breathed another cloud of acid but its halting movements allowed the Riders to dodge out of the way.

This isn't working, Connor thought, sidestepping a mudball and impaling it. He sent his Spectral Sword after the Wisp but the evil faery sneered and slapped it away, sending it spinning into the underbrush.

The Wisp made a circular motion with his hands and the huge tree flared again.

That's it! The tree! Connor darted to the tree. Ignoring the stinging pain of sharp barbs in his back and legs, he hacked into the trunk with Tiuz. The bark burst into flame with gratifying speed and he slashed again.

The Wisp wailed. "No! Not that!"

He spun at Connor, a ball of crackling ice in one hand, but Eric and Dar shot him in the back with fire-darts. Unable to dodge, he lurched through the air, his magic screen flickering as he bounced off a thick tree bough.

The centaurs, Dwarves, Buck and Andyn slammed into the dragon. Blades cut rents in dragon hide, spears plunged deep, and Andyn's mace crunched bones with a golden flare of light. The vacant-eyed drake faltered, drawing back further into the swamp, its claws swiping empty air more often than not.

The Wisp righted itself, eyes wide, looking for Connor, but he jumped on top of a low-hanging limb, lifted himself up and slashed the tree again, setting more of it ablaze. He called for his ghostly sword and it zipped to hover in front of him.

The Wisp spun out of the way of Dar's swing with Rindara and dodged Eric's spear thrust. Khyron charged, sword and dagger burning with white light. He cut the Wisp in one leg, eliciting a howl of pain. The evil faery gestured and a tree limb swung out, walloping Khyron into the bushes.

Connor cut another flaming gash in the tree.

"You can't..." the Wisp gasped, his wings flapping desperately.

"I can, and I will. I am free." Connor's tone was like ice.

He stabbed his blade into the trunk, opening a crack. He pressed down with all his might, Tiuz blazing like a furnace. The tree cracked and split. Connor thrust deeper and something gave. The core of the tree went up like a torch as he jumped to the ground.

The Wisp leaped after him, a wild look in his eyes, but Eric's spearpoint found its mark in the Hell Wisp's side. The evil faery froze, then exploded in a flash of white fire, scattering small bones and flesh in all directions.

Connor stood in the light of the blazing tree for what seemed like a decade. His chest heaved with exertion. Poison burned in his veins and his skin. He couldn't seem to focus on anything but the inferno. A stench of burning corpses filled the glade.

A gentle hand on his head broke his stupor.

Andyn smiled down at him. "Come with us, Connor. You took a few spines there."

A sudden weakness made his knees buckle, but Rorlic held him up. "Steady on, lad," he said, leading him to a rock.

Connor stared at the wild bonfire before him, at the scattered remnants of mud-ball creatures, at the corpses of the lizardkin.

"What about —" he began.

"The Drake?" Rorlic asked. "Aye, it lies slain in the mud, hard by the pond there. You need not worry."

Andyn held her magic mace in one hand and murmured a gentle phrase. Eleison glowed and a wave of warmth and energy filled Connor, dispelling his dizziness and relieving the pain. He became dimly aware of a mild drizzle starting up. A mild humming noise reminded him that his Spectral Sword hovered nearby protectively and he dispelled it back into the brooch.

He eyed the cloudy, darkening sky. "How is everyone else?" he asked, rising.

Andyn sighed, removing her helmet. "We managed to avoid getting killed, though you mind not think it to look at us." She moved towards the others, clustered in a panting heap on the churned earth.

Connor eyed the blaze for a while, then joined Andyn.

"What happened?" Khyron asked, taking a sip from a potion bottle. He grimaced at the flavor.

Connor felt a wave of embarrassment. "I don't know really. One minute I was fighting those little mud creatures —"

"Skitterlings," offered Dar.

"Is that what they're called?" Connor scratched his jaw and shrugged. "Okay. Skitterlings. Then the next thing I knew, Janey was there. It was uncanny and I didn't believe it at first, but the Skitterlings drew back and every time I tried to concentrate, I smelled this odd, sweet aroma and I lost my train of thought. She told me that Rose was waiting for me and after she led me to this tree, she changed into that… whatever it was."

"A Hell Wisp. An undead sprite wizard." Andyn finished applying ointment to a burn on Fantine's flank. The centaur winced.

Connor looked down at his boots. "He reminded me of George Oxbridge. Or Zhinia Margoth."

Eric helped Keldur to stand. "He set a magic trap back by the rock pile with the blue-flowered plant. Probably thickened the mist to help the Skitterling ambush."

"That was a trap?" Connor now felt doubly foolish.

"Well, no one else saw it either," Andyn said, moving over to help Buck. "We've just finished beating ourselves up over it. I just don't know how you managed to break out of it."

Connor gave a little smile. "Hannah's letter," he said, touching his chest.

Andyn smiled back. "The power of love."

His face grew warm. "Well, I'd better make myself useful then. I'm no good at healing."

"Don't go far," Kelaire warned. "We can't afford to chase you again."

Connor drifted behind the now-guttering tree, waving away the acrid smoke as he stepped along firm ground between giant reeds.

The condition of his companions filled him with regret. Andyn's assessment, while given in jest, was pretty accurate.

Boy, I sure loused that one up, didn't I? Well, no use in stewing over it. He set his shoulders. He could help them better by doing a little reconnoitering.

As he slipped through the Harrowing, his thoughts winged back to Janey and Hannah. The Wisp had used his memories of Janey to ensnare him and Hannah's letter had brought him back.

Maybe if I wasn't so conflicted about Hannah and Janey's memory, the Wisp wouldn't have had much to go on.

He sighed. In one fell swoop, the Hell Wisp had managed to bring his unwillingness to move on after his family's death and his reluctance about a relationship with Hannah into sharp focus.

And I'll bet Janey was praying for Hannah's letter to snap me out of the Wisp's spell the whole time. Maybe it was a sign from Heaven.

He paused and looked up at the sky. Yes. It was a sign from heaven.

Ironically, it took the actions of an evil sprite lich to make him realize it. He had his answer: Janey didn't want him to dwell on the past. It was okay to move on.

*Speaking of moving on…*Shaking his head, he continued scouting, heading towards the valley he had seen from afar. Soon, his pathway led upwards. Intrigued, he quickened his pace while keeping to the shadows. The precipitation intensified from a drizzle to a light rain.

Then the stand of massive reeds ended. Drier ground led up a slope to a grassy lawn. Healthy-looking willow trees stood on the hillock, their leaves green against the clouds above.

"What is this?" he breathed, picking his way uphill. At the crest, he stared.

A vast valley stretched out before him, and beyond, mountains loomed in the greyness, their tops swathed in mist. He clearly made out the shape of three sharp peaks on one of the smaller mountains.

The Titan's Crown! Finally! Connor whirled and ran back towards the Harrowing. *Now, if only the weather will hold.*

He heard Khyron's aggravated voice before he entered the glade. "Why did you let him leave?"

"He can handle himself," Buck replied.

"It's not like we don't know where he went," Eric added as Connor approached the Wisp's former lair.

"But I really am sorry I put you through all this," Connor said and stepped around the ruined tree. The entire party jumped, then they all gave exasperated and sheepish grins, even Khyron.

"He's back," Dar said with a wry look.

"I've made up for the trouble I caused, though," Connor announced.

"Really?" Fantine asked.

"Yes. I've found the way to Rainbow Valley…"

Chapter Twenty-Two – Through A Glass Darkly

Father Thomas Williams knew where he was. He had seen three crosses on the hill in many a painting and fresco. However, never had he seen it depicted surrounded by a sea of glass.

The sky roiled grey and gloomy, yet the mirror surface reflected a vast blue expanse with white clouds. He tried to walk forward, yet no matter how fast his feet moved, he never approached closer to the hill. He finally stopped.

Forlorn figures clustered near the middle cross, bringing down the body of a man. Saint John the Apostle held Mary, Mother of Jesus, for a time, then she disengaged from him and knelt. Her head bowed and her body shook with sobs as Mary Magdalene joined her, arm around her in comfort. Saint Joseph of Arimathea, white-bearded, gently removed a crown of thorns from Christ's head. He handed it to Saint John. Father Thomas distinctly saw something small drop to the ground.

Saint Veronica approached and picked up the object, then gently wrapped it in a cloth that bore the image of Jesus' face. She handed it to Saint John, who nodded in thanks.

Voices drew his attention. A golden net of light flashed at his side and vanished.

The Grey Riders strode past him on the glassy sea, heading towards the hill of Calvary. Father Thomas tried to call to them but his voice came out as a whisper. The Riders marched on, free to move while he remained pinned in place. Even the two Alenar sisters walked with them, yet they wore white robes.

His eyes flitted to the glassy surface below his feet. Each of the Grey Riders left a drop of blood in their wake. Where Brandi and Megan and Connor Lomin stepped, their droplets flared golden.

The hill vanished and the Riders continued on into a meadow under bright sunshine.

Thomas Williams gasped and his eyes popped open. He remained frozen for a few moments, caught between his dream and reality. It took him a little while to realize where he was. Early morning sunlight filtered in between the curtains on one side of the room and medicine bottles glinted on tables. Sleeping patients occupied other beds nearby. He touched the bandages on his head.

The images of his dream remained emblazoned on his memory. *Good Lord. What was all that about?* He sat up slowly.

The door on the other side of the room slid open and Sister Karen entered. At the sight of him, she smiled.

"Awake already?" she asked in a whisper.

He nodded, mind whirring.

"How are you feeling?" she asked. She waved a hand and a ball of dim light flickered into being over his head.

"Hmm." He remained lost in thought over the details in the dream.

She frowned. "Last I recall, you were still able to speak. Unless something has changed since yesterday?"

"Oh. Yes. Sorry. I am feeling better." A lot better, he realized. As a matter of fact, he felt only as sore as a man who has done a little too much exercise. His head no longer throbbed with pain.

He said as much.

She cocked her head to the side. "Let's see about that."

She reached into her examination bag and performed a checkup on him as quietly as possible to avoid disturbing the other patients.

"Well, you either have remarkable recuperative powers that I'm unaware of," she said, replacing her instruments, "or someone has been giving you infusions of epic healing magic without my knowledge. I'm willing to bet on the former, based on my dealings with your predecessor."

He didn't answer for a while and she gave him an arch look, waiting.

"Sister Karen, did you ever —" he stopped and started again. "I just had the most extraordinary dream."

She pulled up a chair and gazed intently into his eyes. "Tell me."

He did, leaving nothing out. She listened quietly, nodding occasionally.

"What do you think it means?" he asked.

She gave a quiet chuckle. "It's your dream. I'm more curious to find out what you make of it."

He considered a moment. "Well, it's clear I saw Calvary on Good Friday. The figures are unmistakable. I don't know about the tiny object that fell. And why were the Grey Riders there? Were they approaching their own Calvary? Are the drops of blood symbolic of their martyrdom? Do the blue sky and meadow symbolize heaven?"

She said nothing.

He dropped his hands in his lap. "Frankly, I'm not sure what it means at all. It could be something biological, a reaction to the medications you have been giving me."

She shook her head. "Those medicines do not usually have side effects like that. Maybe it is just your mind, working through your anxieties of the situation and projecting things that worry you. It's undeniable that you have been very concerned about the Riders and their mission."

He frowned, cupping his chin in his hand. "Yes, that could be it. But the dream had so many other odd elements. I think something else is going on. Also, why was there nothing about daemons and war and fire?"

She shrugged. "Who knows what goes on in one's dreams?"

He didn't answer.

Finally, she stood. "Do you feel well enough to talk to Lord Melinor? He is waiting in the antechamber."

"Yes, of course. Let me get dressed and I'll meet him there."

The more he moved around, putting on his trousers, boots and cassock, the better he felt, almost as if he hadn't just escaped death at the hands of an otherworldly evil king and Saren's grandfather.

"You look better." Melinor led him out of the antechamber.

Thomas followed, glad to be moving. "I feel better, though I'm not sure why."

"What did Sister Karen say?"

"She agrees that I'm mending… extremely well."

"Praise God, then." Melinor led him into a side chamber and closed the door. He traced the door outline with his index finger and a blue light followed where he touched. Then he raised both hands from his hips to a point overhead. A glittering cloud, somewhat like dust motes in sunlight, curved above them and adhered to the walls, ceiling and floor.

Father Thomas gave him a look. "Concerned about spies?"

"Yes, actually. We caught another one today, trying to poison a well in Harlinsville. I'm expecting more all the time, particularly with all the people who bought into Ja'al propaganda in the last couple of years."

Father Thomas took a seat at a small round table. "How is everything outside the walls?"

The wizard steepled his fingers in front of his face. "You threw the Dark Wave into a swirl of confusion. I think the daemons are genuinely afraid of you after what you did to Torvu and Tarvener. The enemy has made probing attacks here and there, a few air raids and some attempts at undermining the outer wall. It isn't anything out of the ordinary, considering it's a siege. But the Ja'al are holding back."

For some reason, this gave Father Thomas pause. "Hmm… they're that worried?"

"Let's say they're unnerved. They didn't expect you to be so capable in spoiling their little 'torture the innocents to death' stunt. I think they're trying to figure out a way to counter you."

"Anything else?"

"Militarily?" Melinor let out a deep breath. "Well, the eastern Ja'al force is only two days away but that's given us time to prepare the other sectors of the city. We're as ready as we'll ever be."

"And non-militarily?"

Melinor paused so long that the Nuncio wasn't sure he had heard the question. "You remember the blood tests I did on Brandi and Megan?" he asked finally.

"Yes."

"Well, the results are so unusual, I decided to run an experiment to check out the Stones. I used other Heritage Stones to test the blood of people from families of known and proven lineage."

"And?"

"The results matched. The Heritage Stones are in working order."

Dear Lord. So much hope, and yet so much potential peril. Haven't the Grey Riders been through enough? Father Thomas stared down at his signet ring. "So Megan and Brandi's results are accurate," he said.

"Indeed, though they aren't doing them a bit of good at the moment."

Silence reigned.

Father Thomas' thoughts whirled in his brain: the battle against Torvu, the results of Melinor's examinations, the Grey Riders and their desperate quest... and his dream.

He looked up to see Melinor staring at him.

"I can tell there's something else," the wizard said, leaning back in his chair.

Unlike most dreams, the images from Calvary remained as clear as they had when Father Thomas woke up.

"Melinor, I had a weird dream about the Grey Riders."

"Then tell me about it..."

***

Dar.

The voice echoed in the darkness. He strained to see who it was.

Hello again, Dar.

Instantly, the darkness vanished and he stood in a green glade under cloudy skies. A young man with dark hair and blue eyes in a white robe sat on a tree stump, smiling.

Dar gaped. "You..."

"Yes."

Dar's memories flipped back to over a year ago, when the same dark-haired young man had warned him in a dream of imminent danger in his hometown of Forester. Then again, later, he had seen this same young man in a mystical place called the Chamber of Decision, where Dar had to decide whether to take the easy road to get what he wanted or to take the hard road of sacrifice that would lead many people to peace and happiness – and possibly spell his early death.

"Why are you here?" he asked.

The young man smiled. "Come and see."

The landscape changed abruptly and they stood on a wide sheet of dark glass, spangled with stars.

"Where are we?" Dar asked, but his guide merely smiled again and walked to a specific place on the dark mirror.

"Quaerens voluntatem Dominum," the young man said. "Accedere ad altare Dei."

He stretched out his hand above a very specific pattern of stars. With his index finger, he touched twelve of them in succession. Each star flared brightly and remained that way until they formed an arc. When the twelfth star burned with supernatural brilliance, the young man closed his eyes.

"Consummatum est," he said. The air glowed.

Dar woke up.

At first, he wasn't sure where he was, but the scent of trees and flowering shrubs and the pegasi soon brought him back to his senses. He felt soft grass underneath his blanket, so different from the moist ground and scrubby growth of the Harrowing. The pale light of early morning cast shadows from the towering willow tree above him. The familiar form of Eric Indidarc stood watch among the sleeping mounts.

Dar sat up. He cast about for the centaurs and Dwarves and it took him a minute to remember that they had departed rejoin the other refugees.

He smiled to himself, remembering Kelaire's wistful expression as the Riders bade goodbye and trotted their pegasi toward the Titan's Crown. *A promise is a promise, and I wouldn't want to cross her father either. Besides, she's honorable if nothing else.*

His eyes followed to the dark grey clouds above. To the north, the wide expanse of the valley led towards mountain peaks and to one particular, triple-crowned one.

He recognized a storm pattern when he saw one. They would have to move quickly if they were to get to the Titan's Crown before the rain began in earnest.

Eric strode over to join him. The other Riders stirred and rose, rubbing their eyes and yawning.

"Ready to go?" asked Eric.

"Yeah."

"You okay? You seem kind of distracted."

"I… well, it's nothing significant."

"These days, Dar, everything can be significant."

Connor stood and stretched. "Yeah. Come on, Dar. What is it?"

Dar hesitated. Andyn smiled and motioned for him to speak. With a sigh, he related the details of his dream to them.

Buck groaned and flopped back onto the ground. "More mystical messages? Is this the Song of the Grey Riders all over again?"

"There's no guarantee of that, Buck," Khyron said, rolling up his bedroll. "I wasn't with you back then but I think the two situations are different."

"I don't know," mused Connor. "It sounds like a prediction."

"Which could mean many things, including a rough ride to come," Eric mused. "Remember our visions at the Chamber of Decision. None of that seemed to be all hearts and flowers."

"Freelance sell-swords rarely get hearts and flowers, Eric," said Andyn, lifting her saddlebags.

"As we've found out more than once," Buck replied with a wry look at her.

"Maybe you should write down what the man in your dream said," Connor suggested, hefting his saddle onto Phantom.

"Oh, I will, though I doubt if I'll ever forget it," Dar murmured. "I just wish I knew what it meant."

Eric clapped him on the shoulder. "God will tell us, Dar. He doesn't let things happen for no reason."

Khyron cast his eyes skyward. "Well, mysterious dreams aside, we need to close as much distance as we can. That rainstorm is likely to cut down on our flying time."

Dar sighed. Despite the unease of his dream, he knew Khyron was right. "Agreed. Riders up."

Chapter Twenty-Three – Mother of Sorrows

Well, at least we had a chance to fly for a little while, Eric thought, squinting through the rain.

He banked Niveral as Dar headed down. The other Riders maneuvered to follow. Dar's pegasus led them on a line towards a wooded area on the shore of a small lake in the valley.

A flash of lightning split the sky and Eric only counted three before thunder rumbled.

Definitely need to get on the ground…

He guided his mount in for a landing and cantered to a halt under the overhanging boughs of the trees. Rain dripped down around them but the earth looked relatively dry under the sheltering foliage.

"We took a risk by flying," he noted, pushing back his hood and removing his helmet.

Dar shrugged. "We're on the other side of the Harrowing and we hadn't seen any evidence of the enemy. Besides, with that storm blowing in, I doubt if the Ja'al would have any airborne assets on patrol. Lightning doesn't care if you're a daemon or not. It will fry you just the same."

The sound of hooves thumping into the turf signaled the arrival of his fellows. The Riders lifted saddlebags off their mounts and found places to stow the saddles.

Eric put his hands on his hips, staring into the woods. The wind blew rain across his vision. He watched the heavy, dark stormclouds, gauging their path.

It looks like the worse of it will bypass us, he mused.

Oddly enough, he didn't feel tired. Rather, the quiet peacefulness of the glade set his mind at ease.

"Do you feel anything about this forest, Andyn?" he asked.

She placed a bare hand on a nearby tree trunk and closed her eyes. She smiled. "Only peace and life and beauty, probably more than I've detected in a while. We are in a good place."

He sighed. "Well, I'll scout around anyway. Connor, want to take the north arc?"

The Halfling nodded. "Shouldn't take long."

Despite the evident tranquility, Eric kept his bow at the ready just in case, an arrow in his other hand. He and the Riders had fallen afoul of enough Ja'al plots and ambushes to make him wary.

He examined the ground for tracks, sniffed the air for anything amiss, and paused at intervals, listening intently. Only the sights, sounds and smells of a normal, rainy forest returned to him.

Unbidden, images of Brandi came to mind. He would have thought they would make him melancholy, but he remembered their time together in Forester while hunting down the Ja'al and solving the mystery of the pegasi of Whitehorse Peak. He smiled, remembering the shine of the sun in her red-gold hair.

It took me a little while to see it, but she and I really are soulmates…

The wood opened up into a meadow with a suddenness that made him halt, startled. The rain petered out and stopped altogether.

A white structure of some kind gleamed on the opposite side. He scanned about for signs of danger and even tried a magic spell to detect hidden enemies, but nothing happened.

His brow furrowed. The structure looked like a human figure of some kind, like a statue. A metal plate glinted dully against the green lawn. Intrigued, he advanced.

As he came within ten feet of it, his jaw dropped. It was indeed a statue, pristine and clean despite the bushes, vines and grasses growing in profusion nearby. A woman in a flowing robe stood barefoot on a hemisphere, mournful eyes looking heavenward, tears streaking her face. She held a circular crown of thorns to her breast. A halo of purest white stone surrounded her head. A cube of white marble sat before the statue and a plate of some odd metal lay next to it.

Eric froze. It looked like…

"Mary, Mother of Sorrows…" he whispered.

His eyes drifted to the plate. It looked to be made of a bluish silver metal with some symbols etched into it. Unlike the statue, this had seen the ravages of time, as the symbols had apparently been patterned with some kind of white enamel or paint that had worn off.

He slipped the arrow back into his case and looped the bow over his back. He regarded the statue again. What is this doing here, out in the wilderness? And why hasn't the forest overtaken it?

A chill of both trepidation and wonder ran down his spine. He crossed himself.

Mother Mary, if this really is a sign, please guide us…

He inspected the statue without touching. It was life-sized, as the woman would have been about Brandi's height if standing on the forest floor and not on the ivory globe. The detail amazed him: the folds of her cloth looked real and he half expected her to wipe a tear from her cheek.

He knelt by the plate. The symbols were in Humana, but they spelled out something that baffled him.

"T.A.S. Natividad," he read slowly.

What, or who, is Natividad? And what does TAS stand for?

He stood, looking at the statue of the Queen of Heaven for a long time, then headed back to the campsite.

The Riders turned at his approach. Connor smiled. "All clear to the north."

"Come with me," he said in a distracted voice.

"Eric?" Andyn asked, her voice concerned. "Is something wrong?"

He shook his head, mind still grappling with what he had just seen. "No, nothing's wrong. Everything is… well, you just have to see it."

He turned to go. Dar drew Rindara as they others filed after him. He didn't speak the whole time but his mind whirred.

Who had put a statue of Saint Mary out here, so far from any civilization? What was the meaning of the silvery plate? And what was in the white marble box?

At the meadow, he led them across. The Riders silently joined him at the statue.

"Who is that?" Connor asked. "She looks very sad."

Dar nodded. "It's a statue of Saint Mary, Mother of Christ. It depicts her just after they took her Son down from the cross, after they tortured Him to death."

Andyn gasped. "How heartbreaking. What is that she's holding?"

"A Crown of Thorns," Eric answered. "The ones who executed him fashioned it as a mockery of his claim to be the Son of God, then jammed it on his head."

Khyron's jaw worked and he nodded. "And they killed him in sight of her?"

Dar nodded. "She saw it all."

Buck grunted. "Bastards. No wonder she's crying."

"Why is there a statue here?" Connor asked. "Was there one of your temples nearby?"

Eric spread his hands. "No. That's what makes no sense. And even if it was here only a year or so, the plants of the forest would have overgrown it at the very least. This is the Wilderness after all."

"What should we do?" asked Khyron. "If it's a shrine of your religion, we shouldn't disturb it."

Eric shook his head. "Saint Mary wouldn't mind if we lingered. As a matter of fact, she'd probably like it if we camped here. Besides, the rain is ending and we need a rest."

Buck shrugged. "If you say so. It's your religion. Connor and I can go back and get the pegasi and bring all our gear, if everyone is okay with that."

Eric nodded. Dar slipped up next to him as they departed. Andyn and Khyron strolled around the statue, examining the woods nearby.

"Did you see the plate?" Dar whispered.

"Yes. Do you know what it means?"

"No. I was hoping that you would, Mister Son-of-the-Famous-Wizard."

"Melinor never mentioned anything like this. I'll put it in my pack and bring it back to him, though."

"What about the box?"

Eric shook his head. "Didn't have time to examine it. Want to take a look?"

"Dar! Eric! Come quick!"

They darted around the statue to the other side where Khyron and Andyn knelt in the grass.

"What is it? What —" Eric's question died on his lips as he saw what they examined.

"Is that what I think it is?" Dar asked.

Andyn nodded. "A Coronam Ex Spinis. A Crown of Thorns plant from Celestia."

The Riders stared at it. The main stem of the plant rose up out of the ground a couple of finger-widths, then curled around in a circle before winding back to the center, above the roots. At that point, the stem rose upward, ending in a single bud about the size of a fig. Short thorns and bright green, trefoil leaves grew all along the stem, except where it rose up to meet the flower. The entire plant was small, not more than a hand-span in diameter.

"Megan mentioned one of these," Dar said, squatting down. "It could do incredible things."

"Yes, like disintegrate a Hell Wisp," Eric noted dryly. "Too bad we didn't find it earlier."

Khyron stood. "Well, if it's connected to this Mary person, we should probably leave it. She might be offended."

Dar shook his head. "If it's here, there's a reason. Pick it up, Andyn."

"I'm not sure I should."

"Go ahead," Eric agreed. "The worst that will happen is that it stays."

Andyn gently encircled the stem with her hands and pulled. The plant came free of the earth so easily that Eric wondered how firmly it had been rooted. A large ball of earth came with it.

Khyron produced a leather bag and Andyn deposited the plant inside, then laid it in her backpack.

Andyn's eyes flicked to Eric. "Me again? Your Christian saints seem to have an affinity for me."

He grinned back. "They know a kindred spirit when they see one."

Khyron elbowed Andyn. "Excellent! I'm marrying a friend of Christian holy women."

She hid a smile and stood. "Let see to the camp."

Buck and Connor returned with the pegasi moments later and Eric explained about the Crown-of-Thorns. Connor insisted on taking a look and declared himself impressed.

"How a plant from Celestia made it here, I'll never guess," he commented as Andyn replaced it in her bag.

"You have a lot of company in that," said Dar. "Eric, let's get the plate and look at the box."

Eric knelt with Dar by the box. They peered at it.

It appeared to be crafted entirely of white marble shot through with grey. One cross was etched into the exact center of each face.

"I wonder how you open it," Dar muttered.

"Say please," Connor called over his shoulder. Buck snickered.

"Yeah. Right. Please open the box," Dar said wryly.

To their astonishment, the top of the box sprang up, revealing hinges.

Eric and Dar exchanged a look. The other Riders gaped at them.

"Well, that's creepy," offered Khyron.

"I'm not so sure about this," Dar said. "If my dream felt like the Song of the Grey Riders all over again, then this..."

"I don't like it," Buck said, shaking his head. "Once again, we're being led by the nose along some path we can't see."

Eric lifted the lid. "Yes, but that ended well — for the most part." He peered inside.

A single crystal vial lay on a cushion of purple velvet. Eric lifted it out. It contained a piece of thin, sharp wood. Like the box, there were two simple crosses etched into the vial, one opposite the other.

Eric sat on the moist earth, frowning.

Connor peered at it. "Is it from another Crown of Thorns plant? It sure looks like a thorn."

Eric shrugged. "I can't tell. The light's not really good."

He handed the vial to Dar, who turned it over in his fingers. "Well," Dar noted, "It has a mechanical stopper with a rubber seal, so it's been protected from the elements. Andyn, can you detect anything?"

Andyn joined them, taking the vial. She focused her gaze on it intently and her eyes flashed blue for a second.

She shrugged, handing it back. "Nothing magical at all. Is it something significant to Christians?"

"Well," Eric mused, "Christ was crucified on a wooden cross, and he had a crown of thorns, but if this was anything like that, it would be an extremely holy relic. It would be kept in a very secure location, with all kinds of guards and protections, not sitting out in the middle of the Wilderness in a forgotten glade. I'm convinced this something else."

"Maybe something for a special ceremony?" Andyn asked.

"Your guess is as good as mine." Eric carefully wrapped the vial in a bandage.

Dar put it into his backpack and slipped the plate with the mysterious writing into a sack that joined the vial. "We can ask Father Thomas about it when we get back. Let's set up camp."

Eric rose. "Who's the chef tonight?"

Andyn smiled beatifically. "We're in luck. It's Dar."

Connor rubbed his hands together. "Bless Irial's Name. I don't want to poison anyone again."

"It wasn't that bad," Khyron chuckled, piling wood for a fire. "I've had worse in the Army."

"Really?" Buck raised an eyebrow. "Who was the cook?"

Khyron grinned. "Me."

They had a good laugh over that. The fire burned merrily and produced little smoke. The rainstorm passed swiftly miles away, Dar's meal was particularly good, and the Riders relaxed for the first time in days.

They set up watches and Eric reclined against his saddle, watching the stars overhead.

There they are. One of them is the sun for the world of Celestia. But we need a gate made of stars, whatever that means, and we need it fast. Even when we get to the Titan's Crown, will we even know what to look for? How are we supposed to find it?

The firelight flickered. Mary, Mother of Sorrows, gazed up to heaven with him as if seeking the same answer.

Eric sighed, using his pack for a pillow. The stars remained remote and silent in his mind's eye as he drifted off to sleep.

Chapter Twenty-Four – The Baton Is Passed

Well?" Adina put her hands on her hips, eyebrow arched. She sauntered into Golvadu's command tent.

"Well what?" Golvadu growled`, pouring himself a tumbler of Dwarven bitters. He hated the taste, really, but it always cleared his head. He downed it in one gulp.

Adina fell backwards on a couch, knocking off a couple of silk pillows. "What did His Majesty Torvu say?"

"He needed to confer with Queen Arachnia and King Selaan."

"What for?" Adina yanked another pillow from under her back and flung it on the rug. "We have more than enough to start the attack."

Golvadu snatched the pillows and rearranged them neatly on another couch. "That is *not* our decision," he snapped.

He stalked to the clawed table and tapped the top surface. A three-dimensional image of Oakmoor and its environs leaped up, complete with animated soaring dragons and fluttering pennants.

He gestured at the image and deep purple lights glowed to the east of the city. "There are three reasons to delay. First, this Papal Nuncio has proven to be an unknown quantity. Second, an all-out assault at this stage would not be productive. Our probing attacks have shown that the defenders have enough countermeasures to make it very costly. Their Majesties believe, as I do, that if the city is surrounded and we apply gradual pressure, we can weaken them to the point where the Outer City can be won easily."

"And third?"

"Your paramour, Berek, arrives tomorrow. The Deranese will have to split their attention to both the eastern and western fronts. I firmly believe the order will be given when Arachnia and Selaan arrive."

Her frown remained. "I still don't see why we don't start wearing them down now. Despite our probable losses, they're only Kaftu and Goblins and Ogres and Dark Elves, after all. It's not like we'd be losing the Nightshade Guard or anything."

He looked at her sidelong. "While you might not count the lives of our allies to be worth much, they and their leaders do. And they expect a sizeable reward in exchange for the risk. Without the prospect of riches, the less… devoted members of the Dark Wave may harbor second thoughts."

She shrugged.

"We would have to use a carefully timed, combined attack with artillery, air cavalry, elite units and support troops," he continued. "Our ground cavalry will be of limited effectiveness in the streets and boulevards of Oakmoor. No, Lady Adina, we want to reduce the morale of the defenders, and if they repel an attack, it would only rise. Their spirits are already high enough after the incident with the Christian priest."

She joined him at the diorama. "Speaking of which, has anyone seen him lately?"

Golvadu shook his head, eyes flitting all over the map. He knew there was a weakness — there always was — but it had eluded him so far. No matter. He would find a way to emerge in a position of strength.

Adina touched an image of one of the towers with an elegant finger. "I understand that he was somewhat the worse for wear afterwards."

"What of it? I doubt seriously that he died. For all their idiotic triumphalism, the Christians and their allies are competent healers. I am quite sure that he is in there, waiting."

Adina said nothing.

Golvadu waved at the image and the forces of the Dark Wave moved in a simulated invasion. "No, Lady Adina, we have no need for haste. Their resources, while impressive, are not infinite. They are housing many refugees and noncombatants whom they want to protect at all costs. We will soon have them surrounded. Then the hammer will fall. They will be out of time."

A miniature battle raged in the three-dimensional image and Golvadu brought the eastern army into the mix. Soon, Ja'al forces gained the Inner City.

He smiled and tapped the tallest church, watching with satisfaction as it burst into illusionary flame and collapsed in a cloud of embers. "We will have our vengeance."

***

"Soon," Queen Ahlana announced.

Saren gazed soberly at the hologram of Oakmoor and its defenders and the invaders hovering in mid-air over the tabletop. Even though she had seen the enemy in real life, the illusionary depiction made it look even more like a dark wave of evil.

Melinor nodded, fingers steepled before his face. The other councilors remained silent, intent on the image. Magical lamplight glowed on the polished tabletop and the smooth marble walls.

"You are certain, Majesty?" asked Terenil.

"With the arrival of their eastern army, they will have more than four hundred thousand at their disposal, maybe more. Our resources can only last a few weeks, what with all the refugees in the city. We have at most seventy-five thousand troops at arms — a sizeable number, agreed, but even defending a fortified city it will not be enough. There are too many Fallen Ones. With an overwhelming horde now assembled, they will not wait."

Father Thomas spoke up. "Our spies have confirmed that the Torosc Second Archon, Golvadu Fellhammer, is with them. He has a great incentive to prove to the other Archons that he can get things done. And don't forget that Saren's grandfather is singularly focused on getting her to turn."

Saren controlled a flash of anger. Her eyes narrowed. "As if that would ever happen."

Terenil pointed at the enemy vanguard. "They have massed many of their most powerful units, probably to try to overwhelm Father Thomas, should he appear again."

The Queen nodded. "That has the added effect of making us divert a lot of our forces to that location, leaving other sectors vulnerable." She pressed her lips together and planted her palms down on the tabletop, brow furrowed.

They're waiting for something. But what? Saren wondered.

A sudden fear struck her and she shot a glance at Melinor. "Do you think they've found the Grey Riders?"

Melinor shook his head. "No. If they had already captured or killed them, Torvu — or Tarvener, at the very least — would not have hesitated to mention it. The impact on our morale would have been too valuable to pass up. No, I am convinced that they know little about the Grey Riders other than that they might be in search of the Gate of Stars."

To Saren, it sounded like he was trying to convince himself; after all, even without the Ja'al, the journey was perilous, through uncharted, wild lands filled with unknown dangers. Any number of disasters could have taken their lives already...

She clenched her fists under the table. *They are on their way,* she repeated to herself. *They have to be on their way. If Eric were dead, I would feel it...*

"Nevertheless," King Phillip continued, "with the arrival of the Dark Wave from the east, our position becomes more tenuous. We will have to divide our attention between two very potent attacking forces. And although we have an ace in the hole, as it were, Father Thomas can't be in two places at once... and he's hardly indestructible."

Despite the grim scenario, his eyes twinkled when they alighted on the Nuncio.

Father Thomas smiled back. "I, of all people, will readily acknowledge that. But His Majesty is right. We need a counter."

Saren stared at the image of the city.

"But what?" asked the Queen. "If you remain in one location to keep an eye on Torvu, that leaves us open elsewhere if Selaan and Arachnia show up, as they inevitably will. We had the element of surprise the first time; it won't work again."

Saren's mind spun back to the images of the people in the city: the grim defenders, nervous and frightened civilians, worried officials. She remembered the tally sheets of their supplies and resources. The numbers seemed far too small.

If the Dark Wave gets into the Inner City, or even Outer Oakmoor, they're done for…

"We could try for a pre-emptive strike," Terenil offered. "The military council drew up several scenarios using high-ranking freelancers to strike down elements of the Ja'al leadership. While we doubt if we could cause much trouble for the Hadean gods, we could take out some of the higher-ranking Ja'al leaders, like Adina Tenspire or Berek Lordwain. At the least, it would sow confusion and divert their attention and energies elsewhere."

An animated discussion ensued between the various councilors. Saren only listened with half an ear. A recent memory came into sharp focus: a small, frightened girl struggling to carry a bucket of water, following her two older brothers lugging bracing beams to one of the gates of the Inner City. She still remembered the expression on the girl's face.

"I will do it," Saren said.

Conversation ceased.

"I beg your pardon?" Melinor asked.

Saren locked eyes with Father Thomas. "I will be the counterweight on the other side of the city. His Eminence knows what I mean."

The Nuncio nodded slowly. The others exchanged puzzled looks.

"Saren, what are you talking about?" Terenil asked. He took her hand.

She took a deep breath and gave his hand a squeeze. "The Crown of Saint Alyssa. Father Thomas offered it to me. I accepted, but have not determined the right time to use it. Now is the time."

Queen Ahlana sat back in her chair. "So, the Saint has chosen a successor."

"Wait," Terenil protested. "Saren, we're in a strong position here. And the Crown is not to be used lightly. It drained Andyn Eleandir to exhaustion at the First Battle of Hillton and she nearly had a nervous breakdown when she realized she wasn't able to save everyone."

"I'm not using it lightly, Terenil. Remember the Second Battle of Hillton. Our strategy worked there and will work again."

"Berek will be waiting for it."

She gave a little smirk. "I won't be facing Berek, or the Battle Lords in the east. I'll be in the west."

"No, Saren! Torvu will know by now —"

"Tren!" she said more sharply than she intended. "He might know what

I can do but he has no idea of the power of the relic!"

Terenil's expression darkened and she kissed his hand. "I'm sorry dearest. I didn't mean to bark at you. Just know that Torvu and his command have never had to deal with the holy relic of a saint."

He hesitated and she gazed intently into his eyes. "The overwhelming advantage of the Dark Wave are the Fallen Ones. If it were merely an army of Dark Elves and Skullhead Legionaries, we wouldn't be in this situation. I can disrupt their cohesion and cause turmoil. It will buy time for the Riders."

Terenil's brow remained furrowed and his eyes flashed. "This isn't the same thing! You had Melissa and Simon there with you at Hillton. They aren't here. They went to Madrigal for the… other project."

Saren felt a pang of apprehension. She missed the presence of the two Elohir, yet she knew why they had departed: a very special assignment to protect something of great importance – a potential backup to the mission of the Grey Riders.

I hope we never have to find out if it will work… Lord, please help Eric and the Riders succeed.

"That's why I have to do it," she said. "Without them here, we need someone else to take up the slack. And the time is now, when all the Hadean gods are in one place. Not only will it throw their forces into confusion but it will boost our own morale."

He didn't look convinced.

"Lady Saren is right," King Phillip announced, rising from the table. "Without the Elohir, we need something else to make the Dark Wave think twice. With the Crown, she will do it."

She kissed Terenil's hand and raised her eyes to the Council. "I'll need some help, though."

Melinor smiled and stood. "And you shall have it."

***

Damn it to Hell, Golvadu groused. *Now I have to deal with all three of them.*

Arachnia, Selaan and Torvu lounged on couches of alabaster and gold on the outer portico of his personal pavilion, chatting away and sampling delicacies from silver platters. Occasionally, Selaan would transform into a particularly hideous monstrosity and menace the orderlies, to the amusement of the other two Hadean monarchs.

It's almost enough to make me wish that we would lose and they would go back to Hades…

He raised his eyes to the glittering city before him.

Almost. But I have a score to settle with you, Melinor…

He squared his shoulders. "Your Majesties," he announced with a bow. "All is in readiness. The Dark Wave awaits your command."

Selaan switched from the shape of a gorilla with pincer arms, a goat's head and serpentine tail to a more normal form of a tall human with pale skin and black eyes.

"Ah, yes!" He spun in a circle, knocking a platter to the floor and scattering food on the Gorostoli rug. "Time to chop people into bits!"

He sketched an exaggerated bow to the other two gods. "I must away, per our earlier agreement, to lead the attack on the Eastern front."

Torvu and Arachnia arose and bowed in response. Selaan's form rippled and he now stood two feet taller, heroically muscled. He snapped his fingers and an iron-bound chest of black wood glittered into being before him. With another finger snap, the top popped open.

Selaan held out his arms to the side and black-and-red enameled plate mail shot up out of the chest, settling into place on his body. A greatsword flew to one hand and a helmet decorated with a leering visage shot out to the other.

"Let's see what the Christian chief priest makes of this," he declared, "If he even dares to oppose me." He settled the helmet on his head. "I will see Your Majesties in the Inner City."

Torvu inclined his head, eyes hooded. "We are counting on it, Majesty."

Selaan swept out of the pavilion without a backward glance, mounted a waiting red-orange Dragon outside, and soared off.

What an idiot, Golvadu mused. He schooled his features to neutrality.

Another figure entered the pavilion.

"Ah, Prince Tarvener," said Arachnia. "We understand that your granddaughter is now in the city. I am most anxious to meet her."

"As am I," Tarvener replied. "We have a lot to discuss about the folly of her error."

"Just make sure she doesn't perish too soon."

Tarvener bowed. "That is foremost in my mind as well, Majesty."

"Let's get to it," Torvu growled. He settled his weapons on his hips and held out his arm for Arachnia. She took it and they promenaded outside.

Golvadu followed at a discreet distance. The military, at least, would follow orders to the letter, even if Selaan descended into self-aggrandizing theatrics.

Golvadu would wait for his chance. It would come, Hadean gods or no.

***

"Bear this crown with faith, hope and charity," Father Thomas intoned, his voice echoing in the transept of the church. "Be faithful and stalwart against evil."

Saren knelt before him. She kept her eyes closed, praying with all her might, stomach in knots.

"Take courage, for the battle is the Lord's," he continued, "and remember that vengeance also belongs to Him. Saren Elizabeth DeMey, do you accept this charge as the Lord's Champion?"

"I do."

"Then I transfer the Crown of Saint Alyssa to your keeping, until such time as you surrender it."

The weight of the crown settled on her head. Saren was surprised at how light it seemed. She stood and smiled at Father Thomas, Sister Karen, Melinor and Terenil. Her husband gave her a wink.

All her apprehension vanished. A warm, peaceful presence filled the area and she sighed with relief.

Everything is going to be alright.

"Greetings, sister," echoed a voice in her head.

Saren blinked. To her amazement, the others stood frozen. Even the candleflames held still as if in a painting.

"Uh… hello. I… I am Saren," she replied.

"I know."

A woman appeared before her. She wore a simple white robe with a silver belt. Red-gold hair cascaded waves onto her shoulders and pale grey eyes looked on Saren kindly.

"You're Saint Alyssa!"

Alyssa nodded. Saren knelt.

"Now, now," Alyssa clucked her tongue, lifting Saren's chin and raising her to her feet. "None of that. I am not a queen any longer. I am simply Alyssa."

Saren's eyes shot to the others in the room. "Why can't they move?"

"Time flows at a different pace for you and me. When we are done with our conversation, it will be restored as if nothing has happened."

"Thank you for coming to see me," Saren managed. *Oh Lord, that was lame…*

Alyssa smiled. "And thank you for taking on this task. As I did for your friend Andyn, I am here to instruct you in the proper use of the Crown. We can't have you running around without a tutorial, can we?"

Saren relaxed and smiled back. Her awe and apprehension evaporated.

"Certainly not," she replied. "And I wouldn't want a bad grade."

The saint laughed. The world seemed bright and clean and fresh, like waking up on a clear spring day.

"Well said, Saren Elizabeth! Now, if you will permit me, I will explain a few features that will help immensely…"

Chapter Twenty-Five – How to Use a Holy Relic

H ere they come!" Terenil shouted above the thump of artillery and crackle of magic spells. A crossbow bolt whined past his head and cracked against the wall.

"We are ready, milord," replied a captain at his side. A red-glowing ballista bolt struck the city wall just below them. A ball of flame exploded, curling around the screen of magical protections on the stone surface. Just to the north of them, other bolts struck and the magical screen flickered and died. More missiles blasted chunks of stone out of the wall.

Far below, the Dark Wave seethed and surged. Drums rolled and horns blared, accompanied by chanting in some unknown language. Siege towers rolled towards them and troops marched in orderly ranks, carrying scaling ladders. Curbolgs, Bone Knights, Shock Hind, Blood Satyrs and Deathmists prowled among them. Airborne daemons soared and swooped overhead alongside evil dragons, swirling in dogfights with Iron Thunder, his allies and the defending air cavalry.

Arrows, magic spells and counter-fire artillery slashed into the enemy force, dropping dozens, but they didn't even slow. Occasionally, a hippogriff, pegasus or daemon spiraled down, trailing smoke, to thump into the ground with a sickening crunch.

Terenil gritted his teeth. "Hold this position, Captain. You know what to do."

"Yes sir."

Terenil trotted along the wall, heading towards a bridge that led from the outer wall to towers in the Outer City. He passed troops hidden under tarpaulins, holding nets and ropes with grappling hooks. At one tower, an officer of his company met him.

"All is ready, milord."

"Good. Are the freelance mercenaries in position?"

"Yes sir. They know what to watch for."

"Excellent." He pounded up the stairs to the rooftop, where a squad of his personal guard stood next to Melinor.

"I thought you would be on the other side of the main gate," Terenil noted.

Melinor shrugged. "This is close enough that I can be on the move in case the Hadean monarchs choose to get involved."

"Start preparations," Terenil told his officer. His guards began layering protective spells on themselves. Soon, their armor, shields and weapons glittered as if covered by dew in the morning sun. Terenil followed suit, applying protections against fire, poison, and evil magic.

"How's our air cover?" Melinor asked, looking up at the battle in the skies.

"Holding their own for now." Terenil hefted his shield onto his arm. "The Ja'al can't land any airborne troops in the city without getting carved to pieces. As long as Iron Thunder and the air force hold on, a frontal assault on the walls is the enemy's best option. Where's Father Thomas?"

"Gone to the East Gate. Our scouts reported Selaan heading that way."

The clash of battle intensified and some of the daemons disengaged from their airborne foes long enough to make strafing attacks at the troops on the walls.

Terenil watched the defenders, pride swelling in his chest. Despite losing comrades left and right and faced with overwhelming odds and otherworldly assailants, the soldiers and their accompanying wizards and priests fought back with discipline and skill. Daemons alighted on the walls, laying about them savagely. They were soon forced to retreat under withering counterattacks or died where they stood, exploding in flames.

"There she is, milord!" called his officer, pointing to the main boulevard leading to the West Gate.

Despite knowing what he would probably see, Terenil froze. Time stood still.

His wife strode down the boulevard, unhurried, in her natural form, wearing plate armor of an ancient design embossed with a crucifix on the front chestplate. The Crown of Saint Alyssa sat on her night-black tresses and glowed like full daylight. A similar nimbus covered Saren. Her ivory bat wings gleamed snow white, as did her small horns.

However, his heartbeat accelerated when he beheld her eyes: they were made of light themselves.

As she passed in the street, people stopped and stared. Some fell to their knees, lips moving in prayer. At the main gate, Saren drew a sword and dagger and leaped into the air.

As soon as she soared over the gate, in full view of the Dark Wave, all fighting slackened and ceased. Soldiers stared, open-mouthed. A few attacking Skreets shrieked and flew backwards, retreating towards their lines.

Saren's voice rang out, clear and strong and full of power. "Behold, servants of the Dark One! I am named Saren, a half-daemon, yet I serve the God the Father, his Son Jesus the Christ and the Holy Ghost!"

I bet people on the opposite side of Oakmoor can hear her…

A slow smile crept over Terenil's face, watching the enemy invaders. Fighting slackened. To a soldier and Fallen One, they froze, transfixed by the woman at the gate.

"Be not deceived by appearances," she continued, voice echoing over the battlefield. "Salvation is available to all whose hearts sincerely seek the Lord. But to those who persist in their pride and evil: beware!"

A shriek of fury answered her from the enemy lines. "How dare you!"

Arachnia marched to the front of the Ja'al lines, clad in a sheer gown of deep green and accompanied by Torvu. She glared at Saren. A cloud of green fog churned around her, swirling with figures of giant scorpions, spiders and cobras. She levitated into the air. Two Deathmists, a pair of tiger-daemons and a Battle Lord followed in her wake. Torvu gestured and his boots flared with red light, lifting him up next to Arachnia.

"What gives you the right to spout such blasphemies to my servants?" she announced.

Saren smiled. "God gives me the right, Queen Arachnia."

Terenil watched the daemons nearest the Hadean royalty. Some gripped their weapons tightly, eyes flitting back and forth, looking uncertain. Others glared with undisguised hatred. Still others sneered and snickered to each other.

Good. Anything to break up their cohesion…

"Your god isn't here," Torvu smirked. "You are alone. Soon, you will be dead."

Saren shook her head. "I am never alone. I am living proof that daemons need not serve the Dark One and that we also can repent."

Torvu laughed. "As if we need the mercy of your imaginary god."

Arachnia gestured to the enemy horde. "Then I offer you the same courtesy to repent," Arachnia sneered, "Look upon your grandsire. Prince Tarvener, I believe we have found your errant offspring."

Another daemon with the lower parts of a goat and upper parts of a man strode out of the crowd. "Greetings, granddaughter," he said, lips curving in a gentle smile. Black wings unfurled behind him and he flew up to join the other daemons.

Even if Torvu had not announced him, Terenil would have instantly known that the daemon prince and Saren were related. He had the same dark hair and dark eyes and his handsome facial features were the masculine mirror of her loveliness. He even moved with the same grace, despite his otherworldly physique.

Saren inclined her head. "Grandfather."

"I am impressed," he stated. "You have obviously made the most of your skills and talents. I am sorry you were not here earlier, but I have an offer for you."

"And that is?"

"Claim your full birthright as my descendant. Lay aside your allegiance to these puny beings and claim what is rightfully yours."

Saren shook her head. "I have a family and husband here. I will not leave them, no matter what legacy is offered me."

Tarvener scoffed and waved a hand. "Husband and family? Mere trifles compared to what awaits you. You can have as many husbands and wives and lovers as you like, and riches beyond counting. As my granddaughter, you would command legions and they would obey without question. You will have your heart's desire."

Saren lifted her chin. "I repeat what I said to Verdinon, your assassin, when he came to collect me years ago. Riches I do not want. I have true love, not mere lust. I wish to serve others and make their lives better, not lord it over them. As for my heart's desire, I want to go to Heaven when I die."

Tarvener's eyes flashed. "There is no such place!"

Saren gave him a long look. "That's what Verdinon said."

She turned her face away from him and addressed the daemons. "You can become like me and follow the pathway to salvation. But be warned: if you do not, the Day of Wrath is at hand!"

"Says who?" retorted a Battle Lord.

"Says the God I serve! Repent! *Dies Irae Venit!*" Saren clashed her sword and dagger against each other. The sound echoed over the city. The Crown of Saint Alyssa flashed silvery blue. Triple concentric rings of translucent, golden symbols leapt into being around her, surrounding her in a whirling nimbus of light.

With screams of rage, the Fallen Ones took wing. Saren saluted them with her blades and zipped up into the sky. Tiger daemons, War Fiends, Deathhammers, Skreets, and Dwerrolves soared after her in a dark swarm.

"No!" shrieked Arachnia. "Don't chase her! Return to your posts!"

The daemons raced on, unheeding.

Torvu gestured to several nearby Battle Lords. "Bring them back, you maggots," he bellowed, "or I'll paper the walls of my castle with your miserable hides!"

"And you!" Arachnia spat at Tarvener. "Bring your bitch to heel!"

With a growled curse, Tarvener joined the Battle Lords in soaring after the enraged daemon horde.

Terenil set an arrow to his bow — an arrow with a red-glittering head. Saren darted up into the air, heading for the clouds at the speed of a pegasus. When she was a tiny glowing dot, she looped around and plummeted downwards. The daemons pursued, but the slower ones became entangled with their quicker fellows. Knots of struggling figures formed, then broke apart.

Saren's pursuers blasted a hailstorm of magic spells at her: acid darts, fire balls, lightning bolts, spears of ice, and dark energy beams. The concentric rings of light swiveled around her and the magic detonated or fizzled out on contact. She swooped low over the wooded plains, then soared straight up. A series of bright, sparkling stars glittered in her wake. When the daemon horde passed by them, the stars detonated in bright flashes of light. Fallen Ones exploded, whirled out of the way, or spiraled earthward, trailing flames and smoke.

She banked, turned, then looped back over the city, following the curve of the walls.

Wait for it…

His wife shot past overhead.

Terenil loosed his arrow, not at the daemons, but at the sky. It exploded in a shimmering blast of blue and red. The hidden troops leaped into action.

The daemon squadrons, pursuing at full speed, didn't see the nets and grappling hooks until too late. Their wings ensnared, they slammed into the walls and towers and detonated in fiery, bloody explosions. Some, hooked by the grapnels, swung around off course, screaming until they, too, smashed into nearby structures and burned. Soldiers and mercenaries leaped up from cover and swung halberds and battle-axes, chopping daemons in half as they shot past. Spells from hidden mages and priests shredded ensnared Fallen Ones.

Three War Fiends and a Deathhammer avoided entanglement and veered towards Terenil's tower. Melinor released a storm of fire darts with one hand while a five-forked bolt of lightning blasted out from his staff. Two of the War Fiends detonated and died. The remaining one and the Deathhammer landed on the tower, swinging fiery weapons. Terenil and his guard surrounded them, shields up and glowing with magical light. The daemons fought savagely, but soon bled from multiple wounds, their wings hacked off. As one, Terenil and his guard bull-rushed them, hurling them from the tower to slam into the street below in thunderous explosions.

Riddled with arrows or lanced with spells, Fallen Ones burst asunder in clouds of flame. Saren climbed again, heading for the clouds. Still, the mass of daemons pursued. Battle Lords chased their raging troops, but the daemons paid them no heed. With ringing curses, Arachnia and Torvu leaped into the air, heading towards the angry daemon mob.

The tramp of many boots and jangle of harness drew Terenil's eyes down to the thoroughfares below. King Phillip and Queen Ahlana rode at the head of a massive column of cavalry and infantry, leading humans, elves and Dwarves alike. Terenil even spotted Halfling cavalrymen riding armored centaurs. At the West Gate, the King clashed his swords together and the massive portals opened.

Trumpets blared. With a resounding shout that echoed off the city walls, the sally force charged out the gate.

The Ja'al attackers at the gates surged to meet them but the King's force slammed into them like a tidal wave. The monarchs shone like twin suns. Enemy warriors fell before them like wheat before a harvester's sickle. In their wake, their troops carved a bloody path through the attackers.

Trolls and ogres lumbered forward, accompanied by Skullhead Legionary cavalry, but the momentum of the charge drove them back. A Dwarf riding a red-striped Balar shouted orders in a magically enhanced voice. He loosed dark arrows and lightning at Phillip and Ahlana. The counterattack slowed as the monarchs hunkered down behind magical screens to withstand the onslaught. Oakmoor defenders dropped from the collateral damage.

"How far are they going?" Terenil asked, concerned. "They can't drive off the whole force."

"Only far enough," Melinor replied. "They want the artillery."

As they watched, wizards in the center of the sally force launched fireballs and acid bolts, not at the enemy troops, but at the siege machinery. Towers burst into flame, ballistae collapsed and catapults toppled over.

Ja'al support units converged on the sally force in massive surging waves, but the carnage at the gate and their own forces got in the way. With their own siege artillery out of commission, they slowed under the pummeling from Oakmoor city ballistae and catapults. Golvadu rained spells at the Deranese and his mount breathed streams of frost and ice, but the defenders on the walls concentrated fire at him. Cursing roundly, he retreated out of range.

Another series of trumpet notes rang out and the Deranese reformed into a fighting retreat, with the King and Queen at the rear guard. Light flashed with every swing of the King's swords. Enemies flew away from the Queen as if jerked by some giant hand and enemy spells exploded on her shields. The Ja'al pressed forward, seeking to bring them down, but the defenders on the walls poured down a withering stream of magic, arrows and spears, dropping many. Though some invaders managed to get inside the city before the Gate slammed shut again, these were quickly slain.

Melinor let out a deep breath. "So far so good. Now we have to make sure we recover your wife."

Terenil lifted his eyes. The tiny glowing star of Saren streaked across the cloudy sky, now pursued directly by two dark blots and four distinct and more orderly daemon formations.

Gouts of flame, purple beams, forked lightning and glittering hailstones streamed out at Saren from Torvu and Arachnia. The rotating golden rings around Saren deflected them, but to Terenil it seemed like they were less brilliant.

He swallowed with difficulty and licked dry lips. *She can do this… the Crown will protect her.*

"Steady, my son," counseled Melinor.

Saren reversed course, cutting between two daemon flights. The Fallen Ones launched attacks at her, but she shot past and many of the fire darts, lava spikes and plasma beams sliced into daemon ranks instead. Now close enough for him to see, she flipped onto her back and raised her hands to heaven.

She sang. A series of beautiful notes echoed over the battlefield. Bright clouds of light formed in her wake and the daemons plowed right into them. The lead elements caught fire and spiraled down to slam into the plains. Saren's pursuers diverted and swooped aside.

How long can she keep this up?

As if in answer, she banked and headed back towards the city. Terenil cast a swirling magical light into the air to mark their position and she dove towards them.

"Prepare yourselves," he called to his troops. They saluted, lifting shields and swords to ready position.

"I hear you might need a little help," said Sister Karen, climbing the last few steps to the tower.

"What kept you?" Melinor asked.

"A Deathhammer who wouldn't take no for an answer. He's resting in pieces."

Saren alighted on the tower. Her chest heaved with exertion and, despite the sanctifying light surrounding her, she looked exhausted.

"Get ready for some company," she panted. "I think they're a little peeved."

Terenil put his arm around her and she rested her head on his shoulder. Her limbs trembled.

Torvu and Arachnia soared into range. The city defenders concentrated their fire on the Hadean gods, sending arrows, spells and artillery at them. However, this time, the daemon hordes moved in more disciplined fashion under the command of the Battle Lords. They returned counterfire and city defenders and siege engines began to fall.

"You think you're so smart!" sneered Arachnia. "Behold the might of Hades!"

She clapped her hands together and Torvu followed suit. A dark ball about the size of a grapefruit sprang into being, then darted over the walls at Terenil's tower. With a word from Torvu, the globe burst into a swirling black void, a whirlpool of darkness. Just like a whirlpool, it began sucking in anything within range. The air churned to storm force in seconds.

"Hold on!" ordered Melinor. He lifted his staff and began a spell.

Wood, bits of armor, spent arrows, cloaks, and other detritus of war hissed past them. Terenil braced his feet against the tower walls as the wind took on gale force.

Sister Karen laid her hand on Melinor's shoulder, closing her eyes and chanting with him. A sizzling blue sphere grew over them and expanded to cover the tower and nearby wall. Sweat broke out on Melinor's forehead and he gritted his teeth.

Arachnia broke out in wild laughter. The dead black vortex swept larger. Soldiers, mages and daemons alike clutched at anything solid, but the wind ripped them free to fall, screaming, into the whirling void.

"Enough!" Saren shouted, pulling away from Terenil.

Her eyes flashed brilliant silver and she tapped symbols in the rotating rings surrounding her. Melinor's shield of light tripled in size.

"*Fiat!*" She pointed and a sparkling bead of light shot out from her finger at the vortex. It impacted dead-center.

With a thunderous blast, the whirlpool of death exploded. The ramparts of walls and towers were sheared off and daemons simply vanished in mid-air. Defenders were hurled away from their positions. Chunks of stone crunched into the boulevards below or crushed enemy formations outside the walls.

Arachnia and Torvu wailed in rage as the explosion hurled them through the air. They slammed into their own brigades on the plain below, tumbling and bouncing, scattering their troops like children's toys.

Saren glared at them. "That was for Velucci and Degrance, you cowards!" she screamed.

Then she wavered unsteadily. Her eyes closed and Terenil caught her before she hit the stone floor. Her protective rings ceased their rotation and winked out. The radiant glow of the Crown diminished to a faint glimmer.

Melinor and Sister Karen leaned against the tower crenellations, gasping for breath.

"Saren?" Terenil imparted a healing spell into her, then a second one. Her eyelids fluttered and her breathing became stronger, but she didn't awaken. "What the hell was that thing?" he asked Sister Karen.

"A Nullity Globe," the nun responded, putting her hands on her knees and dropping her head. "It produces a tiny point of immense force in one location. The gravity of it sucks in everything within range until the mass exceeds the capacity of the singularity, at which point it explodes."

Terenil stared out at the wreckage of the outer wall, numb. "And what did Saren do?"

"She used some kind of Celestial magic to disrupt it and blow it up before it was ready, thank God. Who knows how big it could have become?"

"Why didn't the Hadeans use it before?" asked the commander of Terenil's guard. "They could have easily breached the walls."

Melinor pointed out at the enemy formations. "There's your answer."

Torvu and Arachnia slowly dragged themselves to their feet from a pile of wreckage and ruined bodies. Attendants tried to assist them, but they shoved them away with contemptuous shouts that Terenil could hear even from that distance. The Hadean gods limped away towards their pavilion.

Melinor's eyes glittered silver and took on a faraway look. "Yes. I don't think they can use that magic very often. They are both pale and weak. I can see their legs shaking just from the effort of walking."

"My guess is that they decided to use it now, when Saren was tired, to try to eliminate her," Sister Karen finished.

Terenil shuddered, trying not to imagine Saren being drawn into the Nullity to be crushed. He held her tighter.

Saren stirred in Terenil's arms and her eyes opened. She gazed out at the enemy force, now retreating from the walls in organized ranks.

"How are the King and Queen?" Terenil asked.

Melinor gestured down at the West Gate. "They are regrouping, but whole. The King had to use a bit of healing on Queen Ahlana. Golvadu really hammered her."

Terenil bit his lip. "We had better start rebuilding and repairing. This has bloodied them, but it will not stop them. If anything, it will make them more dangerous."

"But first," said Sister Karen, taking Terenil and Saren by the arms. "She needs to rest. And don't protest."

"Wasn't going to," Saren murmured, closing her eyes again.

***

Golvadu wished he was deaf, at least temporarily. The Hadean royalty were involved in a shouting match inside the command tent and he half-expected the walls to burst apart. He counted himself fortunate that he was in a side chamber, at any rate.

Damn it. Those fools are loud enough to wake the undead.

"Can I bring you something, milord?" asked an orderly.

"Some earmuffs," he groused. At the servant's quizzical look, he waved a hand. "Lich's Breath Whiskey, for now."

The flap to the side chamber blew open and Selaan stamped in, muttering obscenities. "Why did I ever let Neralia convince me it was a good idea to come here in the first place?" he screamed at the sky.

Golvadu couldn't resist a smirk. Selaan looked like he had been run through a wheat thresher: burned, bloodied, his armor hanging from him in pieces, limping.

He flopped down on a couch, a surly look on his face.

"Stop your bellyaching," snapped Arachnia. She hobbled into the tent and collapsed on another couch. Closing her eyes, she muttered spells and a pale yellow glow covered her body. "Heal and get your thoughts in order. We need to adjust our plans."

"Now there's a revelation!" Selaan snapped. He placed a hand on his injuries and purple light glowed.

Torvu thrust aside the tent flap and joined them, glowering. After an acid look at his fellow gods, he took a seat himself and began using his own healing spells.

"Your High Majesties," Golvadu bowed. "If you require anything, let me know."

"Some competence would be nice," grunted Torvu.

Golvadu maintained his bow for a few heartbeats, trying to think up an excuse to leave.

"Send for Prince Tarvener," Arachnia ordered. "We have a few pointed questions for him."

The servant returned with the brandy. Golvadu whispered for him to find Tarvener and took a chair at a nearby table.

He sipped the whiskey, formulating various scenarios in his brain. He hated to admit it, but so far, the siege of Oakmoor wasn't going exactly as planned. Certainly, they had their enemies bottled up, and it was only a matter of time before they broke through. However, it was more difficult and taking far longer than he had imagined.

"Prince Tarvener," announced a guard.

Saren DeMey's grandfather entered the tent and bowed deeply. He too, looked the worse for wear. A rapidly-healing scar across his forehead indicated that he had gotten the worst of an exchange with Saren.

"So," Arachnia said, standing. "Why didn't you tell us your granddaughter had access to some kind of Celestial weapon?"

Tarvener gritted his teeth. "I had no idea what it was. It looked like a magical piece of headgear to me. How she got it is anyone's guess."

Golvadu decided to score some points. "It's not a Celestial weapon. It's a Christian relic."

All eyes rotated to him. He shrugged.

"It's called the Crown of Saint Alyssa," he said, sipping his brandy. "One of the Grey Riders used it to destroy Zhinia Margoth last year."

"What's a Zhinia Margoth?" asked Selaan.

"Not what, who. She was a lich princess from the Paragon Age who we awoke in order to provide a diversion from our war plans. She tried to take out the King and Queen of Deran by luring them into a conflict. Her intention was to use a helm of teleportation keyed to herself to get close enough to them to kill them. Instead, one of the Grey Riders brought this Crown relic to the fight and destroyed her."

Torvu's brow furrowed. "This Grey Rider is a high-ranking wizard or something?"

"No. Just an average Veriani priestess. The Crown apparently… amplifies one's abilities by orders of magnitude. A shame, really. Margoth was a good distraction from the Skull Gates and the Dark Wave."

The Hadean gods exchanged looks.

"Is there a way to counteract this relic?" snapped Tarvener.

Golvadu schooled his features to academic disinterest. "None that we know of. We do know that if it's used too much for too long, it drains the bearer to exhaustion, so it's not as mighty as you might believe. It also needs to recharge every morning at dawn. We can wear down Saren DeMey if we just keep after her."

"Maybe we can steal it," Selaan suggested.

Golvadu shook his head. "Not likely. If it's a Christian relic, I doubt any of us — or our agents — can even so much as touch it. But you're welcome to try, if you like, Your Highness."

"I'll pass," Selaan sniffed. "I've had enough of Christians for now, thanks."

They lapsed into silence for a while.

Torvu looked at Selaan sidelong. "What happened to you?"

Selaan ground his teeth, then turned a brilliant smile to the Ja'al god of death. "That Papal Annunciator or whatever he is, that's what. Joined by an entire council of wizards wearing grey robes with a golden star. He was waiting for an attack on the East Gate. I bruised him a bit, but I don't think he's dead."

"Once again, this Nuncio thwarts us," Arachnia mused, "but this time he had help."

Selaan nodded. "He's learning. I brought a lot of firepower to bear on the east side and we almost broke through, but ..." He shrugged.

"We need a new approach," Tarvener said, tapping his chin.

Torvu stood, pacing to a black globe hovering over a redwood table in the center of the pavilion. He tapped it with a finger and the three-dimensional image of Oakmoor sprang to life above it.

"We may have made an error in strategy," he murmured. The others gathered around him. Selaan scowled at the image. "We have concentrated all our most potent force, including ourselves, in one or two locations to try to break through. This has the effect of attracting the most powerful of the defenders to the same place."

Arachnia put her arms around Torvu from behind. "What are you suggesting?" the goddess asked.

"Splitting up," Torvu said.

Arachnia and Selaan exchanged a glance. "Really. That's not a sound tactic," Selaan pointed out.

"In this case, it might be." Torvu continued. "We have many superior practitioners, including you, Selaan. If we disperse our power, maybe we can dilute theirs."

Golvadu's pulse quickened as he realized an opportunity. With their forces split, he wouldn't have to contend with the Hadean gods breathing down his neck.

"You're right. They can't have that many true champions," Arachnia mused.

"They don't." Golvadu sidled up next to Tarvener. "Aside from Saren of Tallemar, the Nuncio and Lord Melinor Indidarc, all the others of rank in the city are no more than above average. Capable in their own way, to be honest, and more than a match for anything below a Battle Lord in power, but they aren't of the same scale as those three. Even that big gold dragon has limitations."

Selaan's scowl faded and he broke out in a smile. "That changes things."

Torvu smiled. "I propose that we split our force so that each of us commands a battle group consisting of eight divisions. I will take one, Selaan another, Arachnia another, Golvadu another and Tarvener a fifth. Then, we move our reserves into position at each of the five attack points to take advantage of any breach. Once a breakthrough is achieved, we charge through. The King and Queen will have to divert forces to close the rift or otherwise retreat."

Golvadu smiled. There was an excellent chance that he himself, considered the weakest of the five, would get the least attention from the defenders — and have an easier path into the city.

They pondered the map for a while.

"I like it!" Selaan chortled. "Capital idea! Let's get to it."

"With all respect, Your High Majesties," Golvadu broke in. "Whereas you are able to use potent healing magic and are ready to try again, our allies among the humans, Dark Elves, Kaftu and the like will need to rest or this will not work. We should take the evening to plan, let them recuperate, and then move in the morning."

Torvu nodded. "Understood. Lord Golvadu, you will handle logistics of all but the Fallen Ones. We will handle them."

Hopefully better than the last time, Golvadu thought.

Instead, he bowed. "It will be so, Great One. Death to our enemies."

And victory for me...

Chapter Twenty-Six – Gate of Stars

ell, thought Buck, *it sure lives up to its name.*

He banked Shadowbane around to the left, following the other Riders. They rode thermals above a massive dome of golden-yellow glass perched in the foothills below three towering peaks. It shimmered in the deepening twilight.

And, of course, we had to arrive here just as night falls…

He kept his eyes on Dar and Eric flying in the lead, waiting for the landing signal. Still, they led the Riders on a vast circle above the Dome of Glass.

Come on. Land already.

Buck didn't see anything moving in the vast expanse of rocky ground surrounding the Dome but the two rangers led them in another loop. After two more circuits, Eric's arm went up and Buck followed them all to land about a hundred yards from the Dome.

"Well? Did you find anything magical on our passes around this thing?" Buck asked.

"That archway is magical for sure." Eric nodded towards the nearest curve of the Dome. "And those smaller structures next to it. But no, nothing else."

Buck's eyes narrowed. A carved stone archway jutted out of the side of the Dome, twice as tall as he and twice as wide. It bore a striking resemblance to the Skull Gates he had seen. Three smaller structures stood next to it, as well as something that glittered like crystal.

I don't know what I was expecting. If the Dome is preventing access to the Gate of Stars, magic is certainly involved.

"What does the Eye of Truth tell you?" Andyn asked Buck.

He flipped down the metal arm on his helmet, positioning a magical gemstone in front of his right eye. He slowly scanned the Dome, the archway and the objects near it. Nearly everything glowed a lurid red. Just to check, he swept over his companions. A mild golden glow shone over Eric and Dar and silver over Khyron, Andyn and Connor. He stowed the armature again.

"The whole place is evil," he growled. "Not that I'm surprised." He leaned on his saddle horn and patted Shadowbane's neck.

"Then let's take some protective measures," Andyn suggested. She guided Medianox to the others, who gathered around her in a circle. She lifted her hands over her head and then back down to her knees four times. Each time, a sparkling cloud of energy drifted down on them, settling and dissipating in a few heartbeats. For good measure, Eric tapped each of them on the head and a silvery shield flared up around them.

"Let's have a look at the archway," suggested Khyron. He walked Zasural forward and together the Riders approached.

As they drew nearer, Buck gripped the handle of Khelios. *What the hell?*

A wide, shallow bowl sat on a pedestal in the center of the archway. Connor could have easily taken a nap in it. Scattered fragments of metal lay within. The statute of a woman in a flowing robe stood several paces from the archway, one hand on a ball of crystal three feet in diameter.

"Well, this is something," Dar said, patting Virasi's nose.

"I'll say," murmured Andyn.

"Khyron and Connor," Dar said. "See if you can find any traps nearby."

"On it," said Khyron, dismounting and joining the Halfling. They prowled the area, eyes moving, inspecting the statue and archway but never touching them.

"The arch is embossed with something," Eric mused.

Buck peered at it. Engravings marched up each side of the archway, ending in an etched metal plate at the top. The first set of carvings depicted people approaching the dome. In the next set, the people laid swords, spears and axes into the basin, then the bowl glowed with a flash of light.

The embossed plate at the top of the arch showed an image of the Dome parting down the middle with rays of light shining forth.

"So we have to give up our weapons to get into the Dome?" Buck asked. "Like hell!"

"Yes, that would be unwise," said Andyn.

"I don't like the idea of giving up anything to get into the Dome if I can help it," Eric murmured, "but if it comes down to a choice between that and getting to the Gate of Stars, I know what I'm doing."

Khyron and Connor rejoined them.

"No traps," the Halfling said with a wary look at the statue. "But I don't like this one bit."

Buck stared at the archway. The carvings mocked him with a promise of success, if only he would do what they depicted… or, knowing the Ja'al, it was all a lie and it was an elaborate trap after all.

Can we really believe anything we see any more? Buck wondered.

No one spoke. The wind blew scattered leaves across the stony expanse.

"We have to do something," Dar said.

"I don't know," Andyn said slowly. "We can't just lay our weapons in the basin. It's too risky. There must be another way."

Their last conversation with the Papal Nuncio echoed in Buck's memory. He set his jaw and faced the others. "While we debate," he said, "the Dark Wave covers all the lands. Every minute we delay puts our families and our nations at risk."

The silence dragged on. Finally, Dar stepped towards the archway. "I know this isn't a great idea, and I know that the Ja'al are liars, so it is not likely to end well," he said, holding out Rindara, "but we have no other choice."

"Wait!" Connor interposed himself between Dar and the basin. He drew Tiuz and it burst into flame. "Rindara, the Changelings and Fidelis are Celestial. Tiuz, Eleison and Khelios aren't. I say we place our lesser items in first, just in case it's enough to open the Dome of Glass."

The others nodded. Andyn carried Eleison towards the basin, the mace shining like a lantern.

Buck held up Khelios before his eyes, lingering on the carvings of the Dwarves on the hilt and the Dwarven runes engraved on the mirror-bright blade.

This was the first and only magic sword I've ever owned. His memory went back to one of his first adventures with the other Riders, more than a year ago, when they had found the weapon hidden in a lost labyrinth.

Is it worth Carine? And the rest of the world?

"Sorry Khelios," he whispered and strode forward to the basin.

Connor and Andyn joined him. As one, they laid Khelios, Tiuz and Eleison down into the stony bowl.

A faint blue light crackled on the archway, lighting up the carvings. The metal plate glowed with an identical light, but faintly. Nothing else happened.

The wind blew, bringing the scent of the nearby forest, still wet from the rains.

Dar set his mouth in a grim line. "Well, we tried the incremental approach. Now for the final step."

He and Eric and Khyron placed their weapons in the basin. With a flash of bright red light, Eleison, Tiuz and Khelios broke into pieces. The Celestial weapons remained unharmed.

The archway flared with light and the azure hue turned sickly and pale. Buck backed up, drawing his dagger. *Holy shit!*

The statue animated. The carved robes became cloth of midnight blue woven through with gold thread. Stony surfaces became tanned flesh and a woman turned bright blue eyes at them.

She smiled, running a hand through long, straight red hair. "My congratulations," she said. "Few have made it this far in ages."

Something about her voice made a ringing sound in Buck's ears and he gave his head a quick shake.

Her eyes flicked to the basin. "Shame about those weapons. But as the prophetic Ja'al verse says:

Gate of Stars and Dome of Glass
Pay the Toll and you may pass."

"Whom do we have the honor of addressing?" asked Khyron, shifting his weight slightly toward the basin.

She laughed. "So polite! Well, my name doesn't matter. Only my proposal."

Buck caught a glance between Andyn and Eric for a split second. Eric gave a slight nod.

"And that is?" Khyron asked.

She eyed them each in turn. "You know that this world is coming to an end. My masters have seen to that. Now, it only remains for you to salvage what you can."

She leaned one hand on the glass ball. "The victory of the Grand Remaking is inevitable, but your prowess has not escaped the notice of the High Kings of Hades. Pledge your loyalty to them, serve as our viceroys on Damora and all you cherish will be preserved for you."

"Meaning what exactly?" asked Andyn, shifting her hands rest on Medianox's withers, near her saddlebags.

"Your families and loved ones will be spared and you will receive enough power and riches to safeguard them for the rest of their lives," she replied. "A fair trade, considering the alternative."

Buck's memory flashed back to the Chamber of Decision. That exact scenario had played out for him in that chamber, and it ended with a rule of evil.

He hesitated. *Did I make the right choice?*

The woman tapped the globe. It glowed golden, just like the Dome of Glass and the surface clouded over. The mist swirled briefly, then cleared to show a map of the known lands. The borders appeared like always, with a notable and ominous difference.

Dark sections of midnight covered the nations like some sort of horrid black mildew. Rokon, far to the north, was completely covered. Most of Eldir and Astarel were consumed. Deran had been deeply invaded from the wilderness and the sea, blotches of darkness extending even to Oakmoor. Terenai had been cut into three pieces by dark slashes and half of Gorostol was obscured by darkness. Every seacoast had black borders, and Hillshire had disappeared under a black wave.

Darkness likewise engulfed major portions of the nations of Derelia, the islands of Erleth, and most of the lands across the Great Sea.

"Impressive, isn't it?" asked the woman.

The image clouded again, then cleared.

Dark green, finned fish-men stormed ashore near a large fortress city by the sea. Dark ships loomed in the background.

Buck recognized the beach where he had played as a child and his heart skipped a beat.

Arrows, firedarts, lightning, and fireballs arced out at the invaders. Dozens dropped, were immolated in thunderous blasts, or had holes blown in them, but they came on, more taking the place of the fallen. Bodies of dead defenders and civilians littered the waterfront.

No! Those bastards!

The mist came and went.

The new view depicted a forest area. In the foreground, many halflings trudged next to overburdened wagons, escorted by Elven and Halfling soldiers. Far in the background, a lurid glow lit the sky.

Evendale burns… Buck realized.

The scene changed again.

This time, the image of Oakmoor filled the glass sphere. The towers of the city were lit by fires from the streets. A great, dark army ringed its walls and more formations marched towards it from north and south. In the sky above, dragons, pegasi and griffons danced on the wind in swirling dogfights, flame and lightning darting from one form to another. Occasionally, one burst into flame and spiraled earthward, trailing a cloud of smoke.

The fog came and went and the Riders looked upon Eleth-Anor. From the small islands in the Bay of Dolphins, pillars of smoke curled skyward from ruined Elven fortresses. Inside the harbor, a wave of troop ships escorted by fish-men surged towards the harbor docks.

Andyn gasped and Buck recognized the vantage point of the view: the Eleandir family home. It was a wide expanse of now-ruined forest and churned lawn next to what had once been a grand estate. Several corpses lay among fallen timbers, ashes and broken glass. Even as they watched, a patrol of hobgoblins tramped through the wreckage, led by three humans on horseback. They began to sift through the debris and poke at the bodies.

Buck looked at Andyn. She clenched her jaw, tears welling up in her eyes.

The mist faded then, leaving them staring at their own white-faced reflections in the crystal globe.

"Seen enough?" the woman asked with a sardonic smile. "There is still time to save them, you know. All you have to do is choose. Give up your quest and join our cause."

Now a verse from the Song of the Grey Riders came unbidden to his mind.

For Good or Evil, All must choose
Or choosing none, their lives to lose.

Buck's mind flew back to the Chamber of Decision those many months ago. As clearly as if it were yesterday, he saw his choices depicted on walls of glass in a room of mist: take the easy path and serve Evil in order to protect those he loved or take the hard path to do what was right and risk the deaths of those he sought to protect. With sudden clarity, he now realized the full implications of the choice he had made to follow the Light and forsake the Dark.

He clenched his fist around the handle of his dagger and his doubts vanished. *I made my decision. More importantly, my family — and Carine — would never forgive me if they knew I betrayed everyone else just to save them.*

Buck met the gaze of the other Grey Riders. Dar nodded to him.

"No," the ranger said.

"No?"

"No," Dar repeated. "We made our choice long ago. We will not go back on it."

The mysterious woman raised an eyebrow to Khyron. "Even you?"

He gave her a sardonic grin and inclined his head towards Andyn. "Wherever she goes, I follow. The answer is no."

"Well," sighed the woman, "That's that, I suppose. You leave me no alternative."

She raised her hands and spun in a circle. Khyron leaped to the basin, flinging Rindara to Dar. He tossed Fidelis to Eric, who caught the spear in mid-air.

The woman's form warped and twisted in a cloud of purple smoke. In a couple of heartbeats, a crowned skeleton in rotting robes burst from the cloud, turning pinpoint eyes of purple fire to them.

Great Earth Mother! A lich…

***

I sure hope this turns out better than the last lich battle, Dar thought, drawing Rindara. The sword blade blazed with the light of a thousand stars.

"Get in the air!" Eric shouted.

Dar reached for Virasi's saddle horn. The lich held out her hands and shouted a harsh syllable. Black tendrils like smoke slithered out from the stony mesa, entangling the legs of the pegasi. The mounts whinnied in fear, their eyes wide, wings beating the air.

"Damn it!" Buck shouted.

Khyron ran past him. "Here!" He flipped his Celestial dagger to Buck, who caught it and unsheathed it in one smooth motion.

"You had your chance!" chortled the lich. "You're overmatched now!"

"Not if I have anything to say about it," announced Andyn, pulling the Crown of Thorns plant from her saddlebag. The rose glowed pure gold.

The undead sorceress recoiled, one hand in front of her face. "What is this?"

Andyn closed her eyes, murmuring under her breath. A misty globe of white sprang up around her and the Riders.

With a vile curse, the lich thrust her hands at them. Arrows of blackest night shot out.

Dar had a flashback to Zhinia Margoth blasting him to death with identical arrows. He braced himself.

The dark arrows hit the white globe and shattered into wisps of dirty fog.

The lich gasped. "Not possible!"

Eric hefted Fidelis. "Nothing will be impossible for God." He threw.

The lich sidestepped, gesturing with one hand. A flash of red fire sent Fidelis off-course to thump into the Dome. With a word, Eric recalled the spear and it flashed back into his fist.

"Nice try," the lich hissed, gesturing with both hands. A cloud of fiery darts coalesced in front of her face and shot out at the Riders.

Dar turned his face aside as a dozen darts exploded against the shields Andyn had laid on them.

Eric cast a lightning bolt. The bolt struck the lich and an invisible screen flared around her. She fired a searing beam of red fire at him, but he tumbled out of the way, leaving a line of molten rock in his wake.

Dar charged. The lich slapped at him with glowing skeletal hands. He ducked and slashed upwards. Rindara Starblade cut through the lich's sparkling shield and cut into her side.

With a hiss, she stepped back and thrust her hands out. A bruising force struck Dar, lifting him up and hurling him backwards. He landed heavily and rolled away from a lance of purple fire. He scrambled to his feet, panting.

Khyron, Buck and Eric leapt at the sorceress, but she gave a short hop and soared up into the air, casting rainbow pinwheels. The swirling missiles struck Buck and Khyron, who recoiled, blinking.

"Amateurs!" the lich laughed. She flew higher, unleashing glittering green stars at them. Andyn called out in Elven and the misty white shield deflected the stars.

Eric hurled Fidelis again, but the lich dodged and the spear returned to him at his call.

Dar shook his head to clear it. *Damn it! How do we hurt this thing?*

Connor activated his dancing sword and the ghostly blade shot at the lich like an angry wasp, stabbing and darting. The Halfling followed it up by loosing arrow after arrow.

The lich screamed obscenities at him, dodging and twisting in mid-air to avoid Connor's phantom blade and his red-glowing arrows. She spat an oath and a black globe of mist exploded in front of her, hurling the ghost-blade into the side of the Dome.

Connor gestured and the magic weapon leaped back into the air again.

"You're starting to annoy me!" the sorceress snapped. She raised her arms, gripping roaring balls of fire in her palms.

Dar gritted his teeth and touched the plate at the throat of his armor. "Habakkuk!"

The universe warped and a distorted image of a skeletal mage wavered in his eyes. Without thinking, he wrapped one arm around her waist from behind and lopped off one of her arms with Rindara.

A horrid scream deafened him. An explosion of intense pain racked his body. Vaguely aware that he plummeted to the ground, he reached out and hit something metallic, yet yielding. The lich was ripped from his grasp and hurled to the side.

"That's the last time I try to catch you," Buck groaned from under Dar.

They struggled to their feet. The lich ran to its severed arm and lifted it back into place. Red light blazed and she flexed the finger bones of her newly attached limb.

"Now I'm mad," she said, eyes flaring. She spat a quick syllable and darted forward — moving twice as fast as before.

Shit! Dar ducked a sizzling grey comet and charged at her. She sneered and slapped him to the side. Head spinning, Dar tried to stab her but tripped over a rock and fell. Her sheet of flame scorched the air above him.

She spun to the others, making grasping motions with her hands. Stones leaped into the air and hammered into the Riders, battering them. Dar took a rock on the helmet and reeled, falling into the Dome.

Andyn gritted her teeth and the Crown of Thorns flared bright white. The lich recoiled, cursing, and her impromptu missiles dropped to the ground.

We need to end this... Dar's eyes flitted around, searching for anything they could use.

His gaze locked on the crystal sphere.

Dome of Glass... globe of crystal? Wait a second! Without another thought, he raced to the globe.

"Dar!" Khyron called out, sidestepping a spitting purple arrowhead. "What are you doing?" He stabbed the lich in the side. She hissed in pain and punched him. A burst of red light flung him backwards to bounce off the Dome.

Dar slammed Rindara into the globe. Light and heat exploded and he flew back, tumbling in a heap.

Through blurry vision, he saw the sphere lying in two pieces. The ground trembled and shook. The archway cracked and split and a great fissure raced up the golden surface of the Dome of Glass.

"What have you done?" the lich raged. "Blasphemers!"

She clapped her hands together and a storm of green spines shot out at them. Dar flattened himself on the ground as the missiles whistled by overhead.

Andyn and Khyron cried out. They collapsed on the ground near the panicked pegasi. Eric and Buck rushed to their sides.

This is going to hurt in the morning, Dar thought grimly, tapping the metal plate at his throat again. "Habakkuk!"

Existence convulsed and he found himself at the lich's side. She whirled on him, reaching out with a hand crackling with electricity. He lopped it off.

The lich uncorked another deafening screech and he staggered backward, ears ringing. Buck and Eric and a ghostly sword charged. She backpedaled, conjuring whirling sawblades of fire with her good hand while her severed one crawled towards her. The Riders parried the blades aside, staggering from the impact.

Andyn limped forward, holding forth the Crown of Thorns. The flower blazed like the sun.

"That's enough!" Andyn's eyes flashed golden like the sunrise. "*Verian, Ald-adani!*"

She plucked off the rose bud and hurled it. The flower took on a life of its own, darting at the undead like a living thing. It blasted through multiple magic screens and struck the lich dead center.

With a horrid shriek, she froze in place. Her bones shone bright white under her tattered royal robes, then disintegrated into ash. With no more than a faint sigh, she disappeared in a cloud of collapsing, dusty cloth. A violent, deafening crack echoed out over the plateau, followed by rumbling and heavy thuds.

For long moments, Dar simply stared at the lich's empty robes, every bone aching, his head throbbing. He lifted himself to his feet and plodded towards figures huddled near the archway. It took him a moment to realize that the Dome of Glass lay in a thousand pieces on the mesa.

He regained enough awareness to cast a healing spell on himself.

Just enough to keep going, he told himself in mental haze.

"Dar!" Buck called. "We need some help here!"

Dar shrugged off his backpack and dropped down next to Andyn and Khyron. Both lay unmoving on the sandy, stony ground. Weariness threatened to overtake him.

Eric returned from Medianox carrying Andyn's saddlebags. "Her healing kit," he said, dropping to his knees beside Dar.

"Andyn?" Dar asked as Eric rummaged through her bags. Medianox minced closer, nudging his mistress with his nose.

Her eyes fluttered open. "Oh. Dar. Where did you come from?"

"Hang on. I have something that will help."

Her hand stopped him. "Where's Khyron?"

"He's right here," said Eric.

Dar's heart froze.

Khyron's skin had the same light-blue pallor as Andyn's and he bled from a dozen wounds like her. He smiled weakly and reached out a hand. She took it and closed her eyes.

"Here," Dar fed her a healing potion. She sipped it, coughing occasionally. A gold light flared in her side and he gingerly removed a bony spine covered with a slick green substance from below her last rib.

"Damn it," Eric said, removing a similar spine from Khyron's calf. "Poison. Will Everheal work?"

Dar nodded. "It's our best bet." He pulled out a jar of silvery ointment and began spreading it on Andyn's injury. Wherever the medicine touched, the ragged edges of her wounds sizzled and smoked. To Dar's dismay, the wounds began to heal, then stopped halfway through.

Andyn's whimpered and her face contorted in pain. "No, Dar. Please."

She put her hand over his. He met her eyes. Already, the irises coalesced into a swirling, lavender void.

"It's an encoded poison," she whispered.

"You don't know that!"

She gave a little laugh. "After trying to help Megan, my dear, I know the signs."

"No! I won't lose you too!"

"Dar," Khyron murmured. "You haven't lost. We've won. The Dome of Glass is shattered."

Dar shook his head, his vision misting over.

"We can't just leave you here!" Eric protested.

"You don't have to," Khyron said. "Take us along, but don't waste time or medicine on us."

The couple looked to each other and smiled.

"It was fun, wasn't it?" Khyron rasped.

Andyn nodded, smiling through tears running down her face. "I would have preferred a less wild wedding reception."

Khyron turned swirling blue eyes to Buck. "You know what to do.

You're a soldier too. Don't let this be in vain."

Buck's jaw worked and he gave a stiff nod, then lifted Khyron in his arms. Eric followed suit with Andyn. He held her near her fiancé and the lovers exchanged a weak kiss.

"Come on, damn it!" snarled Buck in a voice thick with emotion. "The Gate of Stars isn't going to open itself!"

He trudged forwards. The Riders moved as fast as they dared through the field littered with great shards of yellow glass, their mounts following after them. At the center of the area, a shining, raised disk of gold beckoned, nearly eight feet in diameter.

The Gate of Stars! Finally!

Panting, Buck hefted Khyron in his arms just at the edge. "Ready?"

"Ready," Eric answered.

"Wait," said Connor. "It's too small to take us and the pegasi."

"I don't want to split up and go in teams with the mounts." Buck grated. "Khyron and Andyn are running out of time. We have to get to Celestia now.'

Dar nodded. "I'll take care of it."

He kissed Virasi's nose and made a circle with his hand, then pointed up. The pegasi balked, milling together.

"Come on, boy," Dar soothed. "I don't really want you to leave either, but the Gate can't take all of us. Go. We'll be back for you."

With a snort that conveyed his reluctance, Virasi trotted off with the other winged horses following, then soared off into the darkening sky.

"Okay," Dar said. "Go."

Dar and Connor put their hands on Eric and Buck's elbows and everyone stepped onto the disk.

The sky spun and the world lurched. Dar focused on supporting Buck so that he didn't fall.

Firm earth coalesced under his feet. Dar leaned his hands on his knees, fighting the urge to retch. He blinked through bleary eyes.

Too many teleportations in a row… God help me.

A ring of mountains surrounded them and a darkened lake glittered under the light of the stars.

They stood unmoving, staring all around.

"This isn't Celestia," Connor said.

"Damn it!" Dar's heart sank. "Another Ja'al deception?"

"Contact Father Thomas," Khyron wheezed. "Use the Sending Mirror."

Eric reached into his backpack and cursed under his breath.

"What?" asked Buck.

Eric held up a shattered hand mirror.

Dar felt a wave of despair. *No, God! This can't be right. We did everything we were supposed to.*

Eric nodded at the three dark peaks. "I think we're actually at the top of the Titan's Crown."

"Then where the hell is the Gate?" Buck growled.

Dar's heart sank. The lake was at least a mile across and they had no idea of the Gate's location along the shoreline. He could only make out black masses of trees.

"Don't…" Andyn whispered.

"What?" Dar asked.

She lifted her head with difficulty. "Don't despair. It is here. I feel it."

"I'm not leaving you to die alone."

Khyron gave a weak chuckle. "And what am I, Dwarven pastry? Get going, soldier. We're not going anywhere."

Eric and Buck exchanged an anguished glance.

Andyn gasped and coughed. Alarmed, the men put her and Khyron down on the soft earth. Her eyes closed and she went limp.

Eric felt for her pulse. "Damn it! She's fading!"

Dar laid his fingers on Khyron's carotid artery. He felt a faint heartbeat, lessening in frequency. "We're losing them," he whispered, his stomach clenching.

What do I do, God? What do I do? Was all this for nothing? Is it over?

Unbidden, the dream-image of a young man popped into his head. Dar saw his blue eyes and dark hair as clearly as if he were still asleep.

Dar released Khyron and stared at the lake. The details of his dream replayed in his mind. The young man smiled and touched a sequence of lights among a pattern of lights. Dar kept staring at the still waters of the lake, spangled with the stars of the night sky.

Everything suddenly made sense.

Dar's eyes widened. "Oh My God! The Gate!"

"Where?" Connor asked. "Is it on this side of the lake?"

"No!" Dar exclaimed, striding forward into the water. "The Gate *is* the lake!"

"What?!" cried Eric.

Words echoed in Dar's mind. *Accedere ad altare Dei.*

He moved deeper into the lake. "Bring them," he called over his shoulder.

Curiously, the reflected starfield didn't waver or change as he waded in. Instead, the bright pattern remained locked into the surface of the water. He stopped when he could reach every single star he had seen in his dream.

Water sloshed against his midsection as the Riders joined him.

"*Quaerens voluntatem Dominum,*" Dar intoned, reaching his hand to touch the lights. He followed the exact pattern that the young man had used in the dream. "*Accedere ad altare Dei.*"

The stars pulsed at his fingertips. He heard Eric gasp as the lights glowed ever brighter. When all twelve burned with the intensity of lanterns, Dar closed his eyes.

"*Consummatum est.*"

The universe turned around him, not in the abrupt fashion of a teleport, but in a gentle rotating wave. He felt lifted and energized.

He opened his eyes. The surface of the lake, for at least one hundred yards in every direction, now showed a vast green meadow in bright morning sunshine. He moved forward, the Riders at his side.

Without any feeling of transition at all, he stepped onto a grassy lawn. The image of the verdant countryside rotated until he stood with his friends at the edge of a highway of evenly cut paving stones. Graceful, stately trees with white bark and black-and-gold leaves towered overhead. The pathway led through a meadow towards a glittering alabaster city.

He shot a glance over his shoulder. An enormous disk of night sky stood behind them, perpendicular to the ground. The edges crackled gently with silvery light.

"Celestia?" Buck breathed.

"It looks like it," Eric answered.

Somewhere far away, they heard a deep, sonorous gong.

"I think we've been noticed," Connor said.

"Then let's go meet them." Filled with a sudden clarity of purpose, Dar marched up the highway.

Eric kept pace with him, carrying Andyn. Her color remained pale and bluish and her chest had ceased its labored breathing. Dar looked to Buck, who shook his head, jaw tight. Khyron lay limp in his arms.

Dar blinked away tears and his throat tightened. *I'm sorry, Andyn and Khyron. I really did want to be at your wedding. Say hello to Megan for me...*

Something flashed near the city. Soon, Dar made out a flight of creatures racing in their direction.

"I can't believe we're actually on Celestia," Connor said.

"Just a little too late," Eric replied in a voice shot through with bitterness.

"Let's make the most of it," Dar said, halting. He set Andyn gently down on the highway of paved stones. "That way, their deaths won't be in vain."

Buck set Khyron down next to Andyn and straightened, brushing at his eyes.

Too late, again. Dar thought. Despite finally achieving their goal, he felt a vast emptiness. *Megan, Brandi, now Khyron and Andyn...*

The flying creatures resolved into three winged humans in silvery armor. In a gratifyingly short span of time, they alighted near the Riders. A dark-skinned woman with eyes like pearls led them. Her statuesque physique and graceful movements reminded him of Melissa.

"I know not who you are, travelers," she said in the smoothest alto Dar had ever heard, "but you are most welcome if you are the ones who opened yonder gate."

Dar shoved aside his grief and despair. He knew that Kyron and Andyn wouldn't want him to delay on their account.

"We are," he replied, inclining his head. "The Gate of Stars awaits you."

"Blessed be the One!" exclaimed the Elohir. "But who are these two lying on the roadway?"

Eric lifted his chin though his eyes glistened. "They are our friends who gave their lives that we might open the Gate. They were poisoned by venom an encoded by a lich, a servant of Hades and the Ja'al."

"Were they?" The pearline eyes flashed momentarily. "That is unsurprising considering who is behind all this devilry. With your permission, we will attend them."

Dar knelt with her. "But they are dead, Lady."

She knelt by Andyn. Another Elohir woman with blond hair and tanned skin went to Khyron.

The dark-skinned Elohir gently caressed Andyn's bloodstained brow. "We will see about that. What is her name?"

"Andyn."

"I am Lorienne. The woman helping your companion is Alicia. What is the man's name?"

"Khyron."

Lorienne called over her shoulder to the third Elohir. "Johanna, please alert His Majesty that the Gate of Stars has been opened."

A brown-haired beauty with snow-white wings bowed. "Of course, Captain." She soared off, the wind of her passage ruffling Dar's hair.

"Andyn," Lorienne murmured, stroking her hair. "Andyn, I am Lorienne. Come back to us. Your friends await you."

She laid a hand on Andyn's injured side and one on her head, closing her eyes.

The Elohir whispered words under her breath that sounded like singing. Her hands glowed silver and the air around Dar electrified. His vision sharpened, his hearing became more sensitive and his mind cleared.

What is happening? He thought in wonder.

Lorienne opened eyes that had transformed into pools of white light and Dar gasped. She sang a series of notes so beautiful that Dar's heart soared and his eyes stung with fresh tears. Next to Khyron, Alicia repeated Lorienne's actions.

The light in Lorienne's hands faded, as did the unnatural pallor on Andyn's skin. Likewise, Khyron's skin returned to its normal color.

Andyn's eyes fluttered open. She tried to sit and Lorienne gently helped her do so.

If I didn't just see this, I would think I dreamt it.

"Where..." Andyn stammered, eyes darting around. "What's going on? Wait..." A sudden look of panic crossed her features. "Where's Khyron?"

Khyron smiled, scooting over to embrace her. "Right here where I belong."

Andyn began to cry, clinging to her fiancé, body shaking with sobs.

Dar and Lorienne stood.

Dar wavered between stunned amazement, joy and indescribable relief. He struggled for words to say, then settled on simple gratitude. "Thank you. They are betrothed," he told the Elohir.

"Then I am honored to help them." Lorienne's eyes resumed their normal color. "Now, I believe you have some explaining to do."

"We have little time, Lady," Eric interjected. "The Ja'al and their infernal allies make war on our world. A Dark Wave covers much of the Free Lands."

Another gong sounded from the direction of the city.

Lorienne's smile turned sardonic. "Have no fear. We will deal with them with all due haste. But first I think His Majesty wants to have a word with you." She nodded towards the city in the distance.

Dar's jaw dropped. Streams of Elohir soared towards them.

"There must be hundreds," Connor said at his side.

Dar nodded. "Thousands."

Buck grunted. "It's about time. The Dark Wave needs its ass beat."

Chapter Twenty-Seven – Last Stand

Terenil spurred his horse, bowling over a Dark Elf swordsman. A nearby Kaftu raider leaped at him. He blinded it with ball of light on its face and ducked low in the saddle. The creature bounced off Terenil's mount in a jangle of chainmail barding and fell to the ground. One of his knights speared it in the throat.

"They just keep coming," panted the knight.

"Lord Terenil!" called a guttural voice from overhead. A goblin drifted down to him, the bat wings of his cloak fluttering in the smoky air.

"Gorlak!" Terenil grinned. "When did you get here?"

Gorlak landed on a nearby ruined planter. "Yesterday. I come through Ja'al lines disguised as courier from Splitskull Tribe. Melinor send me to you."

An ogre roared at them from an alleyway and thudded forwards, brandishing a great club. Two of Terenil's knights spurred their steeds. The ogre unhorsed a knight with a wild swing but the other one bowled him over. Two nearby Forester militia shot the ogre with arrows and the knight beheaded him as he rose.

Terenil let out a breath. "I'm glad you're here. Get behind me."

Gorlak obliged and Terenil urged his mount forward, accompanied by his guards. They headed down the ruined street at a gallop.

"How does it look elsewhere?" Terenil shouted to him over the tumult of screams, clash of arms and thump of artillery.

"Gorlak no lie. Outer city is lost and Hades gods pushing farther into Inner city. We in big problem, Lord Terenil."

Terenil nodded, turning down a main boulevard. "We can only hope in the Riders, Gorlak. Beyond that, it is in God's hands."

They rounded a corner and charged into the Great Plaza of Oakmoor. Human, Elven, Dwarven, Halfling and Centaur troops took up positions all along the vast open ground, making barricades of wooden beams and over-turned carts. The square encompassed the grounds of the Royal University as well as an enormous market with fountains. It easily covered a square mile, but with so many troops, horses, barricades and field artillery, it looked crowded. Near a great fountain, Iron Thunder raised his head to its full height, Kindri and Tholi at his side. Two silver-and-purple Drakes stood nearby, eyes focused on the skies.

Terenil reined in. "Greetings, Iron Thunder!"

The dragon smiled. "Ah! Lord Terenil! And you must be the Gorlak I've heard so much about."

Gorlak hopped out of the saddle and craned his neck up at the dragon's face, then bowed deeply. "I honored to see you, Great One. Gorlak never meet a dragon before."

"Grandpa, it's a goblin!" called one of the young dragons.

"Yes, Kindri. But he's on our side, if I'm not mistaken."

"Yes," answered Gorlak, smiling at Kindri and Tholi. "But I not sure that I all that special."

Iron Thunder sniffed. "A Christian goblin is far rarer than a dragon."

Gorlak bowed again as Kindri and Tholi slipped up next to him, chatter-ing excitedly.

Terenil led Iron Thunder out of earshot, his mount picking its way among the debris. "How goes it here?"

The dragon scowled. "We are holding our own but the enemy keeps breaking through. We are trying to keep them away from the gate to the Royal District. Any news from elsewhere?"

"Nothing good. Gorlak tells me the Outer City is lost. Harlinsville, Tallemar, The Marketry, and Saint Joseph's have fallen and it is only a matter of time before the Ja'al battle groups link up."

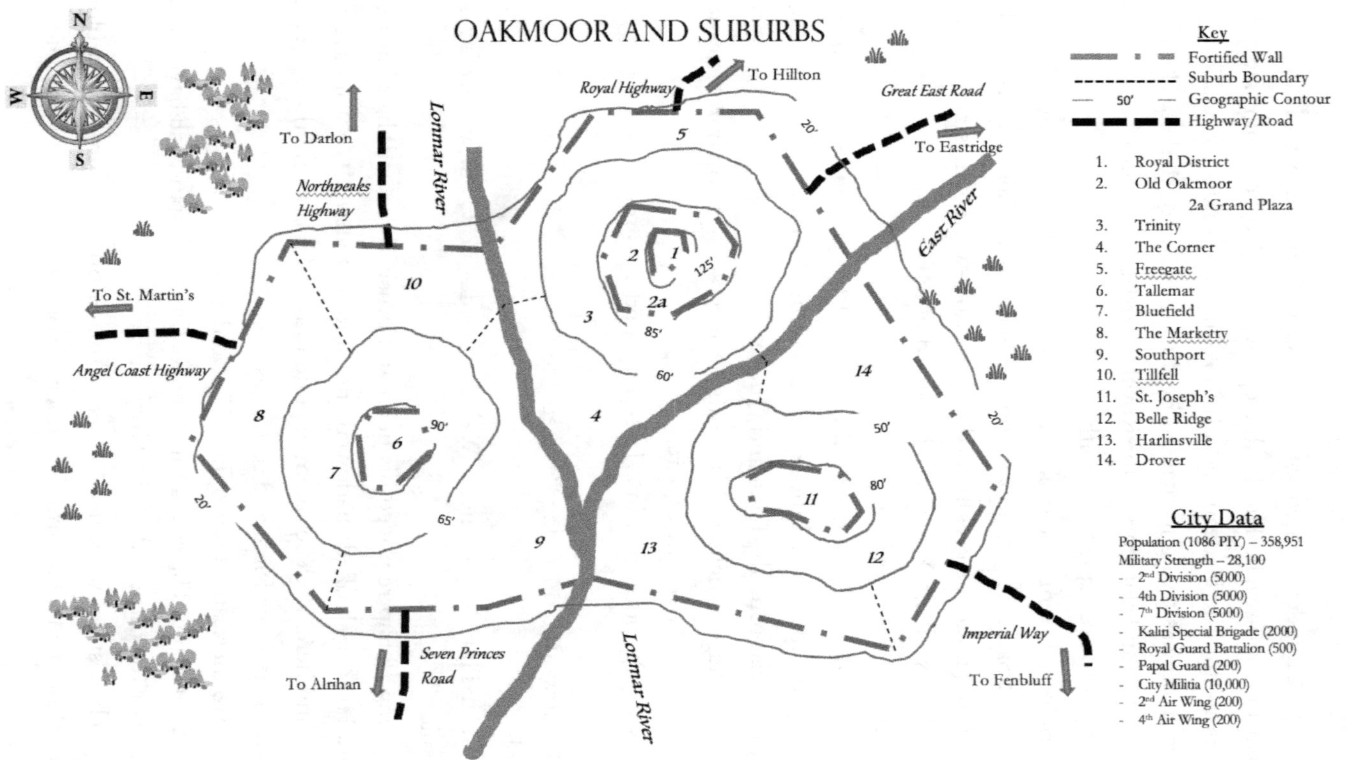

OAKMOOR AND SUBURBS

Key
Fortified Wall
Suburb Boundary
50' Geographic Contour
Highway/Road

1. Royal District
2. Old Oakmoor
2a Grand Plaza
3. Trinity
4. The Corner
5. Freegate
6. Tallemar
7. Bluefield
8. The Marketry
9. Southport
10. Tillfell
11. St. Joseph's
12. Belle Ridge
13. Harlinsville
14. Drover

City Data
Population (1086 PIY) – 358,951
Military Strength – 28,100
- 2nd Division (5000)
- 4th Division (5000)
- 7th Division (5000)
- Kaliri Special Brigade (2000)
- Royal Guard Battalion (500)
- Papal Guard (200)
- City Militia (10,000)
- 2nd Air Wing (200)
- 4th Air Wing (200)

N E S W
To Darlon
To Hillton
Royal Highway
Great East Road
To Eastridge
Northpeaks Highway
Lonmar River
East River
To St. Martin's
Angel Coast Highway
Seven Princes Road
To Alrihan
Lonmar River
Imperial Way
To Fenbluff
125'
85'
60'
90'
65'
50'
80'
20'

"Where is Father Thomas?"

Iron Thunder pointed with a great claw. "He and Sister Karen are pinned down in Southreach. The Ja'al keep swarming to keep him away from the daemons and the Hadean gods. It looks like the strategy is working. The last I heard, he was trying to make it here to the Grand Market. The Knights of the Chalice and elements of the Royal Guard are with him, but it's slow going. I thought to see Lady Saren with you."

Before Terenil could answer, Saren floated down out of the sky, the Crown of Saint Alyssa glowing on her head. "I am here, my lord," she said.

Iron Thunder's eyes flicked to her snow-white wings and horns and he smiled. "Excellent. You come at a good time."

"So do they," Saren replied.

With the tramp of boots, the jangle of harness and clink of mail, a regiment of troops entered the square from the direction of the Royal Quarter. At their head rode the King and Queen.

The dragon inclined his head. "And greetings to your Majesties!" His voice boomed over the Square.

King Phillip reined in. "Iron Thunder! It is good to see you and your kin."

"How are you faring?" asked the Queen, with a glance at Kindri and Tholi.

Iron Thunder frowned. "Well enough for now, but we face an ocean of enemies."

King Phillip removed his helm and brushed his dark hair back over his head. His eyes looked shadowed and tired, but alert. "We will have to make our stand here. If we let them get into Old Oakmoor and the Royal District, they can split our force and scatter us."

"Are there any other options?" asked Saren.

"Not many. The city is surrounded. Our final stand will have to be at the Palace or the cathedral of the Holy Family."

"Then stand we must." Queen Ahlana brushed some dried blood and dirt off her hauberk. "Iron Thunder, if you would assist in arranging the defense."

"Certainly, Majesty."

Terenil dismounted and embraced his wife. She looked into his eyes and he saw the same haunted exhaustion he had seen in the King.

He brushed an errant lock of bloodstained raven hair back under the Crown. "You don't look good, sweetheart."

"I've felt better."

"I have a few potions that might help."

She nodded and he handed them to her, arm around her shoulders as she downed them, eyes closed. Light glowed on her arms and legs and chest briefly, then faded.

She sighed, relaxing into him. "I'm so tired, Terenil. I've tried to split my time between attack, defense and healing, but…"

"But?"

Tears leaked out of the corner of her eyes. When she spoke, it was in the most forlorn voice he had ever heard from her. "Tren, I can't save everyone."

"I know, dearest."

She wiped at her eyes. "Now I understand why Andyn despaired. I have so much power, but I'm only a little person after all."

"Believe me, Saren, God understands. When this is all over, you will meet people whom you saved and they will be very grateful. You will see it differently."

A blond young man rode up on a prancing warhorse. "My lord?"

Terenil broke into a grin. "Detlef!"

The Nuncio's aide bowed in the saddle. "The Nuncio has broken free with the help of some freelance mercenaries and is close by. The Order of the Three Magi accompanies him."

"Thanks be to God." Terenil called to the King and Queen. "Your Majesties! The Nuncio is near! We have a chance to hold them off."

"Praise the Lord!" King Phillip shouted back. The troops hear him cheered.

"How long do we have?" Terenil asked Detlef.

"He was not three blocks behind me when he sent me on."

"Good. Go get some more arrows for that bow and see if there are any magical supplies you can use. The cart over by the Royal Gate has them."

Detlef cantered off and Terenil led Saren to the ledge of a nearby fountain.

"Tren, we really need to —"

"You need to rest for a bit. Don't argue."

He sat with her, the fountain water tinkling in the background. He let his eyes wander to the early morning sky, so blue with white puffy clouds.

How could such beauty coexist with such horror and evil?

He knew the answer. "Beauty is of God. Horror and evil are from the Devil," he whispered.

"Sorry, Tren. What did you say?"

He opened his mouth to reply when he heard King Phillip call out.

"Aha! Your Eminence!"

The Nuncio rode on an armored warhorse to the King and Queen. A company of mixed Papal Guard and Royal Knights cantered at his side and ordered files of infantry and archers trotted behind them.

"Forgive my tardiness," Father Thomas said. "Traffic was horrendous." Melinor, Sister Karen and four wizards wearing grey robes with a golden Star of Bethlehem joined them, riding white steeds.

Terenil recognized them. *At least some of the Order of the Three Magi survived...*

"Are you hurt?" Queen Ahlana asked.

The Nuncio shrugged. "As was said in a famous and very silly dramatic presentation long ago, 'It is only a flesh wound'. Sister Karen took care of me."

Queen Ahlana nodded. "That is good news. We need you at your best. The enemy vanguard approaches. The Hadean royalty are here."

Father Thomas touched his pectoral cross. "Then we will meet them as befits their hideous nature."

Terenil released Saren and set his last five arrows point-down in a nearby flowerbed. She brought his shield from his mount and set it next to him.

"One more time, love," she said, kissing his cheek.

"One more time," he agreed. Closing his eyes, he layered protective spells on the both of them.

He ignored the raucous blare of horns and roll of drums coming from three separate streets leading into the Square. The ground shook with the weighty steps of ogres and trolls and he smelled the distinct, sour odor of brimstone.

"Into your hands, Oh Lord, I commend my spirit," he whispered, then opened his eyes.

Selaan stalked into the plaza from the southernmost street in the form of a giant winged centaur with antlers. A crackling pink sphere of energy surrounded him.

Allied troops loosed arrows and spells but they cracked and shattered on the globe protecting Selaan.

The Hadean god guffawed. "You think to harm me?"

Behind him, Kaftu raiders in vast mobs crowded into the boulevards and parks near the Square, brandishing scimitars, spiked clubs, and javelins. Dark Elves rode giant scorpions, aiming arrows from blackwood longbows. Skull-head heavy infantry marched in formation, their unit banners waving in the morning air.

Saren strode forward and waved a hand. A ring of silvery glyphs raced around the perimeter of the plaza, inscribing an arc between Selaan's growing force and the defenders.

"You will go no further," she said.

"Neat trick," Selaan sneered, altering his form to a two-headed ogre with swirling rainbow-colored eyes. "It won't hold forever. What will you do when we break past it?"

"She, and all her misguided compatriots, will die, High King of Hades," Arachnia announced. She glided into the Square from another street in a swirl of green fog and spectral images of scorpions and spiders. Golvadu strode at her side, the gemstone on his staff sparkling like a malignant red star.

Ranks and ranks of goblins and hobgoblins tramped in her wake, their halberds, glaives and spears glinting in the sunlight. Battle standards crowned by skulls fluttered above them, displaying foul symbols etched in lurid colors.

Trolls and ogres clambered over ruined walls and buildings in a rattle of stone, crunch of splintering wood and clank of splint mail. Battalions of Ja'al knights bore lances at the ready next to platoons of heavy infantry and spear-men. Priests and priestesses of the Ja'al pantheon accompanied each for-mation with wizards and sorcerers at their sides.

"It's only a matter of time," a voice boomed from another street. Torvu marched into the plaza.

Row upon row of skeletons armed with spears and shields clanked be-hind the Hadean god of Death, accompanied by many rotting corpses with great-swords. Near them, blue ghouls prowled, their stench discernible even from a hundred yards. A few vampires sat in the saddles of their Fellsteeds, eyes glowing with hate.

"Or," Torvu continued, "we could just wait here until our air force eliminates the weaklings in the air above us."

"No." Arachnia lifted her chin imperiously. "I want my share of blood."

Terenil shot a glance skyward. Ja'al air units wheeled overhead, locked in dogfights with Deranese riders and Iron Thunder's allies.

"But wait," proclaimed Selaan. "I believe we should allow our beloved sister one last chance, should we not, Prince Tarvener?"

He swept a grand bow to one side and Saren's grandfather strode into the Great Square of Oakmoor. Clad in black studded leather, he carried a battle axe with an edge dripping acid. Glowing sigils of red and pale green whirled over his head.

He raised an eyebrow at Saren. "I will not make the offer again. Leave these pitiful fools and come with me. Your true destiny and your every wish await their fulfillment."

Saren shook her head. "I gave you my answer days ago. I will not leave them."

Tarvener's clawed hands wrung the haft of his weapon and his eyes narrowed. "I don't understand you!"

Saren looked almost sad. "That is the crux of it, grandfather. You don't understand. Evil will never comprehend things like generosity, self-sacrifice, chastity, fidelity and honesty. At this point, I actually pity you. It must be a pale and hollow existence."

Tarvener scowled and his eyes flashed red. "Spare me the sermon and the philosophizing. Will you turn?"

Saren raised her chin and faced her grandsire without blinking. "I would rather die."

Tarvener's jaw worked and he twisted the handgrips of his axe. Finally, he sighed. "I was afraid you might say that. Ziniva was one of my favorite daughters and you have many of her qualities. The shame is that you inherited all her stubbornness too."

Daemons filed into the area from all three directions. Huge Battle Lords soared down to a landing, shouldering aside trees and ogres with equal disdain. Blood Satyrs stalked next to ranks of Dwerrolves. War Fiends prowled, wicked swords glittering with the color of rubies, their wings furled. Deathmists hovered above blackened patches of earth. Blood Satyrs brandished a variety of wicked looking tools of war in their four arms. Bone Knights glowered at the defenders, halberds planted butt-down in the ruined streets. Deathhammers pushed forward, throwing aside the occasional goblin or human unlucky enough to be in their way. Tiger Daemons alighted on ruined buildings and towers, crouching with flaming daggers in their hands.

Tarvener backed up. "High Majesties," he said over his shoulder without turning his head, "I relinquish all claim to Saren, daughter of my daughter Ziniva. You may do with her as you wish. She is no relation to me."

"Thank God," Saren said with a smile. She raised her hands and concentric rings of symbols whirled around her again.

Selaan transformed to a seven-foot-tall human with dark skin, pink eyes and golden hair. He looked down his nose at the Allied forces and sniffed. "Any last words, maggots?"

Father Thomas shook his head. "You are pathetic, Selaan."

"Oh, that's original."

He smiled. "And accurate."

The Hadean gods clasped hands and began a low-voiced chant, the words and tempo accelerating. Terenil didn't recognize the language, but the tone and inflection sounded harsh, brutal, and cruel.

Father Thomas closed his eyes, lips moving in prayer. The air electrified around them and Terenil felt as if a layer of shimmering energy hovered just a finger-span away from his body.

"Get ready!" shouted King Phillip. Queen Ahlana swirled her staff in a circular motion and bright blue light flashed over every defender in the plaza. Terenil raised his bow. Iron Thunder, the Drakes and his grandchildren crouched, tails lashing.

Arachnia, Torvu and Selaan shouted. The air itself convulsed, then Saren's protective ring around the plaza disintegrated. The Ja'al swarmed forwards.

Terenil sighted on a Kaftu witch doctor chanting a spell. A dark mist sprang up around her, concealing nearby Ja'al archers. His arrow zipped through the mist and cracked on her armor. His second shaft hit home in her abdomen. A volley of arrows shot at him. He ducked behind the fountain, then popped out. His next arrow impaled the witch doctor in the temple.

The Ja'al infantry and cavalry reached the barricades. Horses, men, goblins, Kaftu, Dwarves, elves and minor daemons slashed, battered, screamed and died. Sharp detonations marked the demise of the Fallen Ones but the magic protections on the defenders held, deflecting the macabre shrapnel.

Deranese artillery arced overhead at the enemy leaders and generals. Magical screens deflected most of them. Collateral damage felled nearby infantry or archers.

Terenil loosed his last two arrows at a priestess of Torvu casting a spell, then swept up his shield and drew his sword. The blade glittered golden. He murmured under his breath and the shield flared.

Then all became a maelstrom of chaos as Ja'al warriors, ogres and daemons arrived among them. Terenil shield-slammed a goblin lancer off his fellbear, dodged the beast's slashing claws, and split its skull with an overhand strike. Something exploded near him, burning his arm as the flames curled around his magic screens. He stumbled against a dead Elven knight and nearly tripped.

A massive axe swept down and he skipped aside. An armored ogre roared a challenge, drawing back the weapon for another strike. Terenil pointed with the fingers of his shield-hand and a lightning bolt rocked the ogre backwards, its armor smoking. A spear shot past and Terenil knocked it aside with his shield. The ogre swung again. Terenil ducked. The axe hit a nearby barricade.

He thrust upwards. His blade entered under the ogre's chin and exploded out of the top of its skull in a flash of golden light.

Terenil dodged out of the way of the falling ogre. A flash of something in his peripheral vision alerted him and he crouched behind his shield. A blast of dark energy knocked him back and he slammed into a stone bench, tumbling over it. He scrambled to his feet. A Bone Knight advanced towards him but King Phillip cut it in half and his mount kicked the exploding remnants into the enemy ranks.

Shield up, Terenil dodged a charging Skullhead, tripping him into a flowerbed. The enemy warrior rose, stabbing, but two of Terenil's guards interposed themselves, driving him back. A spinning pinwheel of colored lights burst on the Skullhead's helmet and he staggered right into a sword thrust.

Terenil leaped on top of the ogre corpse and clambered to the rim of the fountain. Saren floated above it, the rings of symbols whirling around her. Her chest heaved with exertion as her fingers flew here and there, touching something he couldn't see. With each motion, an enemy spell disintegrated into fragments, a healed defender rose to her feet, or an enemy magic screen winked out.

Golvadu, Tarvener and the Ja'al wizards poured spell after spell at her: ice shards, bolts of black plasma, lightning, flame and firedarts. Ghostly hands clawed or punched at her. Still, she fought on, her shields deflecting or absorbing everything the enemy could conjure.

Sister Karen climbed over a fallen troll, hand up. A burst of light covered Saren and she took a deep breath, some of the color returning to her cheeks.

"Sister! Look out!" someone yelled.

A Tiger-daemon leaped at her. Terenil charged, his sword up, but two young gold dragons slammed into the daemon, hurling it to the side. It sprang to its feet, snarling, a ball of lightning growing in its hand. Two arrows sprouted in its chest and the dragons breathed twin jets of fire. Howling, the daemon stumbled backward and impaled itself on a jagged post, then detonated.

Bones and meat pinged off Terenil's shield. He called up to Saren.

"How are you doing?"

"You're making dinner tonight!" she growled. "I'll be a bit tired."

The three Hadean gods advanced as a team, burst of dark magic hurling aside defenders. Father Thomas barred their path, the hellish blasts curling around a dome of light covering him.

Torvu darted forward in the blink of an eye, swords up. Iron Thunder leaped to intercept him. A massive dragon claw swatted Torvu to the side and he slammed into a barricade, pulverizing it. Arachnia and Selaan uncorked purple fire at Iron Thunder. The dragon held up his forepaws, his shields guttering and winking out. He breathed a jet of flame that curled around the gods, turning nearby zombies and skeletons to piles of ash.

Sister Karen made a pushing gesture with her hands and the daemonic spells deflected to the side, immolating an ogre and a Dwerrolf unlucky enough to be in the wrong place. Melinor and the wizards of the Order slammed their staves into the ground and the ground undulated and bucked, throwing Selaan into the air. The Hadean god bounced and flopped back forty feet, cursing all the way. Arachnia levitated above the magical earthquake but King Phillip and the Papal Guard charged. She backpedaled, blocking their attacks, unable to retaliate.

Torvu leaped at the Nuncio again. Iron Thunder intercepted him, snatching him out of the air like a child's toy. The Hadean god slashed the dragon's wrist with one blade and drove the other into his chest. Iron Thunder cried out and hurled Torvu away. The god of death crunched through a ruined building, cratered a nearby street and slid down an alleyway, leaving a smear of goblin and human body parts and armor bits in his wake.

Gorlak fluttered down to Terenil's side, bleeding from a leg wound. "Too many, my lord!"

"We knew that going in, Gorlak," Terenil managed in a weary voice. Something warm ran down the side of his head. He didn't remember getting hit, but nothing surprised him at this point. Still Saren hovered overhead, healing, deflecting and disrupting. Her rings of golden symbols flickered once or twice.

Gorlak let out a deep breath. "She not go on forever."

Terenil didn't answer, ducking behind his shield as a fusillade of firedarts cracked on it. His magical protections sputtered and died.

The three Hadean gods regrouped. They held hands and shouted a single, vile word. The earth beneath the defenders bucked and vomited forth a hail of black spines, crackling molten rock and whirling metal fragments. Then a deafening boom hit the area. Everything went black for a second.

Terenil lost track of time and place. He vaguely came to the realization that he rested against something hard yet yielding. Struggling to his feet, he wiped daemon ichor and ogre blood from his face. The plaza looked like a vast meat-grinder. The surviving defenders hauled themselves to their feet shakily, leaning against ruined catapults and ballistae. Saren knelt on the rim of the fountain, her whirling rings of magic sigils gone. Father Thomas helped Sister Karen to her feet and Gorlak dragged himself out from under a dead Skullhead swordswoman.

Selaan, Torvu and Arachnia leaned on their knees, gasping. Despite the litter of dead around them, they smiled at one another. More Ja'al troops and daemons filed into the square from the connecting boulevards.

Terenil's heart sank. A third of the defending force lay unmoving in the square.

Golvadu stomped forward, looking somewhat scorched. His eyes blazed and he motioned the Ja'al horde onward. Tarvener cast a healing spell on his thigh and straightened, flexing his leg.

"Finish them off!" shouted Golvadu.

"Silence, worm!" shouted Selaan, straightening. "You're not in charge here! We'll give the orders." He dragged Torvu and Arachnia forward with him.

"No!" Saren stood and threw her hands to the side. Her eyes glowed white and a globe of purest light burst outwards.

The explosion hit the enemy ranks with the force of a tidal wave. The Hadean gods tumbled backwards. Their reinforcements staggered and fell and the daemonic rulers slammed into them.

Saren folded and fell off the fountain.

Terenil clambered over the wreckage and lifted her in his arms, feeling a feeble heartbeat. Despite a now-throbbing headache, he touched her temples with one hand. A blue light flared. He winced from a stabbing pain in his head and Saren gasped, her eyes wide open.

"Saren?"

"I'm here, love," she rasped, gripping his hands and trying to stand. The shimmering light of the Crown faded and then went dark.

"Stay still," he said, gazing out at the scene with bleary eyes. The Ja'al force picked itself up off the bloody ground, dazed. Even the Hadean gods looked disoriented. Black smoke plumed into the sky over the city.

Is this how it ends?

A wail of despair made him jerk his head to the left.

"Grandpa! No!" The two young dragons skidded to a halt next to the body of Iron Thunder, lying prone on the ruined brickwork. The great dragon's chest heaved with difficulty and dark brown blood covered his chest. His right arm had turned to stone and a sickly green pallor glossed over his golden scales.

"Lord Terenil!" Kindri begged, spinning in his direction. "Where is Lady Saren? She can make him better."

Terenil helped Saren limp over to them. Her head lolled against his chest.

He bit his lip, eyes stinging. "She is too weak. I don't know if I can keep her alive."

She moaned in pain and his heart clenched.

"Hang on, sweetheart." He kissed her dirty and bloodied forehead.

God, if you take her home, please take me too. I can't live in this world without her.

"No! Not Saren too!" Tholi cried. He lifted a bloodied and tear-streaked face to the summer sky. "God, can you not hear us? Please don't let them die!"

"I'm sorry, Kindri, Tholi," Saren panted, her eyes clouded with pain. "I have nothing left. I can barely see."

"My children…" Iron Thunder gasped.

"Grandpa?" The two young dragons curled their bodies around their grandsire.

Iron Thunder's eyelids fluttered. "Listen to me. I have a very special charge for you… like guarding the pegasi of Whitehorse Peak. Do you accept?"

Tears streaming down their faces, Kindri and Tholi nodded.

"Then this is my command to you. You are to serve the Papal Nuncio, Father Thomas."

"You can't die! You can't leave us!" Tholi pleaded.

"Everyone dies, my little love. I have the honor of dying for a good cause. Thomas, please…"

Father Thomas limped to their side and leaned against a shattered mangonel. "You have my vow as a priest of God, Donnervassilianelikilandra. I will care for them as if they were my own. And I will give them a task worthy of children of Iron Thunder."

"Thank you. Remember your promise. I love you." Iron Thunder's great golden cat eyes closed and his body relaxed.

"Grandpa!" sobbed Kindri, collapsing on his form.

Melinor clambered over the broken ruins of a great tree, the other mages of the Order behind him. He grimaced and pressed a hand to his side, now darkening with blood. "Saren, I…"

She lifted her head. "I know, Father. I tried. I'm just so tired now. So tired."

Terenil tried to focus enough to put a healing spell into her with the last of his strength. A mild golden light flared over her heart and another lancing pain like a stabbing knife hit him in the temples. He sucked in a breath, grimacing. His head swam.

"No, love, don't." Her hand caressed his face. Burns marked her smooth skin and jagged metal protruded from wounds in her legs, chest and side. A trickle of blood ran from her mouth. The Crown of Saint Alyssa, ever brilliant, lay quiet and dark on her ebony tresses, its light extinguished.

He blinked through blurry vision. "I can't let you die."

She smiled. "I will die someday, love, whether you will it or no. And so will you."

Terenil angrily wiped tears away. An image of her on their wedding day arose in his mind. He remembered her joyful smile the best.

"I love you so much," he choked out.

"As I love you. You have made me so happy. I will wait for you in Heaven," Saren smiled and kissed his hand. Her eyes closed.

Vile curses and the rattle of stone told him that the Hadean royals not only lived but brought themselves back into the fight. Arachnia, Torvu and Selaan stumbled forward, looking ragged, thousands of their followers in their wake. Battle Lords and Deathhammers picked up corpses and hurled them to the side, glowering.

"I've had enough of this!" spat Arachnia.

The Hadean gods put hands on each other, pink light flaring as their wounds healed.

Terenil's eyes wandered to the Ja'al host now reforming and marching towards them. "It looks like it will not be long for me either, my love," he said.

She nodded. Her chest rose and fell, then stilled.

No, God. Please!

He felt no pulse. He tried to summon up enough energy for one healing spell but the pain in his head refused to let him concentrate. All Terenil's weariness and pain and agony overcame him and he let his chin drop. Tears splashed onto Saren's face and armor.

"It looks like you will grant my prayer, Lord," Terenil murmured, lifting his eyes to the advancing enemy horde. "Please let it be swift."

"Come, my fellows of the Order," Melinor said, holding up his staff, a nimbus of power growing over him. "One last time."

Father Thomas and Sister Karen joined him. "There may not be any who will sing songs over our last stand," Sister Karen said, "but we will join the angels in heaven in far better hymns."

The angels must be singing now, Terenil thought foggily. *I can hear them.*

"What that sound?" rasped Gorlak, brow furrowing.

Then Terenil realized he heard actual singing, as if a massive choir with spectacular voices had decided to join them in the plaza.

Wait.

An intense light like a second sun flared in the east with a suddenness that made Terenil lift his head.

What in heaven's name?

A massive Gate, over a hundred yards wide, yawned in the sky above the plaza. Through it soared rank upon rank of Elohir in full armor, singing as they flew.

A stunned silence settled over the battlefield. All motion ceased. The three Hadean gods rattled to a halt. Their troops slowed their march and stopped, staring. An eerie silence descended, broken only by the crackle of flames and an occasional moan from the wounded.

Through bleary vision, Terenil watched a dark-haired, fair-skinned Elohir male in golden plate mail alight next to King Phillip. He wore a simple golden circlet on his brow and carried a spear with a head made entirely of light. Next to him, a dusky-skinned female Elohir with auburn hair in blue-black chainmail and a silver breastplate landed, twin longswords in her hands. Like the male, she also wore a golden coronet. A circle of seven other Elohir surrounded them. Terenil was struck by a family resemblance.

"Is that —" he began.

"Yes!" gasped Melinor. "King Kelson and Queen Ana of Celestia… And their children. They did it. The Grey Riders did it!"

A vast bitterness and unbelievable chasm of sorrow threatened to overwhelm Terenil and he gritted his teeth, eyes flitting to Grandpa lying in the ruined square. The Elohir alighted among the defenders in teams of three.

"Couldn't they have come a few minutes earlier?" he managed in a broken voice, lifting his dead wife in his arms.

Two Elohir women with tanned skin and chestnut hair flew to his side.

"You are the one called Melinor," said one, her tawny eyes sweeping over them.

Melinor leaned on his staff and nodded tiredly. "Yes, Your Grace."

The other woman gazed at Terenil with kind eyes of aquamarine. "And this would be?"

"My son-in-law, Terenil, and my daughter, Saren."

"I am named Rachel," said the one with golden eyes. "This is Sarah. We are here to help you."

"You cannot help us anymore," Terenil said in a dead voice, meeting Rachel's eyes. He felt numb all over.

Rachel gripped his shoulder with a firm hand. "Trust." She joined hands with her sister and closed her eyes. The women laid their hands on Saren's heart and head.

"Arise and walk!" they declared with a suddenness that made Terenil jerk as if awakened from deep slumber. His despair and lethargy vanished.

The Elohir women opened their eyes and a blinding light flashed. Terenil gasped, then relaxed. The pounding migraine headache of mage-sickness disappeared and his every ache receded to a memory. Life and energy surged through every part of his body.

Saren gasped and gripped Terenil's arms. Her eyes fluttered open and she stared at him, taking great breaths. "Terenil?"

Terenil's jaw dropped. "Impossible…" Her terrible wounds had vanished as if they never existed and color bloomed in her skin again. He set her on her feet and she settled the Crown of Saint Alyssa on her head, gaze locked on the Elohir in wonder.

"What have you done?" Saren's lip trembled and she clutched Terenil to her.

Princess Rachel chuckled. She laid a gentle kiss on her head. "Nothing will be impossible for God," she said. The two Elohir soared back to Kelson and Ana.

Terenil gazed out at the scene in the Grand Market. To him, it looked like a painting. No one moved, not even the three Hadean gods. All the combatants on the field had frozen in place, stunned into inaction, and simply watched the entire sequence with Saren.

King Kelson motioned with his spear and the rest of the Elohir Army alighted, interspersing themselves among the Allied force. Six of the Celestial Court carried people in their arms — one of them a Halfling.

Wait... Is that Andyn Eleandir?

Chapter Twenty-Eight – Dies Irae

Andyn took a good look at the Army of the Dark Wave and, despite being among hundreds of Elohir, her jaw clenched and her stomach tightened. She gripped her war hammer.

The Ja'al and their allies stirred restlessly with many a wary look at the Elohir and the remaining defenders of Oakmoor but remained in their places. Even generals and high priests of the Ja'al appeared uncertain.

Yes, to her, the Dark Wave looked nervous - except for the Fallen Ones. These showed no fear or unease, only a weird, ravenous hunger.

This is an old story to them, Andyn realized. *Only the scenery has changed.*

She swallowed with difficulty. "That's a lot of enemies," she said to Princess Kathryn of Celestia.

"It certainly is," mused the Elohir, lifting her shield from her back and strapping it to her arm. She unhooked a mace from her belt and the weapon's crystal head flared blue.

"Plenty for all of us," replied a dark-haired, tanned Elohir next to her, armored in white-enameled plate mail. He winked and hefted his battle axe.

"Just don't get yourself killed, Daniel."

"Your sisterly concern is noted." He strode forward to the front line.

"What means this?" bellowed Torvu.

A cold wave of pure terror washed over Andyn. Her throat constricted and she labored to breathe.

Easy, girl, easy, she thought.

Kathryn's hand squeezed her shoulder.

Torvu pointed a sword at Kelson, eyes narrowed. "What dost thou here, some-time King of Celestia? 'Tis not thy fight."

Kelson smiled. "When thou didst cast out mine own people from these lands and bar us from entering, thence to lay waste to these goodly folk here, thou didst made it my fight, Torvu of Hades."

Arachnia spoke in a sultry, echoing voice. "Come Torvu. We must have at them while we may and rid ourselves of the Elohir scourge. We are many and they are few."

Queen Ana spoke up. "What we have not in quantity, we accommodate in quality, I promise thee, Queen Arachnia. We give thee one chance now. Leave Damora and trouble it no more, or we shall as the servants of the Most High cast you out."

"Thou?" Selaan sneered. "I laugh at thee, insipid weaklings long-bereft of the will to claim overlordship of the Universe! Thou art weak-minded dabblers in magic who take more interest in lower beings than in thine own kin."

Kathryn put her arm around Andyn, a tiny smile on her face. "They haven't changed in five centuries," she remarked. "Still more bluster than anything else."

Something about the Elohir's calm confidence eased Andyn's fear and she relaxed. Sneaking a glance at the defenders, she saw she wasn't the only one so affected. The astonishment still on the faces of many members of the army was now being replaced by sudden, fierce joy. Stout Dwarves grinned, hands gripping war hammers and battle axes. The dwarven women, she decided, looked fiercer than their male counterparts, their braided hair decorated with brightly colored ribbons.

Elves smiled at one another, testing bows, readying spears and shields. Elohir filtered among them, touching one or the other, healing light glowing from their hands.

Human knights adjusted their armor, their faces hidden behind their visors. Next to them, infantry lifted pikes, spears and crossbows with renewed focus, eyes intent.

Arachnia laughed, a seductive sound that echoed in Andyn's head. The Hadean goddess gestured to the Elohir Court.

A sickly-sweet aroma suffused the air and it made Andyn's head fuzzy.

She wondered why she was even out here in the middle of a battlefield in the first place.

What… where am I? Who are the winged people? She struggled to remember something vitally important.

"Come now, Princes of the Elohir," Arachnia soothed. "Tarry here no longer, but hie thyselves to thy fair meadows of Celestia. This fight is unwinnable."

Disjointed thoughts swirled in Andyn's brain. She shook her head, trying to focus. She looked upon the enormous enemy horde and smelled Arachnia's alluring perfume.

She's right, Andyn thought in a daze. *There are so many. Why bother fighting?*

"Spend not thy blood for these pitiful weaklings thou wouldst protect," Arachnia continued. "Are they worth so much to thee?"

"Even one of them is worth more than a universe, in God's eyes," said Father Thomas.

Andyn started, spinning around. The Papal Nuncio took his place at Kelson's side and his eyes flashed. The mesmerizing aura of Arachnia's fragrance faded and vanished.

Andyn shook her head. *What was I thinking?*

Kelson gave a serene smile. Arachnia's eyes narrowed and she pressed her lips together. Her jaw clenched and she took the tiniest step backwards. Torvu's eyes darted to her.

Andyn felt a hot jolt of euphoria. *Ha! Just realized you've lost, bitches!*

"Thy god is false," sneered Selaan. "We do not need the permission of thine imaginary deity to take what is rightfully ours and remake the universe as we choose, by our word alone. We are on the brink of victory."

Prince Daniel laughed. "Thou art deluded, King Selaan. And if thou remainest here, we shall show thee the folly of thy error."

"Enough!" roared Torvu, eyes blazing. A wave of rage surged over the battlefield and Andyn once again felt the chill of terror despite Kathryn's presence. "There is no more to say! Thou hast squandered thine only opportunity to quit the field with both thy honor and thy lives. Know that thou canst not stand against us this day, Kelson of Celestia."

Kelson smiled. "Me? Thou art not to battle me. I serve the One and He guides me." He raised his spear. A shield of light leaped up on his left forearm. "*Deus Vult!*"

"*Deus Vult!*" sang the assembled Elohir in a chorus.

"*Deus Vult!*" shouted the defenders of Oakmoor in a triumphant, thunderous roar around Andyn.

Arachnia, Selaan and Torvu clapped their hands together and globes of pure darkness shot out, transforming to dead black whirlpools in seconds. The cyclones began sucking in everything within range as strong winds suddenly whipped up.

Selaan broke out in wild laughter.

Andyn's heart froze. *Whatever the hell those things are, they are not good.*

The entire Celestial Court sang three notes in unison and a ring of silvery light shot out from them. The light struck the nascent vortices of death. With a mild popping sound, the whirling tempests detonated, blasting everyone nearby with wood and stone fragments and a hot wind.

The Hadean gods staggered, faces pale.

"*Dies Irae Venit!*" shouted King Kelson of Celestia.

From the left and right flanks of the allied armies, Sarah and Rachel held their hands forward and spoke a word.

The Elohir princesses' bodies glowed and disks of bright blue shot out from them in an ever-widening circle with the speed of an arrow. The earth bucked like a horse and Andyn staggered. Wherever the disk touched, goblins, ogres, Kaftu and hobgoblins dropped, their bodies falling like hewn grain. Skeletons exploded, zombies disappeared in flashes of white light and ghouls shredded into tatters. Vampires flew backwards into the air like rag dolls. It was the most breathtaking display of power Andyn had ever seen.

The Elohir princesses wavered on their feet. Nearby warriors caught and held them.

The blue disk of power reached the Riders. Andyn was filled with a sudden, wild courage. She hefted her war hammer, seeking a target. Her eyes lighted on the figure of Selaan.

"You're mine!" Andyn snarled. She stepped forward, but a hand held her back.

The feeling faded and she shook her head. She swallowed. *What the blazes was I thinking of? I was going to charge off and attack a Hadean god!*

Kathryn smiled down at her.

"Easy, Andyn. My famlily have it well in hand. Let others do the fighting."

Accompanied by the rest of their children, the Celestial King and Queen darted straight at Arachnia and Torvu. Daniel and another Elohir Prince darted at Selaan, who backpedaled, blasting magic at them ineffectively. Arachnia and Torvu screamed and dark clouds rent with lightning swirled up around them. The Elohir royal family shot into the clouds without slowing, trailing streams of light like comets. The clouds bulged, rumbled and flashed with lights. The earth quaked.

Led by the Elohir, the defenders charged at the Ja'al lines. Clouds of arrows soared overhead from both sides. Several came close to Andyn, but Kathryn deflected them easily with her shield. From sections of both armies, fireballs soared overhead and detonated with fiery clouds, leaving piles of steaming ash and flaming wreckage in their wake. Lightning and acid sizzled out, tearing holes in each line. Streams of firedarts flickered out, striking warriors from their saddles. Mages dropped, riddled with arrows.

The Alliance met the Army of the Dark Wave and all was chaos. Ranks of cavalry slammed into each other with a thunderous crash of metal and crunch of bone. The allied infantry crashed into the enemy. Flashes from magic became so bright in some areas that Andyn squinted to keep from being blinded. Dragons slammed together in the sky, slain ones spiraling down, trailing flaming comet-tails to crush buildings below.

Groups of darting, dashing Elohir cut through the enemy ranks, silvery magic flashing. Daemons swarmed in red-flaming, black clouds. To Andyn's horror, several Celestials fell, but the onslaught continued.

On the field, and in the air, the Dark Wave gave ground under the onslaught of the Golden Army and a renewed Alliance. Slowly, they began to retreat, leaving piles of dead in their wake.

Selaan changed form to a six-headed dragon. He snapped at the Elohir princes, slashed, and breathed jets of lava, clouds of ice shards, and storms of lightning but to no avail. The Celestials drove him back, bleeding from a dozen wounds. He shrieked a vile curse and a sphere of sizzling black energy burst forth. The Elohir backpedaled, their shields up and flaring.

Then a thunderbolt loud enough to crack stone reverberated over the city. The black clouds surrounding Torvu and Arachnia disintegrated. Andyn lurched to the side and only Kathryn's firm hand kept her from tumbling to the ground. Kelson and his family charged. The Hadean royals retreated, blasting magic and slashing with weapons, then fled. Arachnia cast a greasy cloud of poison gas behind them.

The Elohir paused as Queen Ana dispelled the poison, then zoomed off in hot pursuit.

"Don't leave me hanging, you fucking idiots!" Selaan raged. He took the form of a dark Elohir with bat wings and flew away from the battle, out towards the hills. With a shout of triumph, the princes raced after him.

Horns blared from the enemy ranks and the vast Army of the Dark Wave melted, retreating down the streets and avenues of the city. The Elohir led the defenders, chasing the enemy to the gates of the city and beyond until the Celestials were the only ones with strength enough to continue. Andyn saw distant flashes of light as the Elohir mopped up the remnants of the Ja'al host.

An eerie silence descended on the battlefield. Healers dispersed among the wreckage, seeking the injured.

"Andyn!" Varienne and Altus waved to her, clambering over the wreckage, looking a bit the worse for wear. Andyn waved back, feeling dazed. Father Thomas and Sister Karen joined them, heading in their direction, with Kindri and Tholi following after.

"It's over," Andyn murmured.

Khyron's hand slipped into hers and she leaned into him. "Thank Verian, yes." He kissed the top of her head.

A giant owl swooped down out of the sky and resolved to the figure of Carine Del Rio. She hit the ground running and almost tackled Buck, planting a long kiss on his lips.

Khyron laughed. "Now that's a welcome-home greeting if ever I saw one."

She pinched him and Kathryn joined in the laughter.

Connor looked up at the Elohir princess, brow furrowed. "Why didn't you join the fight?"

The Elohir princess smiled gently, peacefully. "I was tasked to stay here with you. We couldn't have our most valuable 'assets' damaged by some disrespectful daemons, now could we?"

Chapter Twenty-Nine – In Memories, Immortal

Will the young dragons be here, Father?"

Father Thomas blinked, breaking his reverie. "I'm sorry, Detlef. What was that?"

"Tholieros and Kindriana, Eminence. Will they be at the memorial?"

The Papal Nuncio shook his head absently, eyes on a paper on the table. "No. They escorted the body of their grandfather to the wilderness with the other dragons for his interment."

Detlef gave a rueful smile. "I hope they'll be back."

Father Thomas gave him a sidelong glance. "I know they will be. You'll see them soon. Now, please bring the vestments."

"Yes, Eminence." Detlef departed to another chamber of the pavilion, leaving Father Thomas alone for a while.

He sighed, reading over the list. A deep sadness came over him at the sight of recognizable names.

So many…

He heard Detlef return but didn't look up.

"Here you are, Eminence."

Father Thomas remained silent, eyes on the page. *Could we have done something more to save them?*

"Your Eminence?" asked Detlef, laying a stack of white vestments on the chair next to him.

"Oh, yes, I'm sorry, Detlef. Thank you."

Detlef paused, then came to the Nuncio's side. His eyes fell on the list, his face somber. "It's very sad," he said in a quiet voice. "How will we get through this?"

He lost friends too, Father Thomas recalled. *The best I can do for him — and everyone else — is bring them comfort.*

He straightened, putting a hand on his aide's shoulder. "The way we have always come through hard times. With faith, with each other's support and with time."

Detlef blinked rapidly and nodded. The Nuncio gave his shoulder a squeeze. "All the people we cared about who perished in the War of the Dark Wave have gone to a place where there is no war and no pain. We can rest assured in their love and prayers for us who remain."

"It doesn't make it easy."

"No, it doesn't."

Determined not to let the names on the list get him down, the Nuncio turned briskly to the table. "We're going to be late. Please go out to the grove while I get dressed and see if the other presiders are ready. I'll be out in a minute."

"Yes, Eminence."

Detlef lifted up the tent flap and went outside. Thomas glimpsed the meadow and trees outside their pavilion and the people seated on chairs in neat and orderly rows in the shade. They numbered in the thousands.

Thomas couldn't keep his eyes from wandering back to the page as he put on his alb and stole.

Alfred Bydecy, father of Buckminster, he read silently. *Beldryn Torferis, half-sister of Andyn Eleandir, and family (husband Ren, and children, Calindra, Dalris and Khyron). Lawrence Cabot, brother of Dar, and family (wife Cordelia, and children, Elizabeth and Stephen). Perry Lomin, uncle of Connor, and family (wife Georgina, and children, Tanya, Timmon and Larad). Devin DeMey, brother of Terenil. Evan Demaris, brother of Khyron.*

At every memorial service for the last few days, he had to try to provide words of comfort, yet this one hit close to home, with the Riders' family members.

The poison of the Ja'al's hate left no one unscathed. Everyone in Oakmoor has felt at least one loss.

The Papal Nuncio took a deep breath, finished vesting and reached for his notes. He slid them into a pocket under his robes and his fingers touched a small glass vial.

He withdrew the crystal tube and stared at the long splinter inside. Even after careful inspection and magical examination, it seemed to be nothing more than a piece of wood – a thorn from a plant, really.

If it really is from the Crucifixion, then we haven't been keeping good tabs on our relics, he thought wryly, allowing himself a small smile. The very idea, of course, was ludicrous. There was no way that something like that could have ended up on Damora without any of the previous Nuncio's knowing about it.

No, he decided. *It must be something else. We just have to figure out what, when we have the time. In the meantime, we have the important and frustrating dilemma of the Alenar sisters to unravel. That is already enough of a challenge.*

Detlef returned. "They are all ready, Eminence."

"Thank you." Father Thomas took up his crozier and waited while Detlef placed the miter on his head.

Without another word, they exited the pavilion and joined the other clergy in a solemn and silent procession to a wooden altar under the trees. Runners with the symbols of the churches of Christ, Verian, Irial and Kurental draped over the top of it. A Dwarven High Priest of Kurental in silver and white robes stood next to an Elven Patriarch wearing a green mantle with the silver tree of Verian. Next to them, a human woman held a staff surmounted with a gold disk embossed with the Sickle and Wheat Sheaf of Irial. She wore a grey mourning tabard with a gold band from shoulder to hip.

Father Thomas nodded to a bearded man attired in brown robes with a white belt. High Druid Anthan bowed and touched a pendant in the shape of an acorn.

"Our reasons for gathering here are sorrowful," Druid Anthan announced in an augmented voice that echoed out to the farthest chair in the congregation. "Yet they are also triumphant. Our beloved ones have returned to the Earth Mother, as is the fate of all living things, but with great valor and glory to their names. I will not say that tears are inappropriate, for they signify our love for those who have passed from this life, and all things in love are true and good."

He stood to the side, offering the acorn pendant to the next speaker. The other religious leaders took stood forth in turn and addressed the assembly. Father Thomas had already compared notes with them about their remarks to make sure they were all on the same page, as it were. He knew their words by heart and let his eyes roam over the people as he listened.

The Grey Riders sat near the front next to Dar's family, Buck's family, and the DeMeys, in the second row behind King Phillip, Queen Ahlana, and various nobles and officers of the Court. They all wore their grey and black tunics with the symbol of a pegasus on the left breast. The Riders looked somber and tearful, older than their years. Father Thomas reminded himself that they were still very young — even Andyn and Khyron.

Sorrow ages even heroes ...

"So, as is written in the Revelations of Tolan, Chapter Two: Verian the Highest Lord owns all that is Holy," the Elven Patriarch concluded, his sea-green eyes sweeping the assembly. "We also acknowledge that he, in his wisdom, ordains that all things other than himself are mortal and perish, thence to join him in the Kingdom of Forever. There, they live immortal. We should remember this. It is their destiny and they have claimed it with their good deeds. In our memories then, they also remain immortal. May we all merit Verian's Kingdom when our own lives end."

He turned to Father Thomas and bowed.

You'd think I would be used to this after four of them, the Nuncio mused as he accepted the little acorn pendant.

He strode before the altar and regarded the people for a few moments. "I would like to echo the sentiments of all the other faith leaders here in thanking Druid Anthan for allowing us to use this grove for our memorial services. Unfortunately, none of our houses of worship are in any shape to host the solemn memorials just yet, so it is much appreciated."

He nodded to Anthan, who smiled and inclined his head.

Father Thomas let out a breath. "Well, my colleagues have already expressed much of what was on my mind. Our hearts and our most sincere and affectionate condolences go out to you. As Patriarch Moren of Kurental pointed out, the sacrifice paid in victory makes that victory all the more resounding because of the resolve of those who paid with their lives to make it a reality. I could not agree more. Our Irial Matriarch Lindsay's words about the strange and healing path of grief to renewed spirit made me reflect on the fact that our beloved dead do not want us to remain in our sadness but to live for them in the future, to make us proud of them. And Patriarch Minaron's words from Verian's prophet will stay with me for a long time. Indeed, our beloved ones are, in our memory, immortal. Beautiful words indeed, from my colleagues — brilliant, even."

He paused for a moment. "I would only add that our beloved dead are in a realm not limited by time or space. They can see us as we strive to work beyond our grief and try to reconstruct our lives. Never forget that we have them as our advocates, our families, our friends, our beloved ones in Heaven. They are alive more completely than they were when they were with us in this world. They are waiting for us to join them in the next. Let us commit ourselves to living our best lives, to being our best selves, so that we can merit the same reward as they now enjoy. May we turn our sadness into a quiet resolve to follow God's will and make them proud. Then, one day, we will join them in a place where there is only happiness, only love, only peace, only the perfect life that is in God's Heavenly Kingdom."

He smiled. "I know I will so commit myself. I hope you will do so as well, in your own time."

Father Thomas returned to his place with the other leaders, who gave him warm smiles. A choir began a hymn, starting in Elven, shifting to Dwarven, and finally finishing in Humana.

Father Thomas let his mind drift with the music and the words, imagining the spirits of the departed singing along with them, joyful and complete, beckoning them to carry on the legacy that they started with their sacrifice.

If I could only solve the riddle of Brandi and Megan, at least it would give them something to celebrate. There are no easy answers.

He watched Andyn lay her head on Khyron's shoulder, eyes closed, lips moving in prayer.

Yes, Lord. It will be a while before they can heal. Please be with them — and help me find a way to bring them hope.

Chapter Thirty – Vita Nova

I must be crazy, Father Thomas Williams thought. He closed the door behind him.

"Are you going to tell me what we're doing here?" Sister Karen asked.

"I'm not so sure myself," he whispered. The images of his dream replayed in his head, particularly the scene at Calvary. For the fortieth time, he mulled over the significance of the small object that fell to the ground when they took Christ down from the Cross, the Grey Riders walking across a sea of glass, and the golden drops of blood.

For the fortieth time, he had no answers.

Father Thomas regarded the still forms of the Alenar sisters under their Preservation Nets. He gently laid a hand on Brandi's arm. The Net rippled and glowed under his touch.

Sister Karen sighed. "I don't know what you have planned, but I feel our best bet is to keep up with the research and investigations. I've found some Paragon-Era fragments that might be references to counteracting vampirism."

He leaned his hands on Brandi's table, feeling a vast weariness and resignation. "No. We've tried hundreds of references on magical restoration. Melinor and the Order of the Three Magi have scoured every arcane tome they can think of. Nothing has worked. I'm tired, Melinor's tired… and we still have nothing hopeful to offer Dar and Eric." He tried to keep the disappointment from his voice.

She said nothing, gazing at the women on their biers.

"It's time to consider what this really is and what it really means," he said. From a pocket of his cassock, he removed a pair of silk gloves embroidered with a dove and slipped them on. He reached into the opposite pocket of his cassock and pulled out the crystal vial.

"What's that?"

He gently laid it down on a table. "See for yourself."

The doctor peered at it. "Looks like a splinter or a thorn." She frowned. "I'm not picking up any magical auras. Where did you get it?"

"The Riders found it at a shrine, deep in the wilderness. A very old shrine, dedicated to Mary, Mother of Sorrows."

Sister Karen straightened and shot him a look. "No…wait a second. You don't think it's from the True Cross… or the Crown of Thorns, do you?"

He shook his head. "I doubt it. Something that sacred wouldn't just be sitting out in the Wilderness near the Harrowing. I think it would be protected very carefully."

Her eyes narrowed. "Well, God is in the tiny whispering sound, not the earthquake."

"I can't argue with that. But it just seems so improbable…" his voice trailed off. An image from his dream of Saint Veronica stood out in his mind.

"Well, in lieu of more research, what do you want to do?" she asked.

He hesitated, lost in thought. Doubt warred with a growing urge to do something. His eyes flickered to the vial. *I must be getting delusions of my own importance: thorn from Christ's Crown indeed!*

Yet the dream-images of the Riders and the scene at Calvary prodded him. He couldn't shake them. *Is this the sign we've needed — that I've needed? God knows everyone needs something positive after all the death and destruction. We all need hope.*

He waited, but a single word remained on his mind: hope.

Faith, Hope and Love… He set his mouth in a firm line. "Sister, can you open a very small gap in the Nets above Brandi and Megan, like what Melinor used to get their blood samples?"

"Yes, for a few seconds, though I'm not sure how that will help."

"Please. Make an opening above Brandi's mouth."

Sister Karen raised an eyebrow at him. For a moment, he thought she would refuse.

"I promise you it isn't post-traumatic stress disorder, Sister."

"Very well." She led him to the head of Brandi's bier and touched her index finger to the Net. She closed her eyes and murmured under her breath.

Thomas opened the vial and reverently slid the wooden fragment out. Now that he looked at it in the palm of his hand, he saw the resemblance to a broken thorn, stained dark.

A hole appeared in the Net, perfectly placed above Brandi's mouth. Sister Karen nodded.

He brushed the thorn against Brandi's lips. Nothing happened. Sister Karen restored the Net.

"Try it with Megan," he said, trying to forestall a sinking feeling of failure.

They repeated the process and he waited with Sister Karen in the glimmering golden light.

Nothing changed. He slid the thorn into the vial and closed the stopper.

The pair regarded the two sisters for several heartbeats. His heart sank.

Karen made a wry face. "Well, it was worth a try."

"Yes, it was." He let out a deep breath, bitterness growing again. So much loss and sadness and, despite the great sacrifices of the Grey Riders, this one last hope faded into nothingness.

"Maybe we go back to the archives after all," Sister Karen said with a sigh. She didn't sound very confident.

The air in the room glowed. Then it darkened. To Thomas, it wasn't the frightening emptiness of the void, but the comforting, peaceful dark of a summer night sky.

"No, wait," Father Thomas said.

As if answering his thoughts, stars spangled the velvety blackness. He still stood next to Karen, and both biers remained. However, the walls of the chamber had vanished. It seemed that he and Sister Karen hovered in midair next to the Alenar sisters. He looked down. A starfield to infinity stretched out below his boots.

Why am I not afraid? he wondered.

"Greetings, children," said a voice behind them.

They turned.

A young woman in a simple blue gown glided towards them. She stood only a little shorter than Karen and appeared to be about thirty years old. Calm, black eyes regarded him from an aquiline face with a dusky complexion. She lifted back a hooded veil, revealing jet black, curly hair. A wave of peace and kindness banished all his fears and worries.

She looks so familiar. Thomas thought, his mind in a pleasant, dreamlike state.

The Lady moved to the far end of the biers, near the girls' heads. Her expression turned to one of great tenderness and affection. "Do not fear for them," she said in a voice that seemed to make the universe shiver. "All will be made new."

"Do you really think so?" asked Karen in a dazed voice.

The lady lifted her head and smiled at them. "I know so."

Thomas' heart gave a little leap of joy at her smile, a joy mixed with longing. Some of the stars in the darkness whirled and danced and drew near to her, forming a crown of twelve over her head.

His mental fogginess faded and he gasped. They weren't simply lights or some magical illusion. They were actual stars, blazing with the inferno of nuclear fusion. Tiny planets looped in orbit around them: gas giants and rocky planets with moons. Asteroids and comets whirled nearby. His mind reeled.

This can't be happening...

The Lady gently laid her hands on the Alenar sister's heads. The Preservation nets sparkled at her touch. "These daughters are very dear to my Son. I am here to awaken them."

"How?" Thomas managed.

"With the same words my Son used." She kissed each woman on the head. *"Talitha Koum,"* she said each time.

With that, the Preservation Nets vanished. The wooden stake in Brandi's heart disintegrated into a pile of dust. The deathly pallor on her skin faded, replaced by a healthy glow.

Thomas' eyes darted to Megan. The sickly, sallow complexion brought about by George Oxbridge's poison vanished and her cheeks flushed with color.

The Lady raised a hand in benediction and glided backwards, receding into the distance.

"No!" gasped Karen. "Don't go."

"Don't leave us," Thomas pleaded.

The Lady's smile brightened. "I am with you always. And you have tasks to do yet. I will return for you. I promise. Remember…"

"Remember…" Thomas repeated. He blinked, dizzy. His surroundings spun for a moment, then settled.

The room appeared absolutely normal, the way it had been when he brought out the thorn.

Megan and Brandi slept, their chests rising and falling in relaxed rhythm.

***

Dar Cabot marched down the hallway in the Royal Palace. "Did he mention what it was about, Detlef?" he asked.

The Papal Nuncio's orderly shrugged. "No. He just asked that I bring you and Sir Indidarc to the antechamber of the library conference room."

"Did he seem bothered?" Eric asked.

Detlef's blue eyes were thoughtful as he led them through the hallways. "No. He seemed at peace. Happy, even."

Dar exchanged a glance with Eric. His friend shrugged.

I guess we'll find out when we get there, Dar thought.

They arrived in the antechamber. Father Thomas and his personal physician, Sister Karen, stood at the tall windows in the bright sunshine, looking out at something.

Dar bowed. "We are here as requested, Father Thomas."

"Thank you for coming so quickly," the Nuncio replied.

Dar straightened. His brow furrowed. Father Thomas smiled at him beneficently and Sister Karen beamed and dabbed at her eyes with a handkerchief.

What is going on?

Father Thomas opened his mouth, closed it and shook his head. "I had some fancy speech all prepared, but now it seems all so inadequate. Let us show you instead."

He and Sister Karen strode to the double doors that led into the conference room. They pulled them open.

Two women emerged. Time stood still. Dar's heart literally stopped, then started again with a hammering beat.

"Megan?"

Megan Alenar smiled through tears streaming down her face. She wore the same simple white tunic she had worn on the bier. She held her arms out to him and, impossibly, marched across the room.

Next to her, Brandawyn bit her lip, teardrops falling from her eyes. "Eric!" she whispered. Then she raced forwards and hurled herself onto him, wrapping her arms and legs around him in a fierce embrace. Eric staggered, eyes wide, bracing himself against a nearby chair.

Megan darted to Dar and likewise enveloped him. Dar's mind spun. He felt dizzy. As if in a dream, he hugged her back.

"Megan?" he repeated. He tried to say more but his throat constricted and his eyes stung. He squeezed his eyes shut.

Oh my God…

"Yes, it is true," Father Thomas said, voice full of emotion. "It is Megan and Brandi."

Dar tried to speak and his voice refused to work. *How is this possible? What happened?*

He cupped the back of Megan's head with one hand, his fingers combed through her lustrous strawberry-blonde locks. She sobbed once, then stilled. He felt only her gorgeous body, her strong heartbeat, and her breath against his neck.

Lord Jesus, what have you done?

For the next few minutes, all he could do was try to navigate a storm of emotions: wonder, relief and a joy so intense that he couldn't speak. Finally, with an effort, he controlled his breathing. He gently pulled her head away from his neck and gazed into her beautiful face.

"I missed you so much," he managed in a broken voice, searching the depths of her amber eyes. "And you're okay? You're feeling fine?" he continued, convinced he sounded like an idiot.

She gave him the same rascally grin he had missed all these long months.

"What do you think?" she asked in a husky voice, pulling him in for a kiss.

Ecstasy rushed through him and he resolved right there that he wouldn't break the kiss for all the gold in Deran. He would rather stay in her embrace and starve.

In all too short a time, she pulled back.

"Convinced?" she asked, stepping down on the floor and cupping his face in her hands. She brushed her thumbs across his cheeks.

Dar ran his hands over Megan's face and arms. Her complexion looked radiant and healthy. "Your skin is normal again."

She nodded. "The poison is gone." She reached out and took Eric's hand, pulling him and Brandi closer.

"No more vampirism?" Eric asked. Now standing at his side, Brandi nestled her head against his chest, arms wrapped around him. He stroked her hair. She gave Dar the most blissful, beatific smile he had ever seen.

Father Thomas shook his head. "I checked. Gone. As if it never existed."

"How? Did you find a cure?"

"God did, "Sister Karen answered, laying a hand on Eric's shoulder.

"To be precise, God sent his mightiest Saint," Father Thomas interjected. "The Blessed Mother, Our Lady of Sorrows, appeared to us when I touched the thorn from the True Crown to Megan and Brandi's lips."

Dar wavered on his feet. "I...I don't believe it," he managed. "That little piece of wood —"

"— was from the Crucifixion," Sister Karen finished for him.

Dar remained in a daze, barely aware of anything other than Megan in his arms and the bright, warm light streaming in from the windows.

Sister Karen came to their side. "I know this is a lot to process in a short time, but don't forget that the other Riders know nothing of this. We shouldn't delay that reunion overmuch."

Father Thomas gestured to a pair of couches facing the windows. "Have a seat and I'll ask Detlef to get a suitable change of clothing for the ladies."

The two couples eased into the couches next to each other while Sister Karen pulled up a chair. The nun watched the sisters with sharp eyes, almost as if measuring them.

Dar gave her a questioning look and she waved a hand with a little smile. "Just observing. It's the doctor in me. I watch all my patients like a hawk. Just ask Father Thomas."

Dar thought to ask her more but decided against it. Megan maintained her hold on Dar, almost as if afraid to let him go.

He tipped her chin up. "How much do you know about recent events?" he asked.

Her eyes looked sympathetic. "Father Tom summarized while Detlef went to get you: that there was a great war and daemons invaded from Hades via the Skull Gates. Many people died. You and the other Riders brought a Celestial army using the Gate of Stars. Now the War is ended and the Ja'al are destroyed forever."

She paused. "Dar, Father Thomas told me about all the family losses among the Riders. I'm so sorry about your brother and his family. I was so looking forward to meeting them."

A wave of sorrow threatened to overcome his newfound joy. With an effort, he smiled at her through misty vision. "Thank you. I know they would have liked you."

She hugged him tighter.

"What happened to them?" asked Brandi.

Dar let out a deep breath. "During the early days of the siege of Oakmoor, a Ja'al catapult round hit their house and exploded."

"How terrible," Megan said. "Wasn't anyone able to help them? Healers in the area maybe?"

"Unfortunately, not. From what we saw, they probably died instantly," interjected Sister Karen.

"At least they didn't have time to suffer or be afraid, though that doesn't make it any easier," Brandi murmured. "I'm sorry we weren't here to help."

Dar cleared his throat, trying to banish the lump in it. "I don't think you could have done anything, Bran." He struggled for other words to say in an extended, awkward silence.

Eric caught his eye and changed the subject. "That reminds me. What happened after we applied the Preservation Nets? Did you know where you were? Could you hear or see your surroundings?"

Brandi gave him an odd look. "Well, no, dearest. Dead people can't sense anything. And a stake to the heart of a vampire is fairly decisive."

"So, I really did kill you," Eric said in a low voice, looking down at the floor.

"Dearest," Brandi replied, putting a hand on the back of his neck. She kissed him on the lips. "It's all right. I don't blame you. You did what you had to do."

Dar held Megan at arm's length. "We hoped the Preservation Nets would halt the process."

Megan stroked his cheek. "That was the right idea, love, but the poison was too strong. I died."

"Where did you go?" he managed.

Brandi repeated her beatific smile. "To a place of light and peace. We saw our parents and relatives and friends and a host of millions. And He was with us."

Dar simply stared, mind reeling.

"And then?" Eric asked, eyes wide.

Brandi gave a little shrug. "I have no concept of time passing. We were just…there. Jesus told us our task wasn't finished and that we had work to do yet, for Him, very important work. Then Mother Mary appeared and led us by the hand to, well, to this time and place."

"I didn't want to come back," Megan told Dar. "But then I remembered you. I knew that you and I were part of God's plan."

Dar stared into her eyes. Yes, they were the same eyes that had looked upon him those many months ago, but now he saw something else, something he had a hard time describing. It was almost as if she could see into him, into his soul.

This is going to take some getting used to. He could only shake his head in wonder.

"We're right where we belong," Brandi said, laying her head on Eric's shoulder. "Thanks be to God."

Megan rested her head on Dar's chest. He smelled roses and vanilla in her hair.

"Thanks be to God," he repeated.

Long moments of absolute peace passed. Birds flitted by the window and the summer sun shone warm. Despite the sadness of the last few days, he felt completely at peace… and more than a little emotionally drained. A look at Eric's face confirmed his friend felt the same.

Sister Karen watched them with a wry look on her face. She flicked a glance from Dar to Megan, then mouthed the words "Go ahead".

Dar mouthed back "Now?"

Sister Karen made an exasperated face and nodded vigorously. Dar glanced at Eric, who gave him a warm smile in return. He stroked Brandi's hair and nodded.

Dar licked dry lips and his hands felt clammy. *I don't even have a ring.*

Megan sighed in contentment and he looked down at her face. He thought of their letters to each other over the many months, the nights watching the night sky, yearning for her presence. He recalled all the time he had spent in prayer, begging God to return her to him safely.

I thought I'd never see her again, he realized. *Now, here she is, in answer to my prayers, beyond my fondest hopes. How can I let nerves stand in the way?*

Sister Karen cleared her throat. "Do you gentlemen have something to ask the young ladies?" she suggested in a droll voice.

I'm not going to let another minute pass by. Dar lifted Megan's chin again. "Dearest?"

"Yes?"

He stared into her sparkling eyes. "Megan, will you —"

"Yes," she interrupted him. The sun shone in her smile.

Chapter Thirty-One – Reunion

Even the short minutes it took for Brandi and Megan to quickly change into their own Grey Riders garb seemed like an eternity to Dar. He waited with Eric and Father Thomas in the antechamber as Sister Karen helped the Alenars in another room.

"We have to tell the others," Eric said, in a faraway voice. "And Dad."

"They won't believe it," Dar replied.

Eric nodded. "They will when they see them."

"Have no doubts on that score," Father Thomas said. "I called the Riders to one of the guest apartments without telling them the reason. Also, per Megan's request, I had Detlef bring Varienne and Altus to join them."

Dar gave the Nuncio a measuring look. "What was she like? Saint Mary, I mean."

Father Thomas's smile faded and his jaw worked. "I didn't want to stay here," the Nuncio finally said in a voice thick with emotion. "Neither did Sister Karen. But Our Lady said we had to wait."

Dar put a hand on his shoulder. "We're glad you didn't go."

Father Thomas cleared his throat and his eyes twinkled. "Yes, well, I'm sure you'll find some use for me."

The door on the other side of the room opened and Sister Karen led the Alenar sisters in. They wore clothes similar to the other Rider women: black boots, dark grey skirts and blouses embroidered with the silver pegasus at the left breast.

After a warm and deep kiss, Megan snuggled into Dar's side.

"I can't wait to see the others," Brandi said, smiling at Eric.

"There have been a few changes, love," he said, tweaking her nose. "It will take some explaining."

"I'm not in a hurry."

"Then let's go, shall we?" Father Thomas said with a gesture at the ante-chamber doors.

They followed him and Sister Karen through the corridors of the Royal Palace of Mil Tereth. Dar felt as if enveloped by a cloud of happiness, scarcely daring to believe it was real.

If it's a dream, I hope I never wake up...

A quartet of Elven guards saluted as they approached another set of double doors chased in silver.

Father Thomas held up a hand. "Karen and I will speak to them first, but we won't tell too much. We'll call for you." He slipped inside the room with Sister Karen.

Dar contented himself with holding Megan as he waited.

Voices murmured inside the apartment.

"Darius and Eric, come in please."

Dar took a deep breath and Megan's hand and strode inside.

Altus, Varienne and the other Riders gaped at them, wide-eyed. Buck actually staggered and Carine caught him, her expression confused. Connor shot to his feet, looking like he had seen a ghost.

Andyn recovered first. "Brandi! Megan!" she screamed and hurled herself forwards, leaping over a low table.

Megan and Brandi laughed, catching her in their arms.

"Oh my God!" Andyn cupped each of their faces with a free hand. Then her lip quivered and she burst into tears. The sisters held her in their arms, smiling at the others.

Buck and Connor advanced as if sleepwalking. Megan held out one arm while the other kept a tight hold of the weeping Andyn. Connor stepped into her embrace, eyes shiny. Brandi put her arm around Buck.

"Is it really you?" Connor breathed.

"Yes, my sweet friend," Megan said in a calm, loving tone. "It really is."

She raised her eyes to Varienne, who hurried to her side.

"I know not how Irial has done this," the blonde human woman said in a choked voice. She rested her forehead against Megan's. "But I will praise him for endless ages because of it."

Then everyone crowded around, wiping at their eyes and asking questions simultaneously. Dar felt their joy as a palpable thing, something that made the air glow.

Eric introduced Hannah, Carine, Khyron and Altus to the sisters. Dar had a hard time keeping up with everyone's questions, laughing as he tried to answer Khyron and Altus at the same time.

Father Thomas clapped his hands. "I think this will work best if we just explain everything first. Then you can ask as many questions as you like."

Sister Karen nodded briskly and marched to the doors. "And we will need a little Gorostoli jekka and dwarven pastry to keep our strength up." She gave instructions to one of the guards.

Father Thomas had them all sit, then snapped his fingers. "I almost forgot. Sister, would you mind asking the guard to get Lord Melinor?"

She spoke to a soldier at the door and took a seat on a chair.

"Now," Sister Karen said, with a glance at Megan and Brandi, "Father Thomas and I explained about the War and recent events, but we trust the Riders will fill you in on other happenings in their own good time."

"How were you cured?" Khyron asked. "You were both in bad shape when we put the Preservation Nets on you."

Father Thomas explained about the relic from the Crown of Thorns, the appearance of Saint Mary, the miraculous healing and restoration of the sisters to life.

The other young people sat in shocked silence, eyes distant.

"It's almost too much to believe," said Buck, shaking his head.

"And yet, here they are," replied Sister Karen.

"Where is the thorn?" Andyn asked.

Father Thomas smiled. "It's gone."

Dar started. "Gone? Gone where?"

Sister Karen lifted her eyes heavenward and raised a hand. "God only knows. Literally. His Eminence and I searched the room but the only thing we could find was the little crystal vial."

Dar nodded. "Its task was done. Maybe Our Lady took it with her."

"That's entirely possible, but who is to say?" said Father Thomas. "Perhaps it wasn't meant to stay in the realm of mortals any longer. In any event, all has ended up very well, I would say."

"Not for everyone," Buck said with a glance at the others. Carine laid her head on his shoulder and kissed his hand. Khyron and Andyn stared at the carpet, arms around each other. Connor let out a deep breath and Hannah hugged him, her eyes sympathetic. The happy atmosphere turned melancholy in the span of a few heartbeats.

"We know," Brandi said. She gazed at each of them. "Father Thomas told us about your family members." They smiled their thanks, their eyes shiny.

"I am so sorry," Megan whispered, blinking back tears. "My heart goes out to all of you."

Andyn dabbed at her eyes with a handkerchief. "Thank you, Megan. There is nothing anyone could have done."

Dar explained to Megan and Brandi about Hannah's brother, Handor, whom he and Eric had mentioned in their letters but whom the sisters had never met.

Brandi knelt next to Hannah on the couch and Megan joined her. "We are sorry for your loss," Megan said, her hand clasping Hannah's. "We owe him so much for everything he did. Please accept our condolences."

Hannah's gaze dropped to the carpet and she squeezed their hands, then raised them to her lips and kissed them. "My brother met his destiny as set out by the Great Maker of All. He turned aside from evil and helped bring about the eventual demise of the Ja'al. That is enough."

She raised her gaze to the sisters and smiled. "He would be happy indeed to see that you are restored to the embrace of your lovers, his friends."

"I know it doesn't lessen the pain," Brandi added, resuming her place next to Eric, "but Megan and I have been through this ourselves. We are here to help. You need only ask for anything and it's yours. I know all our loved ones are happy now."

Despite his sadness, Dar had to smile. *Still the same Brandi… speaking the truth in love no matter what.*

No one spoke. Finally, Sister Karen nodded emphatically. "You are absolutely right, Brandawyn. Despite the loss and sadness, there is much to be happy about, isn't there?" She nodded at Buck and Carine.

Brandi arched an eyebrow at Buck. "I'm glad someone nice has managed to corral you, Buck."

Carine gave her a coy look. "It took a while for both of us to realize it. He can be a handful but I'm up for the challenge."

Brandi nodded, eyes twinkling. "You have my support. I can always box his ears for you if you need. I never had a brother but I can get into practice very fast."

Everyone laughed. Buck rolled his eyes, the old homespun grin on his face. The somber mood dissipated.

"Those are beautiful betrothal rings, Andyn and Khyron," Megan noted, nodding at the couple.

"Thank you," Andyn replied, eyes bright with excitement.

"I am glad that you have found a good man," Brandi said. "I hope that we can take some small part in the ceremonies."

With a mock scowl on her face, Andyn swatted Brandi's knee. "Small part? Like hell! You and Megan will be among my attendants and I won't take no for an answer."

Megan beamed at Altus and Varienne. "I am overjoyed to see that you two have found each other again."

The couple exchanged a bright smile. "Irial's mercy knows no bounds," replied Altus, "and, apparently, no limits on generosity either. Thank you for including us."

"Varienne and I endured much together," Megan said. "And you protected me when I most needed it, Altus. I'm glad you're here."

"You're going to be busy, Brandi," Varienne said. She shot a look at Connor and Hannah. "Along with Andyn and Carine, there will be a total of four weddings." She held up her hand, clasping Altus'. Matching silver bracelets with red jewels glittered in the morning sunlight.

Megan's eyebrows shot up. "Congratulations! I'm so happy for you!"

"Wait," Brandi said slowly. "Andyn and Varienne and Carine makes three, not four."

Varienne cocked her head to the side, eyes on Connor Lomin. "Care to elaborate, Connor?"

The Halfling held up his own hand, clasping Hannah's. Matching copper bracelets with green jewels flashed.

Dar's eyebrows rose. "Finally got up the gumption, you rascal?"

Connor grinned. "I came to my senses in the Harrowing. Besides, she can be very persuasive." Hannah gave him an impish look and pinched him in the side.

"Well," said Altus, shaking his head. "That's a lot of weddings in a short time."

"Indeed," said Father Thomas, "but unsurprising. With the War ended, everyone feels secure in getting on with their lives. I'm sure that there will be many other marriages to celebrate in the coming weeks."

A pair of orderlies arrived with a cart bearing decanters of steaming jekka and platters loaded with pastries. Suddenly famished, Dar had to hold himself back from taking an entire platter for himself.

Megan steered him away from the cart. "Damora isn't going to run out of pastry, Dar."

He took a bite and a sip. "Between me and Connor, it might."

Khyron sidled over, bearing a steaming mug. "Oh, and I wanted to make sure you knew your pegasi are safe and sound."

Megan beamed. "That's wonderful! In all the excitement I forgot to ask."

"Gorostoli agents found them when they sent out a search party and discovered the remnants of the Gate that you and Daphne and Steven ruined," he continued.

"How is Virasi?" Megan asked Dar. "I'm sure you've taken good care of him."

"He's fine. We had to send the pegasi off to safety when we found the

Gate of Stars but the Elohir brought them back to us after the Battle of Oakmoor."

The door swung open again and Melinor entered. Brandi and Megan set down their cups and leaped forward to embrace him. He staggered and simply held them, eyes misting over.

"What has happened?" he choked out.

Brandi smiled at him. "God."

Father Thomas quickly explained and Melinor nodded slowly.

"Blessed be His Name forever," he managed, brushing at his eyes.

"Amen," murmured Megan, eyes closed and head on his shoulder. For long moments, he just held them. The other Riders remained silent.

Finally, Melinor kissed both girls and cleared his throat. He gestured at the room. "I … it's good to have everyone together again…er.. well, you know what I mean. But I hear that someone ordered jekka. I would be senile indeed if I let Eric and Buck take all of it before I get my share."

They all had a good laugh over that, then congregated back on the couches and sofas.

Megan returned to her seat at Dar's side. Megan and Brandi winked at each other. Megan stared at Dar, eyebrows raised.

He swallowed a bite of pastry. "What?"

Sister Karen cleared her throat. "Gentlemen?"

"Oh, yes, right," Eric replied. "Well, you all should know that Dar and I proposed to Megan and Brandi about fifteen minutes ago. Despite our obvious shortcomings with which you are all familiar, they both said yes."

A chorus of laugher and happy exclamations greeted that announcement and the ladies surged forward to bestow embraces and kisses on the Alenars.

"We have a lot of planning to do," Andyn sighed. "I hope there is enough silk and lace in Oakmoor to do the job. The local seamstresses are going to make a fortune."

"You need not worry about that," Melinor intoned, popping a piece of raspberry tart into his mouth. "The Northern Alliance has already agreed to pay for the weddings for Carine, Varienne, Andyn and Hannah and I doubt if they would object to Megan and Brandi's. Especially —"

He stopped and exchanged a look with Father Thomas, who shook his head. Melinor shrugged.

"Especially what, Dad?" asked Eric.

"Nothing to worry about now," Melinor replied around a mouthful of pastry. "All in due time, son."

Dar raised an eyebrow at Eric, who made a helpless gesture.

"Yes," added Sister Karen. "All that is important now is that the Grey Riders are restored. Praise God."

"Praise God," murmured Dar. He caught the look that passed between her, Melinor and Father Thomas.

I wonder what those three are up to...

Chapter Thirty-Two – Your Heritage and Mine

They are on their way," Detlef said.

Father Thomas nodded, hands behind his back. He breathed deeply of the clean morning air and regarded the brightly lit gardens outside the sun room. "Excellent. See that we aren't disturbed, please."

"Of course."

Detlef departed and the Nuncio continued watching birds and butterflies cavort among the summer flowers. They didn't seem to notice the shattered benches, scorched trees and churned earth marring an otherwise idyllic scene. The local animals seemed to have picked up right where they left off before all the chaos and mayhem.

He heard the doors open behind him.

"Sir Eric Indidarc, Sir Darius Cabot, Miss Megan Alenar and Miss Brandawyn Alenar," announced Detlef.

Father Thomas spun on his heel and smiled at the four young people. They bowed and straightened, curious eyes watching him.

They looked rested and happy, but a bit wary. He didn't blame them. He did notice that both women clutched their men's hands firmly.

"Welcome," he said striding to a cream-and-gold upholstered couch next to a low wooden table. "I hope you had a good night's sleep and breakfast."

Megan smiled brightly. "We did, thank you, Eminence."

Father Thomas gestured to the seats and took one himself. He steepled his fingers in front of his face.

"First, before anything else, I want to see how you are doing."

"Better, Eminence," replied Dar.

The Nuncio noted the momentary pause as he said it but decided to let it pass. *He must grieve on his own time.*

"I must make sure to pay a visit to your parents," he added.

"They would appreciate that, Eminence," Dar said in a low voice. "The upcoming weddings are a bright spot for them, but still…" He trailed off.

Megan kissed Dar's cheek and Eric and Brandi put their arms around him. He nodded. Brandi rested her forehead against his.

Father Thomas extricated a folder from a satchel next to the couch. "I also had something very important to communicate to you."

The young people exchanged curious looks. Father Thomas drew out some papers.

"I have some news," he began. "While Brandi and Megan were in stasis under the Preservation Nets, Lord Melinor and I performed some blood tests on them. We analyzed the samples using the dwarven record-stones and now have the results. There is something important you young ladies need to know about your heritage."

Megan looked confused. "Our heritage?"

Father Thomas waited a couple of seconds. *Let's see how they take this. Surely those who have faced daemon hordes and returned from the dead will be able to handle it.*

"Well, my dear, let me ask a few questions.," he continued. "Are you aware of the real spelling of your last name?"

Brandi nodded. "It was on the ring that Uncle Stephen gave me, the one we sent back using the teleportation bag: Aldenar."

"Quite so. Alenar is a rather common place name, since it denotes a family's place of origin — in this case, an ancient Paragon Kingdom of the south. However, Aldenar is rare. It is an ancient spelling. There are other examples, such as Queen Alyssa's title?"

Dar spoke up. "Saint Alyssa of Tor Haldin."

"Correct. The ancient name of the city of Coastwatch was Tor Haldin. Nowadays it would be Tor Aldin."

He paused. A glimmer of realization shone in Megan's eyes. "You see, don't you? Spellings have changed over the years for places as well as families.

Often, surnames would be altered to look more common to protect someone."

Eric's eyes narrowed. "Protect someone? Protect whom?"

"Royalty." He let that sink in, watching their expressions.

"Wait. You don't mean…" Brandi began.

He nodded. "Yes. We used small sample of your blood in the heritage stones. Both of you ladies are direct descendants of Saint Alyssa."

The four young people stared at him.

Dar found his voice first. "Brandi and Megan are…royal?"

"Yes." Thomas stacked the papers and placed them on the table. "These are the official reports. Everything has been properly documented." The young people read in silence.

Megan looked dazed. "Are you sure? Could this be a mistake?"

The Nuncio shook his head. "As a control experiment, Heritage Stones were tested with people from known royal families and they showed the correct results."

"We're from the royal family of Alenar," Brandi breathed, setting the papers down.

"Indeed. Even more importantly, the tests proved that the bloodline transmitted through your parents is of the line of seniority. Your parents were King Alexander II and High Princess Sedryn III before their deaths, since your father was the older brother of Daphne… er… excuse me — Queen Daphne I."

This was met with stunned silence.

He smiled at them. "With the passing of all the more senior members of your line, you are the next. The throne of Alenar, a Kingdom of the South, currently held in thrall to the remnants of the Republic of Torosc, is your birthright. You, Brandawyn Veronica Therese, as the eldest, are the heir. Congratulations, Your Highness." He inclined his head.

Brandi gripped Eric's hand. "There must be some mistake."

"No, dear one. Once you are crowned, you will be Queen Brandawyn the First, and your sister will be High Princess Megan the Second."

Brandi shook her head. "Wait. I am not a queen. I - I'm not worthy to rule a country. I wouldn't—I can't—I don't know what to do."

"That won't be an issue. There are plenty of people eager to help you.

And yes, by your protests that you are not worthy, I say that you most assuredly are. Saint Alyssa was a very humble person, from what I can glean from the records, and you are much like her. Right now, Alenar needs a good and humble queen."

With one more glance at their astonished faces, he stood, sliding the papers back into the satchel. "There is more, but I will leave you to think on these things for now."

"No, Eminence, please." said Brandi, reaching for his hand. "Tell us everything. I won't be able to sleep a wink if your other news is similar."

He stared at them long and hard. *So many emotions there: awe, excitement, dread, amazement, wonder - and fear.*

He returned to his seat. "Do you remember when you fought the Daemon Lord in Gorostol, just before High Prince Stephen and Queen Daphne died?" Brandi and Megan gave him stricken looks.

He forged ahead. "Recall how he was reluctant to fight any of you? Remember how you vanquished him? I can tell you from personal experience that there is no way the four of you, even with your formidable skills, could have defeated a Battle Lord in your weakened state. The reason you won is because you had an advantage over him."

"What advantage?" Megan asked in a small voice.

"Special abilities courtesy of one of your other ancestors, er, two of them, actually."

"What do you mean?" asked Dar.

"According to the research, one of the Queens of the line of Aldenar was Rianne I. She lived a long time ago, after the fall of the Esten Empire but before the rise of the Archons of Torosc. We think she, well, there's no delicate way to put this. She was half-daemon."

Megan turned pale and shook her head, clutching Dar's arm tightly. "No, that can't be!" she cried. "My skills were from magical contamination. Oxbridge said so!"

Thomas gave her a kind smile. "He was wrong. The records and your blood tests are conclusive. And it's not as bad as you think. Rianne was indeed half daemon, but she forsook her evil nature and became a convert for the love of her life, King Brendan III. She was actually more like Lady Saren. The daemons were reacting to sensing her bloodline in you, a bloodline which is blasphemy in their eyes."

Eric laid his arm around Brandi's shoulders, his features only registering shock. She leaned into him. Dar embraced Megan, his eyes distant as he laid his chin on her red-gold tresses.

In a choked voice, Brandi asked, "Is that all?"

Thomas smiled. "No. Rianne had several children, and her eldest grandchild, Edward — the last of the Aldenar kings prior to the revolt of the Archons — married a woman of rare beauty and kindness named Richenda, the granddaughter of an equally beautiful woman named Kiriel. Kiriel, it seems, was an Elohir in disguise, thus making Richenda herself a half-breed of Celestial origin. From what I can tell, Lady Kiriel returned to Celestia eventually after the death of her human husband and remarried. You saw some of her later descendants at the Battle of Oakmoor."

"We did?" asked Eric.

"Yes, Melissa and Simon are your Elohir relatives. They are Kiriel's grandchildren, through her second husband, and Kiriel was of the royal family, so, technically, you're also related to King Kelson."

They stared at him, stunned. He contented himself with listening to the tinkle of water in the fountain and the birdsong in the garden as they processed this latest thunderbolt.

"I don't understand," Megan finally said.

Thomas Williams nodded and let his hands fall in his lap, giving them a sympathetic look. "I know it is a lot to accept, Highnesses, but your bloodline is part Elf, part human, part daemon and part Elohir."

They sat in silence for a long time. Finally, Megan shook her head and buried her face in Dar's neck. Brandi nodded slowly, her face pale but resolute. A teardrop traced a slow, shiny line down her smooth cheek. She reached her arms around Eric and clung to him.

Thomas met her violet eyes.

"I understand, Eminence," she managed, "I think Eric and I and Megan and Dar need to take some time to think, and talk, and, well, — I mean — we..."

He stood, then gently kissed her forehead. "Take all the time you need."

He kissed Megan as well. "The might of the Northern Alliance stands at your side to protect you and your fiancés. Agents are discreetly stationed near your quarters. Ladies-in-waiting are being assigned as we speak and the Orders of Saint Kira and Saint Michael are sending personal attendants to you. Think, pray, talk, accept. Above all, understand that this changes nothing of who you are - dear children of God and heroes of Damora."

He left the papers with them and took the satchel. Just before he left the room, he turned back and winked. "By the way, don't forget you have weddings to plan. First things first…"

***

Megan stood in front of her mirror, staring at her image, a jumble of thoughts chasing each other through her head.

She looked just like any young half-elven woman with tousled strawberry blonde hair in an elegant white slip of lace and silk. Her eyes strayed down to her bare legs and feet, standing on a soft woven rug from Targanon.

Half-daemon. But I don't have cloven hooves. How can that be?

Part of her wanted to laugh at the sheer insanity of it all. Another part wanted to scream in rage and denial. Another part wanted to sing and dance in wild joy.

For that matter, shouldn't I have wings growing out of my back? And I have Celestial relatives! Related to King Kelson? Have I gone mad?

Princess, part-daemon, part Celestial… yesterday she had only been an ecstatic bride-to-be recently restored from death by the Blood of Jesus Christ Himself, finally reunited with her beloved Darius and looking forward to life with him as Mistress Cabot. Now, the universe seemed to tumble randomly around her. Last night, she had lain in the huge bed and cried herself to sleep, overwhelmed by the enormity of it all. Thankfully, everyone in the palace had let them all sleep as late as they wanted. She felt rested and refreshed, but still dazed.

She stared into the amber eyes of her reflection and touched her image with her fingertips.

She stood there for a long time. "Who *are* you?" she whispered. Her image didn't answer, gazing back at her with those same intent, wondering eyes.

The arched double doors of her room opened a crack and she heard a light Elven soprano. "Does Your Highness need anything at this time or do you wish to remain abed for a while longer?"

Megan sighed and answered in Elven. "I am awake now. Please send Sir Cabot to me if he is up."

Best to have this out as soon as possible, she thought with a twinge of apprehension.

"Yes, Highness. Would you like your ladies to be summoned?"

"Please."

"Should we ask Sir Cabot to remain outside until they arrive?"

She set her mouth in a firm line. "No, that won't be necessary. I will confer with him for only a little while."

Now the face of an Elven maiden showed in the gap of the doors, looking uncertain.

"Forgive me," said the maiden. "But Your Highness' state of dress…"

Remembering how Dar had found her at Oxbridge's beach home, the corner of her mouth quirked in a half-smile.

"It will not be an issue. Sir Cabot is entirely honorable."

The woman hesitated, then nodded. "As you command," she replied, not sounding convinced.

Megan stood gazing at her reflection until she heard another tap at the door.

"Sir Darius Cabot, Knight of Saint Kira's Order."

She steeled herself and turned around.

He looked splendid in a doublet of forest green and silver with matching trousers and black boots. His dear face showed only concern and worry.

He walked within arm's reach of her and then stopped. Suddenly, he broke into a grin. "I'm not really sure how to address you anymore."

Her heart rolled over at his smile and she felt a delicious shiver. "Just Megan, when we're in private or with Bran and Eric. I'm not sure otherwise. There are officers of etiquette to teach us more than we want to know."

"Megan it is then," he said, smile broadening as he stepped closer.

She pressed a hand into his chest, stopping him. "Before another moment passes, Darius, I have to resolve this."

He frowned. "Resolve what?"

She let out a deep breath. "Who I am. And I'm not even sure who that is any more. I do know I'm part Elohir, part daemon, and now a member of a royal line. I don't know what that will mean in coming months and years. I just want to make sure you know what you're getting into and, if you have any reservations, you should voice them now."

He looked confused and hurt for a second. "Reservations? About marrying you? Why?"

Heart pounding, Megan bit her lip. "Because I don't know if my lineage and mixed blood will change anything."

"Oh, that?" He shrugged and his grin returned. "Megan, it hasn't meant anything before. Why should it now?"

She blinked. "But my daemonic heritage — "

"— has always been a part of you," he finished for her, taking her hand. "It was a part of the girl I met in Forester, a part of the woman who said she loved me when she thought she was going to die, a part of the woman who left me to go on a secret crusade and promised on her life to return for me. Nothing has changed. You're still my Megan."

Tears sprang into her eyes and she felt a lump in her throat. "But," she managed in a broken voice, "I don't know how I will - if this will pose more challenges for me."

"Then we meet them together," he said, taking both her hands in his own.

The fiercest love she'd ever felt surged through her. "Then you still want me?"

He laughed, a most glorious sound. "I think the question is if you still want a used-up free-lance adventurer."

She nodded. "With God as my witness, yes."

She suddenly found herself in his arms, gripping him tightly, eyes closed, not caring in the slightest that the only thing between her and complete nudity was a slip of silk and lace, knowing that he would hold her just like this and not ask for a thing.

And she loved him madly for it.

They held each other wordlessly for a while and he kissed her on the top of her head.

"You should probably get dressed and I should wait for you outside," he finally said in a measured tone. "Otherwise, we're going to be physically husband and wife before we can get to a church."

Reluctantly, she released him and stepped back, smiling through her tears. "Of course. Please send my ladies in."

He gently kissed her on the lips and it took a major amount of restraint to keep it at just that. He departed.

She wondered if her daemonic nature provided an extra amount of sexual prodding or if it was just the emotion of the last few days.

God, I've got to get a hold of myself…

Three gorgeous Elven ladies in dresses of teal, plum and gold entered, dropping into deep curtseys.

"What would Your Highness prefer today?" asked one of them, opening her wardrobe and revealing the most beautiful gowns she had ever seen in an amazing palette of colors.

"Oh my," said Megan, eyes widening.

Chapter Thirty-Three – What's In A Name?

Brandi forced herself to stop fidgeting and looked at her reflection in the mirror of the grand hall of the palace.

Well, I said I always wanted to get a few dresses for myself when I had a chance.

She smoothed her navy-blue gown, touching the silver thread at wrists and throat. Tiny white roses encircled the hem and she wore navy slippers with a swan motif decorating the sides. Her personal maid had taken a remarkably short time to comb, braid and coil her hair into a beautiful arrangement on her head with little curls at her temples. She touched the silver circlet on her brow. Her fingers lingered on the tiny shield at her hairline with the praying hands and angel wings of Saint Raphael's Order.

Armored soldiers guarded the doors and her three ladies stayed discreetly in the background. She knew that other agents of the Alliance watched over her from hidden places, ready to surge to her defense at the slightest hint of danger.

Used to a life of self-reliance, all this attention and martial resources at her fingertips made her feel a bit detached and uncomfortable. She hoped it wouldn't dull her edge.

In the mirror, she saw Saren DeMey enter. The guards came to attention and saluted. Brandi's ladies curtseyed. Saren smiled and nodded to them but continued on to Brandi's side. She bowed.

"Your Royal Highness," she said with a twinkle in her eye.

Brandi gave her a mock frown. "Oh, Saren, come off it. We're practically related by now."

Saren smiled. "Don't I know it. How are you holding up?"

She sighed. "Still dealing with all of it. Last night, before going to bed, Megan and I agreed to give Dar and Eric a chance to reconsider."

"As if they would."

Brandi smiled back, remembering her early morning conversation with Eric. As she had hoped and prayed, Eric downplayed any risks from her heritage, pointing out that she had been with him for months in Forester without any signs of evil behavior. He had pledged his devotion to her instantly.

"You're right. It didn't change the outcome, but we felt we had to do it."

The two of them fell silent and Saren turned towards the tall glass doors leading out to the gardens. Brandi's eyes wandered to the flowering shrubs, roses and trees.

"It gets better," Saren said finally. "The more you get in touch with the otherworldly part of yourself, the more you're able to handle the less pleasant parts."

Brandi shot her a look. "Really?"

"Really. You have a strong faith and that helps. As you figure out what skills and talents you have, you'll also start to recognize when the daemonic tendencies come to the fore and how to counteract them or harness and redirect them."

Brandi opened her mouth and closed it. Saren glanced at her sidelong.

"Even the... sexual ones?" Brandi asked quietly.

Saren's smile returned. "Even those. Don't forget that desire for your husband is a good and normal thing, even if it is influenced by daemonic urges. You also have Elohir heritage, which will be a big advantage."

"How do you handle it?"

Saren shrugged. "Constant communication. Every day. We made a pact at the outset that we would talk about it no matter what the time or place or situation and it's worked very well. You and Eric will figure it out, like all couples do."

Brandi fiddled with her belt, an old shame raising its ugly head. "There's that, and I'm a former vampire to boot, with everything that Kelani and Adina forced me to do…"

She fought against the overwhelming guilt of her memories as a vampire thrall. Her hands clenched into fists and she shut her eyes, taking a deep breath.

Saren put a hand on her arm. "I'm sure that Eric has already said this, but it wasn't you doing those things. Adina overwhelmed you and overrode your free will."

"But it still doesn't erase my memories."

"Of course not. But don't blame yourself for something you couldn't control. God doesn't. Neither does Eric."

The wind moved in the trees outside. Brandi exhaled and forced herself to just stand and breathe and listen. Faint birdsong reached her from the nearby gardens. The simple peace of the scene seemed like an answer from the Almighty.

Brandi's mind wandered and she watched her reflection in the glass. *Is that really me? Who am I any more?*

The events of the last few days replayed in her mind, threatening to overwhelm her. In particular, the image of a world map came up in her memory.

Queen of a nation? Me?

She sighed, feeling her stomach clench. "And then there's the small matter of leading an entire country. Good Lord! I have no idea what to do, not to mention that it's currently in a hostile land thousands of miles away."

Saren gave her hands a squeeze. "One thing at a time, Brandi! There are many people in the Northern Alliance who will move mountains to help you, believe me, including me and Terenil and Melinor. And you have my rapscallion half-brother, too."

Brandi's cheeks grew warm and she nodded. "You're right. Thank you, Saren."

Saren turned her head towards the doors and winked. "Speak of the devil.”

Megan glided towards her in a green gown that seemed to be made of emerald itself, her hand clasped in Dar’s, eyes brilliant and face aglow with happiness. Eric marched in right after them, broke stride momentarily at the sight of Brandi, then continued, eyes dancing.

Now she blushed thoroughly as Eric kissed her hand and then held both of hers in his. His eyes said it before his mouth did.

“Brandi, you are stunning.”

Suddenly shy and self-aware, she looked down. “Do you really think so?” she said, giving his hands a squeeze. “I haven’t had much time for dresses.”

To her surprise, he twirled her around and she stifled a gasp and giggle.

“You could have fooled me, dear,” he said in such a warm, comfortable manner that she felt her knees grow weak. “I used to think that my sister looked amazing in a dress and you eclipse her.”

“Oh Eric!” she said, feeling more self-conscious. “Stop! You’re embarrassing me. I’m just not used to all the attention.”

He put an arm around her waist and kissed her lips soundly. “Well, then, you’ll just have to get used to it. But at your pace, of course.”

She felt lightheaded at his kiss but smiled. “Thank you.”

Saren laughed. “I can see everything is well in hand. I take my leave of Your Highnesses and these two rogues. Make sure you manage them.”

With a round of kisses and hugs, Saren departed.

Brandi gestured to the glass doors. “Let’s go outside. There are some plans we need to make and some information I need to give you.”

The men looked surprised, but shrugged and looped their arms in theirs and walked to a pair of glass doors that swung open as they approached.

The summer sun washed the gardens with brilliant warmth. Butterflies flitted from one side to the other. Though the palace staff had tried their best to spruce up the area after the War, she still saw some trees splintered beyond recognition and marked with red paint for removal, as well as crushed fountains and statues. Many of the plants had been replaced, though, and she led the others to a brand-new stone table and benches. Behind them, the ladies-in-waiting followed.

Sitting on a bench with an elegant dress was a new trick for her, but Brandi managed with a little help from one of the ladies.

She held Eric's hand on the table top and smiled at all of them. "Before we begin, Emperor Brion of Terenai has placed wedding planners at our disposal and they have started preparations for a ceremony at Christ the King Cathedral in Oakmoor. Father Thomas insists on presiding."

The others nodded.

"We have a meeting with the planners tonight after dinner," she continued, "so we can figure out all the particulars. I received a note from King Kelson telling me not to be concerned about costs since the Alliance will pay for everything."

She reached into a tiny bag at her hip and produced little squares of paper. "These are your official titles and names after the coronations and weddings."

Dar grinned and winked at her. "What title do I get? Royal Prankster?"

They all laughed. For a couple of seconds, Brandi felt like they all gathered at a picnic at one of the tables outside the tavern in Forester, like so long ago when they first met, just friends and future lovers enjoying each other's company.

"No," she said, "though I'm tempted to make that one up just for you."

Megan, Dar and Eric read. Brandi watched their reactions. Megan shot her a glance.

Eric let out a deep breath. "Are these ceremonial titles or do they actually expect me to rule those areas?"

"Mostly ceremonial, though you are expected to visit at least three times a year. There are occasional duties, but typically the royal family has seneschals or legates to take care of day-to-day administration. Of course, in wartime, the local military are pledged to the Crown, but even then, the king or queen will delegate responsibilities."

Dar folded the little paper and put it into a pouch at his belt. He stared at the tabletop in silence.

"Dar?" Megan asked.

He shrugged. "I feel the same as Eric — and both of you, really. I don't know how to rule anything. Hell, I can barely rule myself most of the time."

Megan smiled and leaned into him with her shoulder. He chuckled, then sobered, taking her hands. "Meg, I promised myself that if a miracle happened and I actually got to see you again, all I wanted was a home by the ocean near Seacrest, my own carpentry business, and a little magic shop for you. I never wanted fame or titles or riches. All I wanted was peace, and now…" His voice trailed off.

Megan raised his hands to her lips. "I know, dearest. It's all I ever wanted too. But people need us and I'm afraid there isn't anyone else. I would feel terrible if we just abdicated. The southern kingdoms have suffered long enough. Brandi and I know what it's like there."

Brandi felt a pang of regret. Her heart's desire was a home with Eric and their children in a place far from war and evil and conflict. All the turmoil and heartache and sorrow of the last couple of years crowded in on her and she yearned for tranquility.

When will we really have peace? she wondered. *Wistfully, she knew the answer. In heaven, just the way I saw it…*

"I understand, Dar," she said. "I want what you and Eric want too, but I agree with Megan. The people of Alenar, and really, all those regions, deserve better. They've been oppressed by evil for a long time."

No one spoke.

"Besides," she added, eyes on the tabletop, "I think this is the task God has put before us: to free the captive lands and bring His hope to everyone there. This is why we were sent back. It is now a solemn duty."

Dar and Eric nodded.

"It has to be your solemn duty too," Brandi pressed. "You have to be committed, just like we are."

The men exchanged a resigned look, then shrugged.

"Well, dear," Eric said, putting his hand on hers. "Dar and I would probably get really bored with a mundane life after a few years and then we'd be out causing all kinds of mischief, so this is probably for the best." His eyes twinkled.

She smiled back. "Don't I know it. And don't forget what Father Thomas said: the Northern Alliance, Merdail and Gorostol are very keen on stabilizing the region, so they will have plenty of people to help us."

He nodded and they sat in silence, listening to the birdsong and the wind in the trees.

"And," she said briskly, "We will have some special help, due to Megan's heritage and mine. A few Elohir will be on hand to train us in the use of our latent powers, which we have only begun to tap, so they tell me."

Dar's eyebrows rose. "I'm not sure whether to be alarmed or overjoyed."

Megan gave him a mock frown and pinched his side. "You better behave, you rascal, or I might just practice on you."

Eric folded his paper and put it away too. "Not to change the subject," he said with a little frown on his face, "but I'm a little confused by something on the paper. It says my full name will be Eric Daniel Indidarc Aldenar."

"Yes," Brandi replied. "Just like mine. Brandawyn Veronica Therese Indidarc Aldenar."

He blinked. "But Indidarc and Aldenar together?"

She smiled back. "As queen, I cannot take your surname as my own. I have to retain the name of Aldenar, but I will bestow it on you when we're wed. However, custom allows me to add your surname to one of my middle names. I did it to honor you and your parents."

He looked stunned.

"Is that alright?" she asked.

He shook his head in wonder. "I am humbled and flattered, Bran. Thank you."

She stroked his face before turning to Megan. "Megan did it too."

Dar whirled on Megan. "You did?"

She giggled again and pushed his shoulder. "Of course, you ninny. I am Megan Diana Marie Cabot Aldenar the Second. Do you like it?"

She received a thorough kiss in response.

Pulling herself away with a laugh, she smiled. "I assume you approve."

"Of course," said Dar with a wicked grin. "And I like kissing you."

"Ahem," said Brandi with a mock severe look at them. "All right. We need to focus, now, please. We have a lot to plan."

Dar gave her a mock bow in his seat and waved his hand in a grand gesture. "Then plan away, Your Highness."

***

"Finished yet, Melinor?"

"This is the last set," Melinor mused, peering into the glass at the blood samples. He gently moved the glass plates aside, attaching labels for each of them: Seamus, Miriam, Connor, Brendan, Deena and Darren.

Father Thomas handed him a wooden case with the Heritage stones. "Maybe it was really just a dream, my mind working through my life's dilemmas, but who knows? For Megan and Brandi, it showed us the truth. How did the other tests come out?"

"King Kelson suggested I check Buck, Khyron, Dar and Eric, but the results were negative."

Father Thomas leaned on the laboratory table. "The only figures in my dream with the golden drops of blood were Brandi, Megan and Connor. I'm willing to bet my last copper that there's something going on with Connor."

"I won't bet against you. The Dark Wave leveled my home and rebuilding is going to cost a lot." Melinor took a drop of blood from Miriam's sample and placed it in a Heritage Stone. He spun it. He and Father Thomas watched, but no lights glowed.

"Maybe the male line."

Melinor nodded, repeating the process with a sample from Seamus.

Bright light lit up the laboratory table.

"Well then."

"I'm glad I didn't take the bet." Melinor copied down the set of glowing symbols on the Heritage Stone. "Please hand me that volume there."

Father Thomas brought a heavy tome and set it down next to Melinor. The wizard leafed through it, stopped at a particular page, then sat back, a satisfied smile on his face. "There you are."

Father Thomas shook his head, eyes on the page. "That changes things."

"We had better tell the Lomin's."

***

"I'm beginning to get suspicious every time someone wants to talk to us but won't tell us why," Connor said, leading Hannah into the library.

"Well," she said, looping her arm in his, "if the results are as positive as the last few times, I'm all for it."

Connor opened the doors and stopped in mid-stride. "Mother? Father?"

Seamus and Miriam smiled at him from their chairs near the big desk. Deena and Darren waved from their places on the laps of Brendan and Cerys.

"What is this all about?"

Connor's father shrugged. "I was hoping you could tell us."

"Lord Melinor is being mysterious again," Hannah opined, leading Connor to a couch. She pulled him to a seat next to her.

"And the answer to the mystery will soon be revealed." Melinor swept into the library from a side door, a sheaf of papers in his hand.

The Halflings made as if to rise but he waved them down, coming to the front of the desk. He leaned back against it.

They waited. Melinor gazed down at the rug for a few moments. Connor's mind raced to all manner of improbably announcements.

Finally, the wizard spoke. "I called all of you here… no, wait. When in the course of human events…Oh, bother! Here."

He handed a page to Seamus.

Connor and Hannah stood and came to his side.

"This can't be right," Seamus said, staring at Melinor.

"It is. The Heritage Stones don't lie."

Miriam read the page, then sat back, eyes glazed.

Connor took it from her. His heart skipped a beat. "Us too?" he asked.

Melinor nodded as Hannah read it. Cerys and her family crowded around.

"Some time in ages past," Melinor said, folding his hands in his lap, "your ancestors migrated to the north from the Kingdom of Loemin, probably near the time of the Fall of Night — which would make sense, since the Archons came to power just about at that time. Evendale would have been remote enough and small enough to be a good hiding place."

Seamus sat back. "How do you know there aren't others? There might be an aunt or uncle."

Melinor shrugged. "It wouldn't matter. The test results show that you are in the primary line of succession: eldest child to eldest child. You are King Seamus III of Loemin."

Connor felt the world spinning. *That means I'm…*

His mother met his eyes and gave a wan smile. "Yes, dearest. You are the Crown Prince."

"You can't mean that we'd actually be able to go down there," Cerys said. "That area is still within the borders of Torosc."

"Torosc as we know it is no more. Kelson's advance force descended on that nation a couple of days ago. With information we shared with them, they were able to track the signatures of the remaining Skull Gates. They have been destroyed and most of the Archons who stood against the Golden Army are dead. We think that only two survived: Golvadu and one other."

"That is good news," whispered Brendan, "But even without daemons to help them, Torosc is still a dangerous place."

Melinor shrugged. "True enough, but it is markedly improved from what it was before the War. With most of the Archons away in other lands managing the Dark Wave, the districts are ready to revolt."

No one spoke. Melinor gazed at each of them in turn.

"Yes, you can reclaim your ancestral homeland," he said. "The Northern Alliance Council has already met on the subject and conferred with Terenai and Merdail and Gorostol. Though there is a lot of rebuilding to do and each nation will be hard-pressed to manage their own recovery, they have already pledged assistance to Nold ac Mithas, Turis Rhi and Alenar to reclaim those lands."

"Would they give assistance to Loemin as well?" asked Seamus.

Melinor laughed and shrugged. "What's one more?"

"I think we have a lot to talk about," Miriam said, rising and taking Seamus' hand.

"Agreed." Melinor straightened. "You should know that Loemin and Alenar have a common border. You'll need to chat with Brandi and Megan…"

Chapter Thirty-Four – To Have and To Hold

Nervous?"

"No." Brandi took one last look in the mirror. She brushed a hand over the surface of her silken wedding gown of white and gold. The twelve-pointed crown of Alenar's queen sat on her head, sparkling in the morning sunlight streaming into the bride's chamber.

More eager than nervous, she thought.

"Good. There's nothing to worry about." Queen Ahlana unnecessarily straightened the shoulder of Brandi's dress.

"Were you nervous?" Brandi met Ahlana's eyes in the mirror.

Ahlana put her hands on Brandi's shoulders. "A little, I must confess. It was five years ago, though, so the events are a little dulled by time, but I was more apprehensive about becoming Queen Ahlana than about being Phillip's bride."

Brandi stood in silence, watching her image. *I certainly don't look like a human-Elf-daemon-Elohir hybrid.*

Ahlana gave a little frown. "There's something else, I can tell."

"I'm part daemon, Your Majesty."

The Queen gave her a look in the mirror. "All right. Well, first, two things. One: You were crowned Queen Brandawyn the First of Alenar yesterday, so my name is Ahlana in private. None of this 'Your Majesty' business. Second: You are part-Elohir. I think that counteracts a lot of Fallen heritage."

"Does it? How many Elohir-daemon hybrids have there been?"

Ahlana laughed. "Your parents, for one! And your grandparents, and everyone on back through time to the children of Kiriel and Edward."

Brandi relaxed, gazing at her bridal bouquet. "I'm being silly, aren't I?"

"Let me ask a more important question. Do you love Eric?"

A wild, intense love surged through her and her throat tightened. "More than anything," she whispered.

"That's all that matters. Now, stop your fussing. Let me look at you."

Ahlana's eyes scanned all over Brandi, from head to toe. She motioned for her to do a slow turn.

"Stunning, as expected," she proclaimed. "Now, let's go. The ladies from Terenai are ready to sing the Alribethyn. It's the ceremony just preceding the processional. And Melinor is itching to walk you down the aisle. Let's not keep him waiting." She took Brandi's arm.

Brandi followed her out of the bridal room. Four Knights of the Chalice came to attention at the door and she nodded to them. The passage to the narthex was lined with white roses and pink carnations and blue sprite-heart from Terenai's deepest forests.

"I wish my parents were here," Brandi murmured. "And Anne. She was the only real mother Eric ever had."

Ahlana patted her hand. "But they are here, darling. This is a church, and God is present. Where He is, there is Heaven. All His faithful servants, including your parents and Lady Indidarc are here as well, watching. Every faithful one who perished in the War can see everything. I know they are inordinately proud of you."

Brandi quickly snatched a handkerchief from the bodice of her gown and dabbed at the corners of her eyes. Ahlana pretended not to notice.

The Queen stopped them in the cathedral foyer. Eleven Elven ladies in formal gowns of their House colors lined the walls, smiling beneficently at them. They curtseyed and Ahlana inclined her head.

A beaming Andyn Demaris entered from the church, wearing a gorgeous dress of dark blue and gold. The six-pointed tiara of a Viscountess gleamed atop her blonde tresses. "Everything is ready. Are you?"

Brandi couldn't resist. "As ready as you were yesterday."

Andyn's eyes twinkled. "That's enough out of you, young lady. You are the last two Riders to get married so let's get to it. We've waited long enough for the combined wedding reception."

The door to the other bride's room opened and Megan entered, accompanied by a smiling Saren DeMey, a nine-pointed Duchess' coronet on her head, dressed in a gown of Megan's colors: emerald and gold. Megan glided to Brandi and gave her a tight hug.

Brandi loved Megan dearly and felt that no man was ever good enough for her lively, beautiful, brilliant sister. Now, seeing her in a dazzling gown of white and silver, her face aglow with happiness, she was convinced that no bride in history ever radiated joy like Megan. More than that, she was thrilled to leave her beloved sister in the loving embrace of Darius Cabot.

"Ah, Megan. You look lovely," said Ahlana.

"Thank you," Megan said with a brilliant smile, touching her smaller, twelve-pointed tiara. Ahlana and Saren huddled for a conversation about something.

"Nervous, Bran?" Megan asked.

"Not anymore."

"Good."

Andyn took her place with the Elven ladies. Brandi held her sister's hand as the assembly in the narthex quieted. Two altar boys swung open the double doors to the church. With an elegant curtsey, Andyn led the Alribethyn, the Song of Seven Blessings. As the choir sang each verse, Brandi and Megan took one step towards the doors and then waited for the next.

Brandi had a hard time holding her composure. The song, eloquently beautiful in a three-part harmony, told the story of a woman from infancy to early childhood, then to her growing time, her teen years and transition to womanhood, then from maidenhood to marriage, then to motherhood, then to the life of a matron of a family and finally passing from this life to Verian's Kingdom of Forever. The verses sang of life's sorrows and joys and enjoined the bride to remember that her life was not her own, that her mission was to care for her husband and to accept his love in return. Each time, the refrain rang out from twelve voices in Elven:

> *"The Master of all Life,*
> *Verian the Highest Lord*
> *Bestows all good things.*

Be therefore his herald
And bring the best of yourself
To your marriage in everything."

They halted ten feet from the doors. Megan let out a deep breath as the echoes of the last refrain rang in the church. "I had better get a hold of myself, or I'm going to be a blubbering mess before we even get to the vows."

"You're telling me. We might need hand towels."

At that, Megan gave a little giggle. "They would have to match the bridal party colors."

Brandi gave her a roguish look.

"Now we just wait for the music," Saren said, taking her place as Megan's matron of honor. Hannah and Varienne gave her brilliant smiles. Ahlana, Andyn and Ellen Hanford took their places in the procession in front of Brandi, wearing Brandi's colors of burgundy and silver.

"Everything is going to be all right, isn't it, Bran?" Megan whispered.

All her mental debates about queenship, marriage and the uncertainties of her future replayed in Brandi's mind. She gave her sister's hand a squeeze. "God is with us, Meg. We didn't get raised from the Gates of Death for nothing."

A choir inside the church started a glorious entrance hymn, accompanied by the music of violins, harps, flutes and mandolins.

"I love you, Brandi."

"I love you, Megan."

The rest of the bride's party arrived. Deena and Darren Loemin looked very serious, resplendent in clothes of deep purple and crimson, small gold coronets on their heads. They processed regally into the church. Melinor sidled up to the two sisters and looped his arms in theirs.

The wizard gave each of them a kiss on the cheek. "Now then, let's get on with it and marry you to those two louts before they change their minds." He winked.

Brandi and Megan laughed and kissed him back.

Deena entered first, scattering flowers of red, white, yellow and pink. Her brother followed, carrying a tiny, gold-chased coffer of whitest ghostwood.

Hannah winked at Andyn and the pair led the procession along the left and right sides of the aisle, followed by Varienne and Saren, Ellen and Ahlana. Finally, Melinor accompanied the two sisters to the high altar.

Hundreds of happy faces in rapt attention greeted them, changing to expressions of awe accompanied by gasps. Some of the congregation held back tears and Brandi saw more than one little girl gazing at her in amazed wonder.

I'd have thought that Oakmoor would be tired of weddings and coronations and parties by now.

"They sure look like angels," one man remarked to his wife, shaking his head in wonder.

Do I really? Brandi thought.

The colored lights of stained-glass windows scattered a rainbow on the red velvet carpet. At the altar, Dar and Eric waited in wedding attire that exactly matched the colors of their brides' gowns. Their attendants flanked them, beaming: Terenil, Altus Volan and Connor for Dar and King Philip, Nolan Hanford and Khyron for Eric.

I am so blessed.

Brandi's eyes flicked to the right of the altar, where Buck and Carine waited, smiling, hand in hand, clad in identical clothes of steel blue.

Wearing vestments of gold and white reserved for high holy days, Father Thomas radiated serenity at the altar and Gorlak stood at his side. The goblin gave her a wink and she smiled at him.

Is this what heaven is like?

Melinor led them to Eric and Dar. He embraced them each separately.

"I don't need to tell you to take extra special care of them," he said briskly, though his eyes shone. "Because if you don't, they are more than capable of correcting you."

"Thanks Dad," Eric said, grinning back. "From past experience, we're well aware of that."

"Good man." Melinor gave each of the sisters a kiss. "Treat your husbands well, Brandi and Megan, and they will move mountains for you."

Brandi swallowed the lump in her throat, unable to speak. Eric took her hand, eyes glowing with admiration. Melinor stepped back.

"All I can say is wow," Eric murmured.

She touched away a tear in the corner of each eye. "You're not so bad yourself."

"Dearly beloved," Father Thomas intoned. "We are gathered together here in the sight of God to join these young couples in holy matrimony: Brandawyn Veronica Therese Aldenar to Eric Daniel Indidarc and Megan Diana Marie Aldenar to Darius Richard Cabot."

With that, the Nuptial Mass began. Brandi wanted to imprint every second in her memory, but the things that stood out the most were the sparkle in Eric's eyes, his smile, the brilliant sunshine through the windows, and the music of the choir.

Father Thomas delivered a short but poignant sermon. "I know you have heard the verses in Saint Paul's letter to the Ephesians about married life. The part that most people don't dwell on refers to the duties of the husband. I quote 'Husbands, love your wives, as Christ loved the Church'. Well…"

He pointed at the crucifix. "There is your model, Darius and Eric. Christ was willing to endure death. You must be willing to endure a similar fate for the sake of Megan and Brandawyn. It is a sobering thought, and, I suppose, a frightening one in a way. But you are not alone in your marriages. Jesus Himself is there with you, as a silent partner, as it were, to guide and help you every day. Pray for the strength to carry out your new vocation and He will give you all that you need."

Brandi stared up at the crucifix, then looked at Eric. He smiled back and gave her hand a squeeze.

Well, that certainly puts it into a different perspective, she thought. *Between that and the Alribethyn, it feels like we're entering holy orders or something.*

In all too short a time, they exchanged vows and the rings. She found herself staring in wonder at the band of gold on her finger.

I'm married. I'm Eric's wife. He is my husband. Am I dreaming this? Or is this an illusion-play spun by a wizard for our entertainment: a tale of a lost girl who became queen and married a shining knight?

As she knelt next to Eric during the consecration, she felt a sudden awe and trepidation.

Dear Lord, please help me be a good wife and a good queen. I cannot do anything without You. Give me what I need to make You proud of me.

Sudden peace and warmth overcame her as she prayed. All her misgivings and worries melted away.

A voice whispered in her head. "You are not alone, dear one. A great warrior of the Light kneels at your side and you have loving friends by the thousands."

Who said that?...

She opened her eyes. Father Thomas raised the chalice overhead, pronouncing the words of consecration.

Brandi's eyes widened and her lips parted. The faint image of Saint Alyssa knelt next to the altar with head bowed. On the other side of the altar, a young man with blue eyes and dark hair likewise knelt. As she watched, great wings of light spread out behind him and he likewise inclined his head.

Brandi shot an astonished glance at Megan, who stared back at her, stunned.

She can see them too!

Eric and Dar, like many in the church, bowed their heads with closed eyes. She considered prodding him, but after a glance at Alyssa and the angel, she relaxed.

Father Thomas lowered the chalice and genuflected. The angel simply vanished. Alyssa favored the sisters with a smile as her image faded away.

Well, I don't know why I'm surprised she's here, Brandi thought as they stood. *She is a relative, after all...*

***

"Rumor has it that witchberries suddenly showed up in the Royal pantry for the reception," Megan remarked to Dar as they waited just outside the Grand Hall of the Royal Palace. Guards lined the entranceway and a hum of many voices within stilled at a metallic rapping sound.

"I'm sure Lord Justin and Lady Cassandra had something to do with that," Dar quipped. "Though Justin will probably deny it."

Megan kept her arm looped through his, floating on a cloud of contentment. She heard the voice of the Royal Herald announcing each of the couples in the combined wedding party.

Megan shot a look over her shoulder at Brandi and Eric, currently exchanging a kiss.

"Hey, you two," she said with a grin. "Save it for our hordes of admirers."

Brandi raised an eyebrow. "This is something I won't get tired of."

"Amen to that," replied Eric, tipping her chin up for a longer kiss.

Megan snuggled closer and nuzzled Dar's cheek. "I'm starving. Are you?"

His warm lips met hers and Megan's world froze in place. She gazed into his eyes, dreamlike.

"If I can have that," he whispered, "I don't need food."

She only nodded.

The Herald's staff rapped again and the line of couples moved forward. He announced the Matrons of Honor and Best Men: Ahlana and Saren with Phillip and Terenil, respectively.

"All right," Megan said, smoothing the front of her gown. "We're next. Try to look regal, dignified, serene. You know: decorum."

Dar gave her a look. "You know who you're talking to, right? The Brush Tramp of Forester?"

She pinched his nose. "You're right. Never mind."

"And now," intoned the Herald, "All rise for the newly-married." Scattered conversation ceased and a wave of ruffling cloth reached Megan's ears.

"I present to you for the first time Megan Diana Marie Cabot Aldenar the Second, High Princess of Alenar, Duchess of Bandar, Baroness of Skybridge and Knight of Saint Terenil, and her husband, First Prince Dar Richard Cabot Aldenar, Duke of Bandar, Baron of Skybridge and Knight Commander of Saint Kira's Order."

The guests broke out in wild cheers and applause. Megan glided in on Dar's arm, trying to look everywhere at once. Despite her earlier words about decorum, she had a hard time containing her amazement at the interior of the Hall. Crystal, silver and polished brass sparkled and shone. Magical lights glittered in lamps in the shape of angels. Flowers decorated the centerpiece of every table and floral garlands looped overhead between massive pillars. More arrangements stood in tall vases near the bridal table, where their attendants, Father Thomas and Melinor awaited them.

She smiled and waved to Buck and Carine with Lord and Lady Dorn. Carine blew her a kiss. Megan tried to turn in all directions at once to acknowledge a multitude of familiar faces in the crowd, but there were too many.

She resolved to visit the other tables when she had a chance.

The cheering subsided as they took their places next to Eric and Brandi's seats.

"They cleaned the Royal Hall quite nicely," Dar remarked.

Father Thomas chuckled. "Just in time, too."

"I thought they were going to hand me a mop and bucket at one point," King Phillip added.

"They ask Gorlak to polish windows," piped up the goblin, perched on a tall chair next to Father Thomas. "But it not problem. Bat cloak make it easy get highest ones." He pointed up at the great windows lining the Hall.

"Don't say that too loudly, Gorlak," Megan told him. "You might be pressed into service again."

The Herald rapped his staff and bowed. "All hail Brandawyn Veronica Therese Indidarc Aldenar the First, Queen of Alenar, Duchess of Khorpoint, Knight Commander of Saint Raphael's Order, Baroness of Kentridge, and her husband High Prince Eric Daniel Indidarc Aldenar, Duke of Khorpoint, Earl of Greymount, Baron of Kentridge and Knight Commander of Saint Michael."

The cheers doubled in intensity as Brandi and Eric marched in, smiling and waving to the guests.

Lord, she looks radiant, Megan thought with a thrill of pride.

The newlyweds took their seats at the table of honor near Melinor. Doors at the sides of the hall opened and attendants swarmed into the hall with platters, plates and dishes bearing a stunning variety of delicacies. A small orchestra in one corner of the room started a lilting tune from Evendale.

"I suppose congratulations are superfluous at this point." Melinor reached across to touch Megan's arm.

"Thank you, Melinor, but I welcome them anyway," Megan replied.

"Tush, young lady. I am Dad to you."

For a second, Megan froze. Her memories flew back to the last time she saw her parents, the night before they died at the hands of the minions of Torosc. Melinor's eyes mirrored the same genial kindness she had seen so many times in her own father's. Her eyes stung and Dar pressed her hand to his lips.

"Thank you, Dad," she managed.

Dar kissed her head. "Enough of this. I'm starved. Let's eat before Connor devours everything..."

Chapter Thirty-Five – Bliss

Did they finally get out of here?" Father Thomas asked, closing the door to the balcony behind him. He joined King Kelson at the balustrade, looking out over the darkening city of Oakmoor. Fireworks boomed and glittered in the sky over the three hills of the metropolis.

Kelson ruffled his wings and leaned on the railing. "Yes, praise God. With all the people vying for their attention left and right, I thought they'd never actually get to their honeymoons."

"Well, at least the most important ones had time with them: family and relatives."

"Agreed." The door opened and closed behind them. Father Thomas turned. "Oh, Saren, thank you for coming."

Still wearing her bridesmaid's dress, Saren sketched a deep curtsey. "Eminence. Your Majesty."

Kelson raised her up and gave her a gentle hug. Saren's eyes widened and she gasped. He smiled down at her. "Among the Elohir, my dear, we go by first names unless in a formal setting like court."

"But I'm not —"

He clucked his tongue. "Now, now! Don't contradict a King." He grinned. "I had a discussion with Ana and my entire family. They spoke to my people here on Damora. The results are unanimous. You are one of us."

Tears sprang up in her eyes. "Your… I mean… you are too kind, Kelson. I am humbled."

His eyes twinkled as he looked down his nose at her. "Just so. If you were a daemon, you'd be puffed up with pride or insulted. That's only more proof that we made the right decision."

"Thank you." Impulsively, she hugged him.

The Elohir king beamed, patting her on the back. He held her at arm's length. "You're very welcome. How is that rapscallion husband of yours?"

Saren sighed. "Trying to get Brandi and Eric into the air for their trip. Tholi insisted on escorting them since Kindri did the same for Megan and Dar. They're the last ones to leave, of course."

She joined the pair at the railing, watching the ongoing celebrations in the city.

Kelson nodded. "It's about time. I hope no one bothers them for at least a month."

"Well, there are security forces encircling each of the locations in a ring of at least a half mile in radius," Saren offered. "They will discreetly patrol to make sure no one intrudes."

The trio gazed out at the fireworks. Father Thomas sighed. *What a blessing to see lights and flashes of colors for a good reason, not in war.*

"I believe there is someone else who gets a vacation, Thomas." Kelson said, clasping his hands behind his back.

"Really?"

"Certainly." Kelson turned his eyes to Saren and Thomas followed suit. She gazed off into the distance for a while until she realized they were looking at her. "Why are you staring — oh! Me?"

Thomas joined in laughter with Kelson.

"Of course, we mean you!" the Celestial King said, putting an arm around her. "You and Terenil gave the last full measure of devotion to helping defeat the Dark Wave. I think you should also have some sort of reward of your own."

Saren shrugged, her face rueful. "Well, Kelson, I don't know. We weren't the only people sacrificing, unfortunately. And there are a lot of things to do in rebuilding. Colonel Benitez says there are still rogue elements out there in the wild places and I know some daemons managed to escape to the south —"

Father Thomas tapped her arm. "Kindly allow me to interrupt. There are many, many people who are more than capable for tasks like that. You and Terenil need a break."

Kelson released Saren. "A very special one. Ana and I are formally inviting you and Terenil to come to Celestia as guests of our family. We have a lakeside bridal retreat that was last used by Kathryn and Elijah after their wedding. We offer it to you."

Saren's eyes became as big as saucers. "Really? To Celestia?" she squeaked.

"Really. Please come, and stay at least three weeks. Melissa and her husband and Simon and his wife have volunteered to escort you."

"I… well… I don't know what to say."

"I think 'thank you, I accept' is customary."

Tears welled up in her eyes again. "You're sure I'll be —"

Kelson faced her and took both her hands. "Our people will be proud to have you there with us. As is said in holy writings, there is more joy over one who returns to the fold than a hundred who never strayed. And you most certainly didn't stray."

"Thank you! Thank you so much!" Face aglow, Saren hurled herself into Kelson's arms and hugged him tightly. "I have to go tell Terenil!"

"In case he is inclined to protest," Thomas added, "Tell him that King Phillip and Queen Ahlana are making it a royal command. Let him try to refuse that!"

She blew him a kiss as she raced off into the castle.

"I do believe she fairly danced out of here, Thomas."

"Haha! That she did! That was well done, Kelson, really."

"And long overdue."

Fireworks burst in the air over the city again, illuminating the pair with colors of red, gold and blue.

"It also may be the solution to their particular problem," Kelson added.

"Which problem?"

"Sister Karen told me that they had been trying to conceive a child for the last six years or so."

"Ah." The Nuncio waited for an explanation but none was forthcoming. "Pardon me for asking, but how will it help?"

"Well, for one thing, they won't have to worry about someone trying to kill them every other day. More importantly, I think that there is still some latent daemonic influence that is preventing pregnancy."

"What do you mean?"

Kelson sighed. "Well, childbirth among the Fallen Ones is highly regulated by the female daemons of high rank, and their designates. They use complex magic spells and curses to prevent other females from conceiving unless they expressly permit it. Think of it as a form of eugenics: more children from the fit, less from the unfit. Well, there was probably a magical lock placed on Saren's mother that her grandmother removed, but since Saren was born here and no unlocking magic was ever used on her, it's possible that some of the latent curse remains."

Father Thomas digested that, mind whirling. "Really. And being on Celestia will correct that?"

"Indeed. More importantly, they will undergo the Nuptial Blessing at the honeymoon site. There is no Fallen magic that can withstand such a blessing, especially if my Ana is the one invoking it."

"Well then, the vacation is a doubly wonderful idea. And thank you. I have been trying to figure out a way to reward them, but they aren't really all that interested in riches or honors."

"Which they will have aplenty anyway."

"True. But a child would be the best blessing of all."

Song and music echoed in the city below, accompanied by laughter.

Father Thomas smiled, watching a trio of children running down a lane, sparkling fireworks held aloft in their hands.

Kelson sighed. "Now, Father Thomas, I have heard of a local delicacy or two that I would like to sample."

"Certainly. What is your pleasure?"

"I believe one is called jekka and the other witchberries."

"Ah. Follow me. I believe I can accommodate you."

***

With a knock on the study door, Melinor poked his head in. "Hello, Father Thomas."

Thomas Williams turned away from the tall window with a smile. "Melinor. Good to see you. How goes it?"

Melinor joined him at the window. Far below, workmen swarmed over ruined walls, collapsed buildings and destroyed homes. Citizens formed long lines carrying away buckets of debris.

This is going to take a long time, he thought.

The Nuncio nodded at the scene. "Restoration is slow but steady Everyone seems to be pitching in. They are remarkably resilient, considering their recent losses. I'm almost afraid to ask, but what is the tally now?"

Melinor sighed. "In Oakmoor? About fifty thousand civilians and twenty thousand troops lost their lives. That doesn't count the wounded. As far as the rest of the world? I don't want to depress you."

"That bad?"

"We've already hit seven digits and counting."

Father Thomas crossed himself, then regarded the scene below. "So many."

They watched in silence. Melinor fidgeted with his belt. "I can't shake the feeling that we failed them."

"Well, you should shake it, and right quickly. No one could have predicted the Skull Gates or the Dark Wave."

"Couldn't we have? With respect, Eminence, you are new to this world. We others have been here all our lives and know of the Ja'al and their tactics and deceptions."

Father Thomas shook his head. "I think you're being a bit unfair. I don't see evidence that anyone was willingly blind or selfish. But you did take the right steps, didn't you?"

Melinor didn't answer. The casualty lists scrolled in his mind.

Father Thomas clasped his hands behind his back. "Let's speak of other, more cheerful things. I think the Riders return from their honeymoons today."

Melinor smiled. "Yes, more cheerful indeed. Saren and Terenil come back from Celestia too."

"Excellent." Father Thomas returned to the desk and sat. "Oh, before I forget, here's the official transcript of the Northern Alliance conference with Merdail and Gorostol." He selected a sheaf of papers and offered them to Melinor.

Father Thomas continued as Melinor skimmed through the documents. "Gorostol and Merdail have volunteered to provide intelligence as a preliminary step."

"Good. That will help." Melinor smiled, handing back the transcripts. "With the Ja'al Cult destroyed and their temples razed to the ground worldwide, we won't have to deal with them."

Father Thomas frowned. "That's something I wanted to ask you about. I heard something quite odd. I heard that Torvu and Arachnia were actually killed. Is that true?"

"Kelson and Ana said so, and I believe them."

Father Thomas shook his head. "How is that possible? I was on the receiving end of their ire. They seemed invincible."

"Well, they are not, I can assure you. Torvu and Arachnia expended much of their power trying to kill us all at the Grand Plaza — and especially in counteracting Saren and the Crown of Saint Alyssa. In their diminished state, they could not stand up to the onslaught of Kelson, Ana and their children."

"Why didn't they just heal themselves and escape?"

"They tried. The Hadean High Royalty possessed significant healing capabilities, true, but they were pursued and under assault without respite for the most part. And don't forget that they were brought via Skull Gate. When all those were destroyed, they had to get to other, older gates used for 'advisors' but the Celestial Court never let them get close."

"That must have been quite a fight."

"Two of Kelson's children were severely wounded and a few Celestial high nobles died, but in the end, the two Hadean gods were indeed killed."

Father Thomas stared off into space. "I'm sorry I was not there. I could have offered them some form of redemption."

"You need have no regrets on that score. Kelson and Ana told me they gave them multiple chances but they were spurned each time."

The Nuncio's expression turned rueful. "Then maybe it was a good thing I didn't accompany them. I don't have the perseverance of the Elohir."

"Neither do I. Despite my desire to see Arachnia and Torvu pay for their misdeeds and the curiosity of seeing evil gods perish, I think it's best we weren't there. I will note that there are two craters, one in the wilds of Derelia and one outside the borders of Rinad, where small hills used to be."

The Nuncio shook his head. leaned back in his chair. "What happened to Selaan? And Tarvener?"

Melinor shrugged. "No one knows. Selaan hasn't been seen or heard from since. Knowing his ability to shape-change at will, it may be difficult to find him. And no one has seen Tarvener since the last battle. Queen Ana thinks either or both of them might have found an Envoy Gate and escaped to Hades."

"We're well rid of them in that case," Father Thomas concluded.

"Agreed. The Ja'al are no more, though some of their adherents might remain. I believe Adina Hightower and Berek Lordwain, for instance, were not among the dead."

They heard a knock at the door.

"Yes?"

"Eminence?" The face of Thomas' aide poked into view.

"Ah, Detlef. What is it?"

Detlef grinned. "The watch commander wanted me to tell you that the Grey Riders are returning. And the Duke and Duchess of Eastridge are already back. They await you in the drawing room."

"Very good news indeed. Thank you, Detlef. You may go."

Detlef departed and Thomas rose from his seat. "Well, let's go see them, Melinor."

Melinor joined the Nuncio in traversing the halls of the palace, wending their way through workmen and soldiers moving equipment and building materials..

Melinor watched the bustle of activity. *A veritable beehive…*

They opened the door to the drawing room to see Saren and Terenil standing at another window gazing down at the city. Saren was in her natural form, ivory wings furled, and had her arms wrapped around her husband.

Melinor marched over to them. "Saren, you imp. Why didn't you just come in to see me?"

She embraced him with a brilliant, peaceful smile. "We didn't want to interrupt you."

"It would have been welcome," said Father Thomas.

She and Terenil bowed and kissed the Nuncio's ring. He laid a gentle hand on their heads.

"Besides," added Terenil. "We both wanted to tell you in person."

Melinor smiled. "Tell me what?"

Saren's expression was so bright and full of joy that Melinor thought she had retained some of the glory of the Crown of Saint Alyssa in her person. She kissed his cheek. "You're going to have another grandchild…"

Chapter Thirty-Six – Knife-Work in the Shadows

Golvadu hunkered down in the corner of the booth, sipping from his mug. His eyes darted all around the tavern.

Many patrons jostled for position and vied for the attention of the two bartenders and pair of serving maids. The noise of many voices in a trio of languages assaulted Golvadu's ears and the smell of stale sweat, alcohol of various varieties and a panoply of cooking odors surrounded him like a cloying, itchy blanket. He wished for the quiet of his tower laboratory.

Not that he had a laboratory any more. If what he suspected had happened, the Elohir had turned it into a smoking pile of rubble by now.

He sipped again, eyes still in motion. At least the ale was good. Of course, in times past, he could just command a servant to bring him his favorite brew and it would appear in mere minutes.

Thoughts of his tower reminded him of all he had lost and he felt the seething rage build. Everything he had worked for, decades of plots and planning and research and carefully laid assassinations: all gone, ruined by a team of former freelance mercenaries in service to the so-called "Faiths of the Light".

He fought to master his anger. He knew that he needed cold, analytical reasoning now, not fury. He would have his chance to exact retribution later, but only when everything was in place. Moving hastily would be his doom, particularly if the rumors were true about a permanent detachment of Elohir on Damora to prevent a recurrence of another Dark Wave.

No, this time he would move with more deliberation and a sober estimation of his adversaries. He wouldn't allow the Grey Riders to take him by surprise again.

A figure entering the tavern caught his eye. It looked to be an old human woman, hunched under a ragged cloak and walking with the aid of a cane. Her gaze flicked in his direction and she limped towards him, navigating the boisterous crowd with surprising ease.

He nodded to the seat across from him and she flopped into it. "Thank you, kind sir," she wheezed.

"Don't mention it."

"Clear skies ahead, so it seems," she opined after a while.

Good. It's her. "Only if one keeps a weather eye on the skies," he replied.

She looked at him. Adina Tenspire's mocking blue eyes met his. "True enough. Wise words from a wise sailor."

"Nice disguise."

"Magic helps."

He took his time, sipping from his tankard. "Where?" he asked.

"An escort will be waiting for you in the town of Wildbrook, Golad. He will take you where you need to go."

Good. The coastal districts weren't secure any more, and rumor had it that some of the Grey Riders might make an appearance. Golad, at least, was still loyal to the Great Remaking and he could count on supporters there.

"When?"

"Three days."

He frowned. "That's not much time."

She smirked as she rose, gathering her cloak around her. "Events will occur with or without our consent, so it behooves us to finish our planning and move quickly. Of course, if you are having second thoughts —"

"No," he interrupted. "I'll be there."

Without another word, she shuffled off into the crowd and soon disappeared.

Golvadu finished his drink. She was right. Though he knew the need to plan carefully, they couldn't delay long.

It's better this way. He stood and swirled his cloak around himself. *Vengeance will not wait. I will not wait. There will be a reckoning. And then we will see who emerges victorious, Grey Riders or no…*

The End

(…for now…)

Sneak Peek – Book 7: Tower of Light

A hard slap brought him to groggy wakefulness.

"Come on, Major," said a cheerful male voice. "No time for dozing."

A cold splash of water left him gasping and alert. Major Adam Tolbert raised gritty eyes to a tall blond man in scale mail armor with the symbol of the Skullhead Legion emblazoned on the chestplate. Oil lamps cast capering shadows in the nearly-empty room. "I'd rather keep my eyes closed, Ormond, if the alternative is looking at you."

"Well, he can still talk, which is useful." A dark-haired woman with smooth, youthful features leaned back onto a nearby table. She wore what could only be described as a chainmail negligee, but Tolbert wasn't fooled. The armor glittered with magic and crimson runes writhed on the head of a war hammer at her hip. She selected a wicked-looking set of pincers from a nearby table. "We need to make him talk about the right kinds of things."

"If he won't talk, I'm sure there are others who will." Ormond smirked. "You have family in Coastwatch, don't you Major? Maybe some of Roshana's coreligionists should pay them a visit."

A momentary panic rushed through Tolbert's mind at the idea of Gudarta fiends plying their sadistic trade on his wife and children. He struggled to keep any hint of apprehension off his face. *Linda knows the signs. They'll get away. We have allies.*

Ormond straddled a nearby chair. "Let's dispense with the song and

"

dance, shall we? We know you aren't an adherent of the Church of Gariil any more than I am. Which one is it? Verian? Irial? Christianity?"

Tolbert didn't answer, keeping his gaze fixed on the door to the adjacent guard room. He tested the bonds on his wrists and ankles to the chair but they were as tight as before.

"We can just pick one," Ormond continued. "It's a death sentence anyway."

"It won't matter," Tolbert answered. "The Ja'al are finished. The deamons are either dead or have escaped back to Hades. Your time is ending and you know it. What religion I follow or don't follow is irrelevant. Your laws won't apply anymore."

Ormond's eyes flicked to Roshana, who shrugged. "It will matter to you," the Gudarta priestess replied. "And to your family. Do you think that everyone will suddenly rise up now and restore the old kingdoms? Many people are still loyal to the Grand Remaking. The People's Republic of Torosc is still strong, despite what you may have heard."

Tolbert chose not to answer.

"It's true we've taken some losses," Roshana continued, laying the pincers down on the table, "but the bulk of our strength remained in Torosc. Additionally, there are still some of our allies from Hades who weren't killed. They're very much alive, as everyone will soon find out."

What? Dear God! Tolbert's mind raced. *If there are still daemons on Damora, no one is safe.*

He thought back to the rumors and stories he had heard. Tales told of a mighty Elohir Army that had annihilated the Ja'al Dark Wave up north. One source maintained that descendants of the rightful rulers of Torosc's many districts had been found and were coming to reclaim their homelands. Some even said the Grey Riders were on their way. Thoughts of the legendary Riders buoyed his spirits.

Daemons or no daemons, he concluded, *it won't matter. The reign of evil in the Southlands will end. It has to.*

"It won't matter when the Grey Riders get here," he retorted.

"Grey Riders!" Roshana laughed out loud.

"That's very funny," Ormond chuckled. "Grey Riders indeed."

Roshana smirked. "Well, you have one thing right, Major. The question of religion is not as important as who is loyal to the Cause. Suppose you start naming those who are no longer supporters of Torosc? It might make a big difference to the health and well-being of your family, not to mention great rewards for you."

Tolbert told her where she could put her rewards.

In one long step, she closed the distance to him and gripped his jaw with her hand. Her eyes blazed. "Don't place so much faith in the Riders. They won't be going anywhere: Shrike assassins will see to that."

She jerked his head to the side, a motion that restarted his headache.

"The pincers or something more brutal?" Ormond asked.

"Neither," she said, standing tall. "I have more elegant methods." She began a harsh, sing-song chant. Ormond took two wax plugs from his belt purse and inserted them in his ears.

Tolbert gasped. The air felt as if were filled with needles. Tingling, intense pain lanced into his ears, eyes, skin and even his brain. He heard someone scream and realized it was himself.

Abruptly, the hellish song stopped. Ormond removed his ear plugs and smiled genially.

Roshana leered at him. "I can keep this up all day. Give up on any lies about anyone coming down to liberate the old lands. It won't happen."

Tolbert breathed deeply, willing the headache and pain to subside. When he could talk he raised his eyes to Roshana's. "The Riders will be here. They are bringing the rightful Queen of Alenar and the High Princess."

Ormond snorted in derision. "Now I know you're delusional. Queen? High Princess? I don't see any either of them, do you?"

A double-thump sounded from the adjacent guard room. Roshana frowned and nodded at the door. Ormond rose from his chair, but before he took more than two steps, the portal burst open.

A figure in a hooded cloak stepped into the room with a young Halfling man. Behind them, Tolbert spotted the prone figures of two Gudarta warriors in the outer guard chamber. The Halfling removed a medallion from around his neck. The air around him shimmered and he transformed into a wiry goblin carrying twin daggers. A silver crucifix lay against his tabard.

The figure lifted the hood. A gorgeous half-Elven woman regarded the room with amber eyes. Her red-gold hair glowed in the firelight. She wore a grey tunic with the figure of a flying pegasus on the left breast and a circlet of silver around her brow. She carried a staff of shiny white wood. She made a fist with her free hand and golden lightning crackled around it. Her eyes became pools of light.

"My name is Megan Aldenar. You were saying?"

Appendix - Glossary

<u>Agent</u> - A spy, bounty hunter or thief, depending on context and the particular agent's morals and ethics. Connor Lomin and Khyron Demaris are ones who tend more towards the "spy" variety. Most agents provide a stealthy component to the groups they support. In military terms an agent would be part of a reconnaissance unit.

<u>Alenar, Brandawyn (Brandi)</u> - One of the original Grey Riders, a half-elven female, trained as a soldier and combat medic/corpsman. The older sister of Megan, she and her family were persecuted for their Christian faith and eventually fled their homeland of Torosc. During her time with the Riders, she fell in love with Eric Indidarc. Later, she was captured by the Ja'al and changed into a vampire thrall by evil magic. When she finally met the Riders again, she insisted that Eric put a stake through her heart to prevent her from seducing and destroying them one by one. A Preservation Net (q.v.) was used on her immediately in the hopes that she didn't die but could be cured of her vampirism someday.

Reserved but kind and devoutly religious, Brandi is quite pretty, with red-gold hair and violet eyes, but doesn't see herself as attractive. Brandawyn is also ambidextrous. Her pegasus is named Amicus (Lat. *"friend"*).

<u>Alenar, Daphne, OF</u> - Ranger Knight of the Falcon (*Orden Falconieri*, OF). The only sister of Megan and Brandi's human mother, she spirited her nieces northward away from Torosc to safety. Sometimes thought of as overly serious (like her niece, Brandawyn), she served as a devoted mother-figure to the sisters after the death of their parents. She perished in battle with Ja'al forces along with her brother, Stephen.

<u>Alenar, Megan</u> - Another of the original Grey Riders and younger sister of Brandawyn Alenar, she fled persecution in Torosc to arrive in Deran. After attending college in Terenai, she graduated as a wizard and scholar. She and Brandi met the Grey Riders in Deran and helped them solve the mystery of *Whitehorse Peak*. When her aunt and uncle died fighting the Ja'al, she was sold into slavery to a Ja'al High Wizard to serve in his laboratory. The Grey Riders rescued her but she was poisoned by an encoded, infernal venom. The Riders used a Preservation Net on her as she died, hoping they were fast enough

and that an antidote could be found eventually.

A strawberry blonde like her sibling, Megan is friendly and outgoing, somewhat vain and impetuous, yet fiercely loyal and brave. She is also very attractive, with strawberry blonde hair and amber eyes, and is fond of baubles and fancy clothes. She loves Dar Cabot and rides a pegasus named Larinor (Elv. *"ranger"* or *"faithful guide"*).

<u>Alenar, Stephen</u> - Uncle of Brandawyn and Megan Alenar, he was the younger brother of Daphne Alenar. In addition to being a scholar, Stephen was also a skilled warrior and wielded potent magic in battle. Known for his teasing sense of humor, he died fighting alongside his sister against the Ja'al.

<u>Alvin, Sir</u> – A Sword-knight set to guard the Bydecy family in Tyler (q.v.), Astarel.

<u>Alyssa of Tor Haldin, Saint</u> – Queen of a petty kingdom during the late Paragon Age, Alyssa ruled over a domain located in present-day Torosc. Her battles against Zhinia Margoth were legendary and all the more remarkable since Margoth was Alyssa's first cousin. After Margoth was finally defeated at the Battle of Three-Nation Lake and disappeared, Alyssa returned to her kingdom. She and her husband and family died ten years later when a combination of wild tribes and opportunistic foreign powers overran her war-depleted nation. She was known for her piety, generosity and forgiving nature.

Her Crown is a relic of jaw-dropping power, bestowing impressive magical abilities, healing capabilities and protections to someone of sufficiently pure heart, though it all comes with a price.

<u>Ambrose</u> – A hill sprite tasked with assisting Hannah Lervion (q.v.).

<u>Ambrose, Lynne, SNJM</u> – A human nun, Sister Lynne is a healer and advisor to the Baron of Sentinel, Gorostol (q.v.). Her stern demeanor masks a gentle and kindly heart.

<u>Ana</u> – The Elohir (q.v.) Queen of Celestia (q.v.), Ana is dusky-skinned and has luminous auburn hair. Like her husband, King Kelson, Ana is clear-thinking and unflappable, even in the face of such horrors as the daemons of the Army of the Dark Wave (q.v.). In battle, she wears blue-black Celestial chainmail with a silver-chased breastplate. She is ambidextrous and uses two swords.

<u>Arachnia</u> – One of the goddesses of the Ja'al (q.v.) pantheon, she hails

from the world of Hades (q.v.) and appears as a tall, raven-haired woman of great beauty and power. The giveaways to her daemonic nature are her fangs and short horns. Though she prefers an understated approach, she can nevertheless fly into a rage when she feels she has been slighted. Her appearance on Damora coincides with the arrival of Torvu (q.v.) and Selaan (q.v.) two other gods of the High Royalty of Hades. Her titles include Mistress of Venom and Treachery and High Majesty of Hades. She is partial to creatures that can poison, such as scorpions, snakes and spiders.

<u>Archon</u> – One of the six rulers of the Republic of Torosc. All are extremely powerful wizards who gained their lofty station by treachery, murder, deceit and blackmail. The High Council is led by the highest ranking (the First Archon), who does not vote but holds veto power.

<u>Astarel</u> - Kingdom to the north of Deran, along the coast. The homeland of Buck Bydecy, it is a seafaring nation with a robust navy and an eclectic society comprised equally of elves, humans, Dwarves and Halflings. It is a member of the Northern Alliance.

<u>Battle Lord</u> – Massive and powerful, these daemonic generals tower over most of their fellows in the battlefield. Possessing an arsenal of magical powers as well as brute strength, they are also highly intelligent and are one of the few creatures able to intimidate large groups of Fallen Ones into obedience. They are also greedy, cruel and arrogant.

<u>Blood Satyr</u> – A type of daemon from Hades, it resembles a smooth-skinned satyr with red skin and stands over seven feet tall. Blood Satyrs have four arms and are formidable wizards, though they can mix it up in hand-to-hand combat as well. They do not have wings but can run very fast.

<u>Blood Sign</u> – An oath taken by dragons signifying that they have declared one or another group (such as a tribe, clan, religion or nation) as enemies. The Blood Sign amounts to a declaration of war, though it is taken by individuals or clans and not all dragons as a race.

<u>Blue Mark</u> – The code name for Rhonin Handor, an agent of the Northern Alliance living in the Elven Empire of Terenai, charged with ferreting out plots and spies against the Alliance.

<u>Bone Knight</u> – Tall, powerful, human-like daemons (q.v.) who wear armor made of bones. They are usually unit commanders and have significant magical abilities, such as warping corpses into undead zombies under their

command. They have four glowing red eyes.

<u>Bydecy ROA, Buckminster (Buck), Sir</u> - Another of the original Grey Riders, Buck is a tall, rangy, sandy-haired human male warrior. He is a native of Tyler, Astarel, and was made a Sword-Knight of the Royal Order of Astarel (ROA) after the Battle of Hillton. His easygoing nature is often mistaken for boredom. He has a particular affection for Carine Del Rio, a druidess. His father is named Alfred and he has a brother (Jack) and a sister (Summer). His pegasus is Shadowbane.

<u>Cabot OSK, Darius (Dar), Sir</u> - An original Grey Rider and native of the border town of Forester, Deran, Dar ran afoul of Ja'al goblin troops in the wilds and headed back to town for help, setting the events of *Whitehorse Peak* in motion. A dark-haired human male, he is a ranger/scout and adept in the woods. He grew to love Megan Alenar during their time together fighting the Ja'al near Forester. He rides a pegasus named Virasi (Elv. *"white star"*). After the defeat of Zhinia Margoth (q.v.) he was knighted into the Order of Saint Kira (*Orden Sancta Kirae, OSK*).

<u>Calder</u> – Gorlak's (q.v.) alias while he guarded the Lomin family.

<u>Chamber of Decision</u> – A mysterious place that the Riders (minus the Alenar sisters) encountered on the way to find the *Helm of Shadows*. Each Rider was separated from the others and shown two paths they could take in their lives— for good or ill. According to the Song of the Grey Riders, they had to choose. All the Riders (except Handor Lervion (q.v.), who attempted to game the system) chose the more difficult path of sacrifice and pain that held the promise of the defeat of evil.

<u>Changelings</u> – A magical sword and dagger forged on Celestia. With the use of a keyword, they transform into weapons of ice, fire, lightning, acid or holy power.

<u>Coastwatch</u> – Seaside metropolis (pop. 150,000) in Torosc where the Alenar sisters were born and raised.

<u>Companion Pin</u> – Enchanted pieces of jewelry, Companion Pins are keyed to a miniature golem resembling a small animal like a rat, hawk, ferret or cat. The constructs are summoned to serve the bearer of the Pin using a secret code word and share their special abilities (night vision, enhanced hearing, camouflage, etc.) with their masters. Stealth (a hawk Pin), owned by Eric Indidarc, is an example of a Companion Pin.

<u>Crossed Swords</u> - Guild of assassins based in Deran and Terenai. Founded and ruled by the Hylar family, the Crossed Swords were used by evil forces to eliminate opposition. Eric Indidarc's real family name is Hylar and he is a son of the guild master; he escaped his former life and was adopted by Melinor Indidarc. In *Assassin Prince*, the Grey Riders joined him in destroying the Guild and bringing his parents to justice.

<u>Curbolg</u> – A hideous combination of cattle and squid, Curbolg daemons are a cross between a beast of burden, a combat mount and a tank. Smaller daemons can sometimes ride them and one of their tentacles can inject a pod into a victim which will spawn into a Curbold newt once the victim dies.

<u>Daemon</u> - Evil to the core, the otherworldly race of daemons spends most of their time trying to overthrow the Elohir (q.v.) or conquer various regions of Damora. They are known as the Fallen Ones because legend has it that they were originally Elohir who turned to the side of evil and worship of themselves (and the Dark One). While many Daemons look like nightmarish beasts, some are very attractive and almost human-like or Elven in appearance. The overriding philosophy of the Daemons is that Damora is a free zone, ripe for the picking. Their home world, Hades, is the 4th planet orbiting the star Beta Hydri (G11 spectral class, 24.38 LY from Earth) and is a combination of stunning beauty and stomach-churning grotesqueness.

<u>Damora</u> - Imaginary world setting for the Grey Riders novels. The fourth planet orbiting the star 82 Eridani, it is roughly 1.15 times the size of Earth and possesses similar climate, regions and flora/fauna. The parent star is a G5V spectral class, main-sequence yellow star approximately 20 light years from Earth. It has two moons, Kaliri and Diometrius, which provide both tidal forces and substantial moonlight for the planet's surface. The technology level of Damora approximates the High Middle Ages of the real world, with significant differences due to the use of magic and scientific advancement.

<u>Darkfire Beads</u> – Small glass beads ensorcelled with a spell of evil energy, they explode when thrown, somewhat like arcane hand grenades. In addition to the concussion and glass shrapnel, they also have the effect of weakening and disorienting their target.

<u>Darkhollow</u> – A haunted wood near the town of Evonald, Terenai. Legends tell of a powerful wizard who dabbled in forbidden magic and destroyed

himself, corrupting the forest in the process. The Hill Sprites who live nearby keep a vigilant watch over it.

<u>Darkspawn</u> – Greater undead made from large creatures such as ogres. The process to create one is particularly awful in that the creature is still living during the ceremony (as opposed to zombies, which use corpses).

<u>Dark Wave</u> – An invasion sparked by the Ja'al cult in Torosc (q.v.), the Dark Wave was supported by daemonic military units teleported in from Hades (q.v.) via the Skull Gates (q.v.). Key to its initial success was the invention of devices (by George Oxbridge (q.v.)) to close existing gates to Celestia (q.v.) that could have been used to bring in Elohir (q.v.) to stymie the assault. The invasion required coordination between many disparate elements such as humans, Dark Elves, daemons, goblins, Kaftu (q.v.) and other evil creatures.

<u>Darlon</u> - Major metropolis in northern Deran, pop ~ 170,000. Home to people of many races, creeds and professions, it is a trading center and university town. Ruled by a duke, it controls trade and access between Deran and the northernmost nations of Astarel, Elder and Rokon.

<u>Deathhammer</u> – A type of daemon from Hades, a Deathhammer is a hulking brutish beast with pig-like features, fangs and white horns. They can use their great wings to fly but are not particularly maneuverable. As their name suggests, they are shock troops. They have a limited magical repertoire.

<u>Deathmist</u> – Daemons from Hades, Deathmists resemble a cloud of grey fog that floats low to the ground and extends silvery tendrils to attack. They radiate extreme cold and can drain the life-force out of someone by grappling them with their tentacles. They do not speak.

<u>Del Rio, Carine</u> – Druid caretaker of one of the many druidical groves near Oakmoor, Deran, she is a mentor and confidant of Buck Bydecy though she is only two years older. Dark-haired and green-eyed, she is a competent steward of the open lands near the city and can shape-change to the form of a black doe. Her mentorship of Buck eventually blossomed into love.

<u>Delvos</u> (dw. "*good worker*") – First Alderman of the city of Sommvik (q.v.) in Merdail (q.v.).

<u>Demaris, Khyron, Major</u> – A former beau of Andyn Eleandir who lost contact with her while on highly-classified missions for the Empire of Terenai, Khyron is blonde and has sea-green eyes. He is almost as stealthy as

Connor Lomin, wields a bow with deadly precision, and is ambidextrous. He is also trained in airborne riding, one of the reasons he is asked to join the Grey Riders. His pegasus is named Zasural (Elv. *"wind-light"*).

<u>DeMey, Saren, Lady</u> - The half-sister of Eric Indidarc by adoption, Saren DeMey was found by Melinor Indidarc (q.v.) as an infant and raised by him and his wife, Anne. A devout Christian, Saren appears to be a complete contradiction in terms as she is half-daemon but fights for the forces of good. Dark-haired and dark-eyed, she transforms to a bat-winged, horned half-daemon at will. Saren continually guards against her daemonic background, as it is a permanent temptation to lust and savagery; however, to the common folk of Deran, she is known to be unfailingly warm, generous, wise and gentle. As the wife of Terenil, the Earl of the Oakmoor suburb of Tallemar, she is a Countess of Deran.

<u>DeMey, Terenil, Lord</u> - The half-elven husband of Saren, he is an earl and the ruler of Tallemar, a suburb of Oakmoor, Deran. A skilled wizard and soldier in his own right, he is adaptable, thoughtful and kind. His devotion to Saren is unquestioned. He has a personal guard of a platoon of magic-wielding armored knights. As part of the Foreign Ministry of Deran, he is privy to information about other nations and is rumored to have an extensive spy network.

<u>Deran</u> - Constitutional monarchy in the northern lands of the Western continent of Damora. A nation built from the remnants of the Esten Empire, Deran is also a meritocracy, where nobles are elected by their peers and the legislature is based on merit and ability more than noble connections. Deran has an advanced network of roads, potent military, and several universities. The seat of the Christian Church, Saint Martin's Town (St. Martin's) is in Deran.

<u>Diometrius</u> – The larger of Damora's (q.v.) two moons.

<u>Dolmide</u> – Halfling hero-saint of the Irial religion. He was a scholar and monk who left a legacy of extensive writings before taking up arms to defend his Paragon-era kingdom when the king was corrupted by evil magic. Despite the exclamation *"Dolmide's Beard"* often used by Irial adherents, Dolmide himself had no beard.

<u>Dome of Glass</u> – A mysterious object or place from antiquity fashioned by the Ja'al and/or their allies to thwart attempts to find the Gate of Stars.

Its location is unknown.

<u>Dorn, Jalek</u> – The lord of the Dwarven community of Dorn's Hall (q.v.), he is on good terms with Nolan Hanford (q.v.) and the two rulers often co-operate to deal with threats from the Wilderness. He is an aggressive but a good tactician with many victories under his belt.

<u>Dorn, Riti</u> – The wife of Jalek Dorn, Lady Riti is fiercer than her husband when defending her people but practical. She is often the more moderate of the two. She has three children.

<u>Dorn's Hall</u> – A small (~500) community of Dwarves on the border of Deran near Forester, it makes its living by mining in the hills nearby, mostly for copper, iron and some silver.

<u>Dragon</u> – Exactly as the name implies, the bat-winged, lizard-like Draconic race is comprised of four sub-groups: Balar, Sarkany, Drakes and True Dragons. The Balar are the smallest (20-30 feet long) and True Dragons the largest (up to 100+ feet long). All can use magic and have a social structure of clans. Evil dragons are marked by a glowing red sheen to their eyes, much like other Dark races (Dark Elves, Dwarves, etc). Iron Thunder (q.v.) is a True Dragon.

<u>Dwarf</u> - One of the major races of Damora. The term "Dwarf" comes from the ancient elvish word, *duarfaen* (Elv. *duar* = 'stone' + *fae/ fey/ fej -* = 'magic', literally "those of stone-magic"). A typical Dwarf male is about four feet six inches tall. Dwarves tend to be burly, sturdy or muscular for their size and can live for almost two hundred years. Males are often bearded (though not all are). They are generally honorable and appreciate strength and resolve in others. Their main talent, as indicated by the name bestowed on them by the Elves, is in stonework and metallurgy.

<u>Dwerrolf</u> – A cross between a wolf and a Dwarf, these daemons can use minor magic such as fire breath. Much like Skreets (q.v.), they are used as light infantry and fly to their destinations, though they usually land to attack. Their voices are often parodies of children's voices.

<u>Earth Mother</u> – Nature-concept deification of the world of Damora as expounded by the Druids. Roughly equivalent to the concept of Gaia in the real world.

<u>Eastridge</u> – A major Deranese city (pop. ~120,000) in the south of the country.

<u>Eleandir SMT, IO, Andyn, Lady</u> - One of the Grey Riders, Andyn is a priestess of the Elven god Verian and a wizard. She has honey-blonde hair and amber eyes, a trim figure and a marvelous singing voice. Rather impatient and quick-tempered, she nonetheless displays unwavering faith, mercy, warmth and a nimble mind. Her husband was killed by Crossed Swords assassins. At the Battle of Hillton, she used a holy relic (the Crown of Saint Alyssa) to destroy Zhinia Margoth. For her exploits, she was knighted by the Elven Empire of Terenai and given the title of Light of Justice and Lichslayer. She is styled as Lady Andyn Eleandir, Servant of Mindra of Terenai, Imperial Order, Light of Justice. Her pegasus is named Medianox (Lat. *"midnight"*).

<u>Eldir</u> – A nation of the Northern Alliance, Eldir is a patriarchate and the seat of the faith of Verian. Possessing a climate similar to Germany in the real world, it used to be at odds with Rokon, a breakaway duchy, until the need for collaboration against the forces of evil caused them to bury the hatchet. It is ruled by the High Matriarch or Patriarch of Verian.

<u>Eleison</u> (Gr. *"have mercy"*) – A powerful magic horseman's mace found by the Grey Riders near Twinspire Mountain during the search for the Helm of Shadows. It strikes against evil with holy power and amplifies healing magic. Andyn Eleandir carries it and another, lesser magic mace; the smaller size of a horseman's mace (as opposed to the more massive footman's mace) permits her to wield them ambidextrously.

<u>Eleth-Anor</u> – (Elv. *"dolphin bluff/ cliff"*) – A major seaport city of the Elven Empire. Home to almost two hundred thousand souls, it commands a sheltered harbor in the Bay of Dolphins (Elethi-Rin). It is Andyn Eleandir's home town and her parents still live there.

<u>Elf</u> - One of the major races of Damora. The term "Elf" comes from the ancient word for their race, *Ellfaen* (Elv. *ell* = 'life' + *fae/ fey/ fej* -= 'magic', literally "those of life-magic"). Elves are more slender than humans and possess intriguing eye colors, such as aqua, amber or violet; they also have a slight point to the top of the ear, though this is not usually pronounced or even noted if the ears are concealed under hair, hat or helm. Elves tend to be a bit more reserved than the other races and have an affinity for magic of all kinds. They possess skills for getting along well with animals and a talent for healing trees and plants. Elves who have turned to evil are named "Dark Elves" and are distinguished by a reddish tint to their eyes.

<u>Elise, Lady</u> – A Shield-knight tasked with protecting Buck Bydecy's (q.v.) family in Tyler, Astarel.

<u>Elohir</u> - Denizen of the planet of Celestia (the 5th planet of the 61 Virginis star, a single G6 spectral class, main-sequence yellow star approximately 28 light years from Earth). Sometimes called "Celestials", they appear to be winged humans. Skin color covers the range of typical shades seen in humans (porcelain, tanned, brown, yellow, dark brown) and their eyes are the color of jewels. Their beauty is often described as 'unearthly'. All possess potent magical and martial skills but are usually reluctant to meddle in the affairs of Damorans. They are uniformly kind, wise, honest and just. Elohir live extremely long lives (~ 1000 years) if not killed in warfare with their evil kindred, the Fallen Ones (or Daemons, q.v.).

<u>Esdan, Lord</u> – A hill sprite (q.v.) nobleman rescued by the Alenar sisters, he is married to Tinira (q.v.). Together with a cadre of other sprites, they assist the Allied nations as reconnaissance troops.

<u>Esten Empire</u> - An empire formed of various kingdoms controlling much of the known world during the second age of Damora (known as the Imperial Age and denoted in calendars by the letters IY (for Imperial Year)). It fell after over a thousand years of rule due to infighting, a breakdown in the social order and the influence of evil.

<u>Evendale</u> - Small Halfling nation southeast of Deran and northeast of Terenai. A republic, Evendale consists of seven districts or counties, each of which have a prescribed number of representatives (aldermen) and senators who draft laws that are approved by the Prime Minister, another elected position. A land with mild climate and productive farmland, Evendale borders on the Wilderness, which means the Halflings are always on vigilant watch, having been invaded by evil tribes from the wild lands multiple times. Its capital city is Lakeview.

<u>Eye of Truth</u> - A magical diamond, the Eye of Truth is actually a sort of lens that allows the owner to see the true nature of things and people. It can detect evil or good auras, see through illusion and discern truth from lies. It was crafted by an ancestor of Buck Bydecy and is owned by him.

<u>Fell-beast</u> – A normal animal warped by vile magic and forbidden scientific knowledge into a servant of evil. Almost any creature can be made fell; examples are fell bears, fell wolves and fell sharks.

<u>Fellhammer, Golvadu, Lord</u> — A dwarven wizard of impressive ability, he is one of the rulers of the Republic of Torosc. As he holds the title of Second Archon, he is surpassed in authority only by the First Archon. Short-tempered, profane and conniving, he is also a creative thinker and a dangerous opponent. He has particular hatred for Melinor Indidarc (q.v.).

<u>Fidelis</u> — A magic spear that can contract to the size of a dagger or telescope to the length of a medium infantry spear, it was awarded to Eric Indidarc by an Elohir (q.v.), Melissa of Celestia. It strikes with great power against evil things and, if thrown, returns unerringly to its wielder's hand via teleport when called. Though Melissa did not say it, there is some speculation that it is from the Paragon Age.

<u>Firedart</u> - A magical attack spell used by wizards and sorcerers. It is essentially a small projectile of flame with a detonable core that looks rather like a tiny comet and has a limited range (about 100 feet or so). It produces the effect equivalent to a 9 mm pistol bullet and rarely misses.

<u>Forester</u> - Large town along the northern border highway of Deran. Forester is ruled by a baron and controls trade along the borderlands. Its defining feature is the central town proper, which is surrounded by a tall, well-built palisade with giant, living trees as its guard towers. It is the hometown of Dar Cabot.

<u>Gariil</u> — (Dw. "*random*") The god of chance and luck sometimes also associated with fertility, Gariil can take on male or female aspects. One of the original religions of Damora, it is still popular in urban areas. The religion is very loosely organized and clergy are often made simply by claiming the title and demonstrating priestly magic. Their temples are often nothing more than casinos or amusement centers. Due to their uncanny ability to turn a profit, they are tolerated in the evil realms of Torosc, Morlan and Jered.

<u>Gate of Stars</u> — A mysterious Gate of unknown nature that is feared by the Ja'al. Guarded by the Dome of Glass, its location has been lost in the mists of time.

<u>Ghost Creeper</u> — An evil, semi-intelligent plant that can detect the approach of non-evil creatures and set up a wailing sound. Their vines wrap around victims and insert a narcotic that makes them sleepy and clumsy. They are often set near Vampire Roses by servants of Darkness as sentries.

<u>Gnome</u> - Half-breeds resulting from the marriage of Halfling and Dwarf,

gnomes possess features from each parent: natural affinity for stone and the underground from the Dwarves and a cheerful disposition and natural talent with all things organic from the Halflings. Somewhat taller than Halflings but shorter than Dwarves, gnomes are industrious and found in all the known lands. They usually have dark hair, tan-to-dark complexions, and brown, amber or grey eyes. A typical gnome lives about 180 years or so.

<u>Goblin</u> - Short, half-simian creatures who often serve as foot-soldiers for the forces of evil, looking somewhat like horned chimpanzees. Extremely agile and able to use any available weapon that is sized for them, they are also good at hiding in shadows. They dislike sunlight. Their social structure is usually in a hierarchical monarchy, with the chieftain or king of a particular tribe wielding absolute authority. Goblins particularly hate Dwarves since the two races compete for underground areas and resources. They are capable miners and are about the size of a gnome or tall Halfling (a few inches short of four feet tall).

<u>Gorlak</u> - A goblin formerly in the employ of the Ja'al, he switched sides after the Battle of Hillton when his life was spared by the Riders. After his captured, he was asked to join the household of the Papal Nuncio (Edward Simpson, who died soon after from pancreatic cancer). Under the Nuncio's tutelage and care, he flourished and now serves as a spy, with devastating success since few would ever entertain the idea of a Christian goblin. He admires the Grey Riders, adores Andyn and Saren, and soaks up new learning like a sponge.

<u>Gorostol</u> (Dw. *"friend alliance"*) – A large and somewhat eclectic nation south of Terenai and north of Torosc. Originally founded by Dwarves, over the years it attracted folk of all races. It is now a buffer state between the oppressive Republic to the south and the Elven Empire to the north.

<u>Grey Riders</u> – The formerly free-lance mercenary group famous for defeating Zhinia Margoth at the Battle of Hillton. The original members were Buck Bydecy, Dar Cabot, Eric Indidarc, Connor Lomin, Andyn Eleandir and the Alenar sisters, Brandawyn and Megan. After the departure of the Alenars, they added Hlerv (Handor Lervion) to their team, but he perished while trying to rescue his sister from the Ja'al. Khyron Demaris, an old beau of Andyn's, later joined the group.

<u>Grey Riders, Song Of</u> – An ancient prophetic poem from the Church of

Irial, it foretold the coming of riders on winged horses who would save a kingdom from a horrible evil. It came true when the real Grey Riders destroyed Zhinia Margoth, a lich princess, at the Battle of Hillton. The prophecy came true in *Helm of Shadows*.

Grue/Grim – Small, minor daemonlings resembling warty, toad-faced humanoids, they are stealthy and annoying but can be very dangerous if encountered in groups. None were sent to take part in the Dark Wave (q.v.) but it was suspected that they scouted locations for constructing Skull Gates (q.v.).

Gudarta - The evil goddess of torture and suffering, the seductive and sadistic Gudarta is a member of the Ja'al pantheon. Her priests and priestesses usually wear revealing and scanty (but highly enchanted) outfits designed to distract and seduce others.

Habakkuk – A suit of magical chainmail with the ability to teleport its owner and one other person for short distances. It is owned by Dar Cabot.

Half-Elf - The offspring of a union between an Elf and human, half-elves are a mix of their parents' heritage: magically talented, strong, adaptable and capable of learning new skills quickly. If it were not for the fact that they are noticeably larger than elves by a few inches in height, they would be indistinguishable from elves due to their predilection to inherit their Elven parent's eye color, hair color and ear shape. Half-elves live to between 100 and 150 years.

Halfling - The smallest of the races, Halflings (from the Elven for "those of hearth magic" - *haliv-fae*) prefer pastoral villages and countrysides to large cities, though they are at home in any setting. As adaptable as humans, Halflings have a talent for craftsmanship (with things other than stone) and farming. They are known for their skill in the kitchen and the durability of their finished goods. Their hair color (blonde, brown or black), skin color (porcelain to dark brown) and eye color (blue, green, black or grey) remind the other races of miniature humans. They live about 100 years or so.

Hanford, Ellen, OSR – The Baroness of Forester, Deran, she originally hailed from Targanon. She has dark skin, dark curly hair and piercing black eyes. She is a wizard of the Order of Saint Raphael (*Orden Sanctus Rafaelis*) and a friend of the Grey Riders. She has two children, Timothy and Alice.

Hanford, Nolan, OSM – The Baron of Forester, Deran, he is a paladin of the order of Saint Michael. He is cautious, prudent and observant. He is on good terms with the Cabot (q.v.) family, whose father served him as clerk for many years.

Harlinsville – A mid-sized suburb of the Deranese capital of Oakmoor, Harlinsville has about 35,000 inhabitants. It was ruled by Lord Dunston and Lady Arlene, Count and Countess — before his murder and her disappearance. A working-class town, it is relatively peaceful but has a shadowy underbelly.

The Harrowing – A treacherous swamp in the Wilderness east of Terenai (q.v.), The Harrowing is so named because of the extreme danger in crossing it. Home to a variety of deadly creatures and tribes of lizard-folk, it is a direct route from the Elven Empire to Rainbow Valley but seldom, if ever, used.

Hell Wisp – A sprite who has turned into a lich (q.v.).

Heritage Stone - A magical item, a Heritage Stone is used to prove paternity and lineage. It uses magical analysis of DNA from a blood sample to ascertain the relationship of the subject to a predetermined DNA pattern associated with a target family or person.

Highpoint – The capital of the Republic of Torosc, Highpoint is one of the largest cities in the world with a population of over half a million. It sprawls along the ridges and foothills of a mountain range in the central province of Silvermount (formerly the kingdom of Gandar). It overlooks a large river and an inland sea (the Great Star Sea).

Hillton - Fortified Deranese city (pop ~ 27,000) perched on a hill along the shores of Sun Lake. It is ruled by a Count. Due to its position on the central plains, it is a major trading center and hub for nearby agricultural areas. It was the site of a siege and battle when Zhinia Margoth invaded Deran from the Wilderness. The battle ended when Andyn Eleandir used the Crown of Saint Alyssa to destroy Margoth. Her army disintegrated without her iron will to keep them from attacking one another.

Human - Humans are much like people in real life, with the exception that they can use magic in the same manner as elves, Dwarves, Halflings and other denizens of Damora. Humans are energetic, adaptable, learn quickly and are endlessly curious about Damora and its people, flora and fauna. The origin of the word "human" has no Damoran equivalent as it does not translate from any Elven or Dwarven syntax.

<u>Humana</u> - Language of the human race on Damora.

<u>Hunt, Barbara, 1LT</u> – An officer in the army of Gorostol attached to Sentinel (q.v.), she is a veteran of many border actions against Torosc (q.v.). She has dark curly hair and dark eyes. She sometimes appears distracted and inattentive but is actually very well aware of her situation.

<u>Incubus</u> – Rakishly handsome male daemons, incubi specialize in infiltration and assassination. Like their female counterparts (succubi, q.v.) they rely on their close resemblance to humans to seduce their victims. They, along with the succubi, arrive as part of the Dark Wave to beget half-daemon children who can be used as spies and secret police once Damora is conquered.

<u>Indidarc SSM, Eric, Sir</u> - One of the original Grey Riders, Eric is the adopted son of Melinor Indidarc (q.v.). Able to use magic and martial weapons with equal proficiency, Eric is cheerful, optimistic and friendly. He treats everyone he meets with the same courtesy and kindness, whether a beggar or noble. His birth parents, the Hylars, were the leaders of an assassins guild from which Eric escaped at an early age. Eric has violet eyes and blond hair and is a half-Elf. His pegasus is named Niveral (Elv. *"snow bright"*). For his role in the defeat of Zhinia Margoth, he was made a Knight of the Order of Saint Michael (*Servus Sancta Michael*). He loves Brandawyn Alenar.

<u>Indidarc OTM, Melinor, Lord</u> - High Wizard of the nation of Deran, Melinor is a nobleman and confidante of royalty in the Kingdoms of the Northern Alliance. He adopted both Eric Hylar/Indidarc (q.v.) and Saren DeMey (q.v.) after his own children were grown. A formidable mage with knowledge of magic, science, medicine, literature and history, Melinor is fluent in several languages. A kind but somewhat absent-minded widower, he is singularly focused on thwarting evil plots in the known lands. He is a member of the Order of the Three Magi, a Christian religious organization composed chiefly of wizards and scholars.

<u>Irial</u> - The Halfling god of harvests, craftsmen and home, Irial is a benevolent deity who sometimes counts elves and humans among his adherents. The precepts of Irial are hospitality, kindness, courtesy, respect for people, animals and nature, and steadfastness in the face of hardship, whether caused by nature or evil designs. Another of Irial's names is Worldmaker.

<u>Iron Thunder</u> – A True Dragon (q.v.) of the Sunfire Clan and mentor,

protector and ally of the Grey Riders, whom he met when they found the pegasi of Whitehorse Peak (q.v.), which he guarded. He is a widower and has two precocious grandchildren, Tholieros and Kindriana. His Draconic name is Donnervassilianelikilandra, though few non-dragons attempt to pronounce it.

Ja'al - Also known as the Manipulator Church (for their penchant for twisting words, lying and otherwise using others callously for their own ends) the Ja'al are one of the evil religions on Damora. The cult is a polytheistic religion worshiping a number of harsh and cruel deities. The precepts of the Ja'al are world domination, rule of the strong over the weak, eugenics, personal gain at the cost of others, and treachery.

Jekka – A drink from Gorostol made from a dark brown bean that grows on vines, it is a cross between coffee and chicory and is highly prized for its invigorating qualities and smooth flavor.

Jered – A large nation south of Torosc (q.v.), it is a confederacy of kingdoms originally established by pirates. Possessing miles of coastline, a multitude of islands, and a tropical climate, Jered is wealthy, powerful, and an ally of Torosc and Morlan in opposing the Northern Alliance.

Kalar, Ahlana II, PhD, OST – The Queen of Deran, she is twenty-nine years old, with a dusky complexion, brown hair and black eyes. A scholar and wizard by trade, she met Stephen at a religious retreat in her teens and never forgot him — nor he, her. She is sunny, optimistic, and resourceful and has an impressive arsenal of magic devices.

Kalar, Stephen IV, OSM – The King of Deran, Stephen is in his early thirties and has extensive experience in both the freelance sell-sword profession and military matters. Ahlana is his wife. A cautious and thoughtful man, he has learned the value of thinking before acting as well as the need to act swiftly if needed. He has black hair and blue eyes and tends to worry over possible outcomes. He is a paladin (a holy warrior dedicated to a religion — in this case, Christianity).

Kaliri – The smaller of Damora's (q.v.) two moons.

Kelaire – The daughter of the chieftain of the Ivory Clan centaurs, she is a bold, and aggressive commander, but young. She is a friend of Khyron Demaris (q.v.) and helped him on several missions when he was in the Special Forces of Imperial Terenai (q.v.).

<u>Kelson, King</u> – The Elohir (q.v.) monarch of the world of Celestia (q.v.). Dark-haired and fair-skinned, he radiates calm and confidence. In battle, he appears with gold-washed Celestial plate mail and uses a spear with a head of pure light that is similar to Fidelis (q.v.) the spear of Eric Indidarc. His queen is Ana.

<u>Kentridge</u> – A city in Torosc from where Altus Volan (q.v.) hails. It is a titular holding of the ancient royal house of Aldenar; the Queen of Aldenar is nominally the Baroness of the city. It has a population of about 25,000.

<u>Khelios (Giantbane)</u> (Dw. *"sharpest"*)- A magical dwarven sword found by Buck Bydecy while on the quest for Whitehorse Peak, it bestows two abilities on its wielder: knowledge of the dwarven language and the ability to detect evil. It is particularly deadly to giants or any creature with giant blood (including cyclops). It has an unnerving tendency to suddenly launch itself at an enemy giant, dragging Buck along for the ride.

<u>Kortos</u> – An alliance of duchies on the great island of Derelia, northwest from Deran across the Great Sea.

<u>Lervion, Hannah</u> – The sister of Handor, Hannah was studying at a military academy at the time of the death of both her parents. She is forthright, honest, friendly and a fierce defender of her family with a high sense of justice. Temporarily reunited with her lost brother in *Assassin Prince*, she tragically lost him while trying to escape from the clutches of the Ja'al and her conniving uncle. A brown-eyed brunette, she is fit and very attractive but acts like the girl next door. She has a deep and abiding affection for Connor Lomin, who finds her irresistible.

<u>Lervion, Handor (Hlerv)</u> - A gnome wizard and spy, he joined the Grey Riders in *Eye of Truth* and helped them clear Buck Bydecy's name and avenge the murder of Andyn Eleandir's husband. He was secretive and somewhat aloof in order to protect his secret identity as the heir of a shipping magnate's fortune. After stealing the *Helm of Shadows*, he escaped to his hometown of Meridian, Gorostol and freed his sister from her Ja'al captors, only to lose his life in the process. In the end, he regretted not appealing to the other Riders for help in his quest and is now celebrated as a hero.

<u>Librarian's Robe</u> – A magical garment, it has the capacity to store a finite number of spells of varying power by use of inscribed sigils on the fabric. A single one can hold up to thirty-six spells which the wearer, often a wizard,

can call up at a moment's notice. It is extremely expensive.

Lich - An undead wizard. Liches are created when a wizard or sorcerer makes a pact with Dark Powers in order to forestall his/her own death, gaining immense magical power and undead status in the bargain. They exude an aura of terror but are greatly harmed by holy spells and items.

Light of Justice – Title given to honor someone who has destroyed a lich – a phenomenal feat considering the rarity and incredible power of that type of undead. Lights of Justice are rare to say the least. Andyn Eleandir was awarded the title for destroying Zhinia Margoth.

Lomin, Brendan – The younger brother of Connor Lomin (q.v.), he almost died in a plague called the Whispering Death, which was loosed from the wilderness by Zhinia Margoth in a bid to depopulate the borderlands so she could search for certain special magic items. Because of the disease, his voice is at half strength. He is the father of Deena and Darren (q.v.).

Lomin, Cerys – The sister-in-law of Connor Lomin (q.v.) and the wife of Brendan (q.v.). Her children are Deena and Darren (q.v.).

Lomin, Connor - Another of the original Grey Riders, Connor is a Halfling who hails from Evendale. Serious, but with a somewhat ribald sense of humor, Connor appears stoic and sober most of the time. He is knowledgeable about traps, curious about ancient ruins and secrets, and wields a broadsword, a rather heavy weapon for a Halfling. Dark-eyed and dark-haired, he has a muscular build but has an almost uncanny skill for moving unseen. His pegasus is named Phantom.

Lomin, Darren – The nephew of Connor Lomin (q.v.), he is about seven years old, adventurous, nimble and clever. He idolizes his uncle and dreams of becoming a free-lance hero.

Lomin, Deena – Darren Lomin's sister (q.v.), she is about nine years old, responsible, cautious and prudent. She often tries to hold back her more impetuous sibling.

Lomin, Janey - Deceased wife of Connor Lomin. Along with her daughter, Rose, she perished in a plague known as the Whispering Death, which is thought to have been released into Evendale by Zhinia Margoth.

Lomin, Miriam – A High Priestess of the church of Irial (q.v.), Connor Lomin's (q.v.) mother is practical, confident and even-handed. As a high priestess, she has significant martial and magical skills and commands a company of ecclesiastical troops of her own in the city of Glen, Evendale.

<u>Lomin, Seamus</u> – The husband of Miriam (q.v.), he is a former army officer who handles security and logistics for his wife's temple district. He is calm, insightful and maintains an even keel under pressure.

<u>Lordwain, Berek</u> – A blond Ja'al wizard of the Fourth Circle, he is highly placed in the cult and often in command of special units or whole armies. While he is an ambitious and smooth operator, he is more practical and less fiery than his mistress, Adina Tenspire (q.v.). He detests the Alenar family but goes along with Adina's scheme to turn Brandi (q.v.) into a vampire.

<u>Margoth, Zhinia</u> - A former Paragon Queen who used fell and evil magics to transform herself into an undead sorceress (a lich) near the end of the Paragon Age. Vicious, conniving, and cruel, she appeared as a skeleton with pinpoint eyes of purple light, clothed in rotting royal robes and wielding a skull-headed staff. Her battle standard was a fanged skull with a crown of flame. She created a cursed magic helmet of teleportation named the Helm of Shadows. Andyn Eleandir destroyed her at the Battle of Hillton, Deran, in the year 1085 PIY using a powerful holy relic.

<u>Marolpeth</u> – (Elv. *"blue grove"*) An Elven city of about 25,000 people in the eastern part of Terenai.

<u>Marta, Lady</u> – A Shield-knight assigned to protect the Bydecy family.

<u>Martin, Cassandra, OST</u> – The Countess of Whitmark, Kortos, she is a former freelance wizard. She is also a friend of several famous retired freelance sellswords, including the Blue Mark and his wife, the Count and Countess of Deorfast, and the Lady and Lord of Sun Plains. A calm, no-nonsense woman, she is the perfect foil for her boisterous, energetic husband, Justin. She is a human woman of average height, with soft brown hair and grey eyes.

<u>Martin, Justin, OF</u> – The human husband of Lady Cassandra, Justin is the fourth son of one of the Dukes of Kortos, a land ruled by a council of sovereign nobility. A Count of Whitmark, Kortos and Knight of the Order of the Falcon with considerable military command experience, he and Cassandra are sent to Deran to help coordinate efforts to thwart the Ja'al's worldwide offensive. Of average height with dark brown hair and eyes, he is inquisitive and good-humored.

<u>McDonald, Fiona, Colonel</u> – A regimental commander in the Astarellian city of Tyler, she is tasked with reconnaissance of Dark Wave forces near the

city.

Meadow – A hill-sprite attached to Hannah Lervion's (q.v.) company.

Melissa - An Elohir (q.v.) knight assigned to watch for the Grey Riders to arrive at Twinspire Mountain in *Helm of Shadows*. She gave the Crown of Saint Alyssa to Andyn Eleandir to use in bringing down Zhinia Margoth. She also provided the angelic sword Rindara Starblade to Dar Cabot, the Elven fire-blade Tiuz to Connor Lomin, and the magic spear Fidelis to Eric Indidarc. She is wise, kind, fierce in defending against evil and seems to be perpetually amused by the Grey Riders, whom she regards with great affection. She is stunningly gorgeous but acts like she doesn't know it. She is married to an Elohir named Coloman and her brother is named Simon.

Meraloy, Caria, OST – An Elven mage of the Order of Saint Terenil (*Orden Sanctus Terenilensis*), she is sent from the Emperor of Terenai to assist Hannah Lervion. She is married to Caridan.

Meraloy, Caridan, Colonel – The husband of Caria, Caridan is a retired freelance warrior and Colonel in the Imperial Elven Army. He travels to Gorostol to assist Hannah Lervion, an agent of the Northern Alliance.

Mercato, Karen, MD, OP, OTM – The personal physician to the Papal Nuncio to Damora and a member of the Order of the Three Magi. She is also an Elven Dominican nun.

Merdail (Dw. "Holy Land") – A large, mountainous kingdom southeast of Terenai (q.v.), it is the Dwarven homeland. Over the centuries, it has become more eclectic as humans and halflings have come to help till the land while the Dwarves concentrate on underground endeavors. It is ruled by a king and queen.

Merfolk – Mermaids and mermen of legend and myth. Despite a somewhat rocky history with land-bound peoples (particularly humans), merfolk communities often form alliances with land nations for mutual protection and assistance. They look exactly as detailed in fairy tales (human torso and fish body).

Meridian – The capital city of Gorostol, it is a large metropolis in the foothills overlooking a beautiful lake known as the Kaljirre (Dw. "*sky mirror*"). It has over 200,000 inhabitants.

Mikman, Kili – A Halfling spy in the service of the Ja'al High Command, Kili has a long history with the Grey Riders. He initially tried to recruit Brandi and Megan Alenar (q.v.) to the service of the Ja'al, but the girls joined the Grey Riders instead. Later, he kidnapped Buck's father in an attempt to slay the Riders but this also failed. He has an intense hatred for Connor Lomin. His nickname is the Death Adder.

<u>Mindra</u> – A Verian hero from the Paragon Age. A soldier in the service of her king, she followed his orders without question until, in a vision from Verian, she realized that he was being manipulated by his councilors into oppressing those who disagreed with him. She rebelled and was pursued but prevailed with the aid of the Church of Verian. She ultimately defeated her enemies, converting two of them and returning the king to the ways of justice. She is the epitome of the concepts of mercy, bravery, wisdom and discernment and is often invoked by those seeking to cut through the lies of the forces of evil. An order of knighthood was established in her honor in Terenai.

<u>Morlan</u> – A nation to the south of Torosc allied with the Dark Powers, Morlan is ruled by a Wizard King. There are many schools and academies devoted to magic. The terrain is hilly or flat plains, punctuated by numerous lakes and rivers. The climate is warm and humid much of the year and it contains vast tracts of verdant jungle. It is allies with Torosc and Jered.

<u>Naeton</u> – One of the three coastal civilizations on the large northern island of Derelia, Naeton is a warlike nation constantly at odds with the Dukes of Kortos (q.v.) and the kingdom of Melen. The country has much mineral wealth, good arable land, and is the base for many organized evil sects on the island.

<u>Neralia</u> - Evil goddess of child sacrifice, murder and domination, Neralia is one of the members of the Ja'al pantheon. Similarities between her church and the defunct worship of Garon-Zith have led many to speculate that the two goddesses are one and the same.

<u>Northern Alliance</u> - A multinational pact similar to NATO in the real world, the Alliance is composed of Deran, Astarel, Rokon, Eldir, Evendale and Terenai.

<u>Oakmoor</u> - The capital city of Deran, home to over a quarter of a million people. Oakmoor is based on three large hills at the confluence of the East River and Lonmar Rivers. It has several suburbs in addition to the main city proper.

<u>Octavio, Arless</u> – An extremely wealthy and arrogant young merchant in the Deranese city of Fenbluff, he has many connections throughout the Northern lands, of both the savory and unsavory varieties. He was turned to a vampire by Brandawyn Alenar (q.v.) while she was still a vampire thrall to Adina (q.v.). He now serves the Ja'al unquestioningly.

<u>Ogre</u> - Large, human-like creatures with fangs and odd-colored hair, ogres are brutish, violent, and not particularly bright. Their leaders are usually the more intelligent members of a particular tribe. Some of their number are smart enough to use magic. They are usually over seven feet tall and three hundred and fifty pounds. Used as shock troops by the forces of evil, Ogres are also greedy and fearless.

<u>Olduvar, Chieftain</u> – The leader of the Ivory Clan centaurs, he is sober and experienced but worries about his impetuous daughter, Kelaire (q.v.). He is a widower.

<u>Oxbridge, George</u> – A Wizard of the First Circle of the Ja'al High Council, George Oxbridge was charged with research and development of the Skull Gates. He purchased Megan Alenar from the Ja'al hierarchy after her capture. He was not a harsh master, but saw Megan and Varienne Walker (q.v.) as simple tools rather than people. He had no attraction to women as such but a keen interest in anything that brings him magical power. He had a burning curiosity about anything mysterious, such as the source of Megan's increasing magical abilities. The Grey Riders killed him in a spectacular battle in Book 5, *The Skull Gates*.

<u>Papal Nuncio</u> – Official human envoy to Damora, appointed by the Pope.

<u>Pass of Eagles</u> – A route into the fabled Rainbow Valley, rumored location of the Dome of Glass (q.v.), it is one of the few relatively passable methods to traverse the rugged mountain range on Terenai's eastern border.

<u>Paragon Age</u> – One of the major epochs of the history of Damora, it was ushered in by the event known as the Skyfire, when humans first appeared and brought Christianity with them. Records prior to this time are sketchy and incomplete. The age is so named because of the rise of rulers of petty kingdoms who were all superior practitioners of a particular branch of a freelance career (i.e. warrior, healer, mage, etc.). It ended when some of the Paragon rulers succumbed to evil influences and tried to expand their nations at

the expense of their neighbors. Alyssa of Tor Aldin and Zhinia Margoth were two Paragon rulers.

Parker, Colin, OT – A knight of the Order of Saint Terenil, he is the aide-de-camp of Nolan Hanford, the Baron of Forester, Deran.

Pegasus – A winged horse. In the Grey Riders novels, they are omnivores due to their part-raptor heritage and can be domesticated. They are wildly expensive to acquire and maintain and are the fastest flying mounts alive.

Preservation Net / Bead – A small bead of amber imbued with a mighty spell affecting spacetime. If broken over an object, it releases a Preservation Net, a magical effect that reduces the flow of time to one ten-millionth of normal for anything it covers. Preservation Beads are extremely expensive and lose their potency after a time period measured in weeks.

Puup - Buck Bydecy's pet pigeon who somehow manages to avoid getting killed despite being in or near several battles. By the time of *The Skull Gates*, he has retired to the gardens of the Papal Nuncio's residence in Saint Martin's, Deran.

Rainbow Valley – The gateway to the Titan's Crown (q.v.), it is known to be a lush and green expanse within the Stonetower Range on Terenai's eastern border. Its remoteness is further isolated by the Harrowing (q.v.).

Rinad – A desert nation on the western continent across the Great Sea. Though sometimes run by extremists, family and tribal connections hold more sway that nationalistic fervor so full-on crusades from Rinad ion have been rare. Rinadis are shrewd merchants and will deal with all who have money; the land is rich in mineral resources and some rare components of magical spells (such as the special mineral-oil combination necessary in constructing teleporters).

Rindara Starblade – A magic bastard sword given to Dar Cabot by Melissa of Celestia. It has a night-black blade that glitters with the light of a thousand stars and is especially potent against daemons and the undead. It was crafted on Melissa's home world.

Rokon – A member of the Northern Alliance, Rokon is one of the smaller nations. Originally a duchy of the Patriarchate of Eldir, Rokon broke away prior to the forming of the Alliance. The two countries have since resolved their differences, attributable to the need for teamwork as required by the Alliance charter. Rokon has a climate much like Norway in the real world.

<u>Ryker's Shoal</u> – A major seaport of Gorostol (q.v.), the city sits near a river delta and boasts no less than four natural harbors. Home to over 100,000 people, it is a major trading and commercial station in addition to hosting two naval bases.

<u>Saint Kira, Order of</u> – Christian order of military scouts, rangers, mages and agents operating worldwide.

<u>Saint Martin's</u> (Town) - Major port city in Deran (pop ~ 80,000). It is the seat of the Christian church and the base of the Curia, the ruling council of Christianity on Damora. The Papal Nuncio makes his residence there.

<u>Saint Michael, Order of</u> - Christian military order of knights and warriors dedicated to protecting the innocent against evil, often used as heavy assault infantry or cavalry.

<u>Selaan</u> – One of the ruling High Kings of Hades, Selaan is known as the Changeable One. He is the god of Trickery, Deception and Chaos and has significant shape-changing abilities. Quixotic and capricious, he seldom remains on one thought for long but his impressive memory makes up for this shortfall. It is thought that his natural form is a golden-skinned, dark-haired man with white wings (in mockery of the Elohir) but since he never retains one form for very long, this is disputed. He greatly enjoys tormenting his victims and causing as much mayhem and destruction as possible.

<u>Sending Mirror</u> – The Damoran equivalent of a cell phone, it can be used to communicate over distances by showing an image of another person who has a similarly designed mirror. Useful range varies. The signals can be tracked, however, and the more powerful the mirror, the easier it is to track.

<u>Sentinel</u> – A large fortified town in southern Gorostol (q.v.) near the border with Torosc (q.v.), Sentinel is one of several outpost designed to keep a watch on the southern lands. It has a population of over 10,000 people.

<u>Shadow Lake</u> – Medium-sized freshwater lake in the wilderness east of Evendale, near Twinspire Mountain. A ruined fortress in the foothills over-looks it; the ruins are where the Grey Riders found the Helm of Shadows (q.v.) and were given powerful magic items, such as Tiuz (q.v.) and the Crown of Saint Alyssa (q.v.).

<u>Shock Hind</u> – Deer-like bipedal daemons, they have serpent tails and can use weapons in their human-like hands. They have several effective attacks, including electrical shock from their tails, goring with their antlers, weapon

strikes and magical spells. They are heavy infantry.

Shriek - A magical infantry sword found by the Grey Riders near Twin-spire Mountain. It makes its wielder stealthier and does great harm to undead. It was owned by Handor Lervion (q.v.); his sister, Hannah, now carries it in his name.

Sirine – Based on the mythical creatures of folklore, they appear as normal humans with a slightly iridescent sheen on their skin. They have gills on the sides of their necks and webbed fingers and toes. They are often allied with merfolk (q.v.) and friendly landbound nations.

Skyfire - A mysterious event from antiquity that changed the face of Damora. Legends say that visitors from another place arrived on disks or globes of fire and brought with them the Christian faith. The location of the actual arrival and the details of the event are lost in history. It is thought to have taken place more than 5000 years before the events of *Whitehorse Peak* (the first of the Grey Riders novels).

Skreet – Small daemons from Hades, Skreets look like a cross between an eagle and a boar. Used primarily as skirmishers, light infantry or air patrol, they tend to swarm opponents. Able to use a variety of weapons, they also have limited magical abilities.

Skullhead Legion - Paramilitary guard force in the service of the Ja'al cult leadership. Known for their brutality, greed and utter disregard for life, they are often used as shock troops. They are fanatical and fight to the death.

Skull Gate – Horrid structures made of iron bars and the bones of sacrificial victims, the Gates are the brainchild of the Ja'al cult. Fully thirty feet tall and twenty wide, they are spacetime portals to Hades (q.v.), the homeland of the daemons (Fallen Ones). Though some Gates were destroyed by freelance mercenary teams prior to the War of the Dark Wave, many remained and became veritable thoroughfares for daemons to enter the world of Damora when the war began.

Sommvik – (Dw. *"Iron Pit"*) A city in the northeast of the kingdom of Merdail (q.v.), it had about 9,000 inhabitants prior to the Dark Wave (q.v.) and was known for rich lodes of iron ore nearby.

Spectral Sword / Sword of the Devoted Defender – A magical blade, it is contained in a small silver brooch. Connor Lomin owns one as a reward for his part in the victory over Zhinia Margoth. At the command word, a misty, ethereal sword leaps into being. The spectral blade defends its owner and attacks any other opponents on command. It can harm apparitions such as ghosts, specters and wraiths.

<u>Sprite</u> – Small (~ 12 inches tall), faerie-like beings, the race of sprites frequent woodlands and wild areas uninhabited by the larger folk of Damora. They keep to their own company and society though they form alliances with Elves (q.v.) or Halflings (q.v.) on occasion and have been known to form friendships with other races. There are four known sub-races, including the more outgoing and martial hill-sprites.

<u>Staff of Power</u> – A magical staff that amplifies the power of spells cast by the wizard bearing it. It can also be used to strike enemies like a quarter-staff, with painful results.

<u>Starpoint</u> – A coastal city in the nation of Gorostol (q.v.), it has a large harbor and is home to some 50,000 inhabitants.

<u>Stealth</u> - Eric Indidarc's enchanted familiar. Summoned from a magic item called a Companion Pin, it transforms to a realistic hawk upon command. When active, it gives Eric the ability to see through his eyes as he flies high above.

<u>Succubus</u> – Seductively beautiful female daemons whose specialties are infiltration, subversion and assassination. Though they are capable fighters, their close resemblance to humans allows them to disguise themselves in order to get close to their targets. Saren DeMey's (q.v.) mother was a succubus.

<u>Summervale, Arlene, Countess</u> – Lady and former ruler of Harlinsville. She is middle-aged, with brown hair and green eyes. Unknown to her husband, she was a secret agent of the Ja'al. When the Dark Wave commenced, she assassinated him and fled to join the invasion force to become a regimental commander. She is ambitious, calculating and cautious.

<u>Sun Lake</u> - Body of fresh water near the Deranese city of Hillton.

<u>Sword-Knight</u> – One of the orders of knighthood of Astarel (q.v.), bestowed by the royal house or nobility. All are hereditary (can be passed along to descendants). Sword-knights are the lowest order, followed by Shield-Knights, Helm-Knights and Crown-Knights (Royal Guard). Buck Bydecy is a Sword-Knight.

<u>Tallemar</u> – A major suburb of Oakmoor, Deran, it is home to more than 30,000 souls. It is ruled by the DeMeys, Earl Terenil and Countess Saren.

<u>Targanon</u> – A nation across the Great Sea from Morlan, its terrain and ecology are as varied as its people. Vast jungles, verdant plains, towering mountains and scorching deserts can all be found within its borders. Though some areas are very civilized, certain others are nothing short of barbaric.

<u>Tarvener</u> – One of the regional rulers of the world of Hades (q.v.), he is a prince in his own right and commands legions of daemons. Nonetheless, he is subservient to the High Kings and Queens (such as Selaan (q.v.)) and, despite serving as the Captain General of the invading Dark Wave, is required to follow their directives. His grand-daughter is Saren DeMey (q.v.), who he means to bring back to Hades with him.

<u>Tenspire, Adina</u> – A female human priestess of the goddess Gudarta of the Ja'al cult, she is beautiful, shapely and blonde (though she changes her hair color on a whim). Intimately involved with the Skull Gates project, she hunted down and eventually captured Brandi and Megan Alenar, keeping Brandi for as her own slave and transforming her through vile magic into a vampire. Adina is the mistress of Berek (q.v.), though she is not above taking her pleasures wherever they present themselves.

<u>Terenai</u> (Elv. "*Realm of the Elves*") - The hereditary homeland of the Elven people, Terenai lies due south of Deran and also shares borders with Evendale, Gorostol and Merdail. A verdant and fruitful land, it is heavily forested in places. It is ruled by an Emperor (or Empress) and is the oldest of the nations on Deran. Its capital city is Mil-Tereth (Elv. "*King's Palace*").

<u>Tinira, Lady</u> – The wife of Esdan (q.v.), she is a hill-sprite noblewoman who helps the people of Sentinel fight off Ja'al invaders. She was rescued from a Hell Wisp (q.v.) by the Alenar sisters.

<u>Tirevlan</u> – (Elv. "Silver Vale") A large city of over 100,000 souls in central Terenai, it is a waypoint for shipping and a major agricultural center.

<u>Three Magi, Order of the</u> - Secretive order of Christian mages and scholars in service of the Papal Nuncio. Composed of extremely skilled practitioners, it counts Melinor Indidarc as one of its number (and he is one of the few publicly acknowledged members).

<u>Tigris Infernalis</u> – (Lat. "*Tiger Hellish*") A breed of half-tiger, half-human daemon from Hades. Winged and capable of using magic, they are also a deadly sword fighters.

<u>Titan's Crown</u> – A mountain of three widely-spaced peaks in the

Stonetower Range east of Terenai, overlooking Rainbow Valley (q.v.).

Tiuz – (Elv. *"fire/ flame"*) An infantry sword resembling a gladius, it is a magic blade of ancient origin wielded by Connor Lomin. At a command word, it blazes to life with a fiery edge.

Torin, Sir – A Sword-knight assigned to protect the Bydecy family.

Torosc – (Dw. *"kingdoms"*) An oppressive land south of Gorostol ruled by a council of six Archons, it is an amalgamation of several petty kingdoms welded together during a time of upheaval. One of its provinces, Coastwatch, was the home of the Alenar sisters prior to the death of their parents. It is the center of activity for evil forces with designs on the lands of the Northern Alliance.

Torvu – One of the High Kings of Hades, the god of Death is a tall, powerfully built man with pale skin, dark horns in his forehead, dead black eyes, and dark hair with a bone-white stripe down the middle. He claims dominion over the dead and has many potent magical attacks in addition to fearsome weaponry. Cold and calculating, he is nonetheless realistic in his appraisal of situations.

Troll - Large, brutish bipedal creatures similar to ogres but taller and heavier. Trolls are hairless and can have four arms rather than two. They prefer mountains and forests and will kill and eat anything edible. Cruel, greedy and selfish, they can nonetheless be outwitted by smarter creatures. Some more intelligent of their species can learn to use rudimentary magic. Trolls have the unnerving talent of being able to blend in with trees and rocks by merely holding still.

Tyler - A major city of Astarel located on the coast just north of the border with Deran It is known for its large harbor, excellent fishing fleet and naval base. It is the hometown of Buck Bydecy (q.v.) and is home to over a hundred thousand people.

Varienne (Walker) – A young blonde human woman from Deran kidnapped by Viper slavers, she befriended Altus Volan, the son of her captors, and captured his heart. George Oxbridge purchased her for her healing talents. She became a helper and confidante of Megan Alenar.

Var-Kird – (Elv. *'Fort Half'*) An industrial city in southeastern Terenai (q.v.) it was so named because it was built on the ruins of an old fortress from the Paragon Age (q.v.); its fortifications only face to the east. The population was about 55,000 at the start of the Dark Wave and contained a sizeable number of Dwarves.

Var-Minrik – (Elv. *"Fort Guardian"*) A massive citadel in eastern Terenai (q.v.) near the Harrowing, it has several major military units and is marked by fortifications designed by Dwarves. It had about 75,000 inhabitants at the time of the Dark Wave.

Verian (Elv. *"Lord-Highest"*)- Elven god of forests and nature. Followers of Verian worship in open structures usually in groves or copses of trees. The organizational structure is somewhat loose, with a council of high priests and priestesses making decisions of doctrine and teachings every year. Verian teaches that liberty, love, kindness, right living, charity and respect for creation are paramount. Andyn Eleandir is a priestess of Verian. The prayer *"Verian, ald-adani"* ("Lord Highest, Heaven's Light!"), is used by Andyn to destroy or repel undead.

Vodyanoi – Half-fish, half-human creatures of the ocean, the Vodyanoi are a parody of merfolk, with the heads of fish, feet that end in fins and human-like torsos and arms. They are almost exclusively devoted to evil but difficult to deal with due to their capricious and independent nature. They are sworn enemies of merfolk (q.v.) and sirines (q.v.).

Volan, Altus – The son of Viper slavers, Altus began to have second thoughts about the family business when his parents captured Varienne. After trying unsuccessfully to purchase Varienne's freedom himself, he left home and joined the Skullhead Legion and became an officer. Further disillusioned by his life, he had a turning point when he and his band captured Megan Alenar. When she was freed by her relatives, they set him free and offered him a new chance at life – which he took in hopes of finding Varienne.

Vortex Bracers – Magical wristbands made of precious metal, these items have the effect of absorbing magical effects and spells, protecting the wearer from their effects. They have a finite capacity, after which they corrode and disintegrate.

War Fiend – Slender, human-sized daemons from Hades with double bat wings and a dragon tail, War Fiends are savage, intelligent and versatile. They are used as anything from combat wizards to medium infantry. They have access to a deadly array of battle magic and are swift, agile fliers.

<u>Whitehorse Peak</u> - A large mountain north of Forester, Deran, so named because its geology and snow-fall pattern reminded the people nearby of a white-maned horse. It is the site of the recovery of the pegasi (as described in *Whitehorse Peak*) that the Grey Riders eventually own. Its dwarven name is Kelematris (Dw. *"Mountain -Horse"*).

<u>Williams, Thomas, Cardinal, CSC</u> – The Papal Nuncio to Damora, "Father Thomas" (as he prefers to be known to his close associates and friends) is a Christian Cardinal sent to Damora upon the death of the previous Nuncio, Edward. He has dark skin, curly hair and piercing green eyes. He is an avid reader and has a healthy respect for the people and creatures of Damora.

ABOUT THE AUTHOR

A route to fantasy fiction through the aerospace industry may seem an odd one to take, but PG Badzey has been writing stories since grammar school and has never stopped, even though his path took an unconventional turn for someone interesting in writing. A trained systems engineer, he kept up with creative writing and coursework throughout a career working on the C-17 airlifter, the International Space Station, the Delta IV Rocket and the James Webb Space Telescope. He has enjoyed and been influenced by JRR Tolkien, C.S. Lewis, Katherine Kurtz, Christopher Stasheff, Terry Brooks and C. Dale Brittain, to name a few. He is the author of the first five novels in the *Grey Riders* series, *Whitehorse Peak*, *Eye of Truth*, *Helm of Shadows*, and *Assassin Prince* and *The Skull Gates*, all of which received 5-star ratings from Readers' Favorite. Other publications include short stories published in *Dragonlaugh*, an online fantasy humor magazine, and *Brevity in Paradise* (the Orange County Writers Guild (OCWG) anthology). PG Badzey has studied martial arts for many years and is active in his parish community. He lives in California, is a member of the OCWG and has taught seminars on fantasy writing in Orange County Libraries.

ABOUT THE ARTIST

A product of Fullerton College's Entertainment Arts Program, Matthew Bostic brings a background in illustration and the comic book industry to his artwork. With a resume that includes apprenticing as an Inker on Ultimate Spiderman and Ultimate X-men for Hack Shack Studios, his vibrant and evocative images bring the world of the Grey Riders to life. "Gate of Stars" is his first novel illustration project. He is a dedicated father and resident of Southern California. His fantasy work can be seen on Instagram @thedragonsmaw.

Find out more about the World of the Grey Riders at
https://pgbadzey.wordpress.com!